T0005879

"Ferociously imagined, incandescent with feeling, this book is urgent and necessary and as exhilarating as a ride on dragonback."

—Lev Grossman, author of the Magicians Trilogy

"Completely fierce, unmistakably feminist, and subversively funny, *When Women Were Dragons* brings the heat to misogyny with glorious imagination and talon-sharp prose. Check the skies tonight—you might just see your mother."

—Bonnie Garmus, author of *Lessons in Chemistry*

"[A] riveting historical fantasy. . . . What's surprising about Barnhill's rare foray into adult fiction is its subversiveness and feminist rage. It's a powerful, searing novel that feels deeply true, despite its magical premise." —BuzzFeed

"Kelly Barnhill's poetic, pointed tale tackles the era's pervasive silence concerning all things female."

—*The Christian Science Monitor*

"Kelly Barnhill couldn't have realized when she wrote *When Women Were Dragons* how prescient it would be. . . . Barnhill's prose is gorgeous and powerful."

—*Pioneer Press* (St. Paul, MN)

"A complex, heartfelt story about following your heart and opening your mind to new possibilities. This novel's magic goes far beyond the dragons."

—*Kirkus Reviews* (starred review)

KELLY BARNHILL

When Women Were Dragons

Kelly Barnhill has written several middle-grade novels, including *The Girl Who Drank the Moon*, a *New York Times* bestseller and winner of the 2017 John Newbery Medal, and *The Ogress and the Orphans*, a finalist for the 2022 National Book Award for Young People's Literature. She is also the recipient of the World Fantasy Award and has been a finalist for the SFWA Andre Norton Nebula Award and the PEN America Literary Award. She lives in Minneapolis with her family.

When
Women
Were
Dragons

Also by Kelly Barnhill

The Ogress and the Orphans
Dreadful Young Ladies and Other Stories
The Girl Who Drank the Moon
The Witch's Boy
Iron Hearted Violet

When Women Were Dragons

A NOVEL

Kelly Barnhill

ANCHOR BOOKS
A Division of Penguin Random House LLC
New York

FIRST ANCHOR BOOKS EDITION 2023

Copyright © 2022 by Kelly Barnhill

All rights reserved. Published in the United States by Anchor Books,
a division of Penguin Random House LLC, New York, and distributed in
Canada by Penguin Random House Canada Limited, Toronto. Originally
published in hardcover in the United States by Doubleday, a division of
Penguin Random House LLC, New York, in 2022.

Anchor Books and colophon are registered trademarks of
Penguin Random House LLC.

Grateful acknowledgment is made to Viking Books for permission to reprint
an excerpt of "O to Be a Dragon" from *The Complete Poems of Marianne Moore* by
Marianne Moore. Copyright © 1957 by Marianne Moore, copyright renewed
1985 by Lawrence E. Brinn and Louise Crane, Executors of the Estate of
Marianne Moore. Reprinted by permission of Viking Books, an imprint of
Penguin Publishing Group, a division of Penguin Random House LLC.
All rights reserved.

The Library of Congress has cataloged the Doubleday edition as follows:
Names: Barnhill, Kelly Regan, author.
Title: When women were dragons : a novel / Kelly Barnhill.
Description: First edition. | New York : Doubleday, 2022.
Identifiers: LCCN 2021051023 (print) | LCCN 2021051024 (ebook)
Classification: LCC PS3602.A777134 W54 2022 (print) |
LCC PS3602.A777134 (ebook) | DDC 813/.6—dc23
LC record available at https://lccn.loc.gov/2021051023
LC ebook record available at https://lccn.loc.gov/2021051024

Anchor Books Trade Paperback ISBN: 978-0-593-46657-5
eBook ISBN: 978-0-385-54823-6

Book design by Maria Carella

anchorbooks.com

Printed in the United States of America
10 9 8 7 6

For Christine Blasey Ford,
whose testimony triggered this narrative;

And for my children—
dragons, all.

The dragon is in the barrow, wise and proud with treasures.

—ANGLO-SAXON PROVERB

They were ferocious in appearance, terrible in shape with great heads, long necks, thin faces, yellow complexions, shaggy ears, wild foreheads, fierce eyes, foul mouths, horses' teeth, throats vomiting flames, twisted jaws, thick lips, strident voices, singed hair, fat cheeks, pigeon breasts, scabby thighs, knotty knees, crooked legs, swollen ankles, splay feet, spreading mouths, raucous cries. For they grew so terrible to hear with their mighty shriekings that they filled almost the whole intervening space between earth and heaven with their discordant bellowings.

—*LIFE OF SAINT GUTHLAC* BY FELIX,
AN EAST ANGLIAN MONK, APPROXIMATELY AD 730,
IN WHICH THE GOOD MONK DESCRIBES THE ORIGINAL
OCCUPANTS OF THE BARROW WHERE THE SAINT
HAD ATTEMPTED TO BUILD HIS HERMITAGE

If I, like Solomon, . . .
could have my wish—

my wish . . . O to be a dragon,
a symbol of the power of Heaven—of silkworm
size or immense; at times invisible.
Felicitous phenomenon!

—"O TO BE A DRAGON" BY MARIANNE MOORE, 1959

When
Women
Were
Dragons

Being the Truthful Accounting
of the Life of Alex Green—
Physicist, Professor, Activist. Still Human.
A memoir, of sorts.

Greetings, Mother—

I do not have much time. This change (this wondrous, wondrous change) is at this very moment upon me. I could not stop it if I tried. And I have no interest in trying.

It is not from any place of sorrow that I write these words. There is no room for sorrow in a heart full of fire. You will tell people that you did not raise me to be an angry woman, and that statement will be correct. I was never allowed to be angry, was I? My ability to discover and understand the power of my own raging was a thing denied to me. Until, at last, I learned to stop denying myself.

You told me on my wedding day that I was marrying a hard man whom I shall have the pleasure to sweeten. "It is a good woman," you said, "who brings out the goodness in a man." That lie became evident on our very first night together. My husband was not a good man, and nothing ever would have made him so. I married a man who was petulant, volatile, weak-willed, and morally vile. You knew this, and yet you whispered matronly secrets into my ear and told me that the pain would be worth the babies that I would bring to you one day.

But there were no babies, were there? My husband's beatings saw to that. And now I shall see to him. Tooth and claw. The downtrodden becomes the bearer of a heavenly, righteous flame. It burns me, even now. I find myself unbound by earth, unbound by man, unbound by wifely duty and womanly pain.

I regret nothing.

I shall not miss you, Mother. Perhaps I won't even remember you. Does a flower remember its life as a seed? Does a phoenix recall itself as it burns anew? You will not see me again. I shall be but a shadow streaking across the sky—fleeting, speeding, and utterly gone.

—From a letter written by Marya Tilman, a housewife from Lincoln, Nebraska, and the earliest scientifically confirmed case of spontaneous dragoning within the United States prior to the Mass Dragoning of 1955—also known as the Day of Missing Mothers. The dragoning, per reports from eyewitnesses, happened during the day, on September 18, 1898, as a lemonade social was underway in the garden of next-door neighbors, to celebrate an engagement. Information and data regarding Mrs. Tilman's case was suppressed by authorities. Despite the sheer amount of corroborating evidence, including the accidental capture on a daguerreotype taken next door which showed in shocking clarity the dragoning at its midpoint, and signed affidavits by witnesses, it was not covered by a single newspaper—local or national—and all studies organized to research the phenomenon were barred from both funding and publication. Scientists, journalists, and researchers were fired and blacklisted for simply asking questions about the Tilman case. It was not the first time such research blackouts occurred, but the sheer quality of the evidence, and the vigor of the governmental effort to suppress it, was enough to trigger the formation of the Wyvern Research Collective, an underground association of doctors, scientists, and students, all dedicated to the preservation of information and study (peer-reviewed when possible) of both spontaneous and intentional dragoning, in order to better understand the phenomenon.

Gentlemen, it is not my place to tell you how to do your jobs. I am a scientist, not a congressman. My task is to raise questions, carefully record observations, and vigorously analyze the data, in hopes that others might raise more questions after me. There cannot be science without the interrogation of closely held beliefs, as well as the demolition of personal aversions and biases. There cannot be science without the free and unfettered dissemination of truth. When you, as the creators of policy, seek to use your power to curtail understanding and thwart the free exchange of knowledge and ideas, it is not I who will suffer the consequences of this, but rather the whole nation, and, indeed, the entire world.

Our country lost hundreds of thousands of its wives and mothers on April 25, 1955, due to a process that we can barely understand—not because it is by its nature unknowable, but because science has been both forbidden from searching for answers and hobbled in its response. This is an untenable situation. How can a nation respond to a crisis like this without the collaboration of scientists and doctors, without sharing clinical findings and laboratory data? The mass transformation that occurred on April 25, 1955, was unprecedented in terms of its size and scope, but it was not—please, sirs, it is important that you let me finish—it was not an anomaly. Such things have happened before, and I will tell you plainly that so-called dragoning continues to this day, a fact which would be more widely known and understood if the doctors and researchers who studied this phenomenon hadn't lost their positions and livelihoods, or faced the horror of their labs and records being rifled through and destroyed by authorities. I know full well that speaking frankly and candidly to you today puts me at grave risk of harpooning what is left of my career. But I am a scientist, sirs, and my *allegiance is not to this body, nor even to myself, but only to the truth. Who benefits when knowledge is buried? Who gains when science succumbs to political expediency? Not I, Congressmen. And certainly not the American people, whom you are honor-bound to serve.*

—From the opening statement given by Dr. H. N. Gantz (former chief of Internal Medicine at Johns Hopkins University Hospital and erstwhile research fellow at the National Institutes of Health, the Army Medical Corps, and the National Science Administration) to the House Committee on Un-American Activities, February 9, 1957

I.

I was four years old when I first met a dragon. I never told my mother. I didn't think she'd understand.

(I was wrong, obviously. But I was wrong about a lot of things when it came to her. This is not particularly unusual. I think, perhaps, none of us ever know our mothers, not really. Or at least, not until it's too late.)

The day I met a dragon, was, for me, a day of loss, set in a time of instability. My mother had been gone for over two months. My father, whose face had become as empty and expressionless as a hand in a glove, gave me no explanation. My auntie Marla, who had come to stay with us to take care of me while my mother was gone, was similarly blank. Neither spoke of my mother's status or whereabouts. They did not tell me when she would be back. I was a child, and was therefore given no information, no frame of reference, and no means by which I might ask a question. They told me to be a good girl. They hoped I would forget.

There was, back then, a little old lady who lived across our alley. She had a garden and a beautiful shed and several chickens who lived in a small coop with a faux owl perched on top. Sometimes, when I wandered into her yard to say hello, she would give me a bundle of carrots. Sometimes she would hand me an egg. Or a cookie. Or a basket full of strawberries. I loved her. She was, for me, the one sensible thing in a too-often senseless world. She spoke with a heavy accent—Polish, I learned much later—and called me her little *żabko,* as I was always jumping about like a frog, and then would put me to work picking ground-cherries or early tomatoes or nasturtiums or sweet peas. And then, after a bit, she would take my hand and walk me home, admonishing my mother (before her disappearance) or my aunt (during those long months of mother-missing). "You must keep your eyes on this one," she'd scold, "or one day she'll sprout wings and fly away."

It was the very end of July when I met the dragon, on an oppressively hot and humid afternoon. One of those days when thunderstorms linger just at the edge of the sky, hulking in raggedy murmurs for hours, waiting to bring in their whirlwinds of opposites—making the light dark, howling at silences, and wringing all the wetness out of the air like a great, soaked sponge. At this moment, though, the storm had not yet hit, and the whole world simply waited. The air was so damp and warm that it was nearly solid. My scalp sweated into my braids, and my smocked dress had become crinkled with my grubby handprints.

I remember the staccato barking of a neighborhood dog.

I remember the far-off rumble of a revving engine. This was likely my aunt, fixing yet another neighbor's car. My aunt was a mechanic, and people said she had magic hands. She could take any broken machine and make it live again.

I remember the strange, electric hum of cicadas calling to one another from tree to tree to tree.

I remember the floating motes of dust and pollen hanging in the air, glinting in the slant of light.

I remember a series of sounds from my neighbor's backyard. A man's roar. A woman's scream. A panicked gasping. A scrabble and a thud. And then, a quiet, awestruck *Oh!*

Each one of these memories is clear and keen as broken glass. I had no means to understand them at the time—no way to find the link between distinct and seemingly unrelated moments and bits of information. It took years for me to learn how to piece them together. I have stored these memories the way any child stores memory—a haphazard collection of sharp, bright objects socked away on the darkest shelves in the dustiest corners of our mental filing systems. They stay there, those memories, rattling in the dark. Scratching at the walls. Disrupting our careful ordering of what we think is true. And injuring us when we forget how dangerous they are, and we grasp too hard.

I opened the back gate and walked into the old lady's yard, as I had done a hundred times. The chickens were silent. The cicadas stopped humming and the birds stopped calling. The old lady was nowhere to be seen. Instead, there in the center of the yard, I saw a dragon sitting on its bottom, midway between the tomatoes and the shed. It had an astonished expression on its enormous face. It stared at its hands. It stared at its feet. It craned its neck behind itself to get a load of its wings. I didn't cry out. I didn't run away. I didn't even move. I simply stood, rooted to the ground, and stared at the dragon.

Finally, because I had come to see the little old lady, and I was nothing if not a purposeful little girl, I cleared my throat and demanded to know where she was. The dragon looked at me, startled. It said nothing. It winked one eye. It held one finger to its lipless jaws as though to say "Shh." And then, without waiting for anything else, it curled its legs under its great body like a spring, tilted its face upward toward the clouds overhead, unfurled its wings, and, with a grunt, pushed the earth away, leaping toward the sky. I watched it ascend higher and higher, eventually arcing westward, disappearing over the wide crowns of the elm trees.

I didn't see the little old lady again after that. No one mentioned her. It was as though she never existed. I tried to ask, but I didn't have enough information to even form a question. I looked to the adults in my life to provide reason or reassurance, but found none. Only silence. The little old lady was gone. I saw something that I couldn't understand. There was no space to mention it.

Eventually, her house was boarded up and her yard grew

over and her garden became a tangled mass. People walked by her house without giving it a second glance.

I was four years old when I first saw a dragon. I was four years old when I first learned to be silent about dragons. Perhaps this is how we learn silence—an absence of words, an absence of context, a hole in the universe where the truth should be.

2.

My mother returned to me on a Tuesday. There was, again, no explanation, no reassurance; just a silence on the matter that was cold, heavy, and immovable, like a block of ice frozen to the ground; it was one more thing that was simply unmentionable. It was, if I remember correctly, a little more than two weeks after the old lady across the alley had disappeared. And when her husband, coincidentally, also disappeared. (No one mentioned *that*, either.)

On the day my mother returned, my auntie Marla was in a frenzy, cleaning the house and attacking my face with a hot washcloth, again and again, and brushing my hair obsessively, until it gleamed. I complained, loudly, and tried unsuccessfully to wriggle out of her firm grasp.

"Come now," my aunt said tersely, "that's enough of that. We want you to look your best, now, don't we?"

"What for?" I asked, and I stuck out my tongue.

"For no reason at all." Her tone was final—or she had clearly attempted it to be so. But even as a child I could hear the question mark hiding there. Auntie Marla released me and flushed a bit. She stood and looked out the window. She wrinkled her brow. And then she returned to vacuuming. She polished the chrome accents on the oven and scoured the floor. Every window shone like water. Every surface shimmered like oil. I sat in my room with my dolls (which I did not enjoy) and my blocks (which I did) and pouted.

I heard the low rumble of my father's car arriving at our house around lunchtime. This was highly unusual because he never came home during a workday. I approached the window and pressed my nose to the glass, making a singular, round smudge. He curled out of the driver's-side door and adjusted his hat. He patted the smooth curves of the hood as he crossed over and opened the passenger door, his hand extended. Another hand reached out. I held my breath.

A stranger stepped out of the car, wearing my mother's clothes. A stranger with a face similar to my mother's, but not—puffy where it should be delicate, and thin where it should be plump. She was paler than my mother, and her hair was sparse and dull—all wisps and feathers and bits of scalp peeking out. Her gait was unsteady and halting—she had none of my mother's footsure stride. I twisted my mouth into a knot.

They began walking slowly toward the house, my father and this stranger. My father's right arm curled around her birdlike shoulders and held her body close. His hat sat on his head at a front-leaning angle, tilted slightly to the side, hiding his face in shadow. I couldn't see his expression. Once they crossed the midpoint of the front walkway, I tore out of my room at a run and arrived, breathless, in the entryway. I wiped my nose with the back of my hand as I watched the door, and waited.

My aunt gave a strangled cry and peeled out of the kitchen, an apron tied around her waist, its lace edge whispering against the knees of her dungarees. She threw open the front door and let them inside. I watched the way her cheeks flushed at the sight of this figure in my mother's clothes, the way her eyes reddened and slicked with tears.

"Welcome home," my aunt said, her voice catching. She pressed one hand to her mouth, and the other to her heart.

I looked at my aunt. I looked at the stranger. I looked at my father. I waited for an explanation, but nothing came. I stamped my foot. They didn't react. Finally, my father cleared his throat.

"Alexandra," he said.

"It's Alex," I whispered.

My father ignored this. "Alexandra, don't stand there gawping. Kiss your mother." He checked his watch.

The stranger looked at me. She smiled. Her smile sort of looked like my mother's, but her body was all wrong, and her face was all wrong, and her hair was all wrong, and her smell was all wrong, and the wrongness of the situation felt insurmountable. My knees went wobbly and my head began to pound. I was a serious child in those days—sober and introspective and not particularly prone to crying or tantrums. But I remember a distinct burning sensation at the back of my eyes. I remember my breath turning into hiccups. I couldn't take a single step.

The stranger smiled and swayed, and clutched my father's left arm. He didn't seem to notice. He turned his body slightly away and checked his watch again. Then he gave me a stern look. "Alexandra," he said flatly. "Don't make me ask again. Think of how your mother must feel."

My face felt very hot.

My aunt was at my side in a moment, sweeping me upward and hoisting me onto her hip, as though I was a baby. "Kisses are better when we can all do them together," she said. "Come on, Alex." And without another word, she hooked one arm around the stranger's waist and placed her cheek against the stranger's cheek, forcing my face right into the notch between the stranger's neck and shoulder.

I felt my mother's breath on my scalp.

I heard my mother's sigh caress my ear.

I ran my fingers along the roomy fabric of her floral dress and curled it into my fist.

"*Oh,*" I said, my voice more breath than sound, and I wrapped one arm around the back of the stranger's neck. I don't remember crying. I do remember my mother's scarf and collar and skin becoming wet. I remember the taste of salt.

"Well, that's my cue," my father said. "Be a good girl, Alexandra." He extended the sharp point of his chin. "Marla," he nodded at my aunt. "Make sure she lies down," he added. He didn't say anything to the stranger. My mother, I mean. He didn't say anything to my mother. Maybe we were all strangers now.

After that day, Auntie Marla continued to come by the house early each morning and stay long after my father came home from work, only returning to her own home after the nighttime dishes were done and the floors were swept and my mother and father were in bed. She cooked and managed and played with me during my mother's endless afternoon lie-downs. She ran the house, and only went to her job at the mechanic's shop on Saturdays, though this made my father cross, as he had no idea what to do with me, or my mother, for a whole day by himself.

"Rent isn't free, after all," she reminded him as my father sat petulantly in his favorite chair.

During the rest of the week, Auntie Marla was the pillar that held up the roof of my family's life. She said she was happy to do it. She said that the only thing worth doing was helping her sister heal. She said it was her favorite of all possible jobs. And I think this must have been so.

My mother, meanwhile, moved through the house like a ghost. Prior to her disappearance, she was small and light and delicate. Tiny feet. Tiny features. Long and fragile hands, like blades of grass tied up with ribbon. When she returned, she was, impossibly, even lighter and more fragile. She was like the discarded husk of a cricket after it outgrows itself. No one mentioned this. It was unmentionable. Her face was as pale as clouds, except the storm-dark skin around her eyes. She tired easily and slept much.

My aunt made sure she had pressed skirts to wear. And starched gloves. And polished shoes. And smart tops. She made sure there were belts properly sized to cinch her roomy clothing to her tiny frame. Once the bald spots began to disappear and my mother's hair returned, Marla arranged for the hairdresser to come by the house, and later the Avon lady. She painted my mother's nails and praised her when she ate and often reminded her that she was looking so much like herself. I wondered at this.

I didn't know who else my mother would look like. I wanted to question it. But had no words to form such a question.

Auntie Marla, during this time, became my mother in opposite. She was tall, broad shouldered, and took a wide stance. She could lift heavy objects that my father could not. I never once saw her in a skirt. Or a pair of pumps. She wore trousers belted high and stomped about in her military-issued boots. Sometimes she put on a man's hat, which she wore at an angle over her pinned curls, which she always kept short. She wore dark red lipstick, which my mother found shocking, but she kept her fingernails trimmed, blunt, and unpainted, like a man's, which my mother also found shocking.

My aunt, once upon a time, flew planes—first in the Air Transport Auxiliary, and then in the Women's Army Corps, and then briefly in the Women Airforce Service Pilots during the first part of the war until they grounded her for reasons that I was never told, and had her fixing engines instead. And she was good at fixing engines. Everyone wanted her help. She left the WASP abruptly when my grandparents died, and worked as a mechanic in an auto repair shop to support my mother through college, and then simply continued. I didn't know this was a strange occupation for a young woman until much later. At work she spent the day bent over or slid under revving machinery, her magic hands coaxing them back to life. And I think she liked her work. But even as a little girl, I noticed the way her eyes lifted always to the sky, like someone longing for home.

I loved my aunt, but I hated her too. I was a child, after all. And I wanted my *mother* to make my breakfast and my *mother* to take me to the park and my *mother* to glare at my father when he was, once again, out of line. But now it was my aunt who did all those things, and I couldn't forgive her for it. It was the first time I noticed that a person can feel opposite things at the same time.

Once, when I was supposed to be napping, I crept out of bed and tiptoed into my father's study, which adjoined the master bathroom, which adjoined my parents' bedroom. I opened the door just a crack and peeked inside. I was a curious child. And I was hungry for information.

My mother lay on the bed with no clothes on, which was unusual. My aunt sat next to her, rubbing oil into my mother's skin with long, sure strokes. My mother's body was covered in scars—wide, deep burns. I pressed my hand to my mouth. Had my mother been attacked by a monster? Would anyone have told me if she had? I set my teeth on the fleshy part of my fingers and bit down hard to keep myself from crying out as I watched. In the places where her breasts should have been, two bulbous smiles bit into her skin, bright pink and garish. I couldn't look at them for very long. My aunt ran her oily thumbs gently along each scar, one after another. I winced as my mother winced.

"They're getting better," Auntie Marla said. "Before you know it, they'll be so pale you'll barely notice them."

"You're lying again," my mother said, her voice small and dry. "No one's meant to keep on like—"

"Oh, come now," Marla said briskly. "Enough of that talk. I saw men with worse during the war, and they kept on with things, didn't they. So can you. Just you wait. You'll outlive us all. After all my prayers, I wouldn't be surprised if you turn immortal. Next leg."

My mother complied, turning away from me and lying on her side so my aunt could massage oil into her left leg and lower torso, the heels of her hands going deep into the muscle. She had burns on her back as well. My mother shook her head and sighed. "You'd wish me to be Tithonus, would you?"

Marla shrugged. "Unlike you, I didn't have a big sister to browbeat me into finishing college, so I don't know all your fancy references, Miss Smartypants. But sure. You can be just like whoever that is."

My mother buried her face into the crook of her arm. "It's mythology," she explained. "Also it's a poem I used to love. Tithonus was a man—a mortal—in ancient Greece who fell in love with a goddess and they decided to get married. The god-dess, though, hated the very thought that her husband would die someday, and so she granted him immortality."

"How romantic," my aunt said. "Left arm, please."

"Not really," my mother sighed. "Gods are stupid and short-sighted. They're like children." She shook her head. "No. They're worse. They're like men—no sense of unintended consequences or follow-through. The goddess took away his ability to die. But he still *aged,* because she hadn't thought to also give him eternal youth. So each year he became older, sicker, weaker. He dried out and shriveled, getting smaller and smaller until finally he was the size of a cricket. The goddess just carried him in her pocket for the rest of time, often completely forgetting he was there. He was broken and useless and was utterly without hope that any-thing could change. It wasn't romantic at all."

"Roll all the way onto your stomach, darling," my aunt said, eager to change the subject. My mother groaned as she read-justed herself. Marla tinkered with my mother's muscles the way she tinkered with cars—smoothing, adjusting, righting what once was wrong. If anyone could fix my mother, it was my aunt. She clicked her tongue. "Well, with this much oil, I can't imag-ine you drying out all that much. But after the scare we had, after you almost—" Auntie Marla's voice cracked just a bit. She pressed the back of her hand to her mouth and pretended to cough. But even then, as young as I was, I knew it was pretend. She shook her head and resumed her work on my mother's body. "Well. Carrying you around with me in my pocket forever doesn't sound half-bad. I'd take it, actually." She cleared her throat, but her words became thick. "I'd take it any old day you like."

I shouldn't remember any of this exchange, but strangely, I do. I remember every word of it. For me, this isn't entirely unusual—I spent most of my childhood memorizing things by accident. Filing things away. I didn't know what any of their conversation meant, but I knew how it made me feel. My head felt hot and my skin felt cold, and the space around my body seemed to vibrate and spin. I needed my mother. I needed my mother to be well. And in the irrational reasoning of a child, I thought that the way to do this was to get my aunt to leave—if she left, my thinking went, then surely my mother would be all right. If Auntie Marla left, then no one would need to feed my mother, or do her tasks around the house, or rub her muscles, or make sure she got dressed, or keep her safe in any kind of pocket. My mother would simply be my mother. And the world would be as it should.

I went back to my room, and I thought about the dragon in my neighbor's yard. How it seemed to marvel at its clawed hands and gnarled feet. How it peered behind itself to look at its wings. I remembered the gasp and the *Oh!* I remembered the way it curled its haunches and arched its back. The ripple of muscles under iridescent skin. The way it readied its wings. And that astonishing launch skyward. I remember my own sharp gasp as the dragon disappeared into the clouds. I closed my eyes and imagined my aunt growing wings. My aunt's muscles shining with metallic scales. My aunt's gaze tilting to the sky. My aunt flying away.

I wrapped myself in a blanket and closed my eyes tight—trying as a child tries to imagine it true.

The earliest known documentation of spontaneous dragoning in recorded history can be found in the formerly lost writings of Timaeus of Tauromenium, written around 310 BC. These manuscripts were discovered originally during the excavation of the vast, underground libraries located in the heart of the Palace of Nestor, but remained unread and unstudied until recently, due to a misclassification of its storage vault. The Timaeus fragments, among other things, shed new light on the historical person of Queen Dido of Carthage: priestess of Astarte, swindler of kings, and trickster of the high seas. The accounts of her life in literature (from Cicero to Virgil to Plutarch and every insufferable boor in between) all vary wildly—each portraying various aspects of an undeniably complex, inscrutable, and fundamentally defiant woman. The accounts of her death, on the other hand, are fairly uniform. Specifically, that Dido—either because of grief, or rage, or revenge, or simply as an act of self-sacrifice to save the city that she founded and built and loved—calmly ascended her own funeral pyre and threw herself upon her husband's sword, breathing her last as the flames engulfed her.

And perhaps that's true.

But the Timaeus writings provide an alternate view. The fragments of Book 19, Book 24, and Book 49 of Timaeus's Historiai provide both brief and casual references to a separate fate of Queen Dido, presented in a way that assumes the reader already knows and understands the story mentioned in the text. This casual referencing, one might argue, is significant, as it implies that the writer does not see the need to argue his view of the events—instead, he simply references a narrative to his contemporaneous audience in a way that suggests it is both accepted and acceptable. Timaeus describes how Queen Dido, flanked by her priestesses on either side, stood upon the shore and watched as the ocean turned dark with Trojan ships, hungry for Carthage's harbor, and riches, and resources, and women. Timaeus describes Carthage as a flowing breast from which Aeneas and his entourage longed to feed, and how the whole city quaked before the terrible hunger of men.

The Timaeus fragments provide tantalizing clues. In Book 19, he describes that the queen and her priestesses opened their garments and let them fall to the ground. "They stepped out of their robes like nymphs, and they stepped out of their bodies like monsters," Timaeus writes, adding that "the sea burned with a thousand pyres." What sort of monsters? And whose pyres burned? Timaeus does not say. In Book 24, he writes, "Oh, Carthage! City of dragons! Woe to you for turning your back on your holy protectresses! Inside a generation, Dido's noble city lay in waste upon the ground." And in Book 49, describing Dido's earlier swindle of King Pygmalion and her subsequent escape across the sea, Timaeus writes, "During her journey, the young Queen traveled to islands that did not appear on any map and bade her men wait for her in the ships as she swam to the land on her own. Each time she returned with women—to be both priestesses and wives, the men were told. The men shivered when they saw these women, and could not account for why. Oh, how their eyes glittered! Oh, how their robes rustled like wings! And oh, how a forcefulness burned in their bellies. They were strong like men, these priestesses. They sunned themselves like lizards upon the decks. The sailors agreed to give the women a wide berth. And those who forgot themselves, who reached lustfully where one should not, had often disappeared by the next morning, their names never spoken again."

Did Dido dragon? Did her priestesses transform? We cannot know. But two things should give us ample reason to pay close attention to the Historiai. First, the Timaeus account is the earliest recording of these events, and therefore less likely to be tainted by the political pressures of revisionism. Men, after all, delight in nothing so much as to recast themselves in the center of the story. And second, throughout history, the occasional and seemingly spontaneous bouts of female dragoning (they are not, in truth, spontaneous, but we will get to that later in this paper) are almost universally followed by a collective refusal to accept incontrovertible facts, and a society-wide decision to forget verifiable events that are determined to be too alarming, too messy, too unsettling. This practice did not start with Queen Dido, and it did not end with her either.

I shall now explore twenty-five discrete historical examples of mass dragoning and their subsequent memory repression, ending, of course, with the astonishing events here in the United States in 1955. Our own Mass Dragoning, while admittedly unusual in terms of its numbers and scope, was not unique in the context of world history. Spontaneous dragoning, I intend to prove, is not a new phenomenon. But given the sheer number of transformations in 1955, it is imperative that we learn from history's mistakes, and chart a different path. It is my thesis that every mass dragoning in history is followed by a phenomenon that I call a "mass forgetting." And indeed, it is the forgetting, I argue, which proves to be far more damaging, and results in more scars on the psyche, and scars on the culture. Furthermore, it is my conclusion that the United States is, at present, in the midst of another such forgetting, with repercussions that are both trackable and quantifiable—and hopefully reversible if coordinated action is taken now.

—"A Brief History of Dragons" by Professor H. N. Gantz, MD, PhD, originally published in the *Annals of Public Health Research,* by the United States Department of Health, Education, and Welfare on February 3, 1956. It was redacted three days later and all copies, except this one, were destroyed.

3

Looking back, I think perhaps my mother had similarly complicated feelings toward my aunt. She loved her sister. And yet. As
my mother recovered, a chilliness spread between them.

"I can do it myself," my mother said in the kitchen as my
aunt kneaded the bread dough. "No need to trouble yourself,"
she said in the bathroom as my aunt scrubbed the grout. She said
it when my aunt tried to braid my hair or when she attempted
to dust the furniture.

"I'll take over, thank you," she said as my aunt read me a
story. She lifted my small body out of Marla's broad lap and
snatched the book away.

And when my aunt called me Alex, my mother's eyes narrowed. "It's Alexandra," she said, her voice flat and final.

The room went cold. My mother held me tight. My auntie
Marla's face went strangely blank. "Of course," she said. Her
words were soft and muffled as snow. "Would you like me to see
to the kitchen?"

My mother's arms squeezed around my body like an iron
vise. "That won't be necessary," she said. "Thank you for your
assistance today," she added, as though my aunt was a trouble-
some employee who needed to be shown the door.

My aunt smiled, briefly and vaguely. She slid her hands into
the deep pockets of her dungarees and rocked back on her heels.
Her eyes flicked toward the window, briefly, and then she turned
toward the door. "Of course, darling," she said. "I can see I'm in
your way. Give me a ring if you need anything."

My mother didn't respond. She just held me tight as she
listened to my aunt's footsteps hitting the wood floor, then the

tile of the entryway. She flinched as the front door swung firmly shut.

Auntie Marla returned the next day, and the next, but even I could tell that something had changed. A storm lingered at the edge of the sky, biding its time.

My mother's color came back and her strength returned—in dribs and drabs at first, and then as a flood. Her hair once again shone. And her patience with my aunt grew more and more thin. Auntie Marla was prone to saying shocking things from time to time. I didn't understand what she meant or why it was shocking, but I did notice that the things she said often made my mother's face turn red. Also, my aunt frequently mentioned my mother's life—her work, particularly—from before she got married. My aunt wanted to talk about it all the time. How proud she was of my mother. And when she did, her face would shine and her hands would clasp together, as though she was praying. My mother, on the other hand, became more brittle and tense and closed—like a clockwork toy, wound way too tight.

"Top of her class, your mother was, Alex," Marla would say, in a voice like the narrator of a fairy tale. "She left everyone in the shade. A mathematics magician. An absolute—"

And then my mother would leave the room, closing her bedroom door with a definitive slap.

Finally, after months of simmering frustration, the voices of my mother and my aunt boiled over. Dishes clattered and a jar splintered in the sink and an open hand cracked against a soft cheek. My mother grunted with frustration. My aunt cried for a single second and the room went terribly still. I hid under the table. I put my hands over my ears. I still remember everything.

Specifically, this: Just before the front door flew open and my aunt stomped outside, my mother paused on the front stoop. She called to her sister's retreating figure, "Come back when you choose a *normal* life. Get a husband. Have a child. Maybe then we can be friends again."

My aunt didn't turn around. I saw her chest expand, hold,

and slowly contract. She tilted her face to the sky. "All right," she said at last. "I'll see what I can do."

The house was silent after my aunt left. For a long time. My mother gave me a stack of paper to draw on and she again retreated to her room.

And while my aunt did not set foot in our house for two years after that, she still accompanied us to church. Marla and my mother sat on opposite sides of my father and me, like bookends—my mother in embroidered dresses, and my aunt in loose-fitting woolen slacks and a blouse that opened at her throat. She was the only woman in slacks in church—which would have been shocking at the time, and probably not allowed in most churches, for most women—but my aunt had a way about her that made people think that whatever she did was perfectly fine. People besides my mother, that is. After all, most women didn't fly planes or work in auto repair shops, but she did both of those quite well, and then once they thought about it *that* way, no one really cared about the pants. Both Marla and my mother wore the matching veils that my grandmother had given them before she died—hand-knotted lace, with complex and beautifully wrought patterns, curling around each of their faces, attached to their hair with bobby pins. Every Sunday, all through Mass, the two sisters gave each other sidelong glances, as though each daring the other to say something.

Eventually, my aunt did exactly what my mother wanted. She got married. To a shiftless drunk. I was only six, and even I knew it was a terrible idea—primarily because I overheard everyone say so. Still. She was a wife now. And, true to her word, my mother and aunt were friends again. Sort of.

They didn't mention the argument. They didn't mention the long separation and silence. They became brisk with one another. Brittle. Vague smiles painted on their faces like the hardened gaze of porcelain dolls. They didn't mention this either.

In any case, it didn't really matter in the end. When my mother went away when I was four years old, her sickness was unmentionable. When she returned it was *still* unmentionable. What happened to the old lady across the alley was unmentionable, too. As was the boarded-up house. People walked by and averted their eyes.

But, whether anyone liked it or not, the Mass Dragoning of 1955 was coming. My family, my school, my town, my country, and the whole world were about to fundamentally change.

And this change, too, would be unmentionable.

4.

Even though my aunt and uncle became regular presences in my house after they got married, my uncle always seemed to me to be a bit of an afterthought—and even more so after my cousin Beatrice was born. Now, all these years later, I can barely remember what he looked like. I just remember his scratchy chin and sour smell and that he was sometimes mean. He became infinitely ignorable once Beatrice came along.

Oh, Beatrice, Beatrice, Beatrice! She came into my life like a rare bird—all color and motion and enthusiastic yawp. She had orange hair and eyes the color and sheen of beetles' wings and skin that turned grubby within seconds of washing. On the day she was born, I swear that the sky froze and the sun stood still and the earth began to vibrate. On the day she was born, no one told me my aunt was heading to the hospital, or that this was the day that the most wonderful human to ever exist would enter the world. But I knew it all the same. The universe became more of itself once Beatrice was in it.

Beatrice and I were made for each other. We were the paired wings of a dragonfly, or lightning with its necessary thunderclap, or the spinning dance of binary stars.

The evening visits from my aunt and uncle felt very different indeed after that. My required presence at the dinner table—to practice social graces, and sit still, and speak only when spoken to—went from a mere annoyance to an interminable chore. What use had I for the world of adults when Beatrice was in the house? Beatrice with her whole fist stuck inside of a drooling smile. Beatrice only just discovering her toes. Beatrice following along with a baby song, her light, clear voice matching my pitch and volume with accuracy and intention, erupting in giggles at the end of each phrase. Beatrice squealing with delight when a toy reappeared. Beatrice was, from the moment she was born, my favorite person on the planet. Sometimes, it felt as though she was the only person on the planet. Or that the two of us were. We were Beatrice and Alex, rulers of the world.

I sat at the table with the adults in my child's chair, painted red, with my hands folded and my napkin on my lap, counting the moments until I could ask to be excused to go to the living room to play with the baby. *Ten minutes,* my mother had told me. Ten minutes I had to sit at the table and *make conversation* though I wasn't exactly sure how, since I was also told that children should be seen and not heard. I watched the clock. Each minute that went by seemed to last a thousand years.

And it was in that moment, when I watched the minute hand creep toward another notch, that I noticed my father's voice becoming hard, and abrupt.

"It's the past," he said, his voice whipping across my face, like a slap. I flinched. "It's not polite to bring up the past." A weighted silence dropped, and my ears began to ring. My mother's skin turned pale, and her shoulders curled inward. My father's face confused me. His jaw clenched and his mouth became hard and grim, showing the serrated edge of his lower teeth. But his eyes told a different story—damp, soft, and pleading.

My aunt began to finger the bracelet on her left arm—a complex pattern of knotted wire that my mother had skillfully made with a crochet hook as a bridal present. She had two, one for each wrist. The metal whorls and twists glinted and flickered in the candlelight, as though they too were made out of flames. "Well, there are several things that aren't especially polite," my aunt said with a swallowed smile. She set down her fork and began to dab her fingers and mouth with her napkin. "But that doesn't stop folks from doing them. On business trips, for example." She winked, and sipped her glass of wine, her red lipstick lingering on the glass, like the ghost of a kiss.

"Can we please not argue," my mother said in a small voice. The air in the room became tight. My father's cheeks clenched and relaxed, clenched and relaxed. The skin on his neck turned red. I looked at the clock. It seemed to have stopped. Beatrice cooed in her baby seat in the other room. Likely examining her toes again. She giggled at something. The air perhaps. Or perhaps her own wonderful self. I bit my lip. Beatrice was being cute and I was *missing it.*

My uncle swirled the dark liquid in his glass and knocked it back. Refilled it in a flash. "Don't make her mad, George," he rasped, casting a bloodshot eye toward my aunt. "You know what they say about angry women."

My aunt gave him a hard stare and the color drained from his face. Her eyes were dark and hot. "And what do they say? Darling," she said with the calmness of a snake about to strike. She gently readjusted her bracelets as though they itched.

His lips were dry. He didn't say anything. He returned his cup to his lips and jerked his head back, pouring his drink down his throat.

"We don't have to talk about this now," my mother said, gathering the plates into a haphazard stack. "It doesn't matter anymore, anyway." She hurried into the kitchen and let the dishes fall into the sink with a colossal clatter.

My aunt swiveled her gaze and let it land directly on me. Her eyes became normal again. "Alex, you've been quiet," she said. "Tell me what you've been thinking about, my love."

I wasn't expecting to be addressed, and her sudden gaze nearly made me jump. "I don't know," I said, falling over my words. "Not the clock," I added, a little too loud, even as my eyes unconsciously flicked back to the minute hand, which inexplicably hadn't moved since we started dinner. I had already been told, repeatedly, that it wasn't polite to stare at clocks when you're at the dinner table. It was unkind to our guests, my mother explained.

"Ah," my aunt said. "I see." She exchanged an amused glance

with my mother, who was now at the door between the living room and the dining room, and who was not, I could tell, amused.

My aunt returned her attention to me. "Do you know what we're talking about, Alex?" she said.

"She doesn't care what we're talking about," my mother said, putting her body between my aunt and me, interrupting the moment. She hoisted the casserole dish and grabbed the soiled utensils, clanking them inside. She bustled back into the kitchen.

"Drop it, Marla," my father said. His voice was cold and flat and unforgiving.

Marla didn't take her eyes off me. "We're talking about your mother. This woman here," she gestured in the direction of my mother's retreating figure. "I believe you've met." She smiled at the table. No one smiled back. She persisted. "Did you know that your mother—*your mother*—graduated top of her class, but the Mathematics Department refused to give her an honors distinction because she was a girl?"

"What's honors?" I asked, even though I didn't actually care. Beatrice was giggling and I thought this conversation was stupid and I wanted more than anything to ask to be excused.

"Honors is when you take a regular degree and make it *fancy*," my aunt said. "Because the person who earned it is fancy."

"Mama already is fancy," I said. My mother patted my head as she hurried back and forth between the table and the kitchen and my father guffawed approvingly.

"You see?" my father said. "Alexandra knows what's what." He lit his cigarette and leaned back in his chair, relaxing a bit.

"It's Alex," I said quietly, with a scowl. No one noticed.

"But do you think that's fair, darling?" my aunt pressed, lighting her own cigarette, and blowing smoke at my father. "Shouldn't her teachers have said she's the smartest, since she actually *was* the smartest? In front of everyone?" Auntie Marla's gaze held me in place. Her eyes seemed a bit larger than normal. The rims of her irises shone like gold. I couldn't move if I tried.

"Obviously," I said. I was in the third grade. I knew about fairness.

"It doesn't matter," my father said, angrily waving the smoke away. "Alexandra, go to the living room." He glared at my aunt. "Who cares about her problem sets and papers? Who cares about honors and awards? No one remembers them. What use is a college diploma for a person who is perfectly happy keeping a lovely home? Foolish use of money, if you ask me. And time. And for what, really? She took a spot at the university that could have gone to a smart boy with a bright future who would likely have gone on to produce something of value. Seems like a waste to me."

The room grew suddenly hot. My aunt was big and loud and *shiny*. Sometimes she laughed louder than any man I knew. I found her thrilling, but terrifying too. She had a way of occupying a room that felt dangerous. She was heat and claw and intentional velocity. Even then.

My cheeks flushed. My aunt ignored my father. She kept her eyes fixed on me, with a tiny curl of a smile hiding in her mouth.

"So there she was, your mother, the very smartest and best in her whole class, a shining star, and she applies to graduate school to study mathematics, and they don't take her. They say no. Not because she's not smart enough, but simply because she was a girl. Well, now. Does that sound fair to you?"

I didn't say anything. But I don't think my aunt was actually talking to me, not really.

"So instead, your darling mama became a clerk at your dad's bank. With her algorithms and slide rules, her lightning-fast figuring. And guess what, she was amazing. She was a sorceress with numbers. She could make any fund—literally any one—grow like magic. She tied spreadsheets together like mystical knots and made numbers expand simply by looking at them." Marla moved her hands in big gestures as she spoke, the bracelets on her wrists glinting as though they were on fire. She closed her eyes and her face glowed.

"You're being ridiculous!" my mother said from the other room. She was upset. I could tell. But I couldn't tell why. Beatrice giggled and my father told me again to go to the living room, but I couldn't seem to move.

My uncle filled another cup. "Lady accountants," he guffawed. "Of all the stupid—"

Marla reached over and swatted him on the back of his head. She did this without altering her position or posture and without looking at him at all.

"Gah!" my uncle choked. "Marla!" My aunt acted as though she hadn't heard him.

"That's magic, my darling," my auntie Marla said to me. "What do you think of that?"

My mother reappeared in the doorway. There were tears in her eyes. I hated it when my mother was upset. I turned on my aunt and glared at her, folding my reedy arms across my chest. *How dare she,* I thought. How dare she upset my mother in this way? Granted, I had no real understanding as to *why* my mother was bothered. Only that she was. And it was my aunt's fault, I was pretty sure. I stuck out my tongue at her. This just made her smile.

"You disagree, Alex?" she said to me.

"It's Alexandra," my father corrected, taking his last inhale of his cigarette and snuffing it out on the ashtray in the middle of the table.

I glowered, but didn't respond.

Marla kept her gaze on me. I felt my skin start to singe. "You dispute your mother's powers, Alex?" she said.

My mother remained in the doorway, like a pillar of salt. The light from the kitchen shone around her.

"Numbers *aren't* magic," I said firmly. I knew this wasn't the reason I was rattled, *exactly.* At times, the tension between adults felt like acid on my skin—no physical wound, but burning all the same. My aunt had made my mother sad. Or maybe my father had. But I couldn't explain how, as the words I knew at the time were unwieldy tools, improperly calibrated for the topic at hand. This only made me more angry. At my aunt, mostly. I scowled to make sure she knew. "Numbers," I said with particular emphasis, "are *numbers*."

My aunt took in this piece of information, clearly impressed. "Agreed," my aunt said. I leaned back in my chair and relaxed. Even back then, I liked *winning*. "But to be fair," she continued, "I never said that *numbers* were magic. I said that your *mother* was magic. A sorceress, specifically, but let's just say magic. It's easier. But here's the thing, Alex, my love. This isn't new information, and your mother isn't alone. All women are magic. Literally all of us. It's in our nature. It's best you learn that now."

My father gave an incredulous grunt, and my uncle, far too deep in his cups, brayed like a donkey. "Well if that isn't—"

And, abruptly, the table fell silent. The sound simply ceased in my uncle's throat. A single glance from my aunt was enough to stop his words at the source. I looked at her, and her eyes were two hot coals. The wire knots around her wrists grew so hot they glowed, and left burns along the edges of her arms. No one moved. No one breathed. My uncle looked pinned in place, as though my aunt's eyes had pierced him in the middle and stitched him shut. He was in her power and at her mercy. She smiled as he went pale.

And then, with a wave of my aunt's hand, the moment passed. My uncle gasped for breath. "You were saying, my love?" my aunt hissed.

My father's hands shook. His eyes were wide. He didn't say a thing. My uncle drained his glass and stumbled toward the door. I learned later he went on what my father called "a bender" (I didn't learn what that meant until much later) and was gone without a word for over a week. No one missed him.

As a preface to the analysis of the various documented cases of mass dragoning in human history that I attempt in this paper, I do wish to add a personal aside, as it will, I believe, assist us in creating the lens through which we must view these events.

On that fateful day in April of 1955, while I, myself, did not experience the shock of a dragoning within my own family, immediate or extended, I did bear witness to one such transformation—Mrs. Norbert Donahue, the wife of one of my colleagues. I had originally known her by her maiden name, years earlier, as she was one of my residents at Johns Hopkins University Hospital, where she went by Dr. Edna Wood. Shortly after her training, she left the practice of medicine to marry and have her children, and thus left her title behind. On the day of the Mass Dragoning, I saw Mrs. Donahue moments before her transformation, as she went streaking through the hallways in a rush, her handbag swinging from her left arm like a pendulum. "Madam," I said, nodding in her direction. She did not stop, nor did she seem to hear me. I did notice that her neck shone. And she seemed taller than I remembered.

She strode into Dr. Donahue's office, screamed something unintelligible, and walked out, sobbing. She had been, I must add, one of my favorite residents, and while it had been many years since the two of us had conversed, I was moved by her obvious distress, and so I approached to see if I could offer comfort, or assistance. "Dr. Wood," I said. "I mean, Mrs. Donahue," I corrected myself. And then I gasped. Her teeth had elongated, becoming razor-sharp. Her eyes, once small and blue, were now the size of fists, dark gold, with horizontal pupils, like twin horizons.

I was astonished. I knew what was happening to her, of course, being well versed in what scant literature existed on the subject. But I had never seen it firsthand, at close proximity. Indeed, few have done so and lived. Since I did not know whether she would be capable of human speech after the process was complete, I thought it prudent to conduct an interview in medias res, and began transcribing my observations as I lobbed questions at Mrs. Donahue—now the subject. The activity was not entirely fruitful, unfortunately. I asked the subject to provide a narrative of her experience, paying close attention to the sensations in the area surrounding the womb—as that, at the time, was my primary focus as the catalyst for such transformations (though later data revealed the flaw in this hypothesis). But also, if she could, an explanation of basic bodily functions would be helpful—respiration, vision, muscle pain. All useful data points. Did she feel flushed, as though with a menopausal hot flash? Did she feel the nausea or muscle cramps associated with pregnancy and childbirth? Was the production of scales accompanied by a burning sensation? Did the eruption of fangs cause bleeding of the gums?

Mrs. Donahue provided no narrative. Instead, she stared at me for a moment. Then she spoke, each word punctuated with a rattling breath: "Everything, is, just, too, damn, SMALL." Her voice was a harsh rasp. She paused, her skin starting to split, an elongating spine pushing out of the back of her dress. Her face snapped forward and she fixed her gaze on me. She smiled. "You should probably run, Doctor," she said.

And so I did.

—"A Brief History of Dragons" by Professor H. N. Gantz, MD, PhD

5.

There is another memory that I still can't make sense of. Even now.

It was a Friday morning in late February. Almost exactly two months before . . . well, before everything changed. I was eight. Actually, I was eight and seven twelfths, I told people, because I was a child who delighted in accuracy. I remember standing at the window, staring at the ice crystals that had written themselves onto the glass, an explosion of geometry and light. I had already finished my breakfast and had braided my hair all by myself (I was rather proud of it) and had put on my school uniform. My mother chased me outside so she could clear the breakfast dishes in peace. Or that's what she told me. In truth, my mother just liked the quiet, an unobstructed space where she could sew or crochet or knit and listen to silence. Occasionally, I would climb up the trellis to peek on her through the window, and watch as she sat, simply tying knots, one after another, each a complex, intricate puzzle. My mother loved string. She loved how a single strand could twist and loop into infinite patterns and infinite possibilities—whole universes could be tangled in a single thread. She made diagrams of each knot in a little notebook that I was not allowed to look at by myself, with corresponding calculations and algebraic expressions that defined the ways in which each wobble, loop, twist, and elbow intersected, interplayed, and bent inside themselves. I didn't understand how the equations worked, or what they meant. She promised she'd explain the mathematics of it to me someday.

(She didn't, though. Of course she didn't. Maybe she never meant to. How can I ever know what my mother meant? Even now, after all these years, she is a memory of a memory of a memory—her own kind of unsolvable, inscrutable knot.)

I didn't have to leave for school for another hour. Normally, this would be my time to sit with my father (usually in silence, as my father read the paper and I read one of my books. We typically interacted best when we didn't speak. This remained true as I got older), but my father was away on a business trip. I noticed the way my mother's lower lip trembled when she said that. I knew better than to ask why.

I had thick woolen mittens that my mother had knitted for me, each painstakingly patterned with her knotwork on the back. In addition to the knots in her craft basket and the knots on my mittens, our whole house was full of lace curtains that she crocheted, and hand-knotted runners on the end tables and sashes on the sofas. She even had special knots that she would slip into my pockets. A knot for safety. A knot for luck. A knot for knowledge. A knot to prevent change. Sometimes, she said that knots were magic. Sometimes, she said they were math. More often, though, she said that both were true, the way a particle can be both matter and light and no one knows why. I thought they were just those things that moms do. Like the notes with hearts stuck in a lunch box.

My mittens were bright red, and stood in contrast to the grey ice and the greyer sky. February in Wisconsin can be like that—a day of warmth will decrease the snowpack, and send melting snow washing into the streets and sidewalks, and then is followed by a frigid blast which encases the world in ice. Partially melted snow piles transform into hard, grey lumps, and the sky becomes dismal. I carefully made my way down the front stairs. My mother had lined my yellow rubber boots with several layers of felted wool, but they were still too big for me—a hand-me-down from another kid in the neighborhood. My feet slid with every step. I let go of the railing and let myself glide down the icy walkway. I spun and glided back.

I would have done that all day, pushing and gliding and balancing and spinning, but an old Ford rumbled down the street and parked in front of my house. My heart lifted. That car had my aunt in it. And with her, Beatrice. Two days a week Beatrice spent the day with my mother, and she spent the other three with a babysitter. I treasured our Beatrice days, seeing her face in the fleeting moments before school, and playing with her all afternoon when I returned home. There was more light and sound and joy in my home when Beatrice was there. I threw open my arms and spun madly on the ice, hoping that Beatrice would notice. She was at this time exactly nine and a half months old. I had a calendar in my room whose only purpose was to mark the weeks since Beatrice's birth and a chart that documented the things Beatrice could do now, along with her changing preferences and dislikes. I was an expert on my baby cousin.

My aunt emerged from the car, the baby on her hip, and a cigarette dangling from her mouth. That was not unusual. She had always smoked, but since the birth of the baby, she smoked even more. I would have asked my mother about it, but I assumed it would be unmentionable.

"Hi!" I said, waving madly. Beatrice squealed back, her feet kicking in her bright red woolen snowsuit that my mother had made. It, too, had complicated knotwork stitched along the sides.

My aunt lifted her gaze to the sky. "Where's your mother," she said, her words heavy with smoke. Her face was grey and her eyes were smudged and puffy. She hitched up her shoulders and rotated them back as she stretched her neck, curling her fingers briefly beneath the base of the skull and pressing into the muscle, as though it hurt.

"She's inside," I said, as I continued to make funny faces at Beatrice. "Doing the dishes. My father is—"

"Yes," my aunt said, sucking in her last inhale and throwing the rest of the cigarette down on the ground, smashing it with her boot. "Business trip, right?" Her face was blank, except for a bit of a scornful curl in her upper lip.

I shrugged. "I guess." I didn't know what else to say.

My aunt's eyes stayed focused upward. I wondered in that moment if she was remembering flying planes. I wondered in that moment if maybe she didn't particularly like her job at the mechanic's shop, where all she did was look down at engines, instead of keeping her gaze on the domed sky above.

"Come inside with me," she said. "I need you to be in charge of Beatrice. I have to talk to your mother."

I didn't need to be asked again. I skated over the icy walkway (my aunt had no trouble with her heavy military boots), and we went inside.

What happened next, I still can't entirely make out.

Beatrice and I settled in the living room, where my mother kept a tub of toys just for her. I often said that they should just move into our house, since my uncle was never home, as far as I could tell. But no one listened to me.

My aunt set Beatrice down and walked into the kitchen.

"Where are your bracelets," I heard my mother say.

There was a long pause. "Gone," she said finally.

My mother said nothing in response. She just banged on the dishes for a while.

This wasn't nearly as interesting as Beatrice. I flattened myself onto my tummy in front of her on the floor, and I built towers of blocks that she knocked over with a squeal of delight. We did this over and over. Beatrice thumped her heels on the ground. She brought her small hands to her round cheeks. She was my favorite person in the whole world.

My mother raised her voice.

So did my aunt.

I made a stack of blocks. Beatrice knocked it over. She had drool on her chin. She picked up one of the blocks and chewed on it desperately, her mouth spreading into a wet smile on either side of it.

My mother's voice was louder.

So was my aunt's.

A glass fell and shattered on the kitchen's tile floor. My

mother cried. My aunt's voice became soft. I built a stack of blocks. Beatrice knocked it over. Her laugh lit the room.

And then . . . *well*. The world became strange.

My mittens, sitting on the ground next to Beatrice and me, began to change. I watched as the yarn unwound itself and rewound differently, writhing gently like a basket of snakes. I inched away, and tucked my hands under my bottom. Afraid to touch anything. Afraid to move. And it wasn't just the mittens. The crocheted curtains and the lace table runners and the hand-made sashes. Each knot began to unravel, and then re-form. The morning light slanted through the windows and spilled onto the floor. I tilted my head and squinted at the curtains. The loops untwisted and unraveled and rearranged themselves. My mittens unwound into a heap of yarn, and then, loop after loop, twist after twist, came back together. Same mittens. Different patterns. I held myself perfectly still. Beatrice knocked a block on another block with a terrific clack. She howled with laughter. She knocked her heels on the ground. Her booties, also knitted by my mother, also with dense, complicated patterns at the toes, rearranged themselves. The patterns became denser, more complex, the tight curls latticing themselves together like an impenetrable lock. Beatrice did not notice. I didn't know what I was seeing, but I still paid attention. I filed each detail away, so I wouldn't forget.

"ENOUGH," my mother yelled. "It simply won't happen."

My aunt, I could hear from the other room, suppressed a sob. I made a stack of blocks. Beatrice knocked it over. The light spilled through the room. The curtains and the table settings and my mittens and the booties, all in flux and transition not moments before, were now stable and whole. As though nothing had happened. The slanted sunbeams glinted with stirred-up dust motes. I hadn't imagined it. I knew I hadn't. But I couldn't ask about it either. How could anyone have words for something like that?

I made another stack of blocks. Beatrice knocked it over.

My aunt in the other room said, "You are my favorite. And you always will be. No matter what happens."

I didn't know what that was supposed to mean.

My mother didn't say anything. She stayed in the kitchen. My aunt strode out and knelt next to me. She put her arms around me and hugged me, and covered Beatrice's face with kisses. She looked at the window, her face brightened by the sunlight. Her eyes were red-rimmed, but so bright they were nearly gold. Had they always been gold? I couldn't quite remember. Then she patted our heads, walked outside, and lit another cigarette as she got into her car. I watched her from the window. I watched as a ribbon of smoke curled out of the driver's-side door, like the exhale from some creature out of a fairy tale. The car rumbled, spurted, and shuddered before sliding down the road and vanishing from view.

6.

This is what we know:

On April 25, 1955, between the hours of 11:45 a.m. and 2:30 p.m. central time, 642,987 American women—wives and mothers, all—became dragons. All at once. A mass dragoning. The largest in history.

My mother was not among the women who dragoned on April 25, 1955. But my aunt Marla was. The distribution of dragoning across the country was haphazard and unpredictable. Six children in my third-grade class had mothers who dragoned. In the grade above me, only two children had mothers who were lost. The grade behind had twelve. There were towns hit hard by the dragoning, and towns that were blessedly untouched. The reasons why remain a mystery. Even now.

The facts, of course, are indisputable, but that did not stop people from attempting to dispute the facts. There were eyewitnesses, photographic evidence, utterly destroyed homes and businesses, and no fewer than 1,246 confirmed cases of philandering husbands extracted from the embrace of their mistresses and devoured on the spot, *in view of astonished onlookers*. One dragoning—from its initial gasp, to the eruption of tooth and claw and wing, to the explosion of speed and fire—was caught on 35mm film, taken at a child's birthday party in a backyard in Albany. Only one of three national news broadcasters attempted to show the film, but it was censured immediately by the FCC (and slapped with a hefty fine for the dissemination of obscene and profane material) and forced to suspend operations for a full week before having its license reinstated. It is assumed that more such films exist, but they were presumably either confiscated by local authorities (and in that case, are lost forever) or simply socked away in stacks of film canisters or hoarded in boxes in basements and are likely decomposed by now. Too embarrassing to look at. Too inappropriate. It's dragons, after all—tainted, it would seem, with feminine stink. Such things are not discussed. Best forgotten, people said.

People are awfully good at forgetting unpleasant things.

The number 642,987 became a source of some consternation and argument. While a full reckoning of the women who dragoned on April 25, 1955—who they were, who their children were, whether their husbands survived, and who they devoured—had been commissioned by both the United States government and the United Nations, several key pieces of information remained conspicuously absent. Foremost was this: with the intense focus centered on the discrete events of the Mass Dragoning of 1955, a national silence persisted regarding the other spontaneous dragonings that happened prior to April 25, *and that still continued after*. It was a silence that led to official censure, blacklists, fines, occasional jail time, the shutting down of scientific journals, and the destruction of careers.

Most officials dismissed the possibility of any transformations prior to April 25, 1955, choosing instead to respond to the occasional reports of possible transformations by simply explaining them away. Those who mentioned dragons were often dismissed as conspiracy theorists or deranged kooks. Or worse: cynical provocateurs. For years prior to the Mass Dragoning, any anomalous occurrence provoked state and local governments to once again distribute pamphlets to help quell the rumors, while daily public service announcements interrupted radio and eventually television broadcasts as a coordinated attempt to curb hysterical thinking. And while each explanation was, indeed, *perfectly rational,* not one was altogether *satisfying.*

Consider, for example, the munitions factory outside Portland, Oregon, which had been destroyed by fire and shock wave, only weeks after the end of the Second World War. According to initial reports, the explosion and resulting fire occurred on the very day the female factory workers learned that they would soon be losing their jobs. The men were coming home and settling down, after all. And the nation was preparing to go back to normal. No one knows what happened inside the factory that day; there were no known survivors. But while the bodies of the foremen and supervisors had been extracted from the rubble (in terrible states, all of them, poor fellows), not a single female corpse was ever found. The official explanation was simply that the female employees, standing too close to the blast, had been incinerated instantly, leaving nothing behind to bury. But that didn't account for the dragon-shaped holes in the exterior walls. And it certainly didn't explain the fact that nearby farmers described what felt like a mighty wind, and an explosion of wings, and a flock of what appeared to be enormous birds, streaking across the western sky.

"Munitions factories," the reports said. "They are basically tinderboxes. Explosions happen. Clearly, better safety protocols are needed." Most accepted this explanation. And the world moved on.

A year later, a young wife sat on a park bench in Kalamazoo, Michigan, staring at the sky while her children played in a nearby playground. Her husband had been an officer in the European theater. A hard man, everyone said. Ill-equipped for civilian life. Neighbors whispered that his return wasn't going very well. And then one day, she left her handbag on the ground and simply . . . vanished. There were other mothers, playing with their own children in the same playground, who mentioned a shadow that briefly covered the sun. But when they lifted their faces, it was gone. They shivered as they recounted the story, rubbing their arms briskly, remembering that sudden, fleeting cold.

"We always knew she was flighty," the president of the Junior League said. "Motherhood didn't suit her. We aren't surprised she left." And again, the world moved on.

And there were the stories—hundreds of them across the country—of brides on their wedding days who shut themselves in the dressing rooms in their various houses of worship, saying they had cold feet. By the time their families pried the doors open, they found a wedding dress in pieces on the ground, and a gaping hole in the wall where the window used to be. Church repair became a booming business from coast to coast.

"Brides," newscasters said in knowing tones. "Sometimes they get away."

And then there was the case of the twenty-five female switchboard operators, working the night shift on the boards at the Feibel-Ross Auxiliary Telephone Exchange Building in lower Manhattan in 1952. There had been, prior to the event in question, numerous complaints filed regarding the behavior of a certain nighttime supervisor—Martin O'Leary. More than a simple case of a boss's wandering hands—an expected workplace hazard at the time—these complaints were serious enough that the authorities were called to take statements regarding whether a criminal violation had actually occurred. Several women underwent examinations by police medical staff and agreed to be interviewed by detectives. In the end, nothing happened. Kind men patted pretty little heads and cases closed. Martin O'Leary and his rapacious smile remained in place, and the employees had reportedly been told that they should simply steel themselves against any advances, to look to the example of the cleverest of mice who always know how to avoid the marauding cat. They were told to count themselves lucky to be in a job at all.

No one knows exactly what happened that night in 1952—other than that twenty-five different people rang the operator, asking to make a collect call, only to be told, "A girl can only take so much, after all." And then the line went dead. The building ripped apart at exactly 11:13 p.m. Every brick was crushed. A search through the rubble uncovered Martin O'Leary's polished wing tips, and not much else. His briefcase was found floating in the East River four days later. All traces of the switchboard girls were lost in the blast.

"Gas explosion," the papers said. "No survivors."

No one mentioned the fact that twenty-five pairs of polished pumps and twenty-five handbags and twenty-five smart dresses in different colors had been found laid out neatly on the sidewalk just outside the crater where the building once was. There was a sign, written in what appeared to be ashes on a piece of discarded desktop. It said SMART DRESSES FOR SMART GALS. WEAR UNTIL THIS LIFE NO LONGER FITS YOU. No one knew what it meant.

The Feibel-Ross girls, the runaway brides, the housewife in Kalamazoo, and the munitions workers were all dismissed as tragedies. Any evidence of dragoning was either lost, ignored, or suppressed. Any questioning was dismissed. Even in the aftermath of the Mass Dragoning, there was little interest in government or academia in pursuing cases outside of that event. The Mass Dragoning happened on April 25, 1955, and 642,987 women (wives and mothers, all) transformed: each name was known, investigated, recorded, and it was determined that there could not be a single one more. The case was closed and the book was written and there was nothing more to say.

The Mass Dragoning of 1955 became simply another day that lived in infamy—studied in school, but with more and more distance, more distaste, and more euphemisms every year. The story became vague, ill-defined, and briefly noted. Which made it forgettable. The other cases of spontaneous dragoning were not to be mentioned.

It was too shocking.

It was too embarrassing.

It was too, well, *feminine.* Words stumbled and cheeks went red and the subject became impolite. And so the world looked the other way. It was, for almost everyone, like any other taboo subject—cancer, or miscarriages, or menstruation—spoken of in tight whispers and vague innuendos before changing the subject.

Still.

While I was only a child when the Mass Dragoning of 1955 occurred, I have spent most of my adult life as a scientist and an academic, and the rigors and clarity of my work make me impatient with euphemistic obfuscation and nonsensical taboo. We spend our lives as adults making sense of the memories we carry with us from our childhoods, but we must still be beholden, always, to the facts. And the facts are these:

On April 25, 1955, the world changed.

On April 25, 1955, 642,987 American families changed.

On April 25, 1955, my own family changed forever.

And I have quite a bit more to say on the matter.

From The Washington Post, *January 23, 1956*

A meeting of the secretive House Subcommittee on Compensation and Resolution briefly erupted in chaos on Tuesday afternoon, as a group of activists who had disguised themselves as janitorial staff invaded the locked committee room and refused to allow the representatives to leave. As usual, no agenda for the subcommittee's daily operation was made available to the public, and no minutes were provided. No members of the subcommittee were available for comment, and the arrested activists have been barred from speaking to the press. The standoff lasted for nine hours before police managed to enter the room, whereupon the assailants were arrested without incident. No further information was made available at press time.

[It should be noted that this story did not appear, as one would assume, in the National News section, but on the last page of the Style and Fashion pages. There was no explanation as to why.]

7.

The Mass Dragoning of 1955 happened when I was at school. We were practicing long division, as I recall. The principal arrived at the door, his face tight and pale. He jerked his head toward the hallway, and he and my teacher hurried out. We could hear their whispers hissing under the door, short and staccato. Within moments, they both returned to the classroom and closed the blinds.

"Eyes on your papers," my principal said. "Don't look up."

They told us to be good children. And we *were*. We didn't make a sound.

We did long division for the rest of the day, worksheet after worksheet, until our pencils wore down to nubs.

I remember the sound of sirens.

I remember the smell of smoke.

I remember taking the school bus home and watching houses burn.

I remember watching large shadows streaking across the ground. Each adult told us not to look up at the sky. We had to keep our gazes tilted down. We were good children, so we did as we were told.

When I got home, my mother made me a snack and asked me how my day was. She moved strangely. Her neck was in constant, writhing motion, like a snake. Her shoulders couldn't stay still. She rubbed her arms briskly and lifted her gaze to the sky, again and again. I remember that the phone rang. I remember my mother bringing her hand to her chest and leaving it there for a long time. She let the receiver fall from her other hand. She brought both hands to her mouth and pressed down hard, as though to keep herself from screaming. The receiver swung back and forth, back and forth, until it eventually stopped.

Finally, after a few deep breaths, my mother walked to where I sat. She knelt down at my feet and took my hands. Her eyes were gold. Had they always been gold? She blinked hard, and they returned to their normal grey. I told myself I imagined anything else. My mother brought my fingers to her mouth, and kissed each knuckle, one by one.

"Mother has to go," she said, in between kisses. "But I am coming back. This is important for you to remember. *Your* mother will always come back. No matter what." I felt the corners of my mouth begin to twitch and the skin of my forehead bunching up, but wouldn't let myself frown, even as I felt that familiar, prickly sensation tangle in my belly and move slowly toward my chest. It became noticeably harder to breathe. No one ever talked about the time when my mother vanished from the house and then came back sick and small. Not even Auntie Marla, who talked about *everything*. The memory of her vanishing felt both unpleasant to encounter and dangerous to hold, but I had no place to put it, no ordered shelf in my mind where it belonged. It remained unmentionable and therefore unclassifiable, which meant I had to carry it, every day, no matter how much it hurt.

"Okay," I said. I folded my hands in my lap, and tried very hard not to move. I wanted my mother to think I was a good girl, even though I wasn't entirely sure.

She affixed her hat with a shiny pin and buttoned her coat, her fingers fumbling slightly. Before leaving, she sat down next to me. "Give me your hand," my mother said. I did so without hesitation. My mother's eyes were wide and bright. Gold again. I told myself that they had always been gold. I told myself that they never had been grey. My skin pricked strangely, and I did not know why. My mother reached into her apron pocket and pulled out a string. She wound it around my wrist and began to tie a knot. I tilted my head.

"Is this a bracelet?" I asked.

My mother smiled. Her smile glittered, just a little bit. "In a sense. Look, I have one too," she pointed to her own wrist. A string, wound around three times, had been secured with a complicated knot.

"That's a pretty knot," I said, because I always wanted to admire my mother's work.

"I agree," she said. "Knots are special. Mathematicians spend their lives studying them. A good knot requires presence of mind to make, and can act as an unshakable force in a shaky, unstable world. Don't take this one off, please."

I already wanted to take it off.

My mother's gaze narrowed into something sharp, something I knew better than to defy. "I mean it. Do *not* take it off."

She told me to do my homework, and she also handed me a stack of paper and some pencils and told me to draw pictures until she returned. She kissed my forehead one more time, grabbed her purse, hurried away, her body involuntarily shuddering twice before she closed the door behind her. I had already finished my homework at school, and I didn't particularly care for drawing anymore, so I invented mathematical word problems instead—planes taking off and trains leaving stations and schools of fish combining and separating and altering their proportions. I tried to make the problems hard enough to be interesting, but clear enough to be solvable. I didn't look at the clock. I didn't look out the window to see if anyone was coming. I kept my eyes on my paper.

Finally, as the sun started sinking low, my mother returned to the house. She had Beatrice on her hip. Beatrice's hair was covered in ashes. Her eyes were wide and somber and she clung to my mother, the fabric of my mother's dress gripped in her fists.

"Beatrice!" I squealed, abandoning my papers and lifting my arms to my favorite person. My mother handed me my cousin, who resisted, but complied. I peered past my mother.

"Where's Auntie Marla?" I asked.

My mother's face became blank. "I'm sure I don't know what you're talking about."

I shook my head reflexively. "Auntie Marla. Where is—"

"There's no such person," my mother said. "Now take your sister into the living room and play. I have things to do."

"But Beatrice isn't—"

My mother held up one hand. She took a slow breath through her nose. *"Take your sister,"* she said slowly, with measured emphasis, *"into the living room to play."* She closed her eyes for a moment, and took a long breath through her nose. "Please," she added. Another pause. "I won't explain it again."

And she didn't. She turned her back to me, tied an apron around her waist, and began cooking dinner. Beatrice kicked and waved her hand. She blew a raspberry on my neck.

"Mama?" she said, pointing to the door.

"Yes, love," my mother said absently as she started washing the potatoes.

"Mama?" Beatrice said again, pointing at the window.

"Your mama's right here. I've always been right here." She gave me a pointed look. "Go play," she said. "Keep your sister quiet. I feel a headache coming on." My mother pressed her lips into a thin, tight line. A small silence fell, like a single pebble dropped onto a hard tile floor—delicate, distinct, and final. There would be no more words on the subject.

And from that moment on, Beatrice was my sister. It was as though my mother could simply will it so. She was my sister. She had only ever been my sister. Any notion to the contrary was clearly ridiculous, and worse: insubordinate. There was no discussion and no explanation. My questions were interrupted or ignored or punished. Photographs of my aunt disappeared from the house. My mother set up a crib and changing table in my room and informed me that it had always been there. And that was that.

The Mass Dragoning of 1955 happened when I was eight years old. Between that time and the day my mother died, six years later, she didn't answer a single one of my questions; she remained tight-lipped to the end. When my mother got it in her head to simply not speak of something, she knew how to go the distance.

8.

We lived in a town in Wisconsin that was about a two-hour drive from Milwaukee. The men on my block worked in the paper factory or they worked in the glass factory or they worked for one of the small fabricators producing particular objects that would eventually get fitted into cars or airplanes or trains. My father worked for the bank. Once upon a time, my mother did too, but then she got married—which, my father often said, was the whole point.

Except that it wasn't. Even then I knew that it wasn't. I had watched how my aunt became, somehow, *less of herself* after she got married. Lines of frustration dug into her face. She was pale and distracted. She worked harder than she did before, and longer hours, because now she had more mouths to feed, and one of those mouths seemed hell-bent on drinking the three of them into poverty. Her marriage gave her the gift of Beatrice, but not much else.

My parents stopped going to church after my aunt . . . *well.* After my aunt ceased to exist. They never applied for the assistance from the Lost Mothers Fund, because that would require them to admit that she existed in the first place. They asked their church to refrain from saying Auntie Marla's name in their yearly Mass with the Litany of the Missing Mothers, but the church refused to comply. Marla was a member of the parish, after all. Her name remained on the list, and so my mother walked out and vowed to never return. For the rest of the spring and all of that summer, Sundays became a day of stasis. We made no plans; we spoke little; even the house seemed to hold its breath. It hadn't occurred to me before that they only attended Mass at my aunt's insistence. One would think it would be the other way around. But without my aunt, my mother had no reason to require that the family rouse themselves early on a Sunday and make themselves presentable, and without my mother's requiring, my father was happy to sit in the backyard and silently read his paper.

We were still members of the parish, officially. I still attended the parochial school, and my mother still went to the Junior League meetings in the church basement, and still showed up to prepare soup for the poor and frozen meals for the shut-ins. She still provided her famously beautiful hand-knotted lace for the Christmas auction. But Mass she could not abide. Not without—

Well. No one could say.

Besides, as a family we were adjusting to our new addition, while pretending that we had no addition and therefore needed no adjusting. We were adjusting to the loss of my aunt while also pretending that I had no aunt. This sort of thing gets exhausting after a while.

And while my mother was busy *not* saying and *not* explaining, I was harboring secrets of my own.

⁓

Three days prior to the chaos of the dragoning, my aunt came over for dinner for what would be the last time. Beatrice and my uncle came with her. Before Beatrice was my sister.

(What am I saying? Beatrice has always been my sister. She was never not my sister. You see? It is so, so easy to lie. Sometimes, it's difficult to stop.)

On this particular evening, it was getting late, and my father and uncle had gone outside to smoke cigars. It was April, but the nights were still quite chilly and damp. They put on their wool jackets with thick scarves and gripped their cigars. They shivered as they guffawed in the dark.

My mother did the dishes. My mother was always doing the

dishes. Beatrice was asleep in the portable bassinette set up in the living room. My aunt usually didn't help my mother with the dishes because my mother was constantly admonishing her for doing it wrong.

"How about I get this child ready for bed. That way you can sit down and have a nightcap when you're done," my aunt said.

My mother didn't reply. She just banged the pots. My aunt took that as a yes. Before we went upstairs, she grabbed her bag, a heavy canvas equipment bag from her Women Airforce Service Pilots days. She slung the strap over her shoulder and followed me up the stairs. She sat silently on the end of my bed while I slipped into my nightgown and brushed my teeth and washed my face. She paged through my notebooks (mostly math problems and pictures of spaceships copied from the comic books that the boys from school read avidly, but that I was not allowed to have for reasons I did not understand). She examined the structures I had made with Popsicle sticks and glue (bridges and castles and a trebuchet), and noted the bin full of discarded dolls shoved off in a corner. I knelt on the ground in front of her and she brushed and brushed my hair, holding it in her fist while she flattened the whole mane of it down my back. Even then, I wished it was short. I often asked my mom if I could have a head full of small, tight curls like my aunt, and my mom would say something about crowning glories and then I would pout.

My aunt assembled my hair into two tight braids. She stood me up and looked me in the face. We remained that way for a long time, just staring eye to eye, while she seemed to try to come up with what she wanted to say. I knew better than to start the conversation. I knew I must be seen and not heard and should never speak unless first spoken to. I was a girl who knew how to wait her turn.

Finally: "You know," she said. She brought her hands to her face and pressed her fingers deep into the plumpness of her cheeks. "When I was a little girl, I had a secret hiding spot in my room, where I would conceal things from my mother. Nothing bad, you understand. I wasn't a bad child. But I had things that were *mine*. I couldn't show them to my mother because they were *just for me.* Do you understand?"

"No," I said.

I did, though. Of course I did. I had been hiding things from my mother for a while. I learned how to pull a piece of the paneling off the inside of my closet, slide it out, hide things inside the gap between the paneling and the main wall, and then slide the panel back in place, making it look like nothing had ever been touched. I had several things hidden in there. Nothing bad. I also was not a bad child. But I kept a sketchbook in there where I drew unkind pictures of my teachers and my parents. I kept three notes written to me by a girl who no longer attended my school and were important to me in ways that I couldn't identify, but I knew in the deepest place in my heart that my mother would not—*and could not*—understand. I had drawn pictures of myself—in a general's uniform, or flying an airplane, or in a business suit, or with a horse's body, or as a robot. These, too, felt both subversive and *private* for reasons that were unexplainable, but true nevertheless. I wasn't about to show them to anyone, my aunt included. I tried to make my face blank. This always worked with my mother.

My aunt's mouth twitched with a smile. "Liar," she said. And then she kissed my forehead. "But I love you. I love you so much. I am going to give something to you. It's nothing bad, and it's nothing you have to worry about. I just don't think your mother would understand. But it's important to me that you have it. Do *you* understand?"

I folded my hands and fidgeted. I didn't know what to say.

My aunt gave my shoulder a little squeeze. She reached into her bag. She pulled out a stack of letters, bound with a particularly intricate knot. And a small booklet called *Some Basic Facts About Dragons: A Physician's Explanation.* And a photo album with a picture on the front cover showing three women in uniforms with their arms wrapped tightly around one another's waists. My aunt was in the center. Her hair was long then, and had been pulled back into a rapidly unraveling bun. Her head rested on another woman's shoulder. They all looked incredibly happy.

She set each thing on my bed. I stared at them. My aunt stood and walked to the door. She paused.

"What am I supposed to do with them?" I asked.

My aunt shrugged. "Maybe nothing. Maybe this is pointless. But no matter what happens in the coming days, I want you to have this. Some things are hard to talk about, and then the world clams up and pretends like it was nothing. Or they act like it never happened in the first place. But maybe that's a mistake. Just because people won't talk about something, it doesn't mean that it's any less true or important."

"Do you want me to read it?" I frowned at the booklet. It had two images on the cover. One was a shape that I had never seen before but I now know is a line drawing of the female reproductive system. The other image was that same drawing transformed and fleshed out as the face of a dragon. At the bottom it said, "Researched and Written by a Medical Doctor Who Wishes to Remain Anonymous." Under that, someone had written, "Also known as Dr. Henry Gantz. You can't fool me, old man." It looked like my aunt's handwriting. I certainly didn't know who Dr. Gantz was. In any case, the book didn't look particularly interesting. "I mean. Do I have to read it?"

Auntie Marla smiled. "It's up to you. You can read the book or you can read the letters, or you can look at the pictures, or you can never look at any of it again. There's a letter to you in there, but you can ignore that too—there's absolutely no obligation here. I just . . ." She paused. Her gaze drifted to the window. For a moment, moonlight lit her face and her eyes reflected the sky outside. She reached her arms around me and gave me a squeeze. "These things are important to me, and I want them someplace safe. You don't have to think about it again. You really don't. It's enough for me to know you have them. Does that make sense?"

"Yes," I said, even though it didn't. She hugged me one more time, and I realized that her chest and shoulders trembled. She pulled away and smiled, but her eyes were wet. She didn't say anything else.

And with that, she closed the door.

I slid the booklet and the pictures and the bundle of letters into the hidden cubby in my closet, and fastened the panel shut.

I never, *never,* told my mother. Even after the sirens and fires. Even after keeping our eyes on the ground as massive shadows streaked across the pavement. Even after the ashes covering her dress, and the smoke lingering in Beatrice's hair. My aunt's treasures stayed where they were—unread, untouched, unmentioned.

It wasn't my first secret. And it wasn't my last. But it was my biggest secret. It still is.

9.

Despite my mother's aversion to hard conversations, the nation went through a short, and only somewhat thorough, reckoning of what had occurred. This was difficult, given the assumed femininity of dragons, and the Mass Dragoning's accepted connection to something as private as motherhood. Embarrassment, as it turns out, is more powerful than information. And shame is the enemy of truth.

But the sheer scope and numbers of the Mass Dragoning of 1955, and the impact it had on the nation's population, workforce, economy, and family structure, did require a national conversation, albeit brief, uncomfortable, and not altogether accurate. At school, after some resistance by the staff, we all worked through a special curriculum distributed by the Department of Health, Education, and Welfare, mandated for all schools, both public and parochial. The curriculum, however, went through many major revisions over the next eighteen months, requiring schoolchildren everywhere to discard out-of-favor workbooks from time to time (in point of fact, we were supposed to burn them) only to replace them with new books with a more up-to-date text, until those, too, needed to be replaced. In those first chaotic weeks after the Mass Dragoning, Sister Margareta, my third-grade teacher, taught us the earliest accepted explanation: that dragons, either escaped from Hell or intentionally released from its Demon Gate by sinister forces in the hidden global war between good and evil (Russian, presumably), had devoured a certain subset of the nation's mothers, for reasons unknown. And likely reasons unknowable. After all, who can reason with a dragon? This was wildly incorrect, of course, but most people were still grappling with the events that day—burning buildings and devoured husbands and half-exploded homes and motherless children weeping in the streets. Newscasters did their best at piecing the narrative together, with patient and firm reporters once again helping America come to grips with difficult things.

There were those in the Department of Health, Education, and Welfare and even in Congress who would have happily preferred the public believing in what was later termed the theory of devouring, as it removed the question of *why*. I truly believe, even now (especially now) that if the dragoning had been smaller in scope, there would have been a more concerted effort at the suppression of news and a more robust campaign of misinformation in those early days. It had, after all, worked before. But it is difficult for any propagandic apparatus, no matter how advanced, to counteract the force of millions of eyewitnesses. Which is why a smattering of facts, as unclear as they were and often poorly contextualized, did make their way out.

By the end of my fourth-grade school year (a little over a year after the event itself), the evening news and the textbooks and the harried teachers had, at last, come to a consistent explanation as to what had actually happened in the Mass Dragoning. Specifically this: that one day, on a perfectly ordinary afternoon in April, exactly 642,987 women were *not* eaten by dragons, as was originally reported. Rather, they *became* dragons. All at once. *En masse.* And then they left everything behind: babies in strollers and roasts in ovens and laundry half-hung on the line.

There were some devourings during those brief hours at the outset, when the dragons, still astonished at their transformations, and wildly acclimating to the needs and modifications of a body that had become so large and sharp and *shiny,* had perhaps overstepped a bit. No babies or children were devoured—though the televangelists claimed, and still claim, otherwise. However, more than six thousand husbands did find themselves swallowed, and another eighteen thousand or so suffered severe burns after their office buildings burned down. Also among the dead: 552

obstetricians; more than six thousand pastors, ministers, rabbis, imams, and priests of various denominations; several score of youth workers; twenty-seven entire parent-teacher associations across nine states; and dozens of office managers, factory foremen, politicians, and police detectives (this is how it became obvious that dragons are bulletproof), not to mention a goodly sum of retired teachers and school counselors.

And then, just like that, the dragons left.

Many went to the mountains, with a preference for the Alps (tourism has never been the same). A large number made their home in the ocean. They were rarely covered in the news, except for the occasional interactions with submarines and radar stations, as it seems the dragons were, and remain, intent on protecting the now-flourishing pods of great blue whales. There were dragons who created communes on otherwise uninhabited islands, and dragons who relocated to Antarctica, dragons who made quiet homes in the jungles, and dragons who launched skyward to explore the cosmos.

There were a few dragons who tried to keep up appearances, reluctant to leave their homes and husbands as their sisters flew away. They attempted to re-don their aprons and oven mitts, busying themselves with laundry and bed-making and dinner preparations until their spouses returned home at the end of the day. Housework, one can imagine, was difficult due to their increased size and razor-sharp talons, and the fact that they emitted flames every time they hiccupped or burped. Nevertheless, they persisted, and greeted their husbands with freshly applied makeup and a home-cooked meal and a tentative "So, darling, how was your day?" as usual.

Unfortunately, the dragons who did so were naturally the sorts of wives who would be married to the sorts of husbands who did not take kindly to great changes in their routines. The husbands who reacted to the dragon situation by scolding and yelling did not, as one might expect, last very long. Still, there were a few who managed to speak softly and kindly, and told their wives in tender voices that they understood, and that they would weather this and all challenges to their marriage, and that they were still very much in love. And in truth, those husbands really did try their best. In the end, though, their dragon wives did not remain suited for a life of homemaking. The lives they lived no longer fit. They found their gaze drifting elsewhere—beyond the limits of the house, beyond the limits of the yard, beyond the limits of the daily tasks of washing and straightening and keeping up appearances. They found that their vision had widened to contain the whole sky, and beyond the sky. The more they looked, the more they longed, and the more they longed, the more they planned, and finally the husbands returned home one evening to dinner in the oven, several meals in the freezer, and notes on the dining room table, still somewhat scorched, saying, "Thanks for trying, my love. But we both know it wasn't going to work anyway."

The husbands looked in vain for their dragon wives, but it was no use. They weren't coming back.

All told, the Mass Dragoning of 1955 was a disaster of unimaginable scope, and it brought the nation, for a moment, to its knees, reeling in a state of loss and confusion and sorrow. There were few people in the entire country who did not know at least one affected family. The country had no precedent for this scale of national grief, and as a result every single coordinated response—on a national level, or a community level, or even at the level of individual families—was neither honest, nor useful, nor kind. We had no guide, you see? No agreed-upon workable models or determined courses of action. This was an unspeakable loss. And many chose to never speak of it.

My mother certainly never did. She never once spoke her sister's name after that day. *Never.* She never mentioned her brother-in-law again. Disappeared. Devoured, presumably. She certainly never discussed the Dragoning. And my father didn't see the need to say anything beyond "A little less noise, there," or "Where on earth are my socks?" She also made sure to sell the family television set, and she "accidentally" spilled coffee on the radio. She threw the newspapers away the moment my father was done reading, and I was not allowed to touch them. My home was a place devoid of information and explanation. All truth, all context, I had to discover myself.

IO.

There are memories that we carry that are not our own.

Or perhaps I am talking about myself. There are memories that *I* carry that are not my own. This should be impossible. And yet.

My auntie Marla was, in the years of my childhood, a towering figure. She stood slightly taller than my father in her low-heeled boots and, prior to her transformation and subsequent disappearance, took up more space than any other adult in my life. I remember her in wide-legged trousers and a sleeveless shirt tied at the waist, her long-fingered hand shading her eyes as she tracked a plane streaking across the sky. She had a sharp jaw and wide, penetrating eyes. She had strong muscles and quick hands and a keen sense of how a thing might be properly put together.

She loved me, and she loved Beatrice, but I think she loved my mother most of all. I think that maybe my mother would always pull my aunt's love toward herself. My mother was the dearest darling of her big sister's heart.

As far as I can figure out, my aunt nearly dragoned at work. She had felt it coming on all day.

Marla was the only female employee at the auto repair shop. Her boss, a blotchy, slumped man with a nervous laugh, tried to fire her more than two dozen times, to give her job to a family man. And every time, he'd beg her to come back, with his oily cap clutched in his hands, because they really couldn't get by without her.

(Besides, they all knew about my uncle. His string of firings. His love affair with the bottle. My aunt, they decided, was as much a family man as anyone.)

On the day of the Mass Dragoning, my aunt sat in a wooden chair in the break room fully slumped over, pressing her chest to her thighs. She curled her hands around her ankles and hung on tight. She tried to shake it off. According to witnesses, she carried a photograph in her hand all day, until it became wrinkly and damp from her hands. It was a picture of me and my mother and Beatrice all sitting on the sofa at my house. Normally, she kept it in a blue frame in her cubby, but one of her co-workers—Earl Kotke, a drinker, sure, but a kind enough fellow, and perceptive, too—said that he saw her take the picture out of the frame and carry it with her. He saw her take it in and out of her pocket and sometimes press it to her heart. He watched as she rubbed her thumb, again and again, over each of the faces.

It was many, many years before I could bring myself to seek out her former co-workers —those who were still alive, that is— and ask about what happened. After all that time, it was too hard for many of them to bring their sense of loss into words. Their hearts were too broken. They loved Marla—everyone did. Most of them simply rested their faces in their calloused hands and wept.

I transcribed each of these conversations. I'm a scientist, after all, and I know that data matters. The interviews meander a bit, and sometimes they disagree, but the central fact they reveal is this: Around one o'clock in the afternoon, Marla rolled the dolly out from under an old truck, laid her tools neatly on the ground and held her hands to her heart for a moment or two. Then she looked at her boss and said, "You boys can take whatever you want of mine. I won't be needing it anymore." And then she walked out the door.

The men didn't understand it. "We figured it was for lady reasons and she'd be back," her boss, Arne Holfenson, told the local newspaper for the single story they ran on the topic. What he told me, years later, was "I saw the look in her eye, and I hoped to God, I hoped with everything in me, that she would come back to us. But she didn't. After all this time, I still beat myself up that I didn't beg her to stay. Maybe she would've if we'd asked. Or maybe she would've gotten confused and eaten us instead of that idiot husband of hers. In any case, I wish she could have known how desperately we wanted her to stay."

Even now, I can see my aunt that day in my mind's eye. I can see her deciding to leave her car at work, striding through the streets toward home. I can see her pausing, watching dispassionately as one house burned, and then another, or as a hapless husband ran out into the yard and down the sidewalk with the seat of his pants blackened and smoking, as an irate-looking dragon pursued him, flying down the middle of the road.

I can see her arriving home.

I can see her sending the babysitter away and gently informing her that she won't need to come back.

I can see her gathering Beatrice in her arms and rocking her to sleep, inhaling the sweet scent of her baby's scalp every time she kissed the top of her head.

I wasn't there. Obviously I wasn't. But I have *seen* it. I have *felt* it. In my head. In dreams. And in those secret places in my mind where the eye sometimes roams. This memory is not mine. And yet, it *is*.

In this not-memory memory, I see my aunt lingering at the crib, letting her fingers drift away from Beatrice's damp curls, and silently closing the nursery door, tiptoeing down the hall. I see her pausing in the living room. Holding her hands again to her heart. Lifting her face toward the window. Stepping out of her men's boots. Stepping out of her coveralls. Stepping out of her underthings. Stepping out of her skin. Stepping out of her life. Greeting her husband with talons and sharp teeth and a refining fire before launching into the sky.

I loved my aunt.

I had no means to mourn my aunt.

And then I had no aunt.

My baby cousin, Beatrice—

I'm sorry. I misspoke.

My sister has always been my sister. I have no cousin as I have no aunt and no devoured uncle.

You see? Lying is easy. When we're awake, that is.

But at night my dreams could not lie. In dream after dream I saw my dragoned aunt, living with other dragons—in the ocean, or the mountains, or the jungles, or the moon. Sometimes I dreamed she was one of the dragons who simply flew skyward, and traveled through the far reaches of deep space, swallowing the universe with her eyes.

Beatrice did not know. My mother never told her. And anyway, it didn't really matter. *Beatrice and I are sisters,* I told myself. *Beatrice and I are sisters,* I informed anyone who would listen.

We have always been sisters.

We will always be sisters.

And that is that.

BETHESDA, MD
POLICE DEPARTMENT
DIVISION _____ PATROL _____
POLICE OFFICER(S) N. Scofield and B. Martinez
DATE OF THIS REPORT: June 15, 1957   TIME: 10:25 AM

The officers were dispatched to 309 Marigold Lane in regards to a warrant issued earlier that morning. This officer made contact with two individuals, one male, one female, both determined to be non-residents, and both in "beatnik" dress. The individuals attempted to prevent the officers from entering the premises, but fled after a brief scuffle. Upon entrance, the officer observed several boxes haphazardly filled with documents, and many shelves were empty. It is unknown at this time how much material had been removed from the premises. Six other young individuals, presumably students, attempted to position themselves between the officers and the remaining boxes. This officer then made contact with Dr. Henry Gantz, a physician formerly at Johns Hopkins University Hospital. He is a known person of interest in the department, and has been interviewed by officers many times. The officers informed Dr. Gantz of the warrant, which gave permission for the officers to seize evidence. Several of the young people protested, and appeared to present a clear threat to the officers, but this was de-escalated by yet another individual, an elderly woman named Mrs. Helen Gyzinska, who identified herself as a librarian from Wisconsin. At an order from Mrs. Gyzinska, the young people vacated without incident. The officers then collected the material in the house as evidence, and arrested the doctor for the possession and dissemination of lewd and obscene materials. The librarian refused to vacate, and the officers were forced to arrest her as well. She waived her right to remain silent, saying that she wanted the following to be recorded in this report, verbatim: "There is nothing lewd about biology, research, or basic facts, gentlemen, and you make yourselves fools when you try to classify the quest for understanding as obscene. The only thing more patently obscene than ignorance is willful ignorance. Arrest yourselves."

II.

Time passed, and eventually I found myself in the fifth grade. My family presented itself to the world as normal, nuclear, and fully intact—a mother, a father, and two little girls.

No one ever mentioned my aunt. She was unmentionable. Instead, they admired the finely detailed dresses that Beatrice and I wore each day, each lovingly sewn by my mother, and the crocheted cardigans she had knotted by hand. They admired my mother's delicacy and beauty—that pale skin, that red lip, that figure so light it looked as though she might blow away in a stiff wind. They admired her hats embellished with hand-made lace and macramé flowers, and the shine of her shoes. They admired my father as the stern and reliable provider for the family. They admired the marigolds my mother had planted in perfectly straight rows along the walkway and the meticu-lously pruned rose bushes contained under the window boxes. Outside, my mother smiled and my father smiled, and Beatrice and I learned how to beam happily while thinking of nothing. My parents never smiled at each other while inside the house. Indeed, I don't recall them speaking much. Not unless it was absolutely necessary.

As for the rest of the world, it shifted, yet again. Enough time had passed since the Mass Dragoning that mentions of dragons had become, once again, simply out-of-bounds, an off-limits topic for any polite conversation. This was true not just in my home. Dragons were a subject avoided in any context. One would sooner arrive at church in one's underpants or discuss menstruation with the mailman or chat about sex on the radio. It simply wasn't done.

Once it became clear that the Mass Dragoning was not caused by any sinister external forces (the Russians, the Chinese Red Army, domestically radicalized Trotskyites who had failed to be rounded up by Senator McCarthy's hearings, and so forth) but were, in actuality, a seemingly biologic process specific to certain women (it was yet unclear how widespread the mutations were), any further discussion of dragons or dragoning or the practical considerations of a post-dragoned world became much more, well, *embarrassing.*

Adults turned red in the face when children raised their hands and asked questions about it.

The topic of dragons suddenly vanished from the evening news.

At the end of September that year, my teacher, Sister Saint Stephen the Martyr, informed us that we would be having a guest coming to class. His name was Dr. Angus Ferguson, and he had an ample beard and dull grey eyes and wore a long, heavy wool coat, even though it was quite warm out. He carried a doctor bag in one hand and a very large leather portfolio pouch in the other, which we would soon learn was filled with visual aids. He gave my teacher a brief bow and proceeded to gaze imperiously over the tops of our heads without meeting our eyes.

We were divided into two lines, one for the girls and another for the boys. While the boys met the visitor, the girls were taken to the home economics room to work on their desk caddies—a project in which we had to fashion sturdy boxes out of pressboard and hand-sewn fabric covers, and assemble each one into a charming little tray. A square box for paperclips and a long rectangular box for pencils and a broad box to hold larger objects like scissors and protractors and the like. We had been instructed to make two—one for ourselves and one for a "friend." The friend, in this case, was a boy from our class. We were each assigned a boy to work for. He would be our assigned friend. I can't even remember which boy I was assigned. All I know is that I did a wretched job on purpose.

When the boys were done with the visitor, we took their place in the classroom. The boys stood in line waiting to exit. Their faces were as red as lollipops, and they could not meet our eyes. One boy shuddered. Another snickered into his hands.

"That's enough, gentlemen," Dr. Ferguson said from his immobile stance at the front of the room. The boys calmed and started filing out.

I assumed that they, too, would be taken to the home economics classroom. I was wrong. They were taken outside. To blow off steam, Sister Saint Stephen the Martyr said, as she herded them away.

We took our places and folded our hands, as we had been taught. The visitor said nothing. He waited for our teacher to return. We knew better than to talk without invitation. Finally, Sister Saint Stephen the Martyr hustled into the room.

"Thank you for your patience," she said to him and not to us. The man with the beard nodded gravely at her, and then inclined his eyes toward the class. "Oh yes," our teacher said, suddenly flustered again. "Ladies. Today's topic is feminine health. Dr. Angus Ferguson is one of the region's foremost experts on the topic. His perspective is very special as he is both a doctor of medicine and a doctor of philosophy. This allows us to discuss both the practicalities of the subject at hand as well as the ethical considerations that all of you are about to face."

Sister Saint Stephen the Martyr paused and cleared her throat, her hand going instinctively to her veil. She frowned and pressed forward. "I'm sure some of you have heard about . . . changes. Others of you are wondering about . . . other changes." She stammered, flushed, and then, by sheer force of will, emptied the redness from her cheeks through the sternness of her expression. She nodded firmly as her face returned to the color of oatmeal, and all became right with the world again.

At our desks, with our hands folded, my classmates and I exchanged puzzled expressions. We weren't invited to raise our hands. But I had questions. Confusion accumulated in the room, like exhaust in a locked garage. If there was one thing I learned from my aunt, is that stuff will kill you if you let it build up. I raised my hand, since clearly no one else was going to. Sister Saint Stephen the Martyr and the bearded guest exchanged a grim look. I raised my hand a little higher. My teacher shrugged and pointed at me.

"Yes, Alexandra," my teacher said with grim resignation.

"It's Alex," I said.

She closed her eyes for a moment, and took in a long breath through flared nostrils. "Alexandra, what is it that you'd like to ask." This should have been a question, but she said it like an accusation.

"Well," I said. I cleared my throat. "I've heard that many girls start wearing . . . *implements* by the time they're in fifth grade, so I'm glad we're finally getting to—"

"That's enough questions for now," Sister Saint Stephen the Martyr said briskly.

"But I was just wondering which sorts of changes we will be discussing. You know, girls-growing-up sorts of changes, or . . . well . . . are we going to talk about the *other* kind of changes? The kind that can destroy a house. Because you see—"

"THAT IS ENOUGH OUT OF YOU." The color in Sister Saint Stephen the Martyr's cheeks deepened until they were scarlet. I half expected her to cross herself, but she didn't.

"Any giggling will result in a four-day detention. Any interruptions will result in suspension. And any *off-color remarks,*" she cast a hard look in my direction, "will require an immediate meeting with your parents, myself, Doctor Ferguson, Mr. Alphonse *and possibly even Father Anderson.*" She let *that* sink in. "When in doubt, pull your rosaries out of your pocket and pray a decade or two, and give it all a good long think. You'll probably find yourselves relieved that you didn't say the very silly thought in your head out loud. Be sure to thank the Blessed Mother for yet again preventing you from looking like a fool in front of everyone. And now, Doctor? You have the floor." She gestured to the podium as she flowed imperiously to the back of the classroom.

The next fifty minutes were a bit of a blur. I still have my notebook from that day, and all my notes. Even then, I was an excellent student. Even then, I took excellent dictation.

We learned quite a bit about pollination. "You see how this relates, obviously," the good doctor said. We didn't.

We learned about the process of seed germination. We learned the purpose of a flower in the life cycle of a plant. We learned about a blossom's private, intricate parts: the brave stamen, whose filaments stood at attention like soldiers; and the dark world of the pistil, the sticky, seductive opening of which was called the *stigma,* which, to my fifth-grade ears, felt like a term that was a bit *on the nose,* to be honest. We learned about metamorphosis in nature—from tadpoles to frogs, and from leptocephali to eels, and from larvae to ladybugs, and from caterpillars to butterflies. He showed us pictures of skeletons from across the animal kingdom and complex diagrams of the endocrine network and a single image of the female reproductive system. I thought about the cover of the booklet, still hidden in my closet, showing a uterus and ovaries superimposed on the face of a dragon. I still hadn't read it. I wasn't sure if I ever would.

The doctor closed his eyes for a moment. He held up his hand. I learned much later that in 1955, he, too, came home to a dragon-destroyed house. I also learned that there had been a message burned into his front door, left for all to see. It said I CONSIDERED EATING YOU, BUT I COULDN'T RISK THE INDIGESTION. THANKS FOR NOTHING. Everyone pretended they didn't notice it. The whole neighborhood averted their eyes. But everyone saw.

"Ladies, I ask you this: Does a butterfly remember its life as a happy caterpillar, content to stay on the leaves of the tree who loves it? Probably not. Does the frog remember its life as a tadpole, swimming without a care in the quiet corners of the swamp under the tender, masculine protection of the sentinel frogs? I can't see that it does. They transform willy-nilly and leap into the jaws of the cruel hawks and storks, and truthfully, most of them die. In nature, not much care is given to the life span of the individual organism. Also in nature, metamorphosis exists as an inexorable force—a caterpillar could no more decline to transform than she could decide to swim the English Channel, or run a marathon. She is at the mercy of her biology. Not so with you. The science remains, well, *fuzzy* at present. But we do believe that the changes to which I refer are *both* biologic *and* intentional. The evidence seems to suggest that it is a *chosen* metamorphosis. And if that is the case—and I cannot stress this enough—I implore you ladies to choose wisely. Wickedness comes in many forms, after all. Some more obvious than others. I don't think we need to open it up to questions. I know I've made myself perfectly clear."

We had no idea what he was talking about.

Later that day, the boys returned and we did our mathematics lesson. As we stood to go to gym, Mary Frances Lozinsky, the girl in the desk next to mine, stood up and realized with shock and horror that the entire back of her uniform skirt was covered with thick, dark blood. She screamed, the girls sitting next to her screamed, and the boy sitting behind her slumped onto his chair in a deep faint. Sister Saint Stephen the Martyr flew to Mary Frances's side, wrapped an arm around her shoulder, and whisked her out of class, speaking softly and gently as they went. The next day Mary Frances was walking funny. She avoided our eyes. She said something about a belt, but wouldn't explain what that was. The day after that, she had six enormous pimples on her face.

Mary Frances *changed*. We could see that she changed. But she was still Mary Frances and could remember the Mary Frances that she was before. Unlike Dr. Ferguson's caterpillar, she *remembered* herself, and remembered her previous life as an unchanged girl. So, the doctor was wrong about that bit. What else was he wrong about? And then, impossibly, Mary Frances continued to change. She started complaining about bra straps. She smelled different. Her face produced more occasional spots, and every few weeks, blue-grey semicircles appeared under her eyes. She started wearing makeup, and getting in trouble for it. She developed a dark, fuzzy shadow on her upper lip. Her body pressed further and further outward, until her uniform blouse stretched nearly to the breaking point and her seams strained to hold everything together. Boys followed her in the hallway like baby ducks scurrying to keep up with their mother.

Every day, she changed a little bit more, becoming less and less of the Mary Frances that we thought we knew, and more and more of the Mary Frances that we would come to know.

And we knew *for sure* that she didn't choose any bit of it.

12.

After the shock of Mary Frances's metamorphosis, each of the girls in my class got our first periods over the next two years, one after another. We learned to anticipate, to steer girls toward the bathroom when the time came, to be quick with a cardigan to tie around someone's waist when the back of their skirt began to darken. We started carrying purses with us, and learned to keep something extra to help a girl out in her time of need. We carried aspirin, and gum, and maybe even a little clutch of tissues. We looked out for one another. Even when we weren't particularly good friends. We all learned that this was the sort of thing that superseded friendship—it was deeper, and older, and more important. We knew that each girl—no matter how many had gone before—would spend time in shock when they changed. From the pain of it. From the redness and abundance of the blood. From the inexorable assault, month after month, whether we wanted it or not. We knew that such shock needed care and understanding.

For me, it happened at school at the very end of sixth grade. Two girls whisked me to the bathroom and clucked and preened over me, speaking softly and soothingly as they helped me clean up. These girls were not my friends before this day, and would not be after. I would still never sit with them at lunch, nor would I be invited to their daily game of foursquare. I was unbothered by any of this. This sort of interaction, I knew without being told, was deeper, and older, and more important than friendship. One girl dabbed my face with a cool cloth while the other showed me how to construct a makeshift belt using shoelaces and a sock to hold the sanitary napkin and how to fasten the whole thing with a series of clever knots under my clothes. It was uncomfortable, but it felt secure enough.

"You should probably tell your mother when you get home," one said—her name was Lydia—as she reapplied her lipstick. We weren't allowed to wear lipstick at school, so she wore a shade that was so close to the color of her own lips that it didn't look like she was wearing lipstick at all. I asked her why, and she said, "Practice."

"I don't think I'll be telling my mother," I said frankly. I explained to them how excellent my mother was at silence.

Lydia considered this. "Do you have any aunties, then?" she asked. "Or big-girl cousins?"

For one brief moment, I found myself thinking, *Auntie Marla.* Almost instantly, a sharp lump formed in my throat and my eyes burned. I swallowed it down, turning away. I winced. Auntie Marla didn't exist anymore, I reminded myself. Or, at least, that Auntie Marla as she *was* didn't exist anymore. Her broad shoulders, gone. Her tight curls and red lips and wide stance and booming laugh, gone. I remembered how she swept me up onto her hip when I was little. I remembered the delicate and tender touch of her calloused hands. I remembered the way her eyes turned gold in the days before her dragoning. If her body changed and became unrecognizable, I wondered, was Marla still Marla? Did she remember us when she shed her old life and stepped into something else—all scale and sinew and rage and fire? I didn't know. And, for that matter, would I still be me with my new breasts and other more unpleasant eruptions? Was my body still my body if I couldn't control what it did?

I shook my head. "No," I said. "There's no one. Just my mother. There's no way I can talk to her about any of this."

Joyce, a very pretty girl whose family had just moved to Wisconsin from California (and who had made a cottage industry of complaining endlessly and dramatically about the cold even though it was well into April and perfectly pleasant out) was sympathetic. "There's no way around it, I'm afraid. Someone needs to shop for things, after all. You'll need extra belts, and no end of pads. There's things you can do in a pinch, but in the end, you'll have the washing to consider, and you'll need to have things on hand, both at home and with you at school, and your mother is the one to help you do that. Here." She reached into her purse, which was so voluminous it could hold an entire library if she packed it right. She pulled out three white, rectangular boxes with blue type on the sides and handed them to me. "I swiped these from the nurse's office. I thought I'd do more good with them than she had managed—she hoards them, you know. I can get more, but you really do need to bite that bullet and tell your mother."

"I will," I said. I felt dizzy and sick. My belly hurt and my back hurt and I wanted the experience to be over. "When I get home. I promise."

I didn't, but Mother managed to know anyway. When I got home that day, there was a stack of cream-colored boxes on my bed along with handwritten instructions. I didn't ask her about it and she didn't say. Which pretty much sums things up between her and me.

Beatrice examined one box—it had blue calligraphy on the side and a silhouette of a lady in an evening dress. She looked at me suspiciously.

"What's this?" she said, holding out the box, her bright eyes narrowing. "Is it a toy?" Beatrice was nearly four, and wished that everything was toys.

"No," I said. I was more snippy with her than usual.

Beatrice leaned on my bed and rested her chin on her folded hands. "Is it for me?" she said.

I shook my head. "No. It's for big girls."

"We are *both* big girls," Beatrice said. She climbed onto my bed and then onto my shoulders, as nimble as a squirrel. "We're the biggest girls," she crowed. I hooked my arm around her tummy and we tumbled to the floor, giggling like mad, allowing me for a moment to ignore the deep cramp in my abdomen.

"Chase me!" she squealed, and darted out of the door.

"In a minute!" I called back.

I took the boxes, and the instructions, and put them on the upper shelf of my closet, in full view. No need to hide what my mother already knew. My head pounded. I lingered in my closet, my eyes drifting toward the removable panel at the back. I suddenly missed my aunt with an intensity that felt like a harpoon in my guts. After all this time, I still hadn't touched the things she left for me. I still hadn't looked at the pictures of my aunt, or read any of the letters, or her letter to me, or looked at the booklet with the face of the dragon on the cover. I wasn't entirely sure why. Sometimes, I had dreams that the panel opened itself up, and all its contents spilled out—my aunt's secrets, my secrets, and the secrets of my mother and father mixed in, broadcast for the whole world to see. Each time, I woke up gasping and sweaty and afraid.

But now . . .

I looked back at the closet. I knelt on the floor, moving closer by inches.

"Alex!" Beatrice hollered from the living room, startling me so bad I nearly choked. "Alex, I NEED YOU THIS SECOND."

Downstairs, my mother shushed her. "Alexandra isn't feeling well," she said with a slightly raised voice. "And she probably would feel better after a bath and perhaps a rest." Her volume ticked up a little higher at the end of her sentence, to make sure I understood. Beatrice started to squeal, and I knew my mother had caught her in her arms and was swinging her around while holding her tight. "Sweet Bea, sweet Bea, sweet Bea," she crooned. "Let's go to the park, shall we?" I heard Beatrice's footsteps thunder across the room. And with that, my mother and Beatrice shut the door behind them, leaving me in peace.

My heartbeat slowed. I sat on the floor for several moments, staring at the closet.

Finally, I forced my eyes away, stood, started the bath, and then went back to my room, where I carefully slid the false panel out of the way and pulled out the bundle that my aunt had given me, three years earlier. My fingers shook a little as I undid the knot. The paper whispered in my hands. One by one I laid the envelopes on the floor, in neat rows. One by one, I slid the letters out, and laid them on top of their envelopes, flattening the paper gently with the backs of my fingers.

I didn't know what I was looking for. I just wanted someone to talk to. Even if she wasn't here anymore.

Marla had saved letters written in loopy, beautiful script from a woman named Clara, and letters written in firm, blocky text from a woman named Jeanne, and letters with exuberant, childlike handwriting from a woman named Edith. She had two letters from a man named Dr. Gantz—the same name Marla had written on the booklet, both chiding and naming him as the anonymous author. The Dr. Gantz letters were completely indecipherable—even his signature was barely legible. I set them aside. I returned to the booklet. It was many pages long and the type was impossibly small. That the illegible letter and the unreadable booklet were written by the same person made sense in a way that felt both obvious and annoying. I flipped through the booklet, focusing only on the subheadings and the pictures. Thanks to that doctor who visited my class in fifth grade, I had a vague idea of what the female reproductive system looked like, but I still didn't understand why they had transformed the uterus and ovaries into a dragon's face. The chapters had titles like "A Birthright of Blood and Fire: The Destiny of Biology" or "The Untapped Power of Female Rage." There were charts and tables and an astonishing number of words in Latin. I was a good reader in sixth grade, but this was outside my scope of understanding.

I let my fingers drift along the surface of the letters, my skin whispering along the paper. I stopped at Marla's letter to me, and my breath caught. I picked it up and held it for a moment, pressing my thumb against my name written in her hand. *Alex.* She never once called me Alexandra, not in my memory. I never thought to thank her for it. The letter was still sealed. The image of her suddenly filled the entire space inside my head. Her pinned curls, her red mouth, her well-worn dungarees and heavy boots, her booming laugh. My aunt with a baby on her left hip and a bucket of tools in her right hand. I imagined her pulling out the paper, with Beatrice asleep on her lap, and writing to me to say goodbye. *No,* I decided. I wasn't ready to open it, much less read it. I needed my aunt to *help* me, but I certainly didn't need her leaving me all over again. Instead I picked up the letter nearest to my hand. The paper was fragile, and the handwriting had the careful strokes of a person who wanted every word to be perfect.

"Marla, my love," the letter said.

It almost happened again, this time while I was in flight. And oh, what a flight it was! The sea below was an aching blue, as was the sky above, with its center of heat and flame. There is a heat and the flame inside me that grows by the day—sometimes by the hour. What part of me is not on fire? My mind, my heart, my body at the thought of you. I had an aunt, you know, who changed like this. No one in my family speaks of it, but we all know. You would have liked her. She raised finches, and sold them out of her house. Bright feathers in all colors, and beautiful songs. She made a good business selling mostly to bored housewives in the nicest part of town—ladies who just wanted something lovely that was wholly their own. My aunt then had her own money, and her own spending power, and her husband couldn't abide it. One day she came home to a den of horrors. Her husband had reached into each cage and wrung each tiny neck, and left their beautiful corpses on the floor. He tossed dead birds onto their marital bed. Terrible thing. Terrible man. She went weeping to her sisters, who were sympathetic, but unhelpful. They told her that a husband is the head of the family. If he doesn't like her work, then what was the point of arguing? My mother uses the same logic to justify all manner of

my own father's sins. Why do women do this to themselves?
What kind of sister turns her back on her own? I have never
understood this. I don't think my aunt did either.

In any case, two days later their house ignited. The
authorities said that a gas explosion ripped off the roof and
left my uncle on the floor with a broken neck. I know better.
I always believed that it was rage that made her change,
and perhaps this is so. But I, myself, feel no rage. And yet,
I feel this change is inevitable all the same. Ever since that
first moment when my hand touched your hand and my lips
touched your lips there is only joy, joy, joy forever and ever. It
is joy that burns me now, and joy that makes my back ache
for wings, and it is joy that makes me long to be more than
myself. But it is love that makes me pause, that tethers me to
this body *and* this *life, that I may always fly home to you.*
My darling Marla, there is a longing now that splits me in
half. I don't know how much longer I can last. No matter
what happens, Marla, please. Always wait for me. Or follow
me. Edith.

I stared at the letter for a long time. I was only eleven years
old. I had no frame of reference. I had no way to understand
what it was that I was reading. And I certainly couldn't ask my
mother. I didn't think I was ready to read anything else. Feeling
more alone than when I had started, I bundled the letters back
together, tucked them into their hidey-hole, and slid the panel
back in place, and went to the washroom to have my bath.

13

I'm not exactly sure when my mother decided to take up gardening. I don't have any clear memories of when it began—only that the garden seemed to suddenly *exist*. There were raised beds, climbing vines, hand-built structures, and a thicket of herbs that kicked out a complex and heady scent that lingered on our clothes and extended almost to the end of the block. My father didn't approve. There was too much dirt, he said. And bees. The garden lacked symmetry, and order. Grass was neater, and what about the lawnmower that cost a pretty penny and why wasn't she more grateful for it? And anyway, why have the distraction? Wasn't the house and family enough? But my mother never asked for permission, so he couldn't exactly forbid it. By the time anyone realized what she was doing, there were already six rows of corn unfurling themselves to the sky, mounds of potatoes, garlic scapes, tomato vines, a growing tangle of squash flowers. The garden shed looked like it had always been there (did she build it herself? She must have), as did the clumps of asparagus and the rhubarb in the side yard.

"When did you even start with this?" my father asked one Saturday afternoon, when he headed outside with a whiskey and a cigar and a newspaper, and my mother handed him a hoe and asked him to tend to the edges. He stared at the hoe for a long time, as though wondering how it worked. Eventually my mother lost patience and did it herself.

"You've been eating out of this garden for quite some time now," she said without looking at him. "But I'm not surprised that you didn't notice."

There was a lot my father didn't notice. His hours at work

grew longer and longer. The older I got, the less he was around. Each day, my father paused at the open front door and kissed us all on the cheeks before he went to work. It was the only time he ever kissed us. When people might see. He whistled as he strolled down the block, the tune echoing as it bounced off the sidewalk and houses and lingered in the air, and fell silent the moment he turned the corner. Every day, my mother scrubbed our house within an inch of its life, and dinner was always served at 6:15 sharp, with a whiskey and rye poured for my father, whether or not he actually arrived.

In any case, my mother insisted that the garden was mostly for Beatrice. She was, back then, a whirlwind of motion and noise, and needed something to keep her occupied. From spring until fall, the two of them spent most of their time in the garden. My mother dressed Beatrice in coveralls that she had sewn herself—

(I had to catch my breath; she looked so much like my aunt.)

(What was I saying? I had no aunt. I never had an aunt. Beatrice was my sister. She had always been my sister.)

—and sent her to work digging out a square of grass, or pulling dandelions, or pushing her wheelbarrow from one end of the yard to the other. My mother planted peppers and tomatoes and carrots and beans. She planted herbs and eggplant and squashes of all kinds.

The summer after sixth grade, the garden dramatically expanded. My mother added new beds and built trellises by hand. She pickled endlessly, and canned constantly, and made whatever she possibly could into jam. Even carrots. And beets. (Both surprisingly delicious.)

The next year, as seventh grade wound to a close and summer opened itself to us, nearly two-thirds of our backyard had been tilled and tamed. Beatrice was now five, and still tiny. Still a whirlwind. She zigzagged between my mother and me, like a firefly, all light and heat and speed. My mother built complicated lattices with complex knots made from willow boughs for peas, and macramé cradles for squash and melons. Cucumbers grew over delicate domes made from balsa wood and chicken wire. Her tomato vines curled around sturdy wood scaffolding. She raked wood chips into neat rows and put in three benches in case she got tired. She worked all day. The house suffered—more so in each successive summer. Her shoulders grew. Her skin browned. She developed freckles across her nose, which made my father wrinkle his.

"This can't be good for you, outside all day," he said. "And where's my lunch?"

His lunch was in the icebox under a doily. Again. My mother told him so. He muttered something about cold food and ill health and my mother ignored him.

It was a Saturday in late June, and very hot. The garden was just beginning to produce. We were still eating the jams and pickles and dried herbs from the summer before, and I was at an age where I just didn't see the point of any of this. Had my mother never heard of a greengrocer? Why must we do all this work?

That day, I had become uncomfortably aware of the fact of my sweat, and worse, the smell of my sweat, in a way that I never had in summers previous. I had certainly sweated before. I knew I had. But I had never known to be embarrassed. The fabric under my armpits was soaked, as was the back of my shirt, as were my underpants. My mother sweated as well, in great gleaming rivulets down her arms, as she turned the mulch and hauled the piles of weeds away. Sweat pooled in the two wells next to her collarbones. I was mortified just looking at her.

My mother had given me a list of chores that I had to complete before I went to my friend's house. Sonja. Sonja Blomgren. Even her name was thrilling to me, with its hidden letters and its ability to coax a smile by just uttering it. Sonja, Sonja, Sonja. She didn't go to my school, because her grandparents were Lutheran. She never mentioned her parents. She never said what happened to them. But I guessed.

Sonja's grandparents used to live on the south shore of Lake

Superior. They both worked as artists, and made beautiful paintings for children's books, among other projects. They moved to our town because it was easier to get Sonja to school if she could just walk there on her own, and because Sonja's grandfather suffered from bad lungs, requiring frequent doctor visits. They rented a house across our alley and down the block—seven houses away from the house where I first saw a dragon (still, all those years later, boarded up and tangled by weeds—home only to the generations of chickens gone happily wild in the remains of the old coop, and the occasional band of feral cats who hunted those chickens).

(Sonja asked me about the house, on the first day we ever spent time together. Of course she did—Sonja was not one to be undeterred by generally accepted silences. I didn't know what to say. I wanted to tell her about the little old lady with the beans and the strawberries and the eggs. I wanted to tell her about the oppressive heat and the coming storm and the quiet, awestruck *Oh!* I wanted to tell her about the silence after, and of my terrible sense of loss. Instead I said, "I'm sure I don't know." I could tell she didn't believe me.)

Sonja had white-blond hair and long, wide-spaced eyes—dark hazel startling the paleness of her skin. She was the only person I wanted to talk to most days. I didn't know why. I only knew I wanted to see her. Or maybe I needed to see her. In fact, the *need* of it was both palpable and insistent. I didn't have words to understand it. I didn't have context. I just needed to see my friend.

I trudged through my endless list of chores, maudlinly imagining myself as Sisyphus rolling that boulder up the mountain. My mother, after years of fatigue following her illness when I was small, now was in possession of boundless energy. Her work in the garden was unceasing, as were her expectations of me.

"Can I be done now?" I said, as I crouched down at the tiny trench I had drawn in the dirt with my finger into which I placed maddeningly small carrot seeds. Beatrice marched through the garden rows, announcing to the world that she was having more fun than any little girl in the whole wide world.

"Bully for you," I muttered.

Beatrice didn't seem to notice my bad mood. Instead she walked over next to me, coming very close, and squatted down, resting her bum on her heels. She folded her hands over her knees and rested her chin on her knuckles. She stayed there for an exceptionally long minute. I didn't look up. I just placed the tiny seeds in the groove in the dirt, one after another after another, cursing them as they stuck to my fingers. I clamped my molars together and flared my nostrils as I bent over my task, trying my best not to scream. Beatrice turned her head, resting her cheek on her knuckles instead. She didn't move.

Finally: "What are those?" she asked.

I let out a sound, midway between a grunt and a groan and a sigh. "Carrots," I muttered.

Beatrice leaned in and squinted at the seeds. "They don't look like carrots."

I carefully pinched a seed from my hand and made a show of placing it carefully in its row in the dirt. "They will. A seed may look like a quiet, lifeless thing—just a speck—but that's just a trick. There is another thing it wants to be. Very soon it will split its skin, sprout out of itself, and become . . . *bigger*." Just saying so made my arms go goosebumped, even though the day was hot. I thought about my aunt. I tried not to think about my aunt. It wouldn't do me any good to think about my aunt.

"Why does it do that?" Beatrice asked. She stood and climbed onto the old tree stump. Sometimes it bothered her to be small.

"Everything does that. Everything changes. Everything starts out as one thing and then turns into another. It's part of being alive. You're not the same as you used to be. I remember when you were so small I could fit you in my pocket."

Beatrice considered this. "Am I a seed?" she said.

"Maybe," I said. I started to pinch the dirt over the seeds, one tiny bit at a time, being careful not to bury them too deep.

"What will I change into?" Beatrice asked.

"A carrot," I said.

"Nuh-uh." She shook her head. "I will not."

"Fine," I finished my row, and pulled myself to my feet, my shoulders aching a bit. "You'll turn into an elephant."

Beatrice laughed. I wiped off my sweaty face and smiled. It was impossible to be in a bad mood when Beatrice was laughing. "*I will not!*" she squealed. She climbed onto my back, and I spun her around until we both landed on the grass.

I pulled my list of chores out of my pocket. I still had to turn the compost and pick the peas. I sighed.

"Okay, then. If you aren't going to turn into a carrot and you're not going to turn into an elephant, then clearly the only possible option is for you to turn into . . ."

I paused for effect, but Beatrice was impatient.

"A DRAGON!" she howled at the top of her lungs. "I WILL BECOME A DRAGON!" She returned to her spot on the stump and threw open her arms, as though they were wings.

The effect was immediate. My mother, without a word, stood, strode over, hooked Beatrice under one arm, and marched her inside. Beatrice was too shocked to cry. I stared at their retreating figures with my mouth open.

I have filed this memory away. I didn't know what to make of it at the time. It was sharp and unstable and *dangerous.* I remember the smell of the dirt. I remember the buzzing of the honeybees as they made their way through the garden. I remember the distant clucking of feral chickens, where my neighbor used to live, but no one spoke of her anymore so it was like she never existed. I remember the calling of chickadees in the great elm trees that guarded the fronts of all the houses on my block. And cardinals. And the occasional crow. I remember how uncomfortable I felt—like my skin was pricking and stretching. Hot and cold at the same time. Like my body was a thing that just didn't fit anymore. A thing to be changed.

I loved my sister. My cousin. *My sister.*

She looked like my aunt. I had no aunt. I missed my aunt.

I wanted to see my friend. My Sonja. My Sonja, Sonja, Sonja. For reasons that I couldn't identify. My skin became suddenly attentive at the thought of her, and my heart tripped over itself beating fast, then slow, then fast again, and it was so good to have a friend.

Friend.

Even then, even on that day, I knew the word *friend* was inadequate in its meaning and scope to explain how I felt, or what she was to me, but I had no language to explain it to myself. No context. It was another thing that was unmentionable.

My mother yelled inside. Beatrice yelled back. I wanted to go see Sonja. But my mother's anger rooted my feet to the ground. I wouldn't have been able to leave if I tried.

There are moments when the bones of the earth feel as though they've rearranged themselves without our permission. I was inexplicably angry. I had never felt rage before. I had read the word *rage* in books, but I didn't know what it felt like. My bones were hot. My belly was hot. I kicked a rock across the grass.

My mother came outside, an inscrutable expression on her face. She stood above me. She seemed to enlarge. That can't be possible. I must be misremembering. My mother was a tiny thing. But in that moment, she towered over me. Her face shadowed.

"*Inappropriate,*" she hissed.

"But, Mama," I began.

"*Inappropriate,*" she said again. "That is *not allowed in this house.*"

"But, I didn't even—"

"How many times must I say it?" She drew a deep breath in through her nose. And then she hit me. Once. Right across the face. It didn't hurt. But it was shocking. My mother had never hit me before. *Never.* I stared at her. Open-mouthed. "*Inappropriate.* Never let it happen again."

But what, though? That Beatrice mentions dragons? She was only five! Surely she didn't mean anything by it. And *I* hadn't done anything. Surely my mother would see how unreasonable she was being. To change the subject, I showed her my neat rows of carrots, each one marked by a string staked into the ground. Except that there wasn't. The knots attaching the string to the stakes had somehow gotten undone, and the string itself had unraveled into bits. And beyond that, the knots holding the twine lattice for the peas loosened, sending the plants into a tangled mess on the ground. And the slings set up to hold the squash. Everything had unraveled. Even the knot in my pocket.

I know because I checked.

And I noticed my mother checking. Her face became wan and tight. She closed her eyes.

"Well. It looks like we have a lot of work to do."

And that's what we did.

I wasn't allowed to see Sonja that day.

In AD 785, *a young priest by the name of Aengus traveled to the fishing village of Kilpatrick on the island of Rathlin, where he took residence in the local church. He was the first parish priest in the village who was able to write, and so took it upon himself to maintain an exhaustive account of his time on that rocky, wild coast. He was not a particularly adept writer—his pen wandered between Gaelic and Latin, adding bits of Old Norse and Welsh, and often twisted the languages beyond comprehensibility. Still, his account is vital, as it is the only surviving account of the Viking attack on the islands, as well as Aengus's own culpability for the disaster.*

During his time on the island, Aengus had become preoccupied with the study of knots. This was not unusual in a fishing community where knotwork had multiple purposes—both practical and mystical. Knots formed the villagers' fishing nets and fencing for their animals; knots secured the rigging and allowed their boats to survive the near-constant storms. They knitted dense knots into the wool of their jackets and heavy cloaks to help shed the rain and keep them warm at sea. The magic of knots was well known, and accepted within the bounds of Christianity. Women tied knots to improve fishing, and knots to protect boats, and knots to keep the sharks away. They tied knots for good weather and knots to make their wombs bear and knots to find a true love and knots to send their rivals away. Each clan had its signature knot, and it was customary for young brides to design a new knot combining her clan with his, to represent the union of families, as well as a knot specific to each of their subsequent children. These she would keep with her always, tied around her waist under her clothes. She would not undo those knots in her lifetime.

Kilpatrick, at the time, was said to be guarded by a number of water dragons who lived in the harbor and in the underwater caves nearby. These water dragons were considered kin, as every year, a certain number of adolescent girls would walk to the water and transform into the wild beasts, sliding into the waves. They never returned to their girl selves. They could be seen from time to time, playing in the surf, or looking after the boats belonging to their fathers or brothers or former fiancés. They minded the sea and kept the beaches free from marauding pirates or the sneaking ships of Greeks or Britons or bloodthirsty Danes. Bards sang songs about these water dragons, and they found their way into carvings on barrows and castle walls, as well as church frescoes and paintings and illuminated texts. Aengus writes of them matter-of-factly, in the same way he might detail the existence of a seabird or a peat bog.

In one entry, a young man named Maol comes to the priest in a desperate state. He is in love with a girl and wants to make her his bride, but the girl has refused. Her parents told him that the girl's older sister had gone into the water and left her skin behind, and that the younger girl was sure to follow, and that was that. Maol weeps and beats his chest. He tells the priest that he can have no other bride, that she is his only love. If she were to enter the waves, then he would follow, though it would mean his certain death. Aengus—alarmed for the young man's safety and soul, for it would surely mean an eternity in Hell—sends Maol home and tells him that the Lord will show him the way. Aengus then turns to his previous research on the practice of knots. After a month of serious study (and exhaustive notes), he travels to the young man's home. He shows him a knot that, once tied around the young woman in secret, will prevent the change from occurring. She will not be able to undo it, such is the power of this knot.

It works. The couple is married within the week.

In Aengus's journal on the date of the wedding, he describes a lovely young woman whose tearful eyes kept wandering away, tilting ever to the sea. He was impressed with her innocence, and her saintly acceptance of her life to come. Word spread of

Aengus's success in saving Maol from certain death by heartbreak, and the priest's knots became something of a phenomenon. Men arrived from villages across the island, and even from the islands beyond, hoping for a knot to prevent change. Or a knot to ensure discipline. A knot for quiet. A knot for obedience. A knot for docility. A knot for happiness in demeanor. And, most important, a knot to help the holder find a water dragon out at sea, to seize her, hold her, and turn her back. Men by the dozens took to the water. Very soon, there were no more shining scales playing in the water. There were no more bright eyes minding the horizon. There were no more wide, ferocious jaws following the fishing boats and keeping them safe. The harbor, for the first time in recorded memory, was unguarded.

The Vikings raided Rathlin in 795. It was a fast, brutal, and nearly complete destruction. The village of Kilpatrick was burned to the ground, including the original church and its adjoining cottage where the priest lived. Nearly every soul was lost. By some miracle, Aengus's journals survived. The last entry was written entirely in Latin—bad Latin, but understandable in its way. In it, the doomed priest says this:

"It was hubris, of course it was hubris, to think that I could have the power to bind that which must not be bound, alter what should not be altered, and change the hearts of those who wish not to be changed. It is my fault, my fault, my most grievous fault, and I do not think that even our Lord who suffers for our sake will suffer my presence in the next world. Perhaps this is as it should be. Instead I must use my last fleeting moments on this earth to declare my sins to those I have sinned against, and beg their pardon. I am sorry, oh glinting, gilded girls of the waves! I am sorry, oh girls of tooth and claw, oh girls of sinew and scale, girls of speed and intellect and power! Forgive me, or not, it is all the same. May my last sorrowful breath be a testament to my wrongs against you, and to the terrible audacity of men."

—"A Brief History of Dragons" by Professor H. N. Gantz, MD, PhD

14.

As Beatrice grew, so did my mother's agitation. Everything seemed to annoy her, but nothing so much as my father.

"Your daughter is speaking," she'd say when my father stopped listening again.

"Hmm?" my father said.

When did my parents' fights begin? It's hard to say. But once they started, they never really seemed to stop. They fought over whether he would read Beatrice a bedtime story and they fought over whether he would help me with my homework and they fought over whether a pat on the head was sufficient and they fought over whether he would attend school functions and they fought over his increasing business trips. Eventually, my mother began sleeping in the same room as Beatrice and me. Sometimes she'd cuddle into Beatrice's bed. Sometimes into mine. But usually she slept curled up on the floor, her face turned toward the window, her eyes glinting with stars.

People remarked that my mother looked more youthful—even childlike—with every passing year. Her hands seemed smaller. Her feet swam in her shoes. As Beatrice and I grew, my mother seemed to diminish. I assumed at the time that this was because she slept with us in our room, that doing so somehow made her become more and more like us. I didn't know what it really meant until it was too late.

Every night, my mother wound a piece of string around each of our wrists—three times around, with a complicated knot tied at the divot between the two bones, right below the heel of the hand. The knots were tiny marvels of twists and whorls and interlocking loops. Sometimes they looked like a flower. Sometimes they looked like a cluster of stars. Sometimes they looked like the diagrams in a physics book depicting time and space. My mother tried knot after knot—different forms and shapes and processes. She consulted her notebook, crammed with computations and diagrams and algorithms and proofs. She consulted her stack of books on knotwork, each one dog-eared and underlined and scrawled with notes in the margins. She said she wanted to find one that would last for a week, at least. More often than not, they completely unraveled during the night. I would find string on the floor, or hanging off the bed, or tangled in Beatrice's hair. Bits of string could be found in any corner of my mother's once-immaculate house.

"Mother," I said one morning, my exasperation getting the better of me, "must you?" I had woken up with string in my mouth, but she insisted on tying yet another new knot around my wrist. I tried to pull my hand away, but she held me firm with a smile.

"Knots are beautiful, don't you think?" She twisted three loops together, and left it at that, which didn't answer the question at all.

"Yes," I said, "But what are they *for*?"

My mother performed a complicated bend, followed by a pattern of sequential clover leaves, each inserted into the one before it. She held the tip of her tongue gently between her lips as she concentrated. Her nostrils flared. When she spoke, it was more to herself than to me. "When my great-great-grandmother emigrated from Ireland, she had a sash that she wore around her waist, which contained the marriage knot for every couple in her family, going back twelve generations. It was a marvelous thing." She squinted as she coiled the working end around the base of the knot. She had no intention of answering my question. I didn't know why I bothered. Still, she continued: "The knots bound them together, you see? And their new family too—each loop, each strand, each twist pulled together into one shape that could withstand any calamity. It's amazing what a knot can do."

"I'd rather not wear it, Mother," I said, "if it's all the same to you."

"You're wearing it," she said, and her eyes became hard, for just a second. Then she softened. "Just think of it as a love knot." She pressed it with the center of her thumb. "Because I love you." And she wandered down the hallway and to the stairs.

I looked at Beatrice's wrist. Hers had already unraveled. It had only been finished for a few minutes. "Well. They're not very good, are they?" I muttered so my mother wouldn't hear.

This didn't stop her from tying more. I didn't ask her about them after that. I certainly didn't ask her about why she was sleeping in our room. It did no use to ask questions in my house. There were no answers anywhere.

Beatrice was to start school for the first time that fall, and my mother pulled out the sewing basket and the measuring tape, and began carefully restitching my old uniform jumpers to fit Beatrice's tiny frame. I was always small in comparison to my classmates, but Beatrice was *dainty*. Light and fast and bouncy. She moved as though she had springs and wings, hopping from room to room like a cricket.

(And *oh!* Memory does funny things to us, don't you think? As Beatrice bounced and vibrated and resisted my mother's attempts to keep her in one place as she attempted to sew, I thought that word: *cricket*. Instantly I found myself pinned—no, *flooded*—by the memory of myself at four years old, listening at the door as my aunt rubbed oil into my mother's scars and my mother told the story of Tithonus. Of true love forgotten and of health and youth shrinking, drying, shriveling into a husk of itself. I remembered the low hum of my mother's voice, and the smell of oil and perfume and illness. The muscles on my aunt's back flexing and releasing as she ran her thumbs up and down my mother's body. My aunt's voice catching at the thought of my mother as a cricket, kept safe in her pocket forever. I shook my head, trying to force the memory away, and yet, still it persisted, the past looped and wound into the present, the two entangled pulled inexorably into an unbreakable knot. No amount of tugging could pry it loose.)

"Do I have to go to school?" Beatrice asked glumly.

"Yes," my mother said as she stitched the jumper. "Also, stop wiggling."

"But do I *actually*?" Beatrice pressed.

"Yes," my mother said, pins in her mouth and her thumb hooked under Beatrice's waistband, trying to keep my sister from dashing about. "Everyone goes to school. It's the law. Also, for god's sake, hold still."

"I am still," Beatrice said as she wiggled and hopped. "I'm the stilliest." She continued to bounce.

The dress had to be shortened two inches and narrowed significantly. I didn't bother asking why my mother didn't simply purchase a new uniform for Beatrice. My father made an excellent salary at his job, and was, as my mother often said, *a good provider,* but he didn't like it when my mother spent money on my sister.

It was late August, and unbearably humid. School was to start in less than two weeks. My father was on a business trip again. Mother refused to mention it. We left the house at two to attend a lemonade social at the school for the brand-new students, and Beatrice was to meet her new teacher. It was for families. The invitation was addressed to Mr. and Mrs. Green, and it said in bold letters that they requested the whole family attend.

"What about Dad?" I asked. I was feeling cross. I didn't want to go either. I wanted to go to the library, but my mother had been forbidding me from going lately, for reasons that she would not name and I could not ask. In prior years, I had been allowed to spend as much time at the library as I wanted and could come and go as I pleased. It wasn't far, and I knew the way, and my mother wanted to encourage my interests. Also, she and the head librarian, an impossibly old woman named Mrs. Gyzinska, once were on quite friendly terms—I would find them, from time to time, deep in conversation in a corner of the library about politics or logic or geometry. I had started a self-study mathematics curriculum, which both my mother and the librarian encouraged, and there was talk of me doing more—something involving the university, but I wasn't sure at the time what it was. I liked the sound of it. I liked math. And learning. And mostly, I just liked the library. I loved running my fingers along the spines and bringing home books that I could hardly understand, but hoped to someday. Also, I knew Sonja spent her weekend afternoons at the library. My stomach flipped just thinking about it. It felt so good to have a friend.

But lately . . . the library had become more and more out of bounds. I could go only when accompanied, and never for very long. It seemed that my mother and Mrs. Gyzinska had some sort of falling-out. Or my *mother* had the falling-out, and then clung to some combination of frustration and resentment, but the librarian didn't seem to notice either way. She greeted my mother the way she greeted everyone else: the sort of brisk benevolence of a person with far more to do than anyone realizes.

At the picnic, I sat by myself off to the side, in a bit of a snit. The knot around my wrist was already coming undone. I tucked it under the sleeve of my cardigan, so my mother wouldn't see. I didn't want to talk to the principal. I certainly didn't want to talk to my teachers. What I *wanted* was to go to the library. I looked over at my mother, who stood apart from everyone else, sipping her lemonade. The other mothers mingled with mothers and the fathers mingled with fathers, and the teachers flitted from group to group, the nuns looking a bit like magpies and the non-nuns looking a bit like small, brown sparrows. Beatrice ran through the throng of children, a blur of speed and force and color. She was faster than everyone else, and more agile. They struggled to keep up.

When it was time to leave, Beatrice's dress was filthy, the braids were undone, and her bright hair wafted around her head like a halo.

My mother sighed.

"Well," she said. "At least we tried." We were about to leave when the principal appeared out of nowhere.

"Thank you for coming, Mrs. Green," Mr. Alphonse said. "A pity that *Mr.* Green couldn't come as well, but perhaps another time. We are so thrilled to be teaching your . . . younger child." The tiniest of hesitations.

"Indeed," my mother said, her face utterly impassive. She blinked her eyes very slowly. Immediately, the air around them became suddenly cold, and tight. Mr. Alphonse blanched, his color draining. He took a step backward. My mother didn't shift in her place. She simply slowly blinked once again. I had never seen a blink more dangerous. Mr. Alphonse cleared his throat, nervously, and his shoulders pulled inward. As tiny as my mother was, it seemed to me that she towered before him. I curled my lips between my teeth and felt the hairs on the back of my neck stand up like soldiers. "I can hardly believe it's here already," my mother continued, ignoring the principal's discomfort. "Time does fly, after all." She smiled serenely. He opened his mouth, as though he was about to say something else, but nothing came out. My mother folded her hands and kept her face impassive. I realized that my back had begun to sweat.

Mr. Alphonse made a series of nonsensical hand gestures, mumbled something about the weather, and then wandered away to shake the hands of various fathers and share a slap on the back along with a loud guffaw, his relief at being far away from my mother radiating from his body like heat. I could feel it from where I stood.

My mother betrayed no feeling. She remained where she was, her hands folded, watching the principal as he retreated. Another slow blink. And on her lips—the tiniest hint of a smile.

We walked home in silence. I stopped dead in my tracks when we reached the walkway to the library and shoved my hands into my pockets. I looked at my mother. Sonja was inside. I could just *feel* it.

"Please," I said. "Just for a little while. I'll be home as quick as I can."

My mother lifted her chin, not looking at me, but rather regarding the library itself. Mrs. Gyzinska stood at the front door, chatting with an older man wearing a brown wool jacket and brown wool pants, even though it was very hot out. They both had buttons on their lapels, but I couldn't read what they said. They greeted people as they nervously approached the library doors, their gaze darting this way and that, as though checking to see if they were being followed. There was a sign on the library door that said MEETING TODAY! I didn't know what sort of meeting. My mother's eyes narrowed. I saw her catch the notice of the librarian, who nodded at her and smiled.

My mother's face was implacable as stone. She shook her head.

"Please, Mother," I said.

My mother turned away, causing a chill in the air that I could feel. "Not today," she said. "And certainly not by yourself." She gripped Beatrice's hand and walked toward home.

She didn't explain. I didn't ask. It wouldn't have made a difference if I had. I shoved my fists into my pockets and followed, my petulance hovering behind me, like a gathering cloud.

15

Although it was considered bad manners to speak of dragons—just as it was bad manners to discuss money or lady parts or certain illnesses—there were indications that the Mass Dragoning of 1955 was not the end of the matter. Despite what they tried to make us believe in school. Despite the fact that a narrative of the events had been widely agreed upon, and the news outlets largely declined to cover any extraneous dragonings—a dragoning after the fact, if you will.

Still, despite these cultural taboos and implicit prohibitions, there were cases of spontaneous dragoning that managed to rise above the reticence of enforced politeness and enter the public consciousness.

In the summer of 1957, for example, two sisters brought nine Girl Guides on a two-week scouting expedition into the Everglades. The girls were all thirteen, and were all the daughters of well-to-do families in Miami. The leaders were both unmarried, both childless, but together raising a motherless nephew—the son of a third sister who disappeared in 1955 and was never mentioned again. One did not speak of such things, after all. The nephew was fifteen, and an avid scout, and while it was not entirely in line with Girl Guide regulations to have him present in the expedition, many of the girls' parents felt some relief that such a skilled and strapping young man would be available to assist throughout this dangerous journey.

The troop did not return. Search teams scoured the wilderness and found nothing. Instead, months later, a group of fishermen exploring the Everglades in their shared flatboat woke early to the sound of a panicked yawp, deep in the thicket of green.

They found a boy, naked, half-starved, and raving by the edge of the water. There was no telling how long he had been alone.

"Gone!" he said over and over, his screams diminished to a painful rasp. "All, all gone."

He had no canoe, no gear, no campsite, no life preserver, and not a stitch on him, aside from a pair of socks that he strangely decided to use as gloves. Rangers tried to glean any information to help guide their search for the missing girls, but the boy's eyes were wide and wild, and his mouth was unable to form sentences. They brought him to a hospital, where he remained for another six months, screaming endlessly for his mother.

A year later, a team of rangers out for the yearly crocodile count found what they believed were the remains of the Girl Guides' final campsite in a tangled, remote area of the wilderness, far afield from the troop's intended route. In their official report—the one eventually leaked to the newspapers—they said that they found a collection of fire-crusted tent poles, three deeply dented canoes, and the torn-apart remains of two more, each ripped in half, as though they were made out of paper. They found the camp seats that the girls had made—each hand-stitched with thick leather threading and embroidered with each girl's name.

What did *not* make the official report, and what I only learned much later, was that each girl had in her knapsack a small diary. The diaries had, originally, been a troop project, to be used toward their badges in book binding and literary arts. Each girl had become, for a few months at least, a faithful diarist, neatly inscribing the date and an explanation of the day's events in small, conscientious handwriting. The entries began in December 1956 and continued until—in every single diary—May 14, 1957. After that, the girls did not write anything down. Instead, they drew dragons. Big dragons, tiny dragons. Dragons destroying skyscrapers and dragons swimming with whales and dragons dancing on the head of a pin and dragons skidding down one arm of the Milky Way. Dragons in school desks. Dragons in cars. Dragons doing dishes. Dragons downing missiles. Dragons laying waste to armies or governments or home economics classrooms. There were no words. No explanations. No statements of intent. Just dragons.

No one ever knew for sure what happened to those girls. There were speculations, of course. But the people who did speculate were roundly criticized. Accused of speaking ill of the dead. Or of falling into the clutches of negative thinking. Some even lost their jobs. The Mass Dragoning was history, after all, and everyone was done with that business. It was so much easier to say that the girls had simply vanished.

"Let this be a lesson to parents everywhere," the newscasters said. And then they let the matter drop.

A little over a year later, in the winter of 1958, a new union formed by the Black female employees of a large fishery in southern Alabama had been striking for several months—demanding fair wages, safer conditions, and an end to the racist abuse at the hands of their supervisors. The company owners, growing tired of the bad press and the union's vexing persistence, contracted with a number of former law enforcement officers and other aggrieved men in the area to make an example of the strikers. They hoped to break the union's will just enough to encourage an amenable contract.

"Who do they think they are?" the company bosses said as they handed out envelopes filled with cash and promises of immunity. "I trust you gentlemen to nip this little problem in the bud."

The envelopes had a pleasant heft in their hands. The men said they would have done it for free as they pocketed the money with a grin.

The strikers had blocked the one road leading into and out of the plant with both barricades and tents, which they used to hold strategy meetings and prayer circles, as well as a distribution center for food and supplies. A separate tent provided shelter for the makeshift childcare center. There were tables heaped with homemade bread and pots of baked beans, as well as a constantly replenishing vat of bubbling stew ready to be dished into crocks for people to take home and feed to their families. The women kept the tents staffed day and night, armed with bats and sticks and righteousness, and the full conviction that justice would eventually prevail. They were prepared to strike forever, if need be.

The men contracted as thugs for the company decided to attack on the night before Christmas. Fewer people there, they figured. And nothing distracts a bunch of women like an impending holiday. This was common knowledge.

"Piece of cake," they laughed as they planned out their course of action. "Like taking candy from a bunch of big babies," they said as they downed bottles of whiskey and headed out loudly, into the night.

The men were never seen again.

There were rumors of shots fired. There were rumors that an unusual tremor sent buildings shaking, knocked dishes out of cupboards and children out of bed, and caused the roads to buckle. People said it could be felt from Heron Bay all the way to Montgomery.

The next morning, the tents had burned and the tables had all flipped and the vat of stew, for the first time in months, was cold. The ground was littered with the remains of broken liquor bottles, and shotguns that had been snapped like twigs, and a scattering of men's shoes. Other than that, the strike line held, and grew. Women from surrounding parishes arrived, helping to clean up, mend what was broken, and lock arms in an unbreakable barrier across the road.

The company, for its part, denied ever meeting with the missing men, denied any knowledge of their plans, denied the envelopes and the cash and the promises, and most important, denied ever disagreeing with the strikers in the first place. "A simple case of miscommunication," they said. They called in the press and signed new contracts with great fanfare, and insisted on photographs showing smiling white men in fine suits magnanimously shaking the hands of Black women in coveralls as they agreed to every single item that the strikers had been demanding for months.

The women in the photographs did not smile. They stood with their faces tilted slightly upward, their eyes obscured by a sudden flash of light.

And then in May of 1959, patrons at a particular bar in Los Angeles reported an astonishing event that occurred during a semi-regular drag ball and performance. Three dancers, each exquisitely coiffed, rouged, and costumed, right in the middle of what was described as the performance of their lives, each bedecked and adorned with color and glitter and light, stepped out of their already beautiful skins in front of a thunderstruck audience. Brand-new dragon bodies unfurled, one by one, onstage, their multicolored scales glittering under the floodlights. They were, all three, so very lovely that the audience had to collectively catch their breath. Some people fell to their knees. Many wept. Given that crossdressing performers at this time in history were particularly adept at making art under difficult, violent, and sometimes outlandish circumstances, it didn't occur to anyone to stop the performance. The music simply played on, the dancing continued, and the drag-dragons didn't miss a beat. They continued their song and continued to dance, finishing to thunderous applause and no fewer than ten curtain calls, before crashing through the leaky ceiling and disappearing into the night. The patrons looked up and watched as the dragons flew in formation, their tremendous bodies growing smaller and smaller, a hard, insistent brightness cutting at the night, until, at last, they glinted among the stars. Onlookers reported that it was the most beautiful thing they had ever seen.

And lastly, on New Year's Eve, 1959, revelers at more than six hundred separate holiday parties across the country reported a transformation or two, all when the countdown to the new year had just begun. There was no damage, no mayhem. Just a sigh, a shudder, and a sudden cry of joy as what was small became suddenly *large*.

Each one took to the sky.

Each one didn't look back.

And none of this was covered on the news. It was, again, unmentionable. And the world kept its eyes on the ground.

16.

Sonja and her grandparents lived in a magical house. Or, at least it seemed so to me. Before they moved in, the house had white clapboard with grey trim and a black roof—virtually invisible on the block. The landlord was a fairly careless bachelor who lived on the other side of town, and didn't much care what colors they painted or how they altered the property, just as long as they paid their rent in a timely manner. Within a month of their moving in, the house had transformed: yellow walls, trim a different color on each window, flowers painted on the door. Inside there were rooms painted with fairy woodlands, and rooms painted in Norwegian meadow landscapes, and rooms painted with mountains crawling with hiding trolls, and rooms painted to look like the shores of Lake Superior—still beloved and longed for. Sonja's grandparents each had separate studios—her grandmother had claimed the main-floor den, while her grandfather transformed the garage into a space with a woodstove and a brightly painted floor and newly installed wide windows and an easy chair for thinking. We were welcome in their studios and welcome to watch them work. (This, in contrast to my own father, whose office I had never once seen. I had no idea what it might be like to watch him work.)

Like Sonja, her grandparents both had wide-spaced, dark hazel eyes. Like Sonja, they once both had white-blond hair, though as they aged, their hair became so white it seemed to glow, and the pinkness of their scalps shone through.

No one ever spoke of Sonja's parents, not once in all my times visiting. There was only one photograph of them in the entire house—a two-by-three-inch snapshot in a plain frame at the bottom corner of a wall full of family pictures in the kitchen. Sonja never mentioned it, and neither did her grandparents. But I knew what it was. It showed Sonja holding her parents' hands on what looked like her first day at kindergarten. She had a wide smile and was missing one tooth. Her father wore carpenter's overalls and held a bucket of tools. Her mother wore smart heels, a pressed skirt with a matching tailored jacket, and a hat pinned into her chignon. She worked (I learned much later) as a research assistant for a psychology professor at the University of Wisconsin, and was apparently indispensable. Sonja had both of her parents' hands in hers, but I noticed the way two of her fingers had reached past her mother's hand to the hem of her mother's jacket, and wound the fabric into her grip. Her father looked lovingly at the top of Sonja's shiny blond head. Her mother's gaze tilted skyward, a look of longing on her face.

Sonja and I spent every moment that we could together, though I vastly preferred spending time at the Blomgren house. There, her grandparents gave us paper and canvas and pots of paint and taught me how to pull a brush toward its destination, and how to find a whole world revealed in a line across an open space. At my house, my mother taught us both how to knit and crochet (Sonja was better at it than I was) and how to carefully follow recipes clipped from *Ladies' Home Journal*. My mother loved Sonja. Beatrice oscillated in her feelings toward my friend, going from outright jealousy to ardent devotion, without much of anything in between. Sonja told Beatrice stories from Norway, where her grandparents had been born (though neither had any memory of it, as they both emigrated as toddlers), and where her father was from. Indeed, it was in the waters between Iceland and Norway where her father's small boat was last seen, and where it is presumed to be resting under the waves.

"What was he doing there?" I asked her once, forgetting myself for a moment.

Sonja pressed her fingers to her mouth for a moment or two. "Looking for someone," she said at last. And then silence reigned.

Sonja also taught Beatrice to draw, showing her the components of a face, the trick to making the eye fill in what the pencil suggests. She showed her the techniques for drawing trees and birds and small mammals, and even fairies and trolls. (These, I noticed, my mother had no problem with. Another thing worth noticing: each time Beatrice attempted to draw a dragon, Sonja would crumple up the paper and throw it away. "Not today, busy Bea," Sonja said. She did this without emotion or scolding or shame. It was simply an indisputable fact of being—like getting wet when it rains.)

As eighth grade began, I spent my school day counting the minutes until the bell would ring and I could see Sonja again. My classwork suffered (though my homework was fine, and I was still miles ahead of my classmates). I wasn't paying attention. I was distracted. I drew. I wrote notes to Sonja. I sketched out plans for adventures that we would embark upon together someday. My teachers fumed, then fretted, and in the first week of October, my parents were called.

Only my mother came. She was, I remember, looking rather pale. Sister Angelica, my English teacher, and Mr. Alphonse, the principal, sat at the table across from her, while I sat at a chair separately, my arms wrapped tightly over my chest and my face pinned into a scowl.

My mother, bless her, came prepared with documents. She explained how diligent I was in my homework. She showed the papers and projects and assignments that I had completed during the month of September, which all received A's. She talked about my trips to the library to watch their fairly substantial collection of filmed lectures on physics and mathematics given by great scholars from places like Harvard and Oxford and other faraway universities. She even brought a letter signed by the head librarian confirming that I was currently working through problem sets in mathematics textbooks that were far beyond what was available to me at school, and recommending me for a program that I didn't entirely understand—and frankly, my mother had not yet agreed to. Still, she thought it important to show my teacher *today*. I didn't mention anything, but I did take note of it. She showed them the work I had done outside of class using textbooks that I had gotten through the magic of interlibrary loan.

"If she's distracted in class," my mother said gently, "I think we should consider the possibility that she is simply *bored* in class, and needs to be challenged more. I had a similar problem when I was in school. I was only fourteen when I was allowed to enroll at the university to study calculus—not much older than she is now. By the time I graduated high school I had already completed more than half of the coursework for my mathematics degree. Perhaps we should consider that this is the path she's on."

Sister Angelica and Mr. Alphonse listened to my mother with indulgent looks on their faces, the way one might listen to a child who was trying to explain why she still believed in fairies.

"And how useful has your mathematics degree been in your career as a housewife, dear?" Sister Angelica said.

The room became ice-cold. My mother's eyes were two dark stones set in a marble face. I held my breath. I felt the knot in my pocket unravel, just a bit.

"And we are not talking about *you, specifically,* Mrs. Green. Of course, everyone is very proud of your accomplishments. But you see, that is part of the problem. We've had to stop posting the exam scores, because the boys see her loafing in class, and yet still claiming that top score, with no thought *at all* to their feelings. I ask you, what does one do with a girl with so little regard for others?"

"So . . . little . . . regard," my mother said slowly, as though her words were heavy weights. My mother's eyes seemed to widen a bit. And elongate. Or maybe I was just imagining it. She pressed her palms together, and dug her fingernails—now sharp points—into the skin on the backs of her hands.

"And then there's this," Sister Angelica said, her thin mouth pressed into a hard line. It was a folder filled with drawings from hours and hours of Sonja's valiant attempts to teach me how to be a better artist. I had pictures of Sonja on the couch, and Sonja on a stool, and Sonja standing in a field of flowers, the ends of her hair winding through her fingers. Sonja dancing on the water. Sonja on the mountaintop. Sonja drifting across the sky. My drawings were unsteady and I lacked an artist's eye. But I still drew faithfully, ardently, desperate in my need to improve, in my need to pin down something lovely and honest and *true*. My breath caught. I couldn't bear to have my drawings in Sister Angelica's hands. I couldn't bear for anyone to see them, or worse, to touch them. Those drawings were *mine* in a way that nothing had been mine before, and *private* in a way that I could not adequately explain. I had written Sonja's name on them, experimenting with different types of lettering, with different stylistic flares. "Sonja," they said. "Sonja, Sonja, Sonja."

Unconsciously, my throat made a strangled cry.

"Who," Sister Angelica said, turning her waspish gaze toward me, "is *Sonja*?"

⁂

I don't remember much of what happened in the rest of that meeting. My mind went blank. My heart went blank. The world became cloudy and diffuse. I was embarrassed and ashamed, but I wasn't entirely sure why. I wished I was at Sonja's house. I wished she was at my house. I wished that the two of us were on a boat, far, far away, sailing toward a more hospitable shore.

A fist landed hard on the desk, startling me into the present moment. *"Young lady are you listening to me?"* Mr. Alphonse barked, the folds of his neck quivering with the loudness of his voice.

I jumped. "What?" I hadn't been listening.

Mr. Alphonse sighed. Sister Angelica's gaze narrowed even more. And my mother's face was as blank as the side of a mountain. I had no idea what she thought. "Just apologize," Mr. Alphonse said. "That's what people do when they know they're in the wrong."

I looked at my mother. She offered nothing. I felt my insides grow hot. Was I in the wrong? I had no idea what for. But I was a rule-following child. A dutiful child. And I hated being in trouble.

"Okay?" I said. "I'm sorry." I felt my skin flush and my stomach turn, but I did not know why. Still, my apology seemed to satisfy my teacher and my principal. They gave each other a curt, grim nod. My mother said nothing. Instead she stood, took my hand, and we walked home.

Mrs. Everly, our neighbor, was at the house, watching Beatrice, which actually meant that she was sitting in the kitchen, smoking my father's cigarettes and enjoying a shot of his whiskey while Beatrice listened to the radio in the living room. Before we walked up the front steps, my mother grabbed my hand and looked at me, hard in the face.

"You need to watch yourself, my girl," she said in a low voice.

"From *what*?" I said. Her sudden urgency was baffling to me. I couldn't tell if I was angry at it, or afraid, or if I wanted to cry. Perhaps it was all three at once.

My mother took in a deep breath, and composed her face. I thought for a moment that she had a slick of tears glistening at the rim of her eyes, but then she blinked, and it vanished. I wondered if I had imagined it in the first place. Finally, "There is a limit to how much we can hold, and how much we can keep in this world. It's not a good idea to cling to the things you can't bear to lose. That's how we break, you see?" She folded her hands together and rested her chin on her knuckles. "*Do* you see?"

"Yes, Mother," I said.

I didn't see. But this seemed to satisfy her anyway. She turned and went inside.

Three days later, my father, at dinner, somewhere between his whiskey and rye and his final cigarette, looked up at the ceiling and did something he never did at dinner. He spoke.

"Mr. Alphonse came into the office to see me today," he said, to no one in particular. And then he went into the den to read the rest of his newspaper.

I looked at my mother. She was very pale. But this was nothing new. She had been so pale lately.

Weeks went by and the matter dropped. Or I thought the matter had dropped. I did my best to appear more engaged at school. I still did my best on papers and homework and quizzes and tests. Sometimes, there would be a note at the bottom of papers, saying, "There is a difference between academic excellence and simply showing off," or a variation on that theme. I did notice that it wasn't written in my teacher's handwriting. I couldn't prove it, but I was pretty sure it was Mr. Alphonse.

One night near the end of October, the winds picked up and blew so hard I thought the house might blow down. The next morning was a Saturday, two days before Halloween. I ran outside to see if everything was still standing, and stood on the front steps for a minute, enjoying the brisk chill in the air, and the warm smell of damp leaves decaying slowly in the morning light. The sun was the color of an egg yolk, set on a wide, blue plate. The colored leaves had all been ripped out of the open-handed trees and cushioned the ground in great, multicolored mounds. I grabbed my jacket from the hook in the entryway and stepped into my shoes and ran to Sonja's house to rake leaves.

Once we finished her yard, we tramped over to mine, singing at the tops of our lungs. What had gotten into us? Neighbors peeked through their curtains, shaking their heads and sucking their teeth. We rested our arms on each other's shoulders, our heads tilted inward, our cheeks nearly touching. I wasn't much of a singer, but I belted out every song I knew, and felt the melody vibrate along the length of my bones. Sonja's arm slid down around my waist, holding me tight. It felt so good, *so good,* I thought, to have a friend.

Sonja waited in the front yard as I went around to the shed to find rakes, my heart thumping pleasantly as I raced back. We had a wide oak tree in the side yard and two maples in front, which meant that the leaves were thick and plentiful. Beatrice came out with her rubber boots and crocheted sweater and took great armloads of leaves, throwing them at the sky. We built a mound of leaves the size of a Ford truck.

"Jump in!" Beatrice yelled, but then she started sneezing and my mother called her inside. My mother was always admonishing Beatrice for nearly catching her death of something.

Sonja and I looked at the pile of leaves. Her hair glinted in the October sun. "Ready?" she said, sliding her hand into mine. The breeze made the empty tree branches groan and stirred up the leaves on the ground, making them spin and twirl around our feet. The air was sweet, and damp—the smell of apples and soil and pleasant rot and everything that once was green loosening and falling and giving itself over to the ground. My breath caught, and I had no words. I just squeezed her hand and we ran, leaped, and landed in the papery softness of color and dust and light.

How do I pin down a memory like this? How do I know how to shelve it or categorize it? It felt impossible to me then, and it feels impossible to me now.

This is how I remember it:

The sky was so blue it broke my heart and the world smelled of something beginning. We landed in the leaves, which pillowed around us. There were leaves in her bright hair, framing her face. The empty branches held up the sky. I remember how they curled around her head like a crown as she leaned over me, catching my arms and telling me I was her prisoner, and oh, Sonja, what a willing prisoner I was! I remember rolling in the leaves, the whispery rustling sound they made beneath me and the paleness of Sonja's arms next to the dirt on my own, and the delicacy of Sonja's tapered fingers next to the stubby brusqueness of my own, and Sonja's cheek against my cheek and Sonja's hair in my hair and Sonja's mouth brushing against my mouth, and oh, Sonja, Sonja, Sonja.

And then she screamed.

My father, standing over us, had grabbed her by her upper arm and wrenched her to her feet.

I remember Sonja's face as she was pulled away—a harsh, livid picture of astonishment and fear and pain. I reached for her, but my father was too fast and my hands clasped at nothing.

"Time to go," my father said.

"But," I began.

"Time to go," he said again, taking great strides across the yard as she stumbled behind.

And he took her away.

───

I wasn't allowed to see Sonja for the rest of that day. Nor the day after. Long days passed.

"When?" I pleaded.

"Never," my father said, his voice quick and final, like a slap.

I told my parents that I would just sneak over, but they informed me that Sonja's grandparents also would not allow it.

"Why?" I asked. The room swam. My eyes swamped. My breath was sharp and heavy in my chest.

"You'll understand when you're older," my father said as my mother stared at her hands.

My father sent me to my room.

17.

My parents grounded me for two weeks. My mother walked me to school each morning and met me on the school steps at the end of the day. I trudged in sullen silence, my hands shoved in my pockets and balled into fists. I would not look at her face. She never once attempted to engage, which just enraged me more. Other kids at school paused and stared when we walked by. No one else had their mothers pick them up. We were in eighth grade, after all. We were practically grown. They knew that the only reason she would do such a thing was because I had done something terrible. None of them could imagine what it could possibly be.

I still didn't understand it.

At home, my mother set me with arduous and pointless and futile tasks. Scrubbing the grout. Sweeping and dusting the basement. Buffing the chrome fixtures. Polishing silver flatware that we never used, and honestly, what on earth was the point. Washing the windows until they gleamed.

She tied a new knot around my wrist, abandoning the yarn, and opting to use a thin length of leather cord instead. It was stiffer than the yarn, so it took longer to tie. Also, it smelled weird. I wrinkled my nose. The leather took effort and tenacity to set in place. It felt like it was meant to stay.

"What's this for?" I asked her.

She shrugged. "It's just a knot."

"Can I take it off?"

"No."

"So what's it for," I asked again.

"It's pretty, don't you think? Look. Beatrice has one, too."

Beatrice worried at hers as though it itched, but didn't take it off even though she clearly wanted to. If there's one person on earth she loved more than me, it was my mom.

Our mom, I mean.

My mother then taught me how to make patterned knots and gave me an impossibly old book called *Lady Sylvia's Book of Macramé Lace* (she had an identical copy of her own, but hers was crowded with notes and equations and bullet points and hand-written papers stuck inside the pages, and I was not allowed to look at it). She also gave me a basketful of yarn and bade me tie knot after knot after knot from a constantly replenishing pile of string. I spent hours each day looping and twisting and pulling tight.

"Why am I doing this?" I demanded after my fingers were raw.

"To hold you in place," my mother said mildly, without meeting my eye.

"I already *am* in place," I roared—only because my father was not at home. "I'm *grounded*, remember? Why are you making me do all of this?"

"You'll understand someday."

I knew this wasn't true.

Beatrice, being Beatrice, did her best to distract and entertain me. She created elaborate pantomimes based on the stories that Sonja had told her. Mountain elves and forest trolls and the Fossegrim in the river who will play his fiddle so sweetly that no creature can resist its song—even the trees will pick up their feet and dance. I'm sure my mother assumed that the stories were coming from Beatrice's own imagination—if she knew their origin, I had no doubt that she'd put a stop to it. Beatrice accompanied her stories with pictures she had drawn to illustrate each moment. A forest troll running away with a stolen baby. The Fossegrim reluctantly teaching a young woman to play even though he knew it would spell her doom, and that everyone she loved would dance themselves to death when they heard her strike the bow. Every story made me miss Sonja more. Beatrice was only trying to help—how could I tell her that each dramatized scene weighed like a stone on my heart.

Beatrice finished her story with a flourish and bow. She waited for me to applaud—I did, even though my hands hurt and my body hurt and the whole world hurt—and then she bowed again.

"Do you feel better?" she asked me, inspecting my face. "I made you feel better, right?" Her face was lit with a ludicrous smile. I smiled back in spite of myself.

"How can I be sad when I'm with you?" I replied. It was a lie. It was entirely true. Both at the same time.

At the end of the two weeks, my restrictions lifted. My mother put the basket of string away. My endless tasks were reduced to my normal chores and I was once again allowed to walk myself to and from school without my mother in tow.

I thought about Sonja. I dreamed about Sonja. I couldn't bring myself to say her name out loud, but my mother saw it on my face anyway.

"The rule is still the rule," she said pointedly, at dinner. My father said nothing. He simply attacked his pot roast and potatoes as though they had wronged him.

"I always follow the rules," I said, dropping my gaze to my lap and clenching my fists.

"Alexandra," my mother said.

"*Alex,*" I whispered.

"The rule is still the rule." She didn't say what this rule was. Obviously I knew. And I had every intention to break it.

The next day, after school, I went straight to Sonja's house.

And I stood on the front walkway for a long time, open-mouthed. I don't think I cried. I had to remind myself to breathe, and when I did, each inhale felt like the blade of a knife. Each exhale was a sputter and a choke, like someone at the edge of drowning.

The colors on Sonja's magical house were all gone. Someone

had painted it white, and badly. There were streaks and lumps and splatters on the windows. The garden beds crowded with flowers native to Norway—salvia and foxglove and snow butter-cups and saxifrage—had all been dug up and covered with wood chips. A sign had been nailed in the center of the yard, its corners fluttering slightly in the breeze. FOR LEASE it said.

And there, at the bottom, was the logo for my father's bank.

Very slowly, I approached the house. The paint fumes were so strong they made me sick. I leaned on the window, cupped my hands, and peered inside. The colors and woodland scenes and images of Norway and trolls and Lake Superior had all been covered over in a thick layer of off-white paint, and Sonja and her grandparents were gone. I stood on their front step for more than an hour, my body trembling with disbelief. Finally, I stumbled back home and barricaded myself in my closet. I didn't come down for dinner.

The next morning, still in tears, I sat in the living room in silence, my book bag slung across my shoulder, counting the minutes until it was time for school. Beatrice, having no idea what was going on, sat next to me and held my hand. My mother came and stood in front of me for a long time.

"It's probably for the best," she said at last. She wouldn't meet my eye.

She handed me my lunch and opened the door. It was November, with its sudden, quaking cold. The kind of cold that sinks straight into your bones. The sky was the color of chalk dust. I pulled my coat tightly around my shoulders, took Bea-trice's hand, and we walked out into the morning.

We were good children. We kept our eyes on the ground.

Testimony of Dr. H. N. Gantz before the House Committee on Un-American Activities, March 12, 1960

CHAIRMAN: The committee will come to order. This morning the committee resumes its series of hearings on the vital issue of the use of American passports as travel documents in furtherance of the objectives of those who seek to disrupt, deform, or otherwise derange the American way of life.

MR. ARENS: Dr. Gantz, I understand that you applied for a passport in order to attend a scientific conference in Communist Prague. Is this true?

DR. GANTZ: Yes, sir, though it should be noted that Communism has nothing to do with it. This conference has long been held in Zurich—or, to be more clear, in neutral Switzerland—but many scientists from nations less free than ours were unable to attend, due to their countries' fear of defections. The conference organizers determined that it would benefit science and the exchange of knowledge if the event was held in a country that was more acceptable to nations . . . less free, in theory, than ours.

MR. ARENS: But your passport application was denied.

DR. GANTZ: This is true.
　　[Transcriber's note: Several moments pass.]

CHAIRMAN: The witness is taking an awfully long time to finish that thought.

DR. GANTZ: Well, there isn't much more to say, is there? I applied for a passport—which is a normal and reasonable act for a citizen to request travel documents from their own government—and those documents were denied without adequate explanation from said government. My entire career has been focused on the expansion of health and science on behalf of my country, an act of patriotism and love of the American system that I still possess even now, despite having been removed from my position at the National Institutes of Health, for reasons that are apparently classified.

MR. ARENS: Mr. Chairman, the witness is engaging in speeches and not simply answering the question.

CHAIRMAN: Dr. Gantz, you are not a revolutionary on a barricade. You are required to simply answer the question. No more speeches, please.

DR. GANTZ: My apologies, sirs. You must understand that this situation has rattled me to my core. My lab has been ransacked and my students and patients have all been questioned by federal authorities—one poor woman was taken by strange men in an unmarked car, right in front of her children, *her children*, sirs, and detained for a day and a half. Unacceptable. No one has explained the rationale for any of this. The fact that my passport was denied is simply another tally mark in a long and vexing series of assaults on personal liberties, perpetrated by my own government, which makes me question the value and health of our freedoms in the United States of America.

MR. ARENS: This is the land of the free, sir! You would do well to show some respect!

DR. GANTZ: Is it? Are you sure? Do you not read the news? Not only are American citizens in places like Little Rock and Greensboro organizing as we speak and demanding that their country grant them a modicum of the basic rights guaranteed in the Constitution, but this very committee has tied itself up in knots addressing threats to this nation that simply do not exist while turning a blind eye as law enforcement commits acts that are not only unlawful, but also un-American. This is happening in American cities. It is happening in American laboratories. It is happening in universities and social service agencies and in the tiny offices of groups dedicated to the notion of justice for all.

MR. ARENS: Mr. Chairman, the witness is both hostile and belligerent.

CHAIRMAN: Dr. Gantz, you would do well to remember where you are.

DR. GANTZ: I know exactly where I am. I'm sitting with some of the very same men who commissioned my research into the phenomenon of spontaneous—

CHAIRMAN: Dr. Gantz.

DR. GANTZ: Spontaneous *dragoning,* and who subsequently destroyed—

CHAIRMAN: DR. GANTZ.

DR. GANTZ: And somehow have declared my work both nonexistent AND classified, which of course is an assault on both reason and facts.

CHAIRMAN: COUNSEL, RESTRAIN YOUR CLIENT. And please explain to him the unpleasant reality of being found in contempt of Congress.

[Transcriber's note: Several moments pass.]

MR. ARENS: Dr. Gantz, when you applied for your passport, you were asked to sign an affidavit declaring that you were not, nor have you ever been, a member of the Communist Party, moreover that you would not ever be tempted to join. You were also asked to sign an affidavit declaring that you were not, nor have you ever been, a member of the Wyvern Research Collective, moreover that you would not ever be tempted to join. Do you remember receiving those documents?

DR. GANTZ: I do.

MR. ARENS: And yet, those documents were strangely absent from your passport application.

DR. GANTZ: They were not strangely anything. I simply chose not to include them.

MR. ARENS: Do you know what happened to the affidavits?

DR. GANTZ: I threw them in the trash.

MR. ARENS: You admit this.

DR. GANTZ: Freely.

CHAIRMAN: Let the record show that the witness admits to tampering with federal documents.

[Transcriber's note: Several more moments pass. Witness's counsel whispers urgently while witness shakes his head.]

DR. GANTZ: I'm not sure why it's such an astonishment. They were my documents. They said clearly at the top that they were supplemental. I looked up the statute, and learned that I was under no obligation to sign them unless compelled by a U.S. court. I was under no such compulsion, so I knew I was in my rights to ignore them. There is no law against throwing trash into the trash.

MR. ARENS: It may surprise you that we have those very documents here.

DR. GANTZ: It does not. Did you read my note?

CHAIRMAN: Let the record show that atop the affidavit declaring an unequivocal renunciation of Communism, that the witness wrote, "Nice try, assholes," thereby necessitating an additional indecency charge. Because what you wrote on the other affidavit is considered classified, it will not be in view of this committee, but will instead be forwarded to the Subcommittee on Foreign and Domestic Threats, to determine whether it is an act of war.

DR. GANTZ: This is preposterous and you know it. This committee is a disgrace and a joke.

CHAIRMAN: The witness is belligerent. We hereby hold him in contempt.

18.

Winter settled in, and the world froze.

And then it thawed.

And then it flooded.

And then, once again, everything overran with heat and green and aching buds and swollen flowers and life in abundance. I was in too foul a mood to notice. Summer hit early that year, and even in early May, we sweltered in our classrooms and sweated through our uniforms, ending each day red-faced and reeking, and desperate for our release in June. At last, eighth grade ended, with its litany of indignities and hurt feelings and oppressive boredom. The school doors opened and we filed out of our elementary school lives and our elementary school selves and we awaited something new. High school. Or something. And though it wouldn't be that much of a change—we were all going to the same place, largely—the transition *felt* significant. We were leaving a part of ourselves behind.

Even the sky seemed to feel it—heavy and waiting.

I missed Sonja. I missed her *so much.* Just thinking of her made my chest cave in and my bones ache.

Despite my learning how to have a friend—a real and true friend—that knowledge never transferred to any of the kids at school. They weren't unkind to me. They were just . . . indifferent. As I was indifferent. I wouldn't see a single one that summer. I wouldn't miss them, nor would I be missed. I say this not out of self-pity, but simply to state the facts.

That summer, my mother's garden was its most productive and abundant. Its swan song, I would realize later. She spent most of her days out of doors—wearing, I noticed, my aunt's old coveralls, with the name patch ripped away, and the sleeves removed at the shoulder, and about five inches from the pant legs cut off to make them fit. In the evenings, she had her bath and put on her stockings and starched skirts and had the table ready for when my father came home. If he came home. She served his dinner and poured his whiskey either way.

I remember noticing that she started to poke holes in her belts to make them fit. I remember noticing the thickness of her foundation to cover the darkness under her eyes. I remember noticing that while our own plates were heaped with food, my mother ate less and less. I remember noticing these things, but I didn't know what to do with that noticing, and so I simply filed them away. I was a child, selfish in the way children are selfish, sure of the world's unchangeability in the way that children are sure of things. My mother was simply my mother. That time when she vanished from me was a thing that occurred in the world of *then*. In childhood, it is difficult to think of *then*. In childhood, there is only *now*.

I missed Sonja. I wrote her letters addressed to her old house, with the instructions PLEASE FORWARD on the bottom. I wrote her every week for my entire eighth grade year. At the beginning of June, right after school let off, the entirety of my letters were returned to me in a great bundle, with the words RETURN TO SENDER, NO FORWARDING ADDRESS stamped across her name. Her grandparents had a different last name, and I didn't know what it was. I had no way to find her.

I took the letters and wrapped them in brown paper that I secured with twine. I hid them behind the false panel in my closet. Just in case.

That summer, my mother often put me in charge of Beatrice when she needed to lie down for a bit—something that was happening more and more. Beatrice, now six, was a whirlwind of activity. She climbed trees and leaped from the branches. She used the back fence as a balance beam. She climbed to the roof of the garage to take in the sun on the shingles. She used the morning glory trellis as a ladder.

I chased her into the storm cellar and I chased her through the neighborhood yards and I chased her all the way down to the end of our road, where it simply stopped at a tangled thicket separating our neighborhood from the decommissioned railroad tracks. At the end of each day, I had to hoist her over my shoulder and trudge her home as she howled with enthusiasm or rage or joy. It wasn't always easy to tell which.

One day in early August, Beatrice made a break for it while I wasn't looking and I had to search for her for hours. My mother didn't know. She was having a lie-down. I searched everywhere, feeling annoyed during the first hour and frantic during the second. I berated myself for not keeping a closer watch. I tried to think how I would explain this to my mother.

Finally, footsore and panicking, I walked through the alley, peeking inside each of the neighbor's trash cans, in case she was hiding, or sleeping, or worse. And that's when I heard Beatrice laughing. I chased the sound of her voice, and came skidding to a halt at the back gate of the boarded-up house. Weeds curled up the fence and bramble tangled through the old garden. I could barely make out the old house, peeking through the green.

Feral chickens pecked through the weeds. Feral cats blinked through the gaps of house where the clapboard had fallen away. And Beatrice lay in a thicket of ivy, its tendrils winding around her arms and legs, making bright green knots against her grubby skin.

"WHAT ARE YOU DOING HERE?" I roared, leaping across the bramble and landing on my knees at her side. She turned her head, blinked a few times, and gave me a mild smile.

"Oh, hi, Alex," she said, as though there was nothing more normal in the world than being away for hours and taking a nap in an abandoned garden. Breaking through the tendriled knots of the ivy, she brought her fists to her face and rubbed her eyes. She yawned. "Did you know there are chickens here?"

I leaned my forehead on my knees and sighed. "Yes, Beatrice." I shook my head. "I did know that."

"And kitties," she said breathlessly. "There are *so many kitties*." As if on cue, two kittens, who didn't look like they had even been weaned yet, ambled over to her feet. Beatrice scooped them up and nuzzled their fur until they struggled and yowled. They weren't altogether used to people. Beatrice kissed their backs and set them gently on the ground.

"I know about the kitties too," I said patiently. "Maybe it's time to go."

Beatrice ignored this. "Why don't we have kitties? They can sleep with me," she added, probably to demonstrate that she had already thought this through.

"Daddy hates cats," I explained. "That's why we can't have one."

"Daddy is *mean*." She stomped her foot and glowered. I had never seen her give my father a cross word. Never in her life. But now she looked like she wanted to kick someone.

I pressed my lips together for a minute. "Mommy doesn't like it when people say things like that." I didn't tell her that what she said wasn't true. But nothing much got by Beatrice. She held my gaze for a moment, and then winked. She returned to the garden, showing me where the blueberries were, and where the chickens hid their eggs. She knelt down next to the tangle of ground-cherries and started peeling back the dry husks and flicked each berry into her mouth, one by one, rolling them around like marbles. She grinned with her mouth full.

Beatrice was clearly in no hurry to leave, so I sat down next to her. The yard was a riot of bright colors, set in a backdrop of vibrant green. Everything the old lady once grew in her garden had morphed into generations of feral offspring. The plants spread, multiplied, and comingled with everything else. A thicket of volunteer squash vines tangled in a mound in one corner, with yellow flowers and all manner of squash sizes and shapes and colors. The strangest cucumbers I had ever seen snaked up the side of the ruined chicken coop—they were round and bright yellow with dark green spots. And wild strawberries were everywhere. The side of the house was impassable with raspberry bramble.

Beatrice reached over and pulled at a wild thyme stem, running her fingernail along the stalk and letting the tiny leaves fall into her hand. The world smelled like compost and green. Two chickens, feeling bold, came near us, pecking at the ground while still marking our movements with a wary eye. A cat watched them from the squash thicket.

"I love this place," Beatrice said with a yawn. "We should come here every day."

"I used to come here every day," I told her. "When I was very little. There was a lady who lived here who used to give me presents."

This got Beatrice's attention. "What kind of presents?" she asked.

"Well," I said, using this as an opportunity to help her to her feet and lead her back home. "Little-old-lady presents. A cookie or some carrots or an egg. One time, she gave me a bag of sweet peas with flowers that you could eat. They tasted like pepper."

"I would like to try one." She looked around, checking for a blossom she could eat.

"Let's tell Mother to grow them. I don't know what they're called, though. Anyway, I used to love it here, but one day the old lady went away, and I haven't been back here since."

"Where did she go?" Beatrice asked.

It had been so long since I thought about it. The man's yell. The woman's scream. The scrabble and the struggle and the gasp and the *Oh!* And then the—

I shook my head. I couldn't even think about it. Every time

a dragon found its way into my mind's eye, I forced it to go blank.

"I don't know," I said. "She just disappeared. Or maybe she just moved."

We paused at the back gate. Beatrice turned and looked at the yard, her gaze keen and searching. "Maybe the dragon knows where she is."

The physical sensation that came over me at Beatrice's words is difficult for me to describe, even now. And it is even more difficult for me to explain. My skin—from my toes to the crown of my head—erupted in what felt like pinpricks—and my vision swam. I became suddenly aware of the sound of my heart beating. And my mind's eye started moving through images faster and faster, like a film projector gone out of control—I could barely make sense of what my mind was seeing. I reached out and held on to the gate for balance.

"What in the world are you talking about, you nut?" I said, trying to keep my voice even and low. "There's no more dragons. They all left and they aren't coming back. Everyone knows that. And no one misses them. It says so right in the pamphlets at school. And scientists write that. Real scientists who work for the actual government. So it has to be true."

Beatrice frowned. "Well, there's a dragon that lives here."

"Don't be crass," I said reflexively. "And anyway, what makes you say that?"

"Well," she shrugged her little girl shoulders. "Just look at it."

I did. A dilapidated house with gaps in the siding like missing teeth. A collapsed henhouse. A shed saved from collapse for the time being by leaning heavily on the trunk of an ancient maple tree.

"All I see is a mess," I said. "Let's go."

Beatrice didn't move. "Dragons love messes. And they love kitties. And chickens. And everyone getting along—they love that part most of all."

"Do they?" I said skeptically. "I think maybe you're just talking about yourself. My understanding is that dragons prefer murder and mayhem and burning down people's farms and villages and destroying families. I mean, that's what happens in stories, anyway. Come on, let's go back. Mother is going to worry."

This actually wasn't true. My mother was likely still asleep. She had been so tired lately, and I was at an age where I only knew how to be aggravated. I was too self-centered to know how to worry about my mother.

"Stories are stupid," Beatrice said. "The people who write stories about dragons have never met a dragon. Dragons like chore charts and sharing and book clubs. Everyone knows that."

"Well, that's news to me," I said as I ushered Beatrice out of the gate.

"It's true," Beatrice assured me. "And anyway, who do you think is taking care of everything? Keeping the chickens fat and the cats happy and scaring the hawks away."

"It looks like you thought of everything. Be sure to keep your ideas to yourself," I said. And Beatrice skipped over to our yard.

And then, not really knowing why, I paused and turned. And looked again at the old lady's yard. It smelled of herbs and weeds and wildflowers, of dirt and rotting wood and generations of cat urine. My eye fell on a gap in the wall—a section of the siding just under the kitchen window that had rotted off or fallen away in a storm. It looked as though the gap opened clear into the house, a window into the yawning darkness inside. A pair of eyes blinked in a gap in the siding, glowing in the dark. I tilted my head. The eyes blinked.

"Hey, kitty, kitty," I said.

The cat—I assumed it was a cat—snorted. It made the wall shake a little bit.

I took a step forward. "Good kitty. Come say hi." I took another step. The eyes blinked again. They were, I realized, much larger than a cat's would be. But they must have belonged to a cat. Weren't some cats simply much larger than usual? And didn't all of their eyes glow?

I took another step forward. I felt the ground beneath my feet rumble a bit. Like purring. Or an engine. Or something else. "Suit yourself," I said. And I turned and walked away, shutting the broken gate behind me.

19.

My mother learned that her cancer returned in March of my freshman year of high school. She didn't tell us at first. She might have never told us, intending instead to simply slip away one day with no warning, but one evening in the middle of April, as she spooned roasted potatoes and canned peas onto our plates, she suddenly collapsed onto the floor, blood leaking from her mouth and nose. My father, who was home that evening, leaped to his feet with a strangled cry and was at her side in an instant. He scooped her up in his arms, whispering and crooning and shushing, as though he was her mother and not her husband.

"Oh, my dear," he wept as he held her body close. I had never seen him speak to my mother this way. He gave a panicked groan as he lifted her up. "*Oh, no.* Oh, my darling. Why are you so light?" His voice was brittle and insubstantial, a thin husk of itself.

My mother's head lolled from side to side as she struggled to stay conscious. My father held her tight, then released her to examine her face, then held her tight again, little moans of anguish erupting reflexively from his chest.

"Why didn't you tell me it was back?" he murmured into her neck. His breath caught and he coughed. "Oh, god, why didn't you say?"

Did my father love my mother? To this day I can't say for sure. Most of the time, I don't believe he did. But in this moment, when I try to pin it in my memory, when I try to observe it for long enough so I can write it down, I think he . . . *yes.* I think, in that moment, as he held her, as he carried her, he loved her deeply.

I stood there, dumbly, watching him. Beatrice came close and took my hand. We followed them as far as the doorway, and stopped when we reached the threshold, unable to move.

My father placed my mother into the passenger seat with a sense of tenderness and care that I had never seen from him before, and never saw again. He smoothed her hair and ran his hand along her cheek and kissed her forehead before closing the door. He patted his pockets, his face suddenly stricken with alarm. He turned to me where I stood in the doorway, his eyes wide and wild and pleading.

"Keys!" he shouted at me.

I scrambled back, sprinted inside, found the keys, and ran them out. My father was already in the driver's seat, holding my mother's hand. His eyes were red. He held his lips together in a pained, tight line. His breath stuttered and caught with each inhale.

"Alexandra," he said. I didn't bother correcting him. "Mind your . . ." He swallowed and shook his head. "Mind the little one. I don't know how long this will take." My mother pressed her fingers to her lips, which had paled to the color of birches. She blew me a kiss, and just doing so seemed to exhaust her—as though each breath was a tremendous effort. My hands were numb and my face was numb and the world felt numb. She was so sick, I realized with a tremendous jolt. How long had she been sick? How had I not seen it before? Why had no one told me?

"When are you coming home?" I managed. I looked at my mother, and not my father.

"Lock the house and make a plan for breakfast," my father said. "It's quite possible that you will be on your own for a bit."

"Mama?" I said, my voice quaking. Or maybe the ground under my feet was quaking. Maybe the whole world shook. When I was a child, my mother disappeared. And the adults in my life didn't explain, they didn't soothe, they didn't provide context to allow me to understand my situation. I was a child, you see? I was supposed to be well mannered and obedient. My eyes on the ground. I didn't need to know anything. And they hoped I would forget. "Mama?" I said again. I reached into the car, past my father.

"I'll be fine," my mother said.

My father batted my hand away, started the car, and sped down the street.

I felt something creeping on my wrist. Looking down, I saw that the knot holding the leather cord around my wrist in place had unraveled. I stood there dumbly as it loosened, opened, and fell to the ground. I didn't pick it up. Instead I looked down the street for my parents' car, but it was gone.

Neither of my parents came home that night. Or the next. Five nights Beatrice and I were on our own.

The doctors said that there was little that could be done, aside from keeping her comfortable.

My mother stayed in the hospital until she passed away on June 5, 1961. Beatrice and I visited her every day after school, while our father was at work. We remained at her side, quietly doing our homework or reading our books or drawing, until the nurses chased us out at five, and then we walked home. I made dinner. I cleaned up. My father stayed at work later and later. Sometimes, he wouldn't even come home until morning, already showered and dressed for the day. He paid the local grocer to deliver the groceries and stock our shelves. He didn't make breakfast (I did that), and he didn't pack our lunches (I did that as well). Instead he patted us each on the head as though we were a couple of Labradors, and told us to be good girls and to say our prayers and obey our teachers. And then he turned and left, whistling on his way to work.

When I asked why my father never came to see her in the hospital, my mother told me that he came every single day during his lunch breaks. But I had never seen it. As far as I know, the only time he went to the hospital was when he stayed by her side for those first five nights. And then never again. Sometimes, all these years later, I do try to be charitable. Maybe he couldn't bear it. Maybe it hurt too much to watch her slip away. Maybe he wasn't raised to be a strong man. Maybe he loved her too much to lose her. Maybe all those things are true, and every other characterization I have for him that is . . . more obvious and less kind . . . perhaps those are true as well. And maybe this is the same with all of us—our best selves and our worst selves and our myriad iterations of mediocre selves are all extant simultaneously within a soul containing multitudes. In any case, I noticed the way the nurses pressed their lips into a thin line whenever they heard my mother speak of my father's supposed kindnesses. I loved my mother, but I knew better than to believe her.

For weeks, I lay next to her on the hospital bed, curled against what was left of her body—cold hands, cold feet, dark hollows where her cheeks had been. She was as light as ashes. She was blowing away. Beatrice lay between us for a while, but eventually, she pulled herself into a little ball on a chair and fell fast asleep. My sister was a tiny thing. All compact heat and potential energy and hidden possibilities, like an egg. My mother used to say the little girl could fit in her pocket. And every time she said so, it made her voice catch.

On the day she died, in those last moments, my mother asked me to read her Alfred, Lord Tennyson's poem about Tithonus. This was not unusual, as she had asked me to read it to her nearly every day during her hospitalization. I didn't know that this time would be different. I didn't know that this would be the last time. How could I know? My mother's hand drifted to my hand. Her eyes were two opaque clouds.

"Read it again," she said. Her voice was small and dry and light, like the husk of a cicada after it has long ago flown away.

She didn't have to say what to read. I already knew. A crumbling book of poems by Alfred, Lord Tennyson sat at the table next to her bed with a bookmark on the page. I opened it up. Beatrice snored in the chair next to mine, her cheeks flushed and her mouth slack. Even her snores were adorable. I cleared my throat.

"The woods decay, the woods decay and fall," I read.

"The vapors weep their burthen to the ground."

My mother opened her mouth in a sigh. I continued.

"Man comes and tills the field and lies beneath." My mother groaned a bit.

"And after many a summer dies the swan."

The poem went on. Tithonus, I felt, got a raw deal. The gods are selfish. And careless. It is a cruel thing indeed to force life onto someone who is ready to die, to rip them away from eternal rest and their supposed reward. And yet. If I could have waved a goddess's hand and made my mother live forever—even if it meant that she would shrivel and shrink, even if it meant she would reduce to the size of a cricket? If I could have held her close for as long as I lived? If I could have kept her with me, even now? Of course I know it wouldn't have been fair. But I would be lying if I said I wouldn't do it.

I watched my mother. She didn't move for a long time after I finished. I felt myself start to panic.

Breathe, I thought at her, as though my thoughts meant anything.

Breathe, Mama, please please breathe.

I watched her chest and put my hand in front of her mouth, looking for evidence of the movement of air. Suddenly, my mother took a deep, hacking gasp, and took my hand. Her fingers were ice-cold. She looked right at me, though I couldn't tell how much she could actually see. Her eyes were cloudy smudges.

"Hey, Mom," I said. My voice was impossibly small. A child's voice. "Do you want me to read the poem again?"

"Stop," my mother rasped. Her fingers lingered on the knotted cord around my wrist. She pinched the knot.

I didn't know what I was supposed to stop. "Do you need medicine?" I asked.

"Stop," she said again. She lifted her other hand a few inches off the bed and then let it drop onto her sheets, as though the effort was too much to bear. I picked it up myself and held both her hands between my palms. Her fingers curled around mine and held on as tight as she could, which wasn't much.

"Okay, Mother. I'll stop." I still didn't know what she meant. But just my saying so seemed to have an effect. She visibly relaxed and sighed a bit.

"I could have done it too, you know." Her eyes wandered. I was pretty sure she couldn't see me.

"You could have done what?" I asked. Her hands were so cold.

"I could have done it too. Any of us could have. I chose—" My mother took a deep breath, but she didn't say anything after that. I waited for another breath. I waited for her to continue. I waited for a long time. And then her fingers unclasped, and she released me, she released . . .

She breathed once more, and then never again.

My mother's hospital room had four beds, two of which were unfilled. One had an old woman who was, at that moment, fast asleep. Beatrice was asleep. My mother was dead. I was the only person awake. People walked back and forth in the hall, but I did not call out. I had no words to explain what had just occurred. I had no frame of reference to make sense of my situation. How can you tell of the death of your mother? I couldn't. It was unspeakable.

I went to the chair and scooped up Beatrice and held her on my lap for a long time, the dense heat of her small body radiating into my skin, warming up my bones. My mother was so still, and growing colder by the minute. I didn't call the nurse. I didn't call my father. Instead I thought about my aunt. I hadn't thought about her for a long time. But I imagined Marla bursting into the room, restarting my mother the way she used to restart old cars. I imagined my aunt punching the doctors who failed us. I imagined my aunt flying into the side of the building and bursting in through the window in a spangle of broken glass, her eyes flashing like rubies, her dragonish scales a brilliant contrast to the thin hospital light, her muscles rippling across her flexible frame. An astonishment of light and heat and violent intellect. I gasped at the thought of it.

But then I shook my head. She wasn't coming. Of course she wasn't. No one in their right mind thought the dragons would ever come back. Dragons never came back. It was one of those self-evident truths. Still. I found myself glancing toward the window all the same.

Beatrice didn't wake up. She just sighed and murmured in her sleep, the warmth of her body heating me through, like I was cradling Prometheus's fire in my arms, carrying it safely home from heaven until the wrath rained down.

~slle~

Exactly one month after my mother passed, my father woke Beatrice and me up early, and told us to get dressed. He brought us downstairs. It was very early. A woman sat on the couch. She wore a generously cut housecoat, which still barely covered her round, distended belly. She looked nothing like my mother. She was very tall, with blond hair, large breasts, and deep-fleshed thighs. Her lipstick was red, like Marla's. She leaned toward the arm of the couch, and rested her cheek on her fist. I remember the way her skin rippled and waved around each knuckle as it sank into the softness of her face. She was beautiful, the way that abundant food is beautiful. My father looked at her hungrily. My mother was fragile and cold, like the etching of frost on a winter window. This woman was nothing like my mother.

"Girls," my father said. "You remember Miss Olson." The woman gave half a smile.

Of course we didn't remember her. Miss Olson was my father's secretary, and perhaps we would have met her if we ever were allowed to visit my father at work. But we never did. We had heard her name, of course, in tight, angry whispers coming from my parents' bedroom.

"It's nice to see you, Alexandra," she said. "Your father

speaks so highly of you." She didn't say anything to Beatrice. I took my sister's hand. I waited for an explanation. None came.

My father tipped his hat, told Miss Olson that he'd be back soon (I should have noticed that he didn't say *we*), and took us to visit Mother's grave. We stayed there for a good long while, my father and I sitting on the bench, and Beatrice stalking through the grass and flower beds, trying to get the squirrels to eat a nut from her hand. Eventually, she gave up and knelt by my mother's headstone, laid a piece of paper over her name, and used an unwrapped crayon to cover the paper with color, allowing my mother's name to emerge in relief.

BERTHA GREEN the paper read. I found myself mouthing my mother's name, rolling it over my teeth and tongue. I had never said her name out loud before. Her name was only "Mother." What else had been taken away from her, I wondered, besides her name?

We didn't go home after that. My father brought Beatrice and me to a small apartment just three blocks down from Beatrice's elementary school and a short bike ride to my high school. He said nothing as he stopped the car. He said nothing as he motioned for us to go inside, and walk up the stairs. The apartment was on the third floor. There was a small Polish market on the building's ground floor, next to an accountant's office, one that dealt exclusively with Polish-speaking clients. I learned this later. I couldn't read either sign. Two men carried boxes in and out, in and out. Some of the boxes said "Girls" on the outside. Another said "Books." One said "Kitchen." One said "Papers." They put a bed in the tiny bedroom—it was little more than a closet. And shoved in a dresser. They brought up my desk.

I stared at my father. I didn't have any words. Where would I even start? Beatrice took my hand and waited, a sense of calm enthusiasm radiating from her body, as though this was simply a normal day.

"Where should we put the other one?" the men asked as they carried up a second bed.

My father looked around. "The corner there, I suppose."

They set the bed down, and soon it was covered in boxes, too.

There was a Sears box with the supplies for a set of ready-to-assemble table and chairs, with instructions. I had never built anything in my life. I looked closely at the box and realized that it had a label affixed to the side with our address. It had been mailed to our house. The date on the postmark was two months earlier. How long had my father been planning this?

Beatrice didn't speak. I didn't speak. My father offered no explanation. He provided no context. He let the facts speak for themselves.

There was a box that said "Beatrice."

There was a box that said "Linens."

There was a box that said "Winter."

There were two boxes of groceries.

There were four lamps and a stack of towels.

He paid the men, and they left. The sink dripped and the refrigerator whined and somewhere down the hall a man and woman shouted at each other. My father looked at his watch.

"Well," he said, patting his pockets and retrieving his keys. "Home sweet home, as they say. I hope you like it." He paused. "It wasn't cheap," he added.

It looked cheap, I thought.

"Where are your boxes, Daddy?" Beatrice asked. She looked up at him, her face betraying not a hint of anxiety. She had no reason to mistrust anyone. "Where will you be sleeping?"

I felt as though I had swallowed a stone.

My father cleared his throat. He met my eye at last. "Surely you understand," he said.

I didn't, and told him so. My ears began to ring.

"Well," my father said, taking a step backward, toward the door. "There's a baby on the way, after all. Considerations must be made. We all have to do our part, and so forth. And anyway,

Alexandra, you have proven yourself more than capable. I really don't understand what the problem is." Another step.

I had to catch my breath. My father seemed suddenly very far away, as though I was observing him through a telescope turned backward. The floor, the whole room, seemed to lean at an impossible angle, swaying back and forth. I felt my stomach lurch as though I was seasick. I closed my eyes and tried to steady myself. "This can't be your plan, Dad," I said, my voice strangely choked. I couldn't swallow. "I can't run a household. Or raise a child." *Obviously I can't,* I wanted to scream. "I mean. What about school?"

My father looked away from me. He looked at the ceiling with its rivets and cracks. He looked at his shoes. His gaze fell on the counters and cupboards in the kitchenette—they were grimy. His mouth curled with distaste. We stood, he and Beatrice and I, in the apartment. It was small, with narrow windows that looked down on the street. I remember the sound of a door whining open and closing with a terrific slam. I remember the sound of footsteps in the hall. I remember a thick, greasy smell coming in from another apartment. My thoughts began to race. Where would the money come from? How would we eat? Where would I *study*? Who would take care of us? *No one.* He wanted me to do this by myself. I had *no one.* I wanted to sit down, but there were no chairs.

"Your mother did it. Without anyone showing her how. Your . . . you know. Your mother's sister did too, after your grandparents passed, she finished raising your mother all by herself. It's not that big of a deal. Anyone can do it. It's just, you know. Nature." My father checked his watch again. The boxes remained unopened. He was not intending to help us put things away. "You have, as they say, instincts for this sort of thing."

"Mom was an *adult* when I was born." I stared at him. "She had gone to college and everything. Plus she had you. And my—" Even then, I couldn't bring myself to say *auntie Marla,* so accustomed was I to lying about it. I shook my head. "She was an adult, too. I can't do this by myself. Dad, *I'm fifteen.*"

"You're quite mature. Everyone says so." He checked his watch.

I leaned back, as though blown by a strong wind. "And what about school, Dad? I'm top of my class. I'm taking extra courses. I *love* school. I *love* learning. And one day I'll go to college and—"

My father's lips curled as though he had vinegar in his mouth. "No one needs a college degree to clean a toilet or get dinner on the table. And caring for a child who is in school most of the day can't be all that hard. I told your mother this all the time. She did all those domestic things, those family things, all by herself even with her cancer—as sick as she was, not that you ever considered that. So how hard could it be, really?" He cleared his throat. He looked at the window, toward the sky. In a brief, wild moment, I imagined it filled with dragons. Burning houses. Burning buildings. Swallowing men whole. I imagined the entire Mass Dragoning happening again, but bigger this time—every city, every town, every block, dark wings and sharp jaws and bright scales crowding the sky. I imagined myself unleashed, unhooked, unraveled, an explosion of heat and rage and frustration. My bones felt hot. My skin felt tight. The air in my lungs seemed to sizzle.

No, I told myself. I closed my eyes and tried to force the vision away. Tried to make myself forget. There is a freedom in forgetting, after all. It didn't matter what happened before. There were no more dragons. They weren't coming back. Everyone knew that. I tried to slow my breathing and quiet my mind. I covered my face with my hands, pressed my fingers to my skin, just for a moment, trying to right myself.

I turned back to my father and refused to look away, daring him to meet my eye. He took two steps backward, toward the door. He paused, leaned back on his heels. He took another step toward the door.

I shook my head in disbelief. "I can't do this alone, Dad," I said. I wasn't much of a crier, even when I was little. But I almost cried then. I clamped my molars together and set my face.

"You won't be alone. I'll be here every day to check on you and see how you're doing. And you'll have all the money you'll need to run a household."

"Do you promise?" My breath caught. Beatrice reached over and curled the edge of my shirt into her hand, pulling it into a fist. She hung on tight. She didn't say a thing.

"I promise." My father said. His voice was thin and vague as smoke. I was not reassured.

He shook my hand, as though we were business associates and not father and daughter. And he closed the door behind him.

My father was a liar. I was alone. He never once came by to check on us.

Only his last promise was true. My monthly allowance was generous and utterly reliable, automatically paid into an account in my name. He paid our rent in a large, lump sum once a year with a little something extra for the landlord's discretion. He set up separate funds in our names at his bank to pay our tuition and bills, and installed clerks to manage them so he didn't have to bother himself. And while he continued to call us most Sundays to exchange awkward hellos and to remind Beatrice and me to be good girls, I didn't lay eyes on my father for almost three years after that. The only time he ever came to the apartment was to leave the occasional package or bag of mail or box of supplies at the door while I was at school.

I nearly forgot the shape of his face.

But I knew exactly what his money looked like.

The Pinsley Mill of Herefordshire, England, was built in 1675 as a corn mill. It was retrofitted in 1744 as a state-of-the-art cotton mill, with one of the first industrial applications of John Wyatt's revolutionary roller spinning machines. Mr. Wyatt, known more for his attempts at poetry than his attempts at engineering, had designed his roller spinning machine to operate using eight donkeys, one ox, one falling river, and approximately 220 very young women and girls—some as young as twelve—to jigger the machinery, as they were able to climb into small spaces when the gears became stuck.

Mr. Wyatt boasted to his friends at the tavern that his secret to the production of the finest possible cloth available on the market was the purity and beauty of the girls in his factory. He insisted that they dress entirely in white, and wash their clothing in lime every Sunday, to remove the dirt of sin. They lived in close quarters in a windowless dormitory, half a league from the factory, where their matron read to them from the Bible each evening, so that they might know what happens to good girls when they forget themselves and fall from grace. At the age of eighteen, they were sent away, before their faces began to coarsen and their beauty to fade—but to where, no one knew. Or if they did, they did not say.

No one in town had ever seen the girls—Mr. Wyatt would never allow it. He arranged that they be brought to the factory in covered wagons from deepest Scotland and darkest Wales. It was whispered that there were even some godless Irish girls somewhere in the mix. Everyone wanted to catch a glimpse of the girls, but Mr. Wyatt turned gawkers away at the door, and set the constable on over-curious young men who tried to penetrate the dormitory. There were rumors, though, that a few people had seen the faces of girls peering from the ventilation shafts near the top of the building, their faces pale as cotton, and their mouths stained indigo from bringing their yarn-dyed fingers occasionally to their lips. "Princesses in the tower," the men at the tavern said, "making cloth fit for a king." Whether these were their own words or quotations from the florid odes that Mr. Wyatt composed in the girls' honor—often while drunk—is still unknown. In any case, the point became moot after the fires.

The first fire occurred in 1754. It destroyed only a portion of the building, and the matron had been able to herd most of the girls out of harm's way. The fire had caused a small collapse in the north wall, and a singeing of the plaster, and the smashing of a few outbuildings (though no one could figure out why, given that fires rarely smash things), and some damage to one of the machines—specifically one of Mr. Wyatt's famous roller spinners. The constable, in his report, wrote, "The illuſtrius machine built by Mr Wyatt, by hand and mind, lay buckled in the middle, as though a Gorgon or a Troll did wander by and miſtook it for a pleaſant ſeat. A shame it was, that ſo noble a creation might be laid low, reduced to nothing but crumpled rubble." Mr. Wyatt, nearly—but not entirely—financially ruined, took to the tavern, screaming of dragons. After several calming drafts of strong spirits, he composed, for all assembled, an epic poem about a crafty businessman who stood firm against the monstrousness of Nature, with the swords of Industry and Modernity aiding in his eventual triumph. Many men in the tavern wept at its conclusion.

That night, the constable took several corroborating statements from the neighbors who lived within earshot of the dormitory, reporting the sounds of whipping and the wailing of girls. But no one could come to their assistance as the doors were, as usual, locked.

Over the next two years, several other fires damaged either the building or the machines, and each one precipitated another drunken ode—for the benefit of the patrons or to put off creditors, no one could say. The final twin fires happened in the middle of the night. According to county records, a monstrous blaze consumed the girls' dormitory, and then later that night, a second fire whipped through the mill. Both buildings were utterly destroyed. The girls, every last one of them, were lost. The matron managed to survive, but at a great loss to her dignity—she was seen, as the brigade raced to the scene with buckets, tearing across the town in the nude. It had been assumed, of course, that her clothing had burned away in the fire, but her skin was curiously unburned. In any case, she spent the rest of her days in the lunatic asylum, as she could not stop raving about dragons. Mr. Wyatt, too, in his bankruptcy hearings, also claimed injury by dragons. But given his preferred career as a poet, this was largely disregarded as a mere metaphor.

From his prison cell, Mr. Wyatt wrote another epic poem about a brave engineer who singlehandedly attempted to quell the beastly nature lurking inside girls and mold them into what Christendom requires—that they be chaste, industrious, obedient, and good. And despite his tireless efforts, monstrous Nature prevailed. His poem acquired few readers and delighted no critics. After all, one newspaper quipped, "the ravings of a debtor are as empty as his purse, and, with neither purchase nor relevance, are easily forgotten." Mr. Wyatt died in prison. He was buried under a simple wooden cross, but this was burned to ashes by an unknown assailant, several months later.

—"A Brief History of Dragons" by Professor H. N. Gantz, MD, PhD

20.

How do I explain the next two years? Honestly, it's hard to remember all of it. Or even most of it. When I try, all I can see is a whirlwind of laundry and textbooks and dishes and lists and letters and breathless worry. I took care of Beatrice. I read her stories at night. I washed her clothes and drew her baths and ironed her sheets and brushed her hair. I took her temperature and gave her medicine and worried over her when she was sick. I kept her in school. I made her flash cards and checked her homework and taught her how to study for spelling tests. I learned to cook and kept her fed. I kept her safe. She was my first and last thought, and most of my thoughts in between, every single day.

Beatrice was my whole world.

I made sure that she arrived at school each day, clean and braided and with her clothes mended and pressed and unstained, her shoes wiped and buffed, and absolutely on time. My father made it clear that I wasn't to draw attention to our unusual living situation. He didn't want anyone asking questions or snooping around. I put up curtains and never played the radio too loud. I trained Beatrice to keep her voice low and not disturb the neighbors. I studied constantly, often staying up well past midnight after Beatrice was asleep. I crammed for exams while cleaning clothes at the laundromat. I took extra classes via correspondence through the university, thanks to an extension program at the library, which allowed me to amass college credits while I was still in high school.

Because I didn't care what my father said. I *was* going to college, no matter what. And beyond that too. The more I dove into mathematics and chemistry and physics, the more I became *more than myself.* The more the world became more than itself. For me, at this time, learning felt like food—and I was starving for it.

The head librarian and my mother's former friend, Mrs. Gyzinska, had taken a special interest in me, and had convinced me to sign up for the university correspondence program, and to stick with it, which gave me the opportunity to study advanced mathematics and history and physics on my own at the library, with professors at the university guiding my progress through the mail. She told me often that she had high hopes for my future, which gave *me* high hopes for my future, in spite of myself. She showed me pictures of universities around the world, and handed me literature on scholarships and special programs. Mrs. Gyzinska proctored my tests and provided me with recorded lectures on 35mm film in the audiovisual room and made sure I had all the materials I needed for each class on hand in the reference section.

My father made an arrangement with the local grocer to leave a box of food and sundries in the lobby of our building every Saturday morning before breakfast. He told the grocer it was part of a philanthropic effort on his part, because we were a "charity case." He knew if I went to the market too often by myself, people would start to wonder at it, and ask questions, and sometimes those questions would be directed at *him,* and that would make him uncomfortable. I didn't mind. It was one thing taken off my endless list of tasks, which meant I had an extra hour each week to study.

It's remarkable how quickly a person can get used to an impossible situation. How terror and panic can start to feel familiar, even ordinary. My father called each Sunday at nine o'clock. He told me not to go running after boys because no one can love a fast girl. I wasn't remotely interested in boys, so this wasn't a problem. He told me to make sure I took the classes on shorthand and dictation so I could be gainfully employed after high school. He told me to make sure I was still a good girl so he could stay proud of me. He said nothing besides a brief hello to Beatrice. Beatrice didn't seem to mind. There were other children in our building, and epic games of Kick-the-Can in the alley, and in the end, talking to a grown-up you can barely remember gets boring after a while. She tore down the hallway at a run.

She ran wild, my Beatrice. I didn't see the point of trying to contain her. She ran faster, climbed higher, and yelled louder than anyone else in the neighborhood. She was also helpful, hardworking, and kind, and always had excellent report cards. I assumed I had nothing to worry about.

Which is why I was surprised that two weeks before the start of my senior year of high school, I found myself, once again, summoned to the principal's office, this time for Beatrice's apparent wrongdoing. I had no idea what Beatrice had done, but given that we were called in before school had even started, I knew it was going to be big.

"Maybe you should just tell me what you did before we head over," I said, reading through Mr. Alphonse's letter for the fifth time. "Just so we can start coordinating our stories now."

Beatrice shook her head and held up her empty hands. "Alex, I have no idea. Really I don't." I wasn't sure that was true. She gulped her milk and made a face as a bit dribbled down her chin, which meant it had turned again. I dumped her glass and made a mental note to pick up milk from the market on the way back. I wondered if the grocer was giving us expired food on purpose and pocketing the difference. I also wondered if he did so at my father's request because he wanted to spend less money on our upkeep. Both seemed plausible.

I sat down next to her at the kitchen table and pressed my forehead against the heels of my hands, trying to stave off a growing headache. I sighed. "How can you possibly have no idea, Beatrice. Surely you have some guesses." I was annoyed. I had too much to do. I still hadn't finished my summer homework (every June, my teachers assigned more and more, making us wonder why they even bothered having a summer in the first place), and my correspondence courses had already begun. I had essays to write for my university applications, a prospect that made me so anxious I wanted to lie down. What would happen to us next year? How would I manage with Beatrice? I had no idea. The only thing I wanted in the whole world was to keep learning, to swallow the entire universe with my brain. The very thought that I might not continue with school made me feel as though I was breaking in half.

"I don't, Alex, I swear I don't. I think he just doesn't like me." The sound of the Sasu boys howling outside—there were six of them in that family. They lived in the apartment across the alley, and they all did whatever Beatrice asked them to do. She loved bossing them around. She looked at me desperately, a mouthed *Please*.

I shook my head.

"Do I have to go?" she asked, her hands buried in the mess of her hair. "Maybe you could just go and tell me what I have to apologize for and I can write a letter."

"If I have to go, you *definitely* have to go. I'm not seeing that man by myself." Beatrice pouted, but I could tell it was just for show.

I told her to wear her sailor dress that Mother made—one that was made and styled for me when I was considerably younger than her but still fit her fine. I figured the meeting would go much more smoothly if Beatrice looked childlike and absolutely adorable. It was a cheap trick, but I didn't mind using it.

It wasn't the first time I'd had to return to my old elementary school. As Beatrice's unofficial guardian, I had to cross the threshold to that building more often than I wished to—for Christmas concerts or spelling bees or when Beatrice played a sheep in the school play. Each time I did so, I made sure to look as presentable as I could. No visible stains, an ironed blouse, a little butter rubbed onto my shoes to shine them up a bit. I wore cardigan sweaters that I had carefully and meticulously de-pilled the night before. My face, as always, was scrubbed clean until it glowed, and my hair, which I now wore short in the back and curling behind my ears, was secured with a headband. This made me look younger than I was, which was not helped by the fact that I, like my mother, was short of stature and narrow in frame. I would never be pretty like her, but she and I were shaped nearly the same. Small shoulders. Spindly wrists. The leather cord that my mother tied and knotted for me years ago had stretched considerably and barely stayed on my hand. It was annoying, but I kept it on as a remembrance. I wished I could have been tall and broad, like my aunt. I wished I could take up space, hoist the world up on my shoulders or look down on it, depending on the needs of the situation. My aunt, better than anyone else I had ever known, knew how to occupy a room.

(Silly me, I had to tell myself again and again. Of course I had no aunt. She never existed. Beatrice was my sister. She was only ever my sister. I clung to this like a life preserver in stormy waters. My mother's lie was the only thing keeping me above the waves.)

My old teachers smiled when they saw me. Or some of them did. They asked me where my father was, but they weren't curious enough to press too hard. When I was little, it was my mother who interacted with the school, never my father. And now, for Beatrice, it was me.

"I was sure he would come for this," a teacher would comment. "It *is* the Christmas play!" Or conferences. Or the choir concert. Or the end-of-year Mass.

"A business trip," I told them.

"My father works too hard, bless him. I do my best to take up the slack."

"He would never say, of course, but it does upset him so, without my mother here."

"A touch of the flu. You know how it goes. But I'm always happy to help out."

"Well," the teachers would remark. "You are a kind sister. I daresay a girl your age would rather be out with her friends. Or perhaps a night out with one of your admirers. Which boy are you going steady with these days? Or is it too difficult to choose just one?"

This I responded to with a vague smile as I moved away to find my seat. They meant this kindly, I'm sure. But honestly, I had no friends. And I certainly didn't have any boyfriends. Who has that kind of time? I had my studies to think of. And my future to consider. And I had Beatrice to take care of. I made her meals and kept her clean and made sure she did her homework and took her to the library each Saturday. I cared for her when she was sick. Beatrice was my whole universe. Our lives were just the two of us. Me and Beatrice, conquerors of the world.

But this trip would include no such positive interactions. This trip was disciplinary. I had been summoned to the school by letter—or, to be perfectly factual, my *father* had been summoned.

"Dear Mr. Green," the letter said. "I have made several attempts to reach you but neither your wife nor your secretary have seen fit to pass the message on. I require a meeting about your daughter, Beatrice, regarding her behavior in class. I insist that this meeting take place before the start of school. If not, I will have to suspend her attendance at Saint Agnes until such meeting occurs. Please contact the school secretary and make the necessary arrangements."

Since all our mail for school went to my father's house (no one knew about our strange arrangement with the apartment, of course), I didn't see the letter from the principal right away. Instead, my father slipped it into our mail slot at the apartment, already opened, with his careless scrawl across the front of the envelope.

"I expect you to take care of this," it said.

I called right away, and we were scheduled for the Wednesday before school began.

"But your father will be in attendance as well?" the secretary asked. "It is imperative that Mr. Alphonse speak to him."

"Of course," I lied. "He wouldn't miss it for anything."

Wisconsin is merciless at the end of August. The days swelter and the nights simmer. Not even the wind gave us any relief. Beatrice and I walked slowly toward Saint Agnes, pausing in every available patch of shade. The air was thick and hot and damp. Our bodies tried to sweat but it didn't do much good—nothing evaporates in a steam bath. The school's brick walls shimmered in the heat.

"Come on," I said.

I walked up the stairs to the school with as much purpose and determination as possible. Beatrice skipped, unbothered by the heat, and when that got boring, she attempted to ascend the steps by hopping on one foot. She missed a step, which sent her sprawling, squealing with laughter.

"Will you please focus?" I hissed. "This is *serious*."

Beatrice tilted her head. "How can it be?" she asked. "I thought you said it was stupid."

"I probably shouldn't have said that out loud." I sighed and sat down next to her. "Are you sure you don't know what this is about? This behavior that's got everyone so worked up. Letters and urgent voices and all."

Beatrice shrugged. She looked genuinely baffled. "I really don't, Alex," she said. "I thought I was a good student. I mean, I mostly am. I get in trouble sometimes, but so does everyone else. Maybe everyone has to go to the principal's office."

I patted her on the back and gave her a kiss on the top of her head.

"Don't worry, Bea. I'm sure it's nothing. Come on." I offered her my hand, and we pushed through the door.

The building smelled like floor cleaner and oil soap and mothballs and summer dust and sweaty adults. I sneezed. Our footsteps echoed on the tile floors. Teachers were in their rooms, airing out their spaces, setting up, or pushing carts between the supply room and the library and back down the hall. I held on to Beatrice's hand very tightly as we walked down the long corridor to the main office. The secretary—an ancient woman named Mrs. Magin—squinted at me over the rim of her glasses.

"Oh," she said, clearly not impressed. "It's you." She looked at Beatrice and looked back at me. "Where is your father?"

I already knew what to say. "He's in a meeting," I said smoothly. "He told me to take excellent notes and report back. He said he'll race over if his meeting ends early, and I'm hopeful that will happen. My stepmother would have come, but the baby is sick." In my various excuses, the baby was often sick. This baby who, I guess, was my brother, and who I had never met. This baby who had an older sibling, who I also had never met.

Mrs. Magin narrowed her eyes. "The letter was very specific." She gave Beatrice a hard look. "That one . . ." She turned her gaze on me. "Some behavior is intolerable. And inappropriate. Her father needs to intervene."

"And he will," I said. "He always does. But as you know, my father never intended to become a widower, just as Beatrice and I never chose to become motherless girls. But we do our best to step up to life's adversities with determination and grace, as we have learned through our fine educations at this wonderful school."

It was my go-to line, and a little overused at that point, I admit, but it certainly got the job done. People seemed to enjoy telling me how *very brave* I was. I gave her what I hoped would be a winning and noble smile.

The secretary pursed her lips together tightly, her lipstick accentuating the ridges and creases, like a bright pink accordion. She tapped her nails on the desk. She saw right through me.

"Well," she said with withering sweetness. "Everyone does love a brave orphan. Why don't you have a seat." With a pink-nailed hand she indicated the hard bench off to the side, and then she returned to her magazine.

We sat, and Beatrice fidgeted. I had attempted to tame her wild curls by harnessing them in the bounds of French braids, but already much of her hair had escaped, and erupted around her head like a fiery halo. I reached into my bag and pulled out her drawing notebook and a pencil, just to keep her occupied.

Mr. Alphonse was late. That was unusual. He was obsessively punctual and expected the little children in his school to be the same. I tried to relax, but my eyes drifted to the clock and marked the time.

Beatrice fiddled with the embroidery along the bottom of the dress. It was dragonflies, originally stitched in gold and iridescent red and pink and green, because I loved dragonflies when I was little and my mother wanted to make me happy. As with every other dress she made for me, as soon as I outgrew it, she carefully washed, ironed, and wrapped the garment in tissue with dried rosemary sprigs and laid it in a box along with the other clothing I had worn that year—all handmade, all with special knots in the pocket, all with a little piece of embroidery in a corner, or on the sleeves, or covering the whole thing, because my mother loved beauty and wanted it to appear everywhere. Now my clothing came from secondhand shops (I was not yet able to bring myself to wear any of my mother's old clothes), and there was little that was beautiful on any of it. I always had Beatrice wear what my mother had made for me, all from boxes from our old basement, with my mother's careful handwriting on the outside: "Alexandra, Age 7." "Alexandra, Age 8." My father mailed each box on Beatrice's corresponding birthday, with a card that simply said, "Many happy returns." It didn't even say Beatrice's name. He gave her no other gifts.

Beatrice fiddled at the embroidery with one hand and drew with the other as we waited for Mr. Alphonse to meet us. Sister Saint Stephen the Martyr had passed away the year before, and her replacement as head teacher, Sister Therese, had been Beatrice's kindergarten teacher. Everyone loved Sister Therese, which made me suspect that her appointment to the head teacher position had not been Mr. Alphonse's idea. Nuns, after all, sometimes do as they please.

"Stop fidgeting," I said to Beatrice.

Finally, I could hear Mr. Alphonse and Sister Therese making their way down the hall. Their footsteps were quick and clipped and they were speaking to each other in low, terse tones.

"Surely, it won't be hard to find a replacement. There are plenty of you," I heard Mr. Alphonse say.

"Nuns don't grow on trees, *Leonard,*" Sister Therese shot back. *"Honestly."*

Nuns are not required to use proper salutations when addressing laymen. I had witnessed this before. And I did like the sound of it. I heard her footsteps—small feet in sensible shoes—squeaking away.

Mr. Alphonse strode in and went directly to Mrs. Magin and rested his hands on her desk, leaning low.

"There's been another . . . incident," he said.

Mrs. Magin said nothing and instead gave a pointed look in my direction as though to discreetly indicate that children were present, but Mr. Alphonse did not pick up on her hinting.

"Teacher's lounge. She's still there—or was when I left—and we lost one window, but nothing else so far. Call the fire department. Nothing's burning, but they will want to be notified."

"Beatrice Green is here with her sister," Mrs. Magin said in a rush before he could continue.

Mr. Alphonse remained perfectly still for a moment before whipping around to look at us. His face was still quite red, but he knew how to let people know he was in charge. He took a step closer and loomed aggressively.

"Where's your father," he said, without a question mark.

"At work," I said. "He's so busy these days, and just couldn't be pulled away. Don't worry, though. I have my steno pad, and I take excellent dictation." At school, all the girls were required to take secretarial training as well as home economics classes. And it was true—I was extremely good at taking accurate and fast notes relaying exactly what was said. It's a skill, I must admit, that I have found useful throughout my life, even though I complained about those classes at the time.

"My letter was very clear—"

I nodded sympathetically. "It *was*," I agreed. "You're *so right*. And *of course* my father *should* be here. He'd say so himself. If he was here. But, unfortunately, I'm afraid it simply wasn't possible for him to come today. There is no one more disappointed than he is. Shall we begin?" I pulled out my pen and paper to show how ready I was.

"Hi, Mr. Alphonse!" Beatrice said brightly. She sat at cheerful attention on the edge of her seat, her hands folded calmly in her lap. Beatrice was never one to feel cowed in the presence of adults. Even when she was in trouble. Especially when she was in trouble. "Is Sister Therese coming?"

Mrs. Magin sat with her fingers hovering over the phone. She looked anxiously at the principal. "Should I call now, sir?" she said, giving yet another pointed look in our direction.

"Of course, of course," Mr. Alphonse grunted. "Tell Sister Therese that we will be starting without her. This way."

And he ushered us into his office, pushing the door shut with his heel.

There are different sorts of men in this world, I've learned since that meeting. Mr. Alphonse, for example, was the sort who would intentionally put short-legged chairs in front of his desk for visitors, while he cranked his own desk chair as high as it would go. I believe he felt that this made him look magisterial. I felt—and still do—it made him look ridiculous. And, even worse, it made him look like a bully. I helped Beatrice into her chair, and as I did so, made sure to inch her chair backward and mine forward—just slightly, and at an angle. I sat primly at the front edge of my chair, my back straight and my chin inclined, using my body to absorb Mr. Alphonse's perpetual glare and deflect it away from Beatrice. My anger at the situation, I noticed, was strangely calming. I took a deep and slow breath through my nose as I smiled sweetly, as I sharpened my tongue.

Mr. Alphonse sat silently for a moment, steepling his fingers under his chin. He waited for me to speak. I didn't want to give him the satisfaction. I was my mother's daughter, after all. I knew how to wait. Finally:

"Did Beatrice admit to you what this meeting is about? Did she say what it is that she has done?" A fire engine's siren howled in the distance and grew closer. Mr. Alphonse's eye began to twitch.

"I don't think she knows what this meeting is about," I said.

"That's impossible," Mr. Alphonse said. The ligaments in his neck bulged slightly. "I was very clear with her on the last day of school. She knows, but she is not saying, which frankly is typical. I have been trying to arrange this meeting *all summer*. Where, again, is your father?"

I laid my hands on my knee, one on top of the other. I blinked my eyes slowly, with deliberation, the way my mother used to do. I turned to my sister. "Do you know what this is about?" I asked Beatrice.

"Nope!" Beatrice said cheerfully.

"Well, then. I think we can rule out any maliciousness, if Beatrice has no recollection of what this is even about. What a relief!" I tapped my pen on my notebook a few times, to show how very settled the matter was.

Another siren joined the first. And a third. Mrs. Magin, in the other room, gasped loudly, and there was an abrupt clatter, like a chair being knocked to the ground. "Sister Claire. *Sister Claire! Not today! Breathe deeply and calm yourself, please.*" We heard running footsteps and the sharp slam of a door.

I looked at Mr. Alphonse and raised my eyebrows.

"It isn't any of your concern," he said, his jaw muscles clenching noticeably. He took another deep breath, as though straining to maintain his composure. Finally, he reached into his desk and pulled out a file. It was thick and overstuffed with slightly crinkled papers. He let it fall onto the desk with a slap.

"Do you know what this is?" he demanded. One of the sirens came to a stop nearby. I could hear the sound of men shouting.

"No idea," I said.

"Your sister has been making *inappropriate images* during the school day. These *inappropriate images* have been made on school-owned paper, and using school-owned materials. She has upset her teachers, upset the other students, and worst of all, she has both demeaned and depraved herself by allowing the brain to linger in places where it clearly should not." He glowered down at us. I looked at Beatrice, my eyebrows raised. Beatrice raised her own in return—in confusion, though, and not with any insubordination. Beatrice, for all of her out-of-boundsness, didn't have a sassy bone in her body.

I turned back to Mr. Alphonse. "Maybe it would help if you said exactly what she's been drawing. I confess we are both a little bit at a loss." I expected him to open the file. He did not.

Mr. Alphonse folded his arms. "Well," he said primly. "I'm not sure I want to say. In mixed company." His cheeks flushed pink.

Interesting, I thought. "Was it . . . bad words?" I prompted.

"I don't write bad words," Beatrice protested. "I don't even know how to spell most of them."

Something crashed in the hallway. Two carts colliding, I thought. Several voices spoke rapidly, all twisting on top of one another. I could hear a woman's voice speaking indistinctly, but in a tone that sounded something like pleading. Mr. Alphonse's cheeks began to color again.

"Look," I said. "It sounds like there is something that you need to take care of. Perhaps you should step out for a moment. It might be a good idea if Beatrice and I have a private chat. That way we can go through the problematic content on our own."

Mr. Alphonse nodded and strode across the room, leaving

without another word. I looked at Beatrice, who shrugged. I shrugged in response. From outside the room and down the hall, Mr. Alphonse's voice boomed—at what, I had no idea. I lifted the file onto my lap. And I opened it.

There are moments, I think, in a person's life, when everything changes. Relationships. Futures. Communities. Maybe even the whole world.

Time, in our experience, is linear, but in truth time is also looped. It is like a piece of yarn, in which each section of the strand twists and winds around every other—a complicated and complex knot, in which one part cannot be viewed out of context from the others. Everything touches everything else. Everything affects everything else. Each loop, each bend, each twist interacts with every other. It is all connected, and it is all one.

But every once in a while, there are experiences that slice all other moments apart—stark, singular things that mark the difference between Before and After. These moments are singular, separate from the knot. Separate even from the thread. They can't be tugged at or loosened. They cannot be wound into something lovely or intricate or decorative. They do not interact seamlessly with the fabric of a life. They are of another substance entirely. Unstuck in time, and out of sync with a life's patterns and processes. I've had many such experiences. The moment I first saw the dragon in the old lady's garden, for example. The moment my mother's knots unmade themselves. The moment when Beatrice became my sister. The moment my father took Sonja away. The moment my mother released that one, last breath, and then went terribly still.

And then there was that meeting in Mr. Alphonse's office.

Prior to this moment, it had always been me and Beatrice, together in the world. We were one mind, one purpose, one heart. It was the two of us, together, in all things. Beatrice was my sister. Beatrice is my sister. Beatrice would always be my sister.

But in this moment . . .

she was something . . .

else.

I began flipping through the file. The first page was a picture of a house. The house was divided into four rooms. A kitchen on the main floor, and what appeared to be a living room. And upstairs was a room with a man and a woman standing next to each other, staring in opposite directions, and a room with a smaller person and an even smaller-than-that person sitting on the floor between a bed and a baby's crib on either side of them. And on top of the roof was a dragon.

"Oh yeah," Beatrice said. She wasn't embarrassed. She looked at the picture of the dragon as though it was a picture of any old thing—a shoe, maybe. Or a tree. The dragon was large and red. Its eyes seemed to shine a bit. She drew it with precision and care. She spent *time* working on that dragon.

My skin felt hot. Even though I thought that the general aversion to dragons was stupid. It was just a thing that happened. There was no reason to get embarrassed about it. Still. I didn't like looking at it. I didn't like the attention that Beatrice had given it. It was too *embarrassing.* Too *female.* I felt ashamed in ways that I couldn't explain. It was as though she had drawn pictures of naked breasts. Or soiled sanitary napkins. "I drew that," she said cheerfully.

"I figured," I said. My voice rasped, and my mouth was dry. I closed my eyes for a second, to shut the image away.

"And Ralphie made a rude noise and Inez started to cry and Sister Claire made me stand in the corner."

I took this in. "I see," I said.

I turned the page. There was a picture of a dragon riding on top of a school bus.

I turned the page. There was a picture of a dragon at a picnic in the forest.

I turned the page. There was a picture of a dragon on a stage wearing a tutu.

I turned the page. There was a picture of a dragon in a cage at the zoo.

"Do you want to see my favorite one?" Beatrice said. I was mystified. How could she have no discomfort? It was all I could do to keep myself from running out of the room.

"No, thank you," I said, my voice barely above a whisper.

Beatrice frowned. She put her hand on my cheek and crinkled her eyebrows in concern. "Alex?" she said. "I don't want you to be mad at me."

I tilted my head back, examining the ceiling, trying to clear my head. "Do you know why these pictures were taken away from you?"

She raised her hands to her shoulders, palms up and tilted forward. "My teacher says they're not appropriate," she said matter-of-factly. I watched as she started to force her face into a façade of meekness. She looked at the ground and folded her hands, though I noticed her eyes occasionally flicking upward as though checking my response. I guessed that this was exactly how she behaved at school. No wonder she was in trouble.

"Do you know what that means?" I clarified. "Do you know what *not appropriate* means?"

"No?" she said with a hopeful smile.

"Oh, *really*," I said drily.

She slumped in her chair and folded her arms. She did too know what *not appropriate* meant. Beatrice was smart. So why was she being intentionally obtuse?

I turned the page. A dragon fixing a car.

A dragon on the beach.

A dragon holding hands with a line of children, heading down the road.

A dragon sleeping in a regular bed.

A dragon eating soup.

"Did Sister Claire punish you every time?"

"Most times," she said. "She'd make me go in the corner, or she would make me write lines, or she would say she was going to call Daddy."

"*Did* she call Dad?"

"I dunno." Beatrice turned her head toward the wall, as though there was a window. Instead, Mr. Alphonse had an anti-Communist poster showing men engaging in fisticuffs with Soviet officers as flames rose up behind them, with the words BETTER DEAD THAN RED emblazoned above. Mr. Alphonse saw most things as possible Communist threats. Perhaps even Beatrice's drawings.

And I was about to comfort her. And I was about to kneel down in front of her and take her hands and tell her that everything was going to be just fine. And I was about to lean over conspiratorially and make fun of Mr. Alphonse and laugh and laugh.

Instead I turned the page.

And instead of a picture, it was a page full of text. The next ten pages were simply full of text. Different styles of handwriting and lettering. Different colors. Different sizes. The same words.

ı am a dragon. *I AM A DRAGON.*
I am a dragon.

I ᴁm a Dragon. *I am a dragon.*
I AM A DRAGON.

A Dragon. **A Dragon.** ***A DRAGON.***

My head swam. My face grew hot. I felt pinpricks on my skin and a line of sweat going down my spine. Even the room started to contract a bit. I sank to the ground, feeling profoundly dizzy. I braced myself, holding on to the seat of my chair with one hand and Mr. Alphonse's desk with the other. I tried to breathe, but it was difficult.

"Alex?" she said, her voice very small. "Alex, what's wrong?"

Now, of course, I know that what I was experiencing was a panic attack. I had no such language then, no such context. All I knew was that my heart pounded and the room constricted around us and my breathing became labored and strange. The papers on my lap felt unreasonably heavy, and my chest felt as though it had been transformed into lead. All I knew was that the words on that page—and worse, the *wish* inside those words—was *dangerous.* I swallowed hard and tried my best to keep from throwing up. I turned the stack of paper over and slammed onto the desk with my fist.

Beatrice jumped. And then she held herself terribly still. She had never been afraid of me. Never before this moment. But now she was. I could see that fear, harsh and livid, pressed into her face. I couldn't take this moment away. Another Before and After.

I remembered my aunt looping her arm around my mother's waist when she first came home from the hospital, gently guiding her to her room. I remembered my aunt fussing over her, and feeding her. Rubbing her skin. Caring for her every moment. And yet. She couldn't be bothered to stay. She left her body and left her life and *left.* And then my mother was alone. And then my mother died. And now we were alone.

There was a reason why my mother didn't want to hear any mention of dragons.

You, a small, shaking voice said, deep in the center of my being as the memory loomed large in my mind. *You left us. You abandoned us.* I didn't know toward whom this was directed. My mother. My father. My auntie Marla. All of them, maybe. A rage I did not know I was capable of burned inside me. I could feel my skin start to bubble with it.

The air in the room electrified.

"Alex?" Beatrice said timidly. I shoved the folder and the papers into my bag. I turned wildly toward my sister. I didn't know the feeling I had right then. But it was hot and sharp and *mean.*

"*Inappropriate,*" I hissed.

Don't leave me, said a voice deep inside me. I ignored it. I didn't think about it. I pretended it wasn't there.

"But—"

"Inappropriate." My voice had edges and weight.

Please don't leave me. You can't leave me. We only have each other.

"But Alex."

"It isn't true, what you wrote." I stood. I paced the room. I felt like I could barely fit inside my own body. I didn't know exactly what was bothering me. Only that I was *bothered*.

"I know, but—"

"It will never, *ever* be true." My voice was hard and sharp and fast. It hit her like a slap. "It *cannot* ever be true."

Beatrice started to cry. "Alex, I didn't mean—"

I grabbed Beatrice by the hand, and we walked out of the room. I wanted to punish her. I wanted to contain her. I wanted to rewind time, to never have to feel this way again. I slammed the door with a terrific crack and Mrs. Magin nearly jumped. I gave her a cold stare.

"He's not back yet," she stammered, but I held up my hand.

"Please tell Mr. Alphonse that I have seen enough, and that I quite agree. This behavior will not continue. Let him know that I am putting a stop to it." I gave Beatrice a piercing look. *"Instantly."* Beatrice began to sob. I ignored her. "This will never happen again."

"But, I don't think you should be—"

"I won't stay in this building for another moment." I strode toward the door and burst into the hall, dragging Beatrice behind.

"Be careful!" Mrs. Magin shouted, but I only half heard her. There were people in the hall talking quickly, and a semicircle of firemen blocking the door to the teachers' lounge. I barely saw any of them. I marched Beatrice to the front door, and we pushed out of the gloom of the elementary school. Into the light.

21.

I felt bad, obviously. I never behaved more like my mother than I did in that moment. It almost felt like it was her voice coming out of my mouth.

After spending over an hour in opposite ends of our small apartment, pouting in silence, Beatrice and I slowly found our way to the middle. My anger had given way to sorrow and exhaustion. I sat on the floor and took her hand.

"I'm sorry," I said to her.

"I'm sorry," she replied.

I didn't say exactly what I was sorry for, and neither did she. I didn't have the language to understand my own feelings. Beatrice laid her head on my lap. My leg was instantly wet from her tears. "Please can we be friends again, Alex," she said. "I won't do anything wrong again. I promise."

I had already thrown her drawings into the trash, but each image remained pinned in my memory. I couldn't look away. *It can never be,* I said to myself, over and over and over again, my discomfort deep and visceral and persistent. I couldn't understand it any better than Beatrice could.

I gently sat Beatrice up and held her gaze as I took her hands in my own and gave them a little squeeze. I kissed her knuckles, one at a time.

"All we have is each other," I said.

"All we have is each other," she responded. It was our mantra. The only thing that was true.

"It's Beatrice and Alex, rulers of the world." She grinned and hugged me, and for a moment, everything was okay. Or okay enough.

To make it up to her, I packed a picnic dinner and we went to the park.

It was one of those fine late-summer evenings, all deep green and yellow. Goldenrod crowded the boulevards and the leafy hollows, and floated lazily in the air, giving everyone red eyes and runny noses. Birds gathered in great conferences in the oaks and elms, making migratory plans in the summer heat. There was enough of a breeze now to make the humidity bearable, and this of course promised a coming storm. Dark clouds gathered along the horizon. It would come, I thought, after nightfall.

"Look how fast I am, Alex!" Beatrice called as she took off across the field. "Look how fast!" And she was—a blur of heat and motion and possibility. Beatrice was uncontainable; she was that moment of change when potential energy becomes kinetic power. I pitied her teachers. I had no idea how it could even be possible to keep such a child in docile lines and sedated rows. How can you teach long division to a whirlwind? And yet, they seemed to do so. And yet. Those pages gave me pause.

I am a dragon, they asserted.

No, you are not, my heart insisted.

I am a dragon. I shook my head at the thought of it. Beatrice, while far from a perfect child, was a fastidiously honest one. She would not have written those words unless she deeply felt they were true.

No. No you cannot. It was a needle in my heart. I couldn't explain it. I *needed* her. Beatrice was my sister. It was me and Beatrice alone in the world. My mother had a sister, and then her sister was gone. And she didn't come back. And my mother, despite her husband and despite her children, died alone. Was I also going to be alone?

I shook the thought away. Beatrice was Beatrice and she would always be Beatrice. She and I were a family, and that was that. All of this would pass. I watched her run, her feet barely touching the grass. The evening sun hung low and blazed brightly around her, the light falling on her skin and making it glow—yellow, orange, gold. Her crinkly hair shimmered, a cloud of whisps and tangles floating above her head. She out-stretched her arms, like wings.

I am a dragon, she wrote.

"Beatrice?" I called, my voice suddenly tight and panicking. *"Beatrice!"*

She stopped, pirouetted on one foot, and struck a pose with a grin.

I was shaking. And despite the heat, my skin was clammy and cold. "Come and eat, sweet Bea," I said, forcing myself to relax. I laid our dinner out on the blanket.

She did, and the two of us ate our sandwiches while lying on our backs, staring up at the sky. We didn't say anything. After a bit, Beatrice reached over, her fingers gently twisting one of the curls over my ears, winding my hair around her knuckles.

"All we have is each other," she said. "Right, Alex?"

I wrapped my hand around hers and gave it a squeeze. "All we have is each other," I said.

It was the only thing that was true.

Later, when I went to the park building to wash my hands, I saw a flyer tacked up to a light post. It had a picture of a dragon on it. It was a reproduction of an old drawing—like a medieval woodcut. The dragon had bat wings and a snakelike neck and a tail wrapped around a tower. THINK IT'S OVER? it said across the top. And at the bottom it said THINK AGAIN. And then, below that, in very small letters, it said THE WYVERN RESEARCH COLLECTIVE: WE KNOW WHAT THEY WON'T TELL YOU.

I stared at it for a long moment. I had heard of that organiza-tion before. But I couldn't remember where.

"What's that, Alex?" Beatrice called from the swings. Her little legs pumped back and forth, back and forth, glinting in the late evening light. The storm clouds were closer now, and I knew we should be going soon.

"Nothing, honey," I called back. "Keep playing."

I reached up, grabbed the flyer, and crumpled it in my hand. I let it fall to the ground, and I didn't look back.

⁓

The next day, as I made breakfast, and folded clothes, and mended clothes, and cleaned the apartment, and made lists for what Beatrice needed to start school, and what I needed to start school, and made endless lists of what we would need and how we would get through the day, I turned on the radio, just to distract myself for a little bit. Beatrice was still asleep. She snored, open-mouthed, in a tangle of blankets, her red hair streaking around her like flames. She was all I had. I loved her so much I felt my breath catch. I laid out her uniform and the socks that needed darning and the cardigans that needed mending as the radio switched to the news.

I stopped cold when the newscaster mentioned Saint Agnes.

"Firefighters were called to Saint Agnes Primary School yesterday, due to a buildup of gaseous substances in the pipes in the teachers' lounge lavatory, which caused a small explosion that shattered a window. Two teachers, both Sisters, were slightly injured in the blast. They will both take early retirement rather than disrupt the new school year. The principal's statement reads as follows, and I quote: 'I hope this puts any and all unfounded rumors to rest. Several theorists and instigators have been attempting to enter the building to further their ridiculous assertions. If they return to school property, I shall alert the authorities. There is nothing to see—nothing strange—at Saint Agnes.'"

It wasn't Mr. Alphonse's voice. It was the newscaster's voice reading Mr. Alphonse's words. But I could hear the principal's bombastic yodel inside each sentence. Why, I wondered. And why had his face been so red in his office?

I shook my head. It didn't do me any good to question anything. There was too much to do. School was starting soon. Beatrice needed seeing to. I had to get food on the table and homework done and somehow make plans for . . . I shook my head again. It was hard to think about the future. My future after graduation was a yawning space. What would happen to us? How could I continue to raise Beatrice while I continued my education? I knew I needed to have both, I knew that they both were *necessary,* but how it would work was a mystery. I had no context to even begin to imagine it. I had no information. It was a hole in the universe where the truth should be, and where my life would be.

And, frankly, I was afraid.

When I was a little girl, they told us to keep our eyes on the ground. They told us not to ask about the houses that burned. They told us to forget. And we were good children. We followed the rules.

And now I realize, there is a freedom in forgetting.

Or at least it is something that feels like freedom.

There is a freedom in *not* asking questions.

There is a freedom in being unburdened by unpleasant information.

And sometimes, a person has to hang on to whatever freedoms she can get.

At this point in the paper, I feel the time has come to make a confession: I was once a member of a long-secret and underground group of researchers, scientists, doctors, and librarians called the Wyvern Research Collective. The scientific work conducted by this group has remained, for legal reasons, cloistered from the rest of the scientific community. Our findings are discussed and reviewed in the shadows and thus are prevented from shedding light on vexing conundrums in other aspects of biology, reproductive science, physiology, and aeronautics. The silencing or obscuring of any aspect of nature—due to cultural taboo or fear or general squeamishness—harms science. I do not regret my work with this group, or the advances we made. I do regret that any research we disseminated had to be done in secret, and anonymously, which prevented our discoveries from finding their place among the larger conversations in the scientific community.

In the fall of 1948, I published a pamphlet called Some Basic Facts About Dragons: A Physician's Explanation. I published this pamphlet anonymously, as we always did, but because of the concrete and universal applications of the findings, I did my best to disseminate the information as widely as I could, and without our usual precautions, and outside of our usual network. This was done without the blessing of the collective, which prompted a parting of ways. The observational data I collected on dragons for this project were a bit of an accident—an unexpected set of findings from the research I conducted on a group of Women Airforce Service Pilots at the beginning of World War II, funded by the United States Army. The topic I was originally tasked with investigating was not dragons—clearly not! The military could barely bring itself to mention the existence of its female recruits, much less discuss anything so delicate and profane as dragons. Instead, I was supposed to monitor the physiology of the female pilots, likely as a pretense to bar them from service entirely. (In this my superiors were disappointed. I found no evidence to prohibit women from serving. My subjects thrived.) Scientific research is a curious beast, however. Any researcher worth his salt will tell you that the things we discover are rarely the facts we set out to prove. A good scientist must remain curious, open-minded, humble, and above all, obedient to the data, and to the facts.

The women I studied were young, healthy, and resilient. Bright sparks, each one. They took to flying in a way that alarmed their superiors—not to mention their male colleagues. They greeted the sky each morning, and gazed at it ruefully as evening fell and they returned to their barracks. My research was only underway a month when, quite unexpectedly, one woman dragoned—a nineteen-year-old girl from Iowa named Stella. Her dragoning was fairly consistent with the other cases documented over the years by the WRC. By all accounts, she transformed in a state of rage. Four airmen perished instantly. A fifth man—an older mechanic by the name of Cal—was the only witness. He said that he saw the men surround Stella. He called it "hassling." He heard her yelling to be left alone, and had headed toward her at a run, hoping to help. Instead, he heard her scream, and saw her transform in a terrible burst of fire. The blast was so strong, it blew him a full twenty feet backward. The ground shook like they had been bombed. The men had been blown apart. It wasn't clear if either the transformation or the subsequent death of the airmen was intentional. The mechanic did not believe so. When the dragon came to her senses, she noticed Cal staring at her, wetting himself with fear. She patted his head and flew away.

The next two dragonings were less typical. One occurred while the woman in question was in flight. I was in communication with her via radio link, getting data every fifteen minutes regarding her respiration, perspiration, vision, hearing, verbal acuity, and cognitive reasoning. Her answers, as recorded in my

log, were notable in that they demonstrated a consistent eleva-
tion over time of her sensations of optimism, cheerfulness, and
a strange, fierce joy. After she had been flying for two hours in
a long oval around and around the base, she stopped and said,
"I'm sorry, Doctor. It's just . . . too wonderful up here. It's all
just . . . too wonderful." I asked her what that meant, and was
met with the sound of the emergency release and the pilot eject.
Fearing the worst, we ran outside, expecting to see debris rain-
ing down. Instead we saw that she had cut the engine while still
human, and, in dragon form, she held the aircraft in the vise
of her talons, unfurled her wings, and was flying it back to its
base. She was an impressive specimen—dark green with gold
on the underbelly, and strikingly large. She shone so brightly it
was difficult to look at her straight on. Normally, it was army
policy to shoot dragons on sight (not that this did any good,
and often ended in friendly-fire deaths from ricocheting bullets),
but this was so extraordinary that the soldiers simply stared in
astonishment as she gently set the plane down on the tarmac,
paused a moment, and then launched into the sky. I remember
the scene quite well: the chaotic questioning, the men running
back and forth, and a group of WASP recruits standing outside,
together in a line, their faces lit in the morning sun, and their
eyes gazing up.

The next dragoning transpired one week later. This incident
is a bit more delicate to relay, and so I must do so in a more
oblique fashion. Two WASP recruits in the study were close
friends. Two peas in a pod, as they say. I never saw one without the other. Their devotion was an obvious fact. Like sisters,
you see. But closer than sisters. An intimacy that—well, perhaps even that is too much. What I can say is this: I saw them
both on a Tuesday for our regular check-ins, where I took data
points on their weight, heart rate, basal temperature, blood pressure. I took their blood for study, asked them about their mental
states, asked about the regularities of their menstrual cycles, and
checked their vision. Both were as healthy as they had been the

week before, but I did notice that one of them—a young woman named Edith—had an increased heart rate. I made a note of this, in case it signified an infection. The two left my office and went off alone. It was their R&R, and they had made a picnic and had a couple blankets, and wished for privacy. Later that day, only one returned, a woman by the name of Marla. I interviewed her, despite her tremendous grief. Her testimony is not entirely useful, as it had all the hallmarks of a woman who has suffered a devastating loss. I will note, though, that in her report, she said, "Edith was happy. She was so happy. It couldn't be contained." Why did Edith dragon? I am still not entirely sure. The data remains inconsistent and unclear. The female pilots were all temporarily grounded for a number of months after that, for safety reasons, and would have remained so had not the need for qualified pilots superseded those concerns. As for my research, it was terminated the next day, and the army sent me home.

The army informed me that my findings were classified, and that my materials would be confiscated. The only reason I retained any records at all is because of my lifelong habit of always having two sets of notes and exact copies of everything—and the men who ransacked my workspace didn't check everywhere. Both the National Institutes of Health and my university cast a dim view on my research on dragoning and encouraged me to drop it in favor of more important—and less embarrassing—pursuits. The WRC forbade me from attempting to disseminate my findings, claiming it would put the collective at risk. But I disagreed. My research demonstrated that dragonings were far more common than people thought—and that they were increasing. I published Some Basic Facts About Dragoning later that year. I sent it to every medical school in this country and throughout Europe. It was banned and censored almost instantly.

I could not have known what was in store for this country, nor could I have known what we were heading toward in 1955. I do know that our only hope, our only way through this and any other calamity, is a faithful return to questioning, testing, *observing, and drawing conclusions. We must be servants to the data and helpmeets to the facts. Science, I truly believe, is humanity's only hope, and it is in science, today and always, that I will put my trust.*

—"A Brief History of Dragons" by Professor H. N. Gantz, MD, PhD

22.

School began with its litany of indignities.

One more year, I told myself, but my breath caught at the thought of it. I was speeding headlong to the edge of a cliff, with no concept of what was awaiting me when I got there. A bridge? A ladder? A series of ropes and pickaxes? The void of space? Certain doom? Or maybe even a pair of wings . . .

I shook the notion away. Worry wouldn't get the dishes done, as my mother used to say. And it certainly wasn't going to help us make it through the year.

On that first day, I walked Beatrice to school. She had complained that she was old enough to do it herself, but I insisted, and still she held my hand the whole way, just as she always did, as I balanced and guided my bicycle with my other hand. Mr. Alphonse met us on the front steps of Saint Agnes, his arms rigidly folded across his chest, his face strangely puffy and bloated. Beatrice, in honor of the first day of school, was so clean she practically glowed in the dark. I had soaked her blouse and bobby socks in borax and bleach and hung them in the sun to dry. I had used men's pomade to keep her crinkles and curls in check, and a fine-toothed comb to attack the snarls, and corralled her hair into two tight French braids, wound so close to her skull that the skin of her scalp announced itself in harsh relief. No one was going to accuse me of neglecting Beatrice's appearance or letting anything slide. No one would have any reason to look too closely at our strange living arrangement—no grown-ups, no guidance, no extra pair of hands. Our own little universe. It was best that no one knew.

As we approached the building, Beatrice let go of my hand and skipped around the corner and up the walkway, thrilled as always to see her friends and teachers. She skidded to a halt when she saw Mr. Alphonse. I had been expecting this, however, and I was ready. I put my hand on Beatrice's shoulder and stepped between my sister and the principal. I took an envelope out of my pocket. I turned to face Beatrice and winked so only she could see.

"Now Beatrice," I said sternly. "I expect you to go straight to Sister Claire and hand her this letter of apology." I held my hand up as though she was about to protest. "No complaints!" I gave her another secret wink. "Now, scoot!"

Beatrice took the envelope—which, truth be told, actually did contain a letter of apology, written under duress and with me looming over her shoulder, the day after our meeting at the school—and scampered up the stairs, taking care not to make eye contact with her principal, her relief at not having to talk to him radiating from her body in waves. She disappeared through the open doors. I looked up at Mr. Alphonse, my body matching his stance and arms and jutted chin—only because I knew it would bother him. His forehead creased. I gave him what I hoped was a winning smile.

"Beatrice has written a heartfelt apology, of her own volition in an earnest desire to put the past behind her and make amends," I said. "You were right, Mr. Alphonse, and you deserve my thanks for bringing the issue to my attention. My father thanks you too, and says so constantly." I had practiced this, obviously. "It's a new year, and a new start. I'm glad we both agree."

Mr. Alphonse looked terrible. He had dark circles under his eyes and his skin, while still blotchy, was generally the color of oatmeal. His dress pants sagged even as his belly loomed over his belt. I wondered if he was ill. He frowned and took a step toward me.

I checked my watch. "If you'll excuse me, I would rather not be late for my first day of school." I turned, secured my book bag, and mounted my bike.

"I insist that your father return my phone calls and appear in my office," he said. "It is most—"

"Happy first day of school, Mr. Alphonse!" I said as I pedaled away.

"We are not done here, Miss Green!"

We'll see, I thought to myself, noticing with a start that my voice inside my head sounded more and more like my mother's voice every single day.

~

I arrived at school early enough to go straight to the girls' bathroom, and I sat in a stall for about ten minutes, my bottom perched on the edge of the toilet, my forehead resting on my knees, choking on the cloud of hairspray left by the other girls before me. I breathed in and out, bracing my hands on each wall—not exactly enjoying this one moment of solitude and quiet, but certainly appreciating it. I sighed, stood, dabbed the sweat off my face and armpits with a wad of toilet paper, changed into my uniform, and switched out of my sneakers into my flats. I paused, just breathed for a minute, trying to steady myself. I could hear kids hollering and laughing outside.

(I *had a friend once,* I found myself thinking. *She lived in a magical house.* I shook my head, trying to force the image of Sonja's face away. It had been so nice to have a friend. But that was over now. I didn't need friends—I had Beatrice. And I had my schoolwork. And my work beyond school. There was so much to learn. I had to live in the present. It did no good to ask questions.)

I washed my hands and slid into the hallway, making my way past groups of boys leaning against the lockers and groups of girls walking shoulder to shoulder, always moving in packs.

I held my books close to my chest and kept my head down

until I reached the main office. As with previous years, my schedule had been mailed to my father's house, so once again I had to go to the office, lie, and say I had lost my schedule (*like I would ever lose a single thing,* I thought huffily) and get a copy.

I kept my eyes down as I walked in. They still had the honor roll posted next to the door. My name should have been at the very top. Everyone knew it. Instead I was number seven. "A clerical error," the dean had informed me then. "We'll fix it as soon as we can." But they never did.

The woman who ran the front office, an ancient nun named Sister Kevin, smiled brightly when I arrived. "Alexandra!" she said. "As I live and breathe!" If it weren't for her nun's habit, her bright eyes and face like a wizened apple might have made her look like one of the trolls in Sonja's picture books that she showed me when we were children. (And just thinking so made my breath catch and my eyes sting. I took a deep breath, to calm myself down, and forced the thought away.)

"Good morning, Sister," I said, my voice suddenly thick. I cleared my throat. "I'm sorry to say I've mislaid my schedule. Any chance I could get a copy?"

"You know we were talking about you all morning," she said as she pulled out the card with my handwritten schedule already filled out. She had been expecting this, it seemed. "I'm sure your ears were just burning." She clapped her hands together and beamed. I had heard that back when she was a teacher, she was a bit of a menace. All demands and bombast and disappointment and yelling. It was hard for me to imagine. Now she was all smiles and endless enthusiasm.

"My ears are just fine, thank you, Sister." I looked at the schedule and frowned. "I'm sorry, there seems to be a mistake." I showed it to her. "I'm scheduled for calculus. But I shouldn't be. I already took it in the correspondence program, in ninth grade. I have already amassed credits at the university." She didn't take my schedule. She simply maintained her delighted expression. "I got an A. And I was the top student in the class.

The professor wrote me a letter congratulating me and everything. In the spring I spoke to Sister Frances—"

"Who is no longer the principal, dear," Sister Kevin said, kindly. "Sweet?" She offered up a jar of hard candy. I shook my head.

"She's not?" That was news to me. "Since when?" I checked myself. It did me no good to get snippy. "I mean, I'm surprised. No one said anything last year. Did she retire?" I squinted, trying to pin down what Sister Frances's age might have been. It was difficult for me to tell with most people, but even more difficult with nuns.

Sister Kevin fished out a lemon drop and popped it into her mouth. "No. She just, you know, flew the coop, as they say. Stretched her wings. I mean her legs. She had always wanted to do some traveling, dear heart, and so we decided not to stand in her way." She closed her eyes and rolled the lemon drop in her mouth. I could hear it rattling against her molars. This didn't make any sense.

"Is she coming back?"

She smiled, her shoulders bouncing a bit. "Who's to say, really. Are you sure you don't want a sweet?" I shook my head. "In the meantime, Mr. Alphonse—from Saint Agnes—will be acting principal for both schools, until the diocese makes a replacement." She pursed her lips for a moment. "It's a lot for any man. I hope he doesn't work himself to death, poor thing."

Great. I sighed. I laid my schedule out on the desk. I pointed to the spot that said "Calculus." "But you see. I took this class. Already. In ninth grade. And then I took multivariable calculus and then I took discrete mathematics, and now I'm taking linear algebra and probability through the university. These classes are quite difficult, and Sister Frances and I decided that it would be helpful for me to have a free period in order to study."

"Sister Frances isn't here, dear," she said indulgently.

"I know," I said, trying to keep my frustration in check. "But see, she already said. We *decided*. Sister Frances signed off and everything." I paused. "In pen," I added lamely.

"Sister Frances isn't here, dear," Sister Kevin repeated, with no change to her tone or expression.

This was going nowhere. I decided to take it up with the teacher instead. "Thanks, Sister Kevin. It's always so nice to see you."

"As it is for me with you!" she said, blowing me a kiss. I turned to go. "Oh! And how everyone was gabbing about you this morning! So many opinions! That friend of yours came by with her stacks and stacks of information and pamphlets. She made everyone take it whether they liked it or not! Such a force of nature she is! She has high hopes for you, my dear. The sky is the limit, she said, which made me giggle a bit. Imagine being limited by the sky!" She chuckled.

Sometimes, Sister Kevin gave me a bit of a headache. "I'm sorry?" I said. "Who came by?"

"You know," she said. "Your librarian friend. 'No shortcuts for this one, oh no,' she told us. She'll only be happy if you land in the highest ivory tower that ever was. You will be our little philosopher king. Or queen, I suppose. Dear Helen. She always was a browbeater when we were in grammar school. It's nice to know that some things never change!"

She popped another lemon drop into her mouth. And then another. They rolled about like a marble tournament. She still attempted a lumpy smile.

I didn't know what to say to any of this. "Thanks, Sister," I said.

My head swam, but I decided to ignore it. I had been planning to head to the library after school, regardless. Maybe Mrs. Gyzinska would explain Sister Kevin's ramblings then.

By third period, I understood why I had been placed in the calculus class. Not only was I the only girl, but the teacher, Mr. Reynolds, had never actually taught calculus before, and hadn't taken the class since college. By the end of the class, he had asked me to come to the board no less than nine times to explain sample problem after sample problem, and had asked me to correct everyone's pretests. He also asked me to take attendance, answer questions, and wipe down the board at the end. I tried to explain my situation at the end of class, but he didn't want to hear it.

"Correspondence is *not the same* as learning in a classroom," he said huffily. "I thought you were smart enough to know that." He pointed to the corner. "Would you mind emptying that trash before you leave?"

"But I took the same final that they take at the university. And it covers more topics than what we learn here. All these boys will have to retake this class in college, but I will not. And sir. You just saw me explain these concepts after not studying this for over a year. Clearly I learned it. This seems like a waste of time."

"Learning," he said primly, "is *never* a waste of time. I'll see you in class tomorrow. I expect you to work just as hard as the boys. No special treatment."

I asked again, and the answer was no. I asked if I could simply be his teaching assistant—that's what he wanted anyway—and then I could be helpful, but still have the time to study while everyone else was working their problem sets. The answer was still no. I left in a frustrated huff.

The day didn't improve from there.

I walked home under a cloud, guiding my bike with one hand, making mental lists of what I had to accomplish before I went to bed that night. Beatrice needed to be fed and entertained. She probably had homework. The sink needed fixing again, and it did no use to ask the landlord to do it. Thanks to some helpful reference books, and a fairly functional set of old tools given to me by the kindly janitor at the library after his were replaced, I had by this time a rudimentary understanding of how to fix a pipe or a toilet, how to solder a wire and fix a circuit, how to screw together a highly functional—though, admittedly, not particularly attractive—bookshelf. And so forth. I knew how to find the studs in the wall and how to protect myself while working with electricity and what to do when the refrigerator stopped working.

I needed to get dinner together.

I had homework to finish.

I had a paper to write.

I had problem sets and reading to complete for my correspondence courses.

And Mrs. Gyzinska had told me that the time had come to start preparing my applications for universities. My stomach clenched at the thought of it. How would I do it? What about Beatrice? What was going to happen?

Beatrice was already home, her book bag tossed in a heap on the building's front stoop. There was a narrow yard between our building and the one next door, and a small green space in the back, which led into the alley. Beatrice, two girls, and six boys came tearing around the corner. They looped around the building, and disappeared around the other side. They didn't notice me. Beatrice had an object in her hand—two pieces of wood, one long and one short, that had been diagonally lashed together with twine at the hilt to form a makeshift wooden sword.

"Prepare to meet your doom, you finks!" Beatrice howled, and the other children squealed in response.

They came around again. I held up one hand and they skidded to a halt, red-cheeked and panting.

"Hi Alex," Beatrice said.

"We're heading to the library," I said. "Come inside and get your things."

"*Now?*" she whined. "Not this *second*. I had to be in school *all day*."

As did I, but I didn't say so. I sighed. Maybe the library could wait. Beatrice, after her gleaming cleanliness this morning, was now a raggedy mess.

"Fine," I said. "Play if you need to, but not for very long. I need to stop by the library no matter what. I need to pick up some materials. You can be with your friends for a bit longer, if you'd like. Just come inside when I call, and we'll have an early supper."

That was all she needed. "ONWARD!" she bellowed, and the other children bellowed along with her and they all streaked around the building again, and out of sight.

I picked up Beatrice's book bag and slowly climbed the stairs, nearly collapsing on my bed in the corner, which also served as our couch during the day. I heated the creamed chicken on the stove and made the rice, slicing radishes and cucumbers on the side. I laid out my work for after Beatrice's bedtime and put what I'd need at the library back in my bag. I made a list, checked things off, remembered the broken sink, added it to the list, remembered that Beatrice would certainly need a bath, added that to the list. I looked at the clock. There weren't enough hours.

The phone rang. I jumped. The phone *never* rang, except when my father called on Sundays. When he remembered to call on Sundays. Which was less often all the time. I almost didn't answer it.

I picked up the phone and listened to silence for a moment. Then I heard my father cough.

"Dad?" I said. He coughed again. And again. "Dad, are you there?"

He made an impatient, grunting sound. It was definitely my dad.

"It's nice to hear from you," I said. "Did you know it's not Sunday? I mean. Not that I mind."

Finally: "Mr. Alphonse came by the house today. I forgot how much I disliked that man."

We're not done here, Mr. Alphonse had said.

Anxiety bit at the back of my neck. I tried to rub it away.

"And it was just a social call?" I asked.

He ignored this. "He phoned the office and heard that I was recovering at home," he coughed, swore, and coughed again.

"Are you all right, Dad?"

"That's none of your business." He cleared his throat. "So he just invited himself right over. He wondered where you and . . ." He paused. "Well, he wanted us all to chat together about some goddamned thing. It upset my wife. You understand the position this puts me in. I expected you to take care of this sort of thing. I am relying on you to keep that child in line. Your mother would have wanted it so."

I could feel my cheeks become hot. I curled my empty hand into a fist and pressed it against the wall, knuckles first. I knew it didn't do me any good to get angry, and yet. I closed my eyes and breathed deeply, trying for the life of me to tamp down the growing heat in my chest. A siren whined outside. That had been happening a lot lately. There was that fire at Saint Agnes and a fire at the Odd's-N-End's store and a fire in a grain elevator about fifteen miles from town. And at an old folks' home in Eau Claire. And then at some bar at the Minnesota border. Each time, they were put out quickly. They were only briefly mentioned on the news.

"I do understand your position, Dad. I'm so sorry your . . ." I paused briefly. "I'm sorry your wife was upset. What was her name again?"

"Don't be cheeky."

"Sorry, Dad." Another siren. It was too hot in the apartment. The library wouldn't be much better, but at least the basement would be cool and I could work there. Every minute I was working, studying, writing, proving, figuring, or patiently tying complex mathematical expressions into neat, elegant knots—as long as I was doing *something,* it gave my mind a reprieve from worrying over what would happen next. Next year. Another world. What was my father's plan? I was afraid to ask. "Listen, I have no idea why Mr. Alphonse felt the need to come over and see you. I have the situation handled. Beatrice was spending too much time drawing things and not doing her work. She apologized, and now everything is fixed."

"He said you sassed him."

"I did nothing of the kind."

"He doesn't like your short hair. You know what they say about girls with short hair."

I scowled. "They spend less money on hair spray?"

"*Cheeky!*" my father admonished me again.

"I retract my cheek," I said. "Listen, Dad. Don't worry about any of this. I have it handled. I've *always* handled these things. And anyway, I graduate this year. With honors, it looks like. Which means maybe we should talk about what happens when I—"

My father coughed again. "You're really going to fool with that business? You could start working now, have a career. A high school diploma is just a piece of paper. Something for college boys, and that's about it. If you ask me, it's much more important to have men in the industries see what you can do, and position yourself accordingly. There isn't an office in America that wouldn't be over the moon to have a girl like you sitting at one of their desks. In any case, you'll be married soon enough, so it doesn't much matter in the end."

Married? My stomach lurched at the thought. Who did he think he was talking to? "Dad, that isn't the point. And that's not even part of the plan. I'm in the middle of—"

"You know, I just had a meeting with the guy who owns the radio station, and I told him about you. He's got a secretary job for you if you want. All you have to do is ask."

"*What?* Dad. I'm not even trained as a secretary. People get those jobs after they go to secretarial school. Plus, they have their high school diplomas—not just *a piece of paper*. Honestly. Plus, I am applying for—"

My father interrupted me again. "He's a good man. And it's a good job. And this is a bird in the hand—you'd be silly to throw an opportunity away. But your mother did raise you with all matter of silliness, so it's tough to say what you'll do. Who cares about a piece of paper when you have an employer that wants to hire girls young and pretty and too green to know any better, handing out opportunities like candy." My father didn't explain what this meant. But I guessed. "It's like skipping the line. My guess is that you'd be running the place in a month, head like yours. You should think about it."

I took a deep breath and tried to clear my head. This wasn't going well. My father had another coughing fit. I waited for it to pass. "What I'm *thinking* about, Dad, is pursuing a degree in—"

Again he interrupted me. "Well, it's been good to hear your voice, Alexandra, but I have to go." He coughed one last time—a hard, hacking expulsion. "Be good. Stay good. Don't embarrass me. Think of what your mother would have wanted and don't disappoint her."

"I won't," I said, but he had already hung up, and didn't hear me.

⁓

Two days later, a letter arrived from my father. It had no post-mark and no stamp. It had simply been slipped under the door to our apartment and set on the floor. Had my father been by and refused to say hello? Had he handed the letter to our landlord so he didn't have to see us? I'm not sure which one was worse.

"Dear Alexandra," the letter said.

I noticed an implicit question in your wheedling during our conversation the other day, and it appears that you have a bit of a misconception. I thought I had made myself perfectly clear on the subject of a university education for young ladies. But since there is still some confusion, allow me to clarify:

No, I will not fund, assist, or in any way support any attempts at higher education for you, past high school. I do not intend to support either of you after you graduate in June, as I believe you are more than capable of doing so on your own. Finishing your education through graduation is what your mother would have preferred, so yes, in deference to her memory, I will reluctantly support it to its end, arbitrary as that milestone is. Your apartment is paid through the end of August, at which point you will have income of your own, and will be able to take over. I've been more than generous, all things considered. I made a promise to your mother, regarding your "sister," and I pride myself for seeing it through, though I know you and I disagree over my methods. You'll understand that when you're older. I have a new family, after all, and concessions had to be made.

I am proud of you, Alexandra. Surely you must know that already. I know your mother would be proud as well. I will wish you well when you graduate.

Regards,
Dad.

I read it. I read it again. I crumpled the paper and threw it into the trash.

So, I thought to myself. *That was that, then.*

On the day before the Mass Dragoning of 1955, a group of twenty-five well-heeled literature majors from Vassar College took the train to Manhattan and paid a visit to the block where the Feibel-Ross Auxiliary Telephone Exchange Building used to be.

They didn't tell anyone where they were going. Nor did they seem to have planned their trip in advance. In interviews with both professors and students who were not part of the twenty-five, all report the same phenomenon—that each student, either in class, or in the library, or in the middle of field hockey practice, simply stood up at 9:35 exactly, and exited without a word. They massed on Main Street and made their way to the Poughkeepsie train station, where they boarded the 11:25 to Manhattan.

The Vassar students assembled themselves on the sidewalk, facing the empty lot. They had good posture and clear eyes and a grounded stance. They had spent their whole lives, in their preparatory schools and finishing schools, in their tutoring sessions and ballet lessons and piano recitals and art history lectures, training to become women of substance, like their mothers. They stood in silence before the empty space that once was the Feibel-Ross—another hole in the universe. Their faces were bright, witnesses reported, and beautiful. As one, they lifted their gaze to the sky. And then, all at once, and all in a long, neat line, they took out their notebooks, and began to draw.

No one paid them much mind. The Feibel-Ross lot glared like a missing tooth in the middle of a mouth. It was a loud sort of emptiness. People quickened their steps and lowered their eyes. No one noticed themselves doing this.

The Vassar students remained for the entire afternoon. They drew and drew, well into the evening. People remembered this later, though they couldn't for the life of them explain why it was important. Why their presence—standing perfectly still in a line along the curb, their faces tilted toward their notebooks in concentration and consternation or tilted toward the sky with an expression that could be interpreted as anticipatory or concerned or flooded with wild joy depending on the viewer—was noteworthy. Or why they didn't take note of it until it was too late.

The next morning, in the early hours before the Mass Dragoning had begun, people all across Manhattan found—strewn on park benches and on subway staircases and lining the gutters—drawings of women. Thousands of them littered the streets. They blew into the windshields of cars like autumn leaves and swirled outside skyscraper windows like birds. Women in business attire. Women in housedresses. Women in coats. Women manning machinery. Women in cockpits. Women at the plow. Women in their underwear and in the nude. Women at the beach. Women in bridal gowns and in marital beds. Women holding babies. Or swelled with more babies. Or wiping noses. Women on the school steps. Women waving goodbye. The drawings were everywhere.

No one knew what this meant.

And every once in a while, there would be a piece of paper with nothing drawn on it at all. Simply a sentence composed in a lovely hand: "The Martin O'Learys of the world have it coming."

No one knew what that meant, either.

The Vassar girls never made it to the train that night and did not return to their dormitories. Panicked house mothers called the police and called families and notified the papers. The girls did not return. Ordinarily, this would have made the evening news the next day, of course, but it didn't. The nation watched its mothers transform in a mass demonstration of rage and violence and fire. Suddenly, there were other things to think about. And so the world forgot about the Vassar girls.

Mostly.

—"A Brief History of Dragons" by Professor H. N. Gantz, MD, PhD

23.

Over the next month, I started seeing tiny flyers in odd places. Stuck inside the mailbox door or taped on a bicycle rack or strewn on the steps in front of the school. They were small, about the size of my palm.

> *FREE CLINICS FOR THE CURIOUS*
> *Having symptoms you can't explain?*
> *A feeling that the inside is larger than the outside?*
> *Our CLINICIANS have answers.*
> *We provide HONESTY in place of lies,*
> *INFORMATION in place of obfuscation.*
> *No appointment necessary.*

I paused as I opened the front door of my apartment, noticing a card stuck to the glass. I pulled it off to see if there was an address on the back, only to have it snatched out of my hand by Mr. Watt, my landlord. He was a short man with a head that balded only in patches, leaving frail wisps clinging randomly to his deeply freckled scalp. They looked like feathers on a wrinkly baby bird. He had a stubbled, gnarled face, pressed permanently into a scowl.

"If I catch you looking at that filth again, I'll tell your father." He was constantly threatening to tell my father things. As far as I could tell, he never had.

I folded my arms. "I have no idea what you mean. It was just sitting here on the door. What was I supposed to do with it? I thought *you* had left it there." I hadn't, but I didn't care for his tone.

"Hmph. Loony outsiders with their loony ideas. More Madison liberals, if you ask me. Or worse." His face grew grim. "*Californians.* Well. Not in my town, no sir." His gaze darted up and down the road, as though at this very moment, hordes of trucks crammed with West Coasters were bearing down on our streets.

He tore the paper into pieces and shoved them into his pocket.

"But, do you at least know what it's even about? I keep seeing these cards all over town."

"I ain't saying nuthin'," he said. "I sent a note to your father about that girl of yours. Running wild again. It's the last thing I need. Keep her under control, or find a new place to live." It was an empty threat, I knew, but it unsettled me all the same. He pushed past and hobbled down the stairs to his apartment.

I shook my head.

Clinics for the curious.

I had to admit, I was rather curious.

The next day, in French class, three girls in the row ahead of me examined three cards—each slightly different but advertising the same clinics. I tapped the shoulder of the closest one—a tall girl named Emeline, who wore her hair in a high bun to show off her long neck, and who flashed her new engagement ring to whoever came too close. She never wore makeup—that wasn't allowed—but she always did seem to glow.

"Excuse me," I said.

"Yes"—she swiveled to glow in my direction, extending her hand with a pretty flourish to show me her ring—"it is real, if you were wondering." She flashed an indulgent smile.

"Sorry?" I said. "Actually, no. I wasn't. But I *am* curious about those cards. Is there an address?"

The girl next to her, Marie-Louise, I believe her name was, peeked over Emeline's shoulder and rolled her eyes. "They can't just *advertise* something like that," she explained. "That's how they get shut down. You know." She glanced over her shoulder. "By the *government.*"

"Why would the government shut them down?" I asked. Sister Leonie entered the room. She was a tiny thing, with a face like a walnut and small grey eyes that shone like two brand-new nickels. Her shoes creaked as she waddled up to the blackboard. She needed a long stick with a rag on the end in order to clean it up to the top.

Marie-Louise quickly gathered the cards and shoved them in her pocket. "Use your head," she whispered. "Why *wouldn't* they? But if you're really curious, I suspect you'll find out more soon enough."

"How?" I asked.

Marie-Louise said nothing. She just tapped her nose.

Sister Leonie turned. *"Silence, s'il vous plaît,"* she said, not unkindly.

We opened our books.

Before I knew it, September wound down and October asserted itself, all bright colors and bright skies and stiff breezes. Beatrice behaved at school and came home with glowing comments on her papers and each day I breathed a sigh of relief. Maybe the dragon drawings were just a phase.

Beatrice didn't complain when I took her to the library for long hours, nearly every day. I let her do exactly what my mother denied me. I let her roam without limits and read whatever she wanted. I praised her for her curiosity. Mrs. Gyzinska had several assistants who checked in on Beatrice, sometimes bringing her to the children's room to make arts and crafts, and she would come home wearing outlandish crowns with glitter, or bright bangles covered in tin foil, or a pair of brightly colored wings. (The wings I threw away. She was a child; I hoped she would forget. I hated myself for doing it.)

As for me, I kept to myself at school. I kept my eyes on the ground. I was used to being alone. More than once I thought

I saw Sonja, just out of the corner of my eye. Sitting alone at a lunch table. Or standing in a doorway. It was never her. But each time, I felt my heart crack, just a little bit. I had a friend once. But my father dragged her away. There was more to that story, but it hovered just out of my reach, insubstantial as smoke. I tried to force it from my mind. It didn't do to dwell on the past, after all. There is a freedom in forgetting. Or that was the story I told myself then.

On the first Saturday in October, Beatrice and I walked to the library, my back bent under the weight of my book bag, and Beatrice running ahead of me. She kept her arms and outstretched, like wings.

"I'm flying, Alex!" she cried. "I'm really flying!" Her hands fluttered prettily, like a dancer's. She hopped onto a concrete wall and leaped off. Any other time, I would have taken a moment to admire her strength and agility and grace. But on this particular day, I felt weighted down, and afraid. *How was I going to get it all done?* I asked myself for the hundred thousandth time that day. *What would happen to us next year?* I fussed. Each question felt like a stone on my back. I started walking with a persistent hunch.

"Little girls don't fly," I said.

She stopped and glared at me. "Why do you always have to ruin things?" she pouted.

I didn't have time for this. "It's not ruining. It's science. Little girls don't fly. They walk, just like big girls."

We said nothing more until we reached the library steps.

Our town's library had been built in the 1890s by Mr. Carnegie and then expanded in the thirties. Mrs. Gyzinska, who had been head librarian even way back then, had also finagled a way to get the Civilian Conservation Corps to send over a couple of artists to paint murals in the children's section and another in the reading room—richly detailed forest scenes with woodland creatures ambling through leafy, wide-branched trees, as well as the occasional fairy or brownie or troll peeking out from clever hiding places. There was also a ceiling littered with galaxies and stars over the science shelves. She had . . . unusual connections for a small-town librarian. She took the helm when she was quite young, and simply never left. And lucky for us. It was the prettiest building in the whole town. All roads seemed to lead to the library.

Beatrice skipped inside and waved brightly at the assistant librarian.

"Hello, Mr. Burrows!" she said far too loudly, but he didn't shush her. She fluttered her arms. "Do you like my wings? Today I am a—"

"Little girl," I said reflexively, and also with more volume than I had intended. "Today she is a little girl. Just as she is every day." I thought about my mother in her overalls, hauling Beatrice inside when she said something wrong. I grimaced, forcing the memory away.

Beatrice glared at me. Mr. Burrows gave a wan smile but uncurled smoothly to his feet. He was, most of the time, an unflappable young man.

"Everything about you is lovely, Beatrice," he said diplomatically. "Wings or no wings. And anyway, the library has some new materials in the arts and crafts room, and I have been anxious to give it a go." A clear lie, but I didn't say anything. "Perhaps we can make a pair of wings for your sister. Or for me. Can librarians have wings? Perhaps everyone should have wings."

"Alex doesn't need wings," Beatrice sidled over to Mr. Burrows and she took his hand. "She only walks. Like a *sucker.*" She shot me a hard look, but I could tell she was temporarily placated. She skipped to the back stairs.

I made my way to the stacks.

I had been working for well over two hours when Mrs. Gyzinska approached the desk where I sat slumped over a particularly vexing problem set.

Ever since my mother passed, and I started spending more and more time at the library, Mrs. Gyzinska made a point to come and sit with me. Sometimes offering a chat, but usually she would just sit for a good long time, without saying a thing, painstakingly addressing her paperwork or simply reading a book. I appreciated this. It sounds strange, but I appreciated not having to explain myself. I appreciated not having to talk, but also not being alone. Every once in a while, she'd walk with me out to the back garden and we would talk for a long time about mathematics or chemistry or Jane Austen. I enjoyed her company.

I never actually told Mrs. Gyzinska about our living situation. She certainly knew that I was in charge of Beatrice. She often inquired after the well-being of my father and my stepmother, and I always said, *"They're fine, thanks for asking,"* even though really I had no idea, and each time she pressed her lips together in a thin, tight line.

"Well," she'd always say. "At least they have their health."

Which was an odd thing to say. I never remarked on it. We just let it stay there, between us, untouched.

I didn't look up as she approached my desk. As usual, she said nothing. Mrs. Gyzinska was fastidiously true to the rule of silence in the stacks. She rapped her swollen knuckles on the old oak desk to catch my attention. She waved at me to follow her and then walked toward the back workroom. Despite the curve of her shoulders and the crick in her spine, despite the slight limp of her left leg, she still maintained a swift pace. I hurried to keep up.

Mrs. Gyzinska was very old (it was hard for me to say, really, how old she was) and had been a widow for most of her life. When she was young, she secured a scholarship to attend a prestigious university out east, where she eloped with the young scion of a prominent family (squarely against his parents' wishes). Old money, as they say—the kind of wealth that has its own weather system. And then her husband died young, not long after their wedding, and under embarrassing circumstances. I never found out what those circumstances were, exactly, only that the family used it as a way to prevent her from inheriting his portion of the family fortune. To keep her quiet, they offered her a small, but self-sustaining, fund to ensure a comfortable living, as well as a separate, much larger account to fund whatever organization she wished to attach herself to, knowing that philanthropy would open more, and grander, doors for their former daughter-in-law than a degree ever would. It was because of the deep pockets of this family—with no connection to my small town in Wisconsin whatsoever—that we had such a well-funded and excellent library system. Everyone in town knew this story, and everyone pretended it was a huge secret. Mrs. Gyzinska became head librarian and chief commissioner for the county system when she was only twenty-four years old, and maintained the library's excellence until the day she died.

In the workroom, Mrs. Gyzinska closed the door and told me to sit down at the long table that was usually used for sorting books or gluing split spines. She went to the corner and poured out two cups of very hot coffee. It burned my mouth, but I appreciated it all the same. She had books to show me, as she had made several purchases for the reference section. I began paging through them eagerly. Mrs. Gyzinska watched me as she slowly sipped her coffee. Her skin softly bunched around itself, like petals, and her eyes were small and bright and keen. She held a stack of envelopes on her lap. She held them up for me to see.

My stomach clenched a bit.

"I've taken the liberty," she said slowly, "of sending out for information in your name." She let the envelopes slip from her fingers onto the table, one by one, paper whispering against paper, like the sound of wind in the trees. I stared at the envelopes. "They are scholarship applications. You're a good candidate. Your sex will work against you, I'm afraid, because the world remains in its current state, but your accomplishments speak for themselves. I know every professor working in the correspondence program—if any one of them hesitates to write you a recommendation, leave him to me, and I will handle it. There are very few who do not owe me a great debt. May I suggest you call yourself Alex and simply . . . *forget* to check any box that might identify yourself as female, and let them figure it out."

"I would have done that anyway," I said. Ever since I started my correspondence classes, my professors knew me as Alex and not Alexandra. They sent me evaluations heaped with praise. To this day, I'm not sure some of them would have done so if they had sent it to Alexandra.

I forced myself to thumb through the envelopes, forced my face into a neutral expression, but all the while anxiety gripped my insides like a vise. My vision swam a bit and I could feel the back of my neck begin to sweat. What about Beatrice? How would I manage it? I didn't know, and I couldn't say it out loud. Mrs. Gyzinska seemed to hear me anyway. She shifted her weight in her chair, squeaking its legs against the floor. I cleared my throat and looked at the envelopes. I noticed that she had placed an envelope from her alma mater on the top. I imagined it must look like a castle, all covered with ivy.

I handed that one back to her.

"This one can't happen," I said flatly. "Even if I got in, there's no way."

Mrs. Gyzinska regarded me silently. She sipped her coffee. She didn't ask.

The silence held until I couldn't stand it anymore.

"I mean," I said. "I appreciate it. I really do. And I'm definitely going to school, it's just that . . ." My voice trailed off.

Mrs. Gyzinska set her cup on the table. Her face was mild and pleasant. She didn't look uncomfortable in the slightest.

I swallowed, and tried again. "It's so far away. And wherever I go, I have to bring Beatrice. So."

Another interminable silence.

"Beatrice won't live *here*," Mrs. Gyzinska said finally. "With your father. And your stepmother. That's what you're saying." She steepled her fingers and held them under her chin. "Her family is—"

"Me," I said. I looked at my hands. "It's me and Beatrice, together. That's what it will always be. My father is not interested in me going to college, and said so, so we will do it on our own steam. It's a tall order, but it's even taller at a rich kids' school. If you understand me. They don't have a lot of people in my situation. It's hard to imagine that they would understand, much less accommodate me."

Her expression flickered a bit, but then was as implacable as ever. "Well," she said, waving her hands casually, "I fear you may be right about that. No matter. In any case the letter of recommendation that I have already written for you will work just as well at the University of Wisconsin as it will anywhere else. I have considerable pull there too. The issue, of course, is how we can compel them to allow you to live in married and family housing, since, after all, you and Beatrice are a family unit, rather than having to navigate securing a place to stay in a city you do not know, and with limited resources. No one should have to do that on their own. Especially not a"—she pursed her lips—"a *mathematician*." She frowned. She would have preferred me to study philosophy, I think.

There was a sudden splashing outside. I looked out the window and saw Beatrice and Mr. Burrows mucking through the marsh in Wellingtons. Mr. Burrows held a rack full of test tubes, and Beatrice held a long syringe.

"Now, you see," I could hear him explain, "we have to be careful and thoughtful about exactly where we wish to draw our samples, that way we can—now Beatrice, that is the opposite of what I . . . Oh, heavens."

Mrs. Gyzinska rolled her eyes. "This is why I never had children," she said, shaking her head. Then she noticed me, checked herself, and patted my hand. "I don't have your skills," she added diplomatically.

I sighed. Rested my forehead on the heels of my hands. "I'm not sure I do either," I said. It was so much. It was so, so much.

I opened my textbook and started reading. I wasn't trying to be rude. I just had work to do. And precious little time to do it in. I tried to quiet the swirl of anxious thoughts tangling inside my head. The very notion of pausing the pursuit of my studies felt, to me, like the end of the world. Who was I, after all, without the clarity of mathematics? Who was I without theorems and equations and angles and variables? Who was I without careful measurements and reasoned analysis? I thought about my mother, about her cancer eating her from the inside. In my imagination, her tumor looked like a dragon. I imagined myself in armor like a knight. I imagined traveling into the depths of my mother's body—tracking it, finding it, engaging with it, and killing it. I underlined passages and made margin notes in my textbook with such force that I nearly split the paper.

Mrs. Gyzinska didn't move.

She sat there for a long time.

Beatrice continued to splash in the marsh with Mr. Burrows following fussily behind. She hooted with laughter.

Mrs. Gyzinska tilted her head to the left. "She's a wild one, your Beatrice," she said.

I didn't reply. What was there to say? Was she wild because I was bad at this? Maybe, but I didn't think so. Beatrice has always been herself.

"Tell me about her mother," Mrs. Gyzinska said gently.

My head snapped up. "Our mother is dead," I said. My words were quick and fast, like a slap.

Mrs. Gyzinska sat in silence for a moment. "I mean . . ." She paused. "I mean. Tell me about her *other* mother," she said, her voice barely above a whisper.

We didn't speak for a good long while. I became intensely aware of the whoosh of blood through my veins, and the ringing of my ears. With each breath, I felt the heat of my body begin to surge, until I worried I might burst into flames. I clenched my fists tight, and my nails dug into the heels of my hands until they bled.

How do we remember the moments when we fall apart? Time doesn't work the same when we become frightened or frustrated or enraged. Moments loop over themselves and split apart, like a knot fraying from the inside out. What happened in that moment is a tangle. I've spent years trying to unwind the thread of memory, and lay it flat, but it is an impossibility. What I do know is that my reaction to her question was swift, defiant, and utterly out-of-bounds. I remember raising my voice. I remember throwing a book against a notice-covered wall. I remember the smell of glue in my nose, and the sound that the legs of the wooden chair made as they screeched across the floorboards, and the smack of my hands on the table. I remember Mrs. Gyzinska with her hands folded in her lap, her head tilted slightly to the left, her softly rumpled face gazing at me in a look of mild curiosity, and without any anger in response—which just made me angrier. I remember stomping into the stacks and slamming the door behind me. I remember feeling ashamed of myself.

Indeed, it is the shame that I remember most.

As I raged and swore, as I swung my bag onto my back and stomped out of the workroom, I became suddenly flooded by memory. Memories of my mother. Memories of my aunt. They came thick and fast and sharp, like an assault. I remember thinking about the dinner table at my house—the uncomfortable adults, my aunt needling my mother about her skills and accomplishments and my mother shutting it down.

My mother didn't dragon—but could she have?

My aunt did dragon—but what if she hadn't? What if she had stayed, and Beatrice and I could have lived with her after my mother died, with her wide stance and wider smile? With her competent hands and keen observations?

And I was *angry*. I was *so angry*. At my mother. At her cancer. At my father. At his abandonment. And I was angry at my aunt. For leaving my mother. For leaving Beatrice. For leaving *me*. Because I needed her.

I scrambled up the stairs as Mrs. Gyzinska strode behind. She appeared calm and unhurried even as she moved swiftly and kept up. This made me mad as well.

"Beatrice has no mother," I said without turning around. "I have no mother. We only have each other."

That is not all I said. I know I said more than that. Hurtful things. Hateful things. I don't remember most of it. I remember that I called her a nosy old bag and a busybody and a snobby bore. I didn't think those things before, and I don't believe I even thought them then. I just said them to be mean. Even though Mrs. Gyzinska believed in me. Maybe she even loved me. My bag thumped against my hip. I needed to find Beatrice.

"I'm merely saying—" she began.

"There's nothing to say," I nearly spat. I strode through the library, looking for my sister.

"I just feel that it's worth mentioning," Mrs. Gyzinska soothed, keeping pace with me despite her age and the shortness of her legs.

"Beatrice!" I called. Loudly. Even though we were in the library.

"That some outreach could be possible. Do you understand what I'm saying? Your aunt, in whatever state she's in, could be—"

"Where is that girl?" I groaned to myself. People in the library looked up.

"You're going to need all the help you can get. In whatever . . . *form*. So it's worth . . ."

"*BEATRICE,*" I shouted. They weren't in the children's section. I looked out the window. They weren't outside anymore. I turned on my heel and hurried to the arts and crafts room.

Mrs. Gyzinska was *so old.* And yet. She kept trying to stand in front of me, cutting me off as I raced through the stacks. Mothers took their small children by the hand and got out of my way. "This is difficult to talk about, I grant you, given the ridiculous situation our culture puts us in. Suffice to say, though, there *are* researchers who are patiently, carefully, and, alas, secretly studying these sorts of situations. It isn't easy. Congress has been ardently investigating everyone these days. In any case, it is possible that options exist. Do you understand me? There is a precedent, Alex, a *precedent*. This is what I'm trying to tell you."

I ignored this and ran down the stairs and found Beatrice elbow-deep in fingerpaint. "Come on," I said. "We're going."

"But I just started!" Beatrice said, bringing her hands to her cheeks in dismay, leaving two large handprints on each cheek—one red and one blue.

"Wash up," I said curtly. I gave Mr. Burrows a hard look. "Can you please help?" Mr. Burrows, unflappable as always, guided Beatrice toward the sink.

"But!" she said, not even attempting to complete the sentence.

"Alex, will you please *listen*," Mrs. Gyzinska heaved behind me.

I didn't know why I was so angry. I thought about my aunt standing in her dragon-destroyed house. I thought about *how much* I had wanted her to appear in my mother's hospital room. Avenging her. Avenging us. An elemental force of rage and violence and righteous fury. My skin felt hot. My bones felt hot. The library was *too hot*.

"Get your things," I said to Beatrice.

Mrs. Gyzinska composed herself. She folded her hands and rested them calmly on her bulbous belly and took a long breath. Even her calm seemed to infuriate me.

"This is your library, Alex dear. It always was and it always will be. I apologize for making you upset. I do think, however, that you might be interested in reading some of this research. I have it available, if you wish to glance through it. It was suppressed, you see? Shut down by the same entity that funded it. I can put you in touch with some of the scientists doing this work if you are interested. But what you need to understand is that what happened in America was not the first of such events. This is a well-known phenomenon. And it is important to note *that they do not always stay gone.*"

"Who doesn't?" Beatrice said as she skipped over to Mrs. Gyzinska to give her a hug, as she always did.

"The dragons of course, darling."

I felt, suddenly, pinned in place. Without breath. Without time or motion—like a butterfly stuck to a board with a needle through its thorax. What is anger, anyway? What does anger do? My mother was not an angry person. Or at least I don't think she was. My aunt was so angry that it became too much for her own body. It destroyed her house and swallowed her husband and left a broken family behind. I didn't want that, but I didn't know what to do with my anger. I felt world shake, and I felt my skin burn, and I let out a volcano of words that rattled my teeth as they came out.

I don't remember what I said. Only that it was cruel. Only that it made poor Mr. Burrows go quite red and then say, *"Language!"* Only that it made Beatrice cry.

I grabbed Beatrice's hand and left the library.

She didn't speak to me the whole way home.

24.

Where did it come from, this anger? I wasn't raised to be an angry person.

And yet.

As I walked home, my anger didn't dissipate. It coiled inside me like a set spring, straining to release.

It was warm for early October, and the leaves were just starting to turn, splashes of candy red or deep gold shooting through the green. We walked by one house with a tree at the edge of its yard, heavy with apples, and a sign that said PLEASE PICK. We both ignored it, though we usually didn't. Beatrice wouldn't hold my hand. She walked a little bit ahead of me, her steps slow and stunned.

I waited for her to say something. Something accusatory. Something angry. Something reproachful. Anything at all. I remembered my mother's face when she came down hard on us for stepping out of line. I remembered my mother's face at the moment of the slap. When does fear become anger? When does anger become fear? Or were they the same?

"Beatrice?" I faltered. She quickened her steps. "Beatrice, I——"

Beatrice simply increased the distance between us. I didn't really know what I wanted to say, anyway, so I just let the matter drop. My anger didn't go away. It shifted and adjusted itself. It wound its way through my belly and spiraled around each of my bones.

We walked in silence the rest of the way home. Beatrice was a good girl. She kept her eyes on the ground. I did too, out of habit. And yet. I had to fight my gaze from inching upward, as though it was somehow magnetized to the sky.

Around midnight, long after Beatrice and I ate our dinner and I put her sullenly to bed, long after I heard the beginning of her nightlong snoring in the other room, I stood, slid my feet into my boots, hugged my coat onto my back, and stepped outside. I left a note for Beatrice on the entry table just in case. I locked the door behind me.

I'm ashamed to admit it wasn't the first time I'd gone out by myself at night, leaving Beatrice on her own. As young as she was. What if she woke up? What if there was an intruder? What was I thinking? If I had children now, I would never do this in a million years. But I was a teenager, and thoughtless in the way teenagers are thoughtless, and impulsive in the way teenagers are impulsive. And restless. Ever since the beginning of school my restlessness had increased—it felt itchy, somehow, as though my skin didn't fit right on my body anymore. The world was an uncomfortable piece of clothing with stiff fabric and harsh seams and an unrelenting tag. I wanted nothing more than to shrug the whole thing off, but replace it with *what,* I didn't entirely know.

I turned on Spencer Street and walked toward the river. The town-side riverfront back then was a mixture of abandoned industry and undeveloped lowland scrub that had been slated to become industry someday. It was a waiting place, and quiet. On the opposite bank was a broad cranberry bog, punctuated every once in a while by small stands of tangled willow trees. In the summertime, the bog rang with the full-throated voices of frogs singing their lust and hope and yearning in the dark. Now, though, the bog was quiet, save for the hiss of wind through the marsh grasses, and the groan of willow limbs in the unrelenting breeze.

The nuns told us to be careful down there. Never go to the river alone, they said. There were men there, after all, hiding in the shadows and squatting in the ditches. Winos. Vagrants. No-goodniks who couldn't find jobs due to bad skills or bad character. Beatniks with their un-American thoughts and lascivious devotion to poetry and chain-smoking and jazz (granted, no beatniks had actually been spotted in this part of Wisconsin in 1963, but everyone knew that if any ever *did* show up, one would likely find them by the river). But I loved being next to the river. I still do. The remains of the old paper mill, from before they moved it upstream, still stood, giant and hulking and covered with birds. There had been talk of converting it to a park, but the lovers of industry couldn't bear the thought of the river decoupled from masculine notions of productivity. Best to wait, they said. In case another captain of industry came along and wished to use that space. And so, it sat, existing solely as a haven for mink and foxes and dark clouds of crows. I hooked around the edge of the complex and walked out to the flood wall. It was usually empty. Every once in a while, I'd see a group of students from the University of Wisconsin taking water samples or soil samples, or gazing at the dark skies through their telescopes.

I walked along the flood wall to a place where a set of stairs led to the river. It looked like no one was there, which was a relief. I sat halfway down, leaning back on my elbows, and staring into the dark. The marsh and cranberry bog on the far bank were invisible. Even the river slid and rippled by in darkness. With the town lights behind me blocked by the hulking old factory, the night sky opened up, and the stars, one by one, asserted themselves.

It's dangerous by the river.

Girls aren't safe on their own.

And maybe they were right. Still, it felt good to be silent. And it felt good to be alone. And it felt good to be *uncontained,* the way a bird must feel when it realizes that the thing constraining it was nothing more than an eggshell—delicate and fragile, and just waiting to be cracked open.

I was angry, but not, I realized with a start, at Mrs. Gyzinska. So who *was* I angry at? I didn't even know where to begin.

Something moved in the bog on the other side of the river.

Something large in the tangle of birch. I couldn't see, but assumed it was likely a cow escaped from one of the farms not too far out of town, though it could be a deer or a moose. Whatever it was, it moved about in the muck with a lumbering gate and a heavy step. I leaned back on my elbows and looked up. It was cold, and getting colder, and the breeze bit my skin. But the stars shone sharp and clear above, an aggressive clarity. My embarrassment over my behavior that day settled on my chest like a heavy weight. I groaned, loudly.

"*Hush,*" a voice said, a ways off to my left. "You'll scare her."

I scrambled to my feet with a yelp.

"*Shhh,*" the voice said. I squinted in the dark. Not thirty feet away, a man sat on a small folding stool at a tiny desk—just a rectangle barely larger than his lap, on extendable legs. He held a device that looked a bit like a pair of binoculars, but larger and heavier—they needed to rest on a stand, which sat on the desk. He also had a steno pad open in front of him, and a small penlight. He looked through his strange binoculars. He took down notes. Again and again.

I wasn't exactly sure how to respond. Was I interrupting him or was he interrupting me? "I'm sorry?" I said at last.

He waved me away. "No need," he whispered. "I don't think she heard you."

I looked around. I didn't see anyone else. Of course, earlier I hadn't seen *him* either. "She?" I asked.

He pointed across the river. The birches swayed. I could still hear the sound of deep, wet footsteps in the muck. "Over there," he gestured. The moon was thin, but what light there was bounced off the water. The man was very old. He wore a thick sweater and what looked like a military coat. His warm cap was pulled down over his ears. "Isn't she beautiful?"

I squinted again. "I don't see anything," I said. "Is it some kind of animal?"

"No more than you or I," he murmured. He underlined whatever he was writing and then sat up straight, turned, and faced me. "My apologies," he said with a smile. "I'm being terribly rude. My name is Henry. Henry Gantz."

Why did I know that name? "Hello," I said, ignoring the itchy feeling at the back of my brain. "I'm Alex." I didn't tell him my last name.

His smile widened. "Ah! Of course! The orphan. I've heard of you. The librarians all speak so highly of you. All day long, they pepper me with stories about the bright girl with the brighter future." He paused a moment. "I assume they must be correct, but I would need data to verify their assertions."

"Oh," I said. "Thanks?"

"You're quite welcome." He smiled indulgently. "They've taken me in, your librarians, and your library, I suppose, and given me space for my research. I'm a bit of an orphan myself, but of the scientific variety. And a political orphan too, I suppose, but that is another tale."

I didn't know what any of that meant, but I bristled a bit at being called an orphan—though functionally, it was true enough. The word, I knew, originally meant "bereft," a fact I filed away after I learned it in school. And while that was an accurate enough word—I lost my mother, after all; my father was absent; I had an aunt who no longer existed; I had to do this alone; *bereft* basically summed it up—at least I had Beatrice. We had each other.

I shoved my hands into my pockets to warm them up. "I don't think *orphan* is a very nice word," I said primly.

If he heard me, he didn't act like it. "I also heard about your little outburst at the library today," he chuckled. "They're all talking about *that,* too."

Shame churned through my stomach. I was going to have to apologize to Mrs. Gyzinska. And to Mr. Burrows too, probably. But not for a bit. I decided to change the subject. "You work at the library?" I took a step closer, trying to get a clearer look at his face. I didn't recognize him. "I've never seen you there."

"Not exactly," he said, writing something down in his steno

pad. "And I'm not surprised you don't recognize me. I do my *work* at the library, if you understand me, thanks to the generosity of dear Mrs. Gyzinska. God bless that woman. The world doesn't deserve her. But I don't wander about in public very often. My work is best done with a low profile, you see, so my office is a bit out of the way. I have the run of the place after hours. But that isn't so bad for those of us who are curious for a living."

I stood there quietly for a long time. The man didn't notice me puzzling over his words. He looked through his contraption and took more notes. I wanted to look at what he was writing.

"So . . . you're a professor?" I asked.

"Once upon a time, I was," he said as he kept one eye pressed against the viewing lens of his device. "Back when people called me Doctor. Doesn't that sound nice? *Dr. Gantz.* Now they just call me old man." He wrote a word and underlined it with a firm stroke.

"You can probably still call yourself doctor," I said. "If it makes you happy. It seems like once a person becomes a doctor they must stay a doctor. Right?" Admittedly, I had no idea how it worked.

He ignored this. "Please. Keep your voice down. I don't want you to startle her." I looked back across the river. All this for a cow?

"What makes you think it's a she?" I asked. But then I felt silly saying so; every dairy farm I had ever seen was entirely female, with males only trucked in every once in a while when it was time to make them all mothers. Of course it was a *she*.

He turned the page and started writing again. "Well, that is an excellent question! Very astute! It's true they mostly are female, though, to be fair, not entirely—though that's a controversial take, and there isn't a lot of agreement on that point, thanks to the lack of scientific exchange and the strangulation of the community of ideas, but don't get me started on that!" He swallowed a laugh, as though this was an inside joke between the two of us. I had no idea what he was talking about. "To answer your question, I know this one is female because I've been watching her for the last several hours. Fascinating creature. Quite old. This sort of thing takes longer when they're old, which is true for pretty much everything, if I'm being honest, but you have many years before you have to learn about that. In any case, the slow pace is a gift, actually, and fantastic for my research. Lots of opportunity for observation."

He was an odd man. Off-putting. He seemed to be having a conversation with himself, and not really with me. I didn't want to be there anymore. "Well. Nice to meet you. I have to go." I gave a wave.

He looked up from his notes. "Oh, but must you so soon? If you stay, you can see her launch. It is amazing, watching them use their wings for the first time."

I blanched. *"Wings?"* I said. The river gurgled and the bog burped and the wind shook the grasses and the trees. I shivered. I heard a sigh coming from somewhere, but I couldn't tell where. Animal? Or just the breeze exhaling through the empty windows of the building behind us. "Oh. It's a bird over there? It was making such a racket, I thought for sure it must be a c—" I didn't want to say what I thought. Why would a cow be in the cranberry bog? I didn't want him to think I was silly. "So. A bird, you say." I wasn't making a particularly good impression.

He paused for a long moment, his mouth pursed slightly to the side. "Sure," he said. He wrote something down. "A *bird.*" His voice was flat. "Have a wonderful night." He turned back to his binoculars and began drawing without looking at the page. I turned and left without a word.

I shoved my hands in my pockets, sharply aware that our conversation had reached an abrupt, and awkward, end. I walked away in the dark.

Why did I know that name? *Gantz.* It wasn't particularly common. I racked my brain, thinking through classmates and teachers. Maybe the author of a textbook. Who else? And also, I wondered, why on earth would an old bird be using its wings for the first time?

I walked up the stairs toward Spencer Street. The moon hovered low over the trees, its thin light casting long shadows stretching across the ground. Dry leaves skittered along the pavement as I walked. I paused, looked up at the sky, and marveled at the stars, the darkness, the quiet of night, the thin moonlight, the wide expanse of bog. I saw the silhouette of wings rising above the birches and soaring upward—a dark shadow against the spangle of light. Using her wings for the first time. *Good girl,* I found myself thinking as I turned and walked toward home.

It wasn't until later that I realized it was the most enormous bird I had ever seen. I shook my head. *Probably just a trick of the light.*

25.

On April 15, 1947 (eight years prior to the Mass Dragoning), five academics and one librarian were summoned by congressional subpoena to testify before the House Un-American Activities Committee. Or, more specifically, they were summoned to testify before a subcommittee of a subcommittee of HUAC. Both the name of the subcommittee and the sub-subcommittee—as well as the names of the congresspeople who sat on each—were secret at the time, and are still unknown, and likely unknowable, lost in a sea of redactions. The testimony, too, remains sealed, despite the current efforts among historians and researchers to gain an understanding of the ways in which science was stifled and silenced in the years leading up to the Mass Dragoning and in the decade after.

The sub-subcommittee intended the hearings to be a quiet affair. The subpoenas themselves were given under seal, and the six individuals were subjected to a court-mandated gag order. This order was largely respected by the five academics. The librarian, on the other hand, fully ignored the order, and while the major news outlets avoided contacting her out of fear of being blacklisted, she cheerfully gave interviews with several underground newspapers dedicated to Socialism, racial justice, and sexual equality—*Cultura Proletaria, The Liberator, La Fuerza, The Daily Worker,* to name a few. She did this knowing that it could land her in prison for contempt of Congress, but also knowing that most members of Congress don't bother reading the underground presses anyway, and that her interviews would likely not even come to public consciousness until after she returned to her home in Wisconsin.

Following the closed-door testimony, four members of the sub-subcommittee expressed frustration that they were not provided with any information that could tie the group to "larger global efforts to upend our way of life," which was of course taken to mean Communism. One member said, off the record, "All I know is that we all just spent a lot of damn time learning nothing of consequence, except what it feels like to get your ass handed to you by a goddamned librarian." It is unknown, exactly, to what the representative is referring. Or to whom.

Of the six individuals interviewed, three were forced to plead the Fifth rather than give the names of their colleagues, and were sentenced to three to four years in prison. All five academics were removed from their university posts and blackballed in academia after that.

It was rumored that they all were hired in library jobs. At the same library.

As for the librarian, robust efforts by a particular Wisconsin senator to remove her from her job did not bear fruit: it turned out that the librarian in question was the single largest funder of her own library's system, and managed a high-yield endowment that would keep the organization not only flush with cash but wealthy enough that it regularly handed generous grants to other, more needy districts. She was, it seemed, untouchable. She faced no penalties and served no time. She simply returned to her library.

And if it was up to congressional norms and processes, her identity would never have been revealed. It is only thanks to the underground press (and her library's commitment to the cataloguing, preservation, storage, and access to those newspapers) that we know her name at all: Helen Gyzinska.

I did not know any of this at the time. Mrs. Gyzinska was not the sort of person who advertised all that she knew, nor did she tout the various causes of which she was a dynamic part. She simply did the work and didn't much fuss about it. I didn't know any of this until after she passed away.

How many underground scientists did she shelter? How many blacklisted academics did she secretly fund? As of this writing, her impact on the preservation and continuation of science, fostering connections between researchers around the world, compounding what was known and energizing the questions being asked, is still being unraveled and uncovered—the web of her influence was broad, and varied, and intricately complex.

It's not a bad way to live, actually.

26.

I stayed away from the library for a full week after my outburst. I was more irritable as a result. I missed the library so much. I scowled as I brought Beatrice to school and I snapped at a boy in calculus who complained about his grade on the quiz and I eviscerated a girl who told me I'd be prettier if I let my hair grow longer and I told my literature teacher to go sit on a tack. I'm not exactly sure why, but that's what got me sent to the main office.

I didn't mind, because I thought I'd see Sister Kevin. Instead I found a harried-looking woman at the desk with a button on her sweater that said VOLUNTEER.

"Hello," I said. "I was sent down for poor behavior. Is Sister Kevin here?"

The volunteer looked like she might cry. "No," she said. "Sister Kevin hasn't been seen in days. I'm sure she's, you know. Doing . . . whatever it is that nuns do. Feeding the poor or something. Just forgot to leave a note. Nothing to worry about. I do wish she had left some instructions, though. I don't know how anything works!"

I felt a twist of anxiety in my stomach. I liked Sister Kevin. "Is she okay?"

"Of course she's fine. You've met her. She's just . . . *flighty.*" She searched the desk drawers. "There is a form I'm supposed to fill out, I just know it. Why did no one leave me instructions?"

"Maybe you should ask the principal?" I said. We both turned to the closed door of the principal's office. Mr. Alphonse was in there, shouting at someone on the phone. The volunteer went pale. I grimaced.

"Or?" I offered. "I could . . . just go back to class?"

The woman nodded gratefully. "Yes, I do think that would be best. Whatever it is that you did, don't do it again!"

"I promise," I said.

With each day that passed, I regretted my behavior at the library more and more bitterly. I had a midterm exam coming up, and I had to take it in the audiovisual room, with Mrs. Gyzinska proctoring. She had to sign it when I was done, and stamp it with her university seal. I would eventually have to go back.

Each day my questions increased. *How did she know?* About my aunt. About my situation. About all of it. *How did she know?* And what did she mean about *precedents*?

I tried to force the thought away. There were no answers to my questions.

Each day, I studied and worked. I fed Beatrice and bathed Beatrice and helped her with her homework and read her a story and insisted on her consistent bedtime. I had papers to write and novels to analyze and a textbook to read and a problem set to finish and scientific theories to commit to memory. Each day we woke up and started over. No one was coming to help us. We were entirely on our own.

The following Saturday evening, I made rice and canned beans and sliced in hot dogs. I heated up some frozen spinach and mixed it with cream of mushroom soup. Beatrice would hate all of this, but food was food. And then I went out to find her.

In the alley, there was a large dumpster that the three apartment buildings shared. It was always full, and stinking. I called for Beatrice.

"Coming!" she yelled from far away.

There was a flyer taped to the dumpster.

YOU HAVE QUESTIONS, it said. WE HAVE ANSWERS. THE WYVERN RESEARCH COLLECTIVE. No pictures. No symbols. No phone number. It was getting annoying, actually. I pulled it off the dumpster and shoved it in my pocket.

Beatrice hollered her goodbyes to her friends and came striding around the corner, flushed and filthy. We looked at each other for a long moment, neither speaking. I hated this. I hated the strangeness between us.

"Dinner's on the stove," I said. I turned and walked toward the apartment. Beatrice followed. I wanted to say something. I didn't know what to say. We climbed the stairs in silence. I stood at our apartment door for longer than was entirely necessary. I couldn't quite force myself to go in. I didn't know why. Beatrice slid her hand into my own.

"Alex?" she said. Her voice was small. I hadn't told her about my worries, of course. She was just a little girl. And she deserved to be a little girl. I forced my face into a smile. I gave her hand a little squeeze.

"Are you angry at me?" Beatrice asked.

I walked into the apartment, shut the door, sat on the floor, and invited Beatrice onto my lap. She needed no other prompting. I curled my arms around her and held on tight. She was such a tiny thing—a cricket, practically. I imagined carrying her around in my pocket, and all at once the thought became too much to bear.

"I'm not angry," I said to her. "I'm never angry. I overreacted and made a fool of myself, that's all."

"Why?" she asked.

What could I say? I wanted to tell Beatrice the truth, but I didn't know where to begin. Maybe start with the fact my mother forced me to lie and lie and lie, and how we built our family on that lie, and eventually mostly believed in that lie. Beatrice was my sister. I had no aunt. We do not speak of dragons. My mother was gone, but her rules were *still here*. And, frankly, it felt comfortable to keep living with her rules. And safe.

"I don't know," I said, which was mostly accurate. "I love you," I added, which was entirely true.

Beatrice rested her head on my shoulder. We only had each other. There was no other family than this.

How hard can it be? my father had said.

Really hard was the answer. He had no idea.

Later that night, I allowed myself the freedom to lose myself in my work. It was a profoundly pleasant feeling—outside of time, outside of place, outside even of *myself.* Beatrice breathed in the other room and the faucet dripped and down the hall, two men shouted at each other, their voices muffled through the walls. None of that mattered. Each problem, each proof, was a universe unto itself—balanced, intricate, and whole. I finished each one with a rush of deep satisfaction. I could have worked all night and would have never gotten tired.

A knock on the door sent me sprawling back into the world, startling me like a slap on my face. I nearly yelped. I looked at the clock. Twelve-thirty. Was it that late so soon? And who on earth was knocking at my door at this hour?

My heart rattled and my skin pricked. My father had warned me about strange men, but he was also quick to point out that I wasn't as pretty as my mother, which meant, he explained, that I wouldn't have to worry quite so much. Still, he supplied me with a baseball bat and told me to keep it by the door, just in case. I didn't—Beatrice would have used it to break a window during a temper tantrum, I was pretty sure—but I did keep it on top of the refrigerator, and grabbed it now. I stood at the door, not unlocking it.

"Who is it?" I asked, gripping the bat, trying to feel tougher than I was.

"Mrs. Gyzinska," said the voice on the other side.

The room swam for a moment.

"I'm sorry?" I said.

"It's Mrs. Gyzinska," she said again. "Now open up and let me in. Your neighbor is staring at me through a crack in his door, and I'm sorry to say that I don't like the look of him. Perhaps someone should tell him no one likes a peeper." There was a silence, and then the sound of the closing and locking of a door somewhere in the hall. She wasn't wrong about Mr. Hanson. He was an odd one.

I still had my hand on the lock. I still hadn't opened it. "But," I began. I swallowed. "How on earth did you know where I lived?" Even the schools didn't know where we lived. All our mail went to my father's house.

"I'm a librarian," she said curtly. "This sort of thing goes with the job. Now, open up."

And I did.

My apartment, I should explain, was tiny. It had a main room that served most purposes, and a tiny bedroom at the back. The bedroom was hardly more than a closet—one small window, with just enough space for Beatrice's bed on one side and a long closet rod along the other side. We kept our dresser in the main room, which was eight paces, wall to wall, with a kitchenette along one side. A chrome table with two chairs occupied the center of the room, and the walls were lined with bookshelves, most of which I had made myself using cast-off lumber and old bricks that I had braced together with brackets I had fabricated in metal shop, when I was the only girl in metal shop.

I turned on the kettle, because that's what my mother would have done, and set out two teacups with bags of Lipton. My mother would have also put out sugar cubes and wedges of lemon, but I had none, and so we drank our tea with puckered lips instead. Mrs. Gyzinska hadn't spoken since she entered the room and neither had I. I hung her coat in silence and she sat at the table in silence and I made the tea in silence and we sat, facing each other, sipping in silence.

Finally:

"I am sorry, dear," she said. "About what happened last week. And I'm sorry for not coming sooner. I kept expecting you to return to the library. I apologize. I should have known to be more . . ." She thought for a long moment. Beatrice snored loudly in the other room, a gentle, undulating wave. "In my younger days, I knew how to tiptoe into a conversation. How to listen both to what is said and unsaid. It was a skill that once served me well, and I'm afraid I'm a bit rusty. My long career has allowed me to stomp rather than sashay, and it appears this time I stomped right into it." She folded her hands and rested her chin on her knuckles, peering at me intently. "I didn't want to upset you, Alex, I truly didn't. And it breaks my heart that I did."

And then we were silent again.

I looked down at my hands. The gas stove hissed and the kettle rattled.

"Listen. I haven't always been the feisty old lady who lives in a library, though I'm sure it must seem that way to you. I understand you, Alex, just a little bit, because I used to be a lot like you. I was only thirteen when my teacher told my immigrant parents that I needed to go to college, and so the parish priest took up a collection and off I went. I didn't know what I was in for, but I took that qualifying exam and I blew it to pieces, just like you will. There was absolutely no question that I *deserved* to be there and there was no question that I could outthink and outlast anyone who coasted in on their granddaddy's wealth." She scowled, apparently just thinking about the people she went to school with. "But I still needed someone to help me get there. One of the teachers at my Podunk school knew that world, and she knew it wouldn't be easy, because the doors to ivory towers don't open automatically to the daughters of poor farmers." She closed her eyes for a moment, taking in a long slow breath through her nose. "She knew the value of opportunity, and she wrestled that opportunity into submission and handed it over to me. I trusted her. My parents trusted her. I often think of what would have happened if we didn't." She took a sip of her tea. "I need you to trust me, Alex. I need you to *trust* me. And I know that's a lot to ask."

Beatrice, dreaming in the other room, sighed and snorted and rolled over. Her bed creaked. I craned my head and perked my ears and Mrs. Gyzinska watched me watching. Beatrice returned to her soft snoring, and I relaxed.

"Your situation, of course, is different. It's much trickier. You have a cousin who is your sister who is your child. I know that's not how you see it, but that is the fact."

I shook my head. "I have a sister. My mother is dead. My father does what he can."

Mrs. Gyzinska waved this away with a snort. "You have a mother who you almost lost when you were little, and who almost left again during the dragoning—oh, don't look so shocked. It's just biology. Are caterpillars disgusted by butterflies? No. Of course not. People's aversion to that whole business makes *no sense*. And obviously, I know all about what happened. I'm a librarian, for god's sake. It's my job to catalogue information. You lost your mother for good at possibly the worst time for anyone to lose their mother. It wasn't her fault, and she tried her best, but there it is, and you were left alone. And you have a father who has abdicated his responsibility to a *teenager,* which is the lowest thing a man can do. And the only reason why I haven't called social services—and trust me, I considered it—is because I couldn't bear to be the person who separates you and Beatrice. It is a real possibility, if they involved themselves, and it would be a true calamity. I won't let it happen."

I looked at my textbook. It was a library book, but Mrs. Gyzinska had allowed me to take it for the whole year. "I know you're good for it," she had said. "And anyway, I know where you live," she had added with a wink. I assumed at the time that she was talking about my father's house. How long had she known?

My thoughts swirled and tangled and then became incredibly still. What do you say in a situation like this? What's the response? My mother always knew what to say—she knew how to be unflappable and poised and precise always. I shook my head, utterly at a loss. I felt like the quiet remnants of a house after a tornado tore it to shreds and left it behind. I had no pieces to connect, nothing that made sense, no way to impose order on the chaos. But I needed to say *something.* "Would you like anything to eat?" I managed after a long moment.

Mrs. Gyzinska smiled. "No, dear. But thank you. There is a great deal more to discuss, but I won't overplay my hand just yet. I will bring up the issue of dragons again, so brace yourself—and yes, I know that it makes you uncomfortable, and maybe a little angry too. It's understandable, after all you've been through— but I want you to notice that your feelings are complicated by cultural factors that are, let's face it, a little ridiculous. There are people who have problems with women, and alas, many of them are also women. That is because of something called the patriarchy, which I'm sure they have *not* discussed in that school you go to, but that doesn't stop it from being an unnecessary and oppressive obstacle, and best disposed of as soon as possible. The point is this—I am working on your behalf. And on Beatrice's behalf. And I'm trying to find the solution to your continued education, which absolutely *must* be maintained, as well as the preservation of your family. And I think I may be onto something. I won't go into it now. Just know this: Things are afoot. We are on the brink of something big. And no one is talking about it on the news. But they will."

She patted my hands and stood.

I stood too.

"I—" My throat hurt. I tried to swallow but it felt like sand. "I just want . . ." My eyes were hot.

Mrs. Gyzinska refastened her hat and slid her arms into her nubby pink coat. "You don't have to say anything, dear. Just trust me."

I pressed my hands against my forehead to keep my thoughts from spinning. "I am sorry, though," I said. I couldn't look at her face. I looked at her shoes instead. They were brown and leather with neat laces and sturdy heels. "I . . . I don't get angry." I shook my head. "I don't usually get angry. But lately . . ." The words died there.

Mrs. Gyzinska gently cupped her hand against my cheek and tilted my face upward so I was forced to meet her eyes. They glittered strangely. "Anger is a funny thing. And it does funny things to us if we keep it inside. I encourage you to consider a question: Who benefits, my dear, when you force yourself to not feel angry?" She tilted her head and looked at me so hard I thought she could see right into my bones. She raised her eyebrows. "Clearly not you."

I blanched. I had never thought of it like that.

She glanced around the room. "Look at where you're living. Think of what you're being asked to do. You're not angry? Hell. I'm angry on your behalf. I'm going to be out of town for a bit—there are some people I need to see and some conversations I need to have. Mr. Burrows will proctor your exams while I'm gone. I have more to say on the subject, but you have school in the morning. You don't have anyone telling you it's time to go to bed, so I'm telling you right now. You need to take care of yourself. The world is changing, and it needs you to be well. Go to bed. Get some sleep. And start keeping your eyes *up*. The skies are full of promise. You are less alone than you think."

She gave my cheek a soft pat, and she turned and let herself out.

I stood in the center of the room for a long time. The clock ticked. The refrigerator rumbled. Somewhere deep in the building the pipes banged. I heard Mrs. Gyzinska's car door creak outside and I heard her car rumble away.

Then I did as I was told. I curled under my blanket and was asleep before I even lay down.

27.

Winter came early that year. On the morning of October eleventh, the sky dulled and the wind blew and snow fell in great heaps on the ground. Farmers scrambled, and crops were ruined. The cold settled deep into the ground and our boots squeaked across the compacted snow and grey ice. Beatrice and I stuffed old socks into the gaps around the windows, and I cooked endless pots of soup. We arrived at school each day wound in layer upon layer of scarves, our faces rigid against the cold.

I called my father to ask for extra money to replace Beatrice's coat and boots and snow pants, since she had finally outgrown her winter gear. Plus all our mittens that I had in our winter box in the storage area of our building had been attacked by moths. My father gave me my monthly allowance, of course, and we had enough for incidentals, but coats were expensive. So were boots.

I dialed the number. Unfortunately, my stepmother answered.

"Your father's not here," she said. A baby and a toddler screamed in the background. Siblings of mine that I had not yet met. As of this writing, I still have not met them. Some grievances are long.

"Oh," I said. "Is there a better time when I might reach him?" I had exchanged phone pleasantries with my stepmother only a handful of times. But I had learned that it didn't do much good to leave a message.

"It's hard to tell," she said. Her voice was flat. "Maybe you should leave your request with me."

I paused. I could barely remember what she looked like. She had once been a secretary. My father's secretary. I imagined a woman in a smart suit and her yellow hair in a tight chignon, with ink smudges on her fingers and high heels that clicked against the floor so you might always know if she was coming or going. I imagined smooth stockings and a pressed blouse and an expertly drawn curve on her brow accentuating the eye. I guessed she didn't look like that anymore. She lived in my mother's house and cooked in my mother's kitchen and likely dug up my mother's garden to plant something boring, like petunias or grass. I knew that she slept in my mother's bed. Other than that, I didn't know a single thing about her. I never thought it was strange until this very moment.

"Okay," I said. The baby's scream increased in pitch, and the toddler opened up its throat into a siren-like wail. I decided to talk fast. "Normally, when unexpected expenses crop up, I let Dad know, and he puts a little extra money in the mail."

"Oh. *Does he now,*" my stepmother said, her voice a quiet seethe. Something crashed in the background, but it didn't seem to faze her. I heard her draw in a long, slow breath, like a flat hiss.

I kept my own voice light. "Yes," I said. "Beatrice is wearing last year's coat and boots—actually two winters' ago—and they are absolutely too small. I'll need to buy new ones. I'm wondering if Dad can send the extra money to help with that."

Or maybe he can show up with it, I thought bitterly, *in person. Like he promised.*

"I'm not sure that will be possible," my stepmother said.

"Why not?" I asked.

"You know," she said, changing the subject. And then she paused, a sibilance marking the silence between us, like a breeze across a field of grain. "We have several boxes of your mother's old things. Clothes and coats and shoes. I can't wear any of them—she was no bigger than a child, after all. And her books too. So much . . ." Another pause. Another crackling, hissing sound. *"Math."* I could hear her look of disgust. "Why don't you come by this afternoon and pick them up?"

I held the phone to my ear for a moment or two. In that moment, I had completely forgotten about the money. "My mother's . . . old . . . things," I said, trying to make sense of it. "How many boxes?" I asked.

"Five or six. I'm assuming some of the boxes belong to you, as well. I haven't looked that closely. And perhaps also to your . . ." Another pause. "Your little friend."

"Beatrice," I prompted. "My sister?"

"Sure," she said.

So she knows too, I thought. *Of course she does. I wonder who else?*

My stepmother coughed. "I had attempted to bring the lot of it to the secondhand shop, but your father prevented this." Another whirring hiss. Was it her breath? I imagined her nostrils flaring. "He said that he thought it should go to you when you are more fully on your own. And no longer a burden to . . . others." Another hiss. I realized she was probably smoking a cigarette. My mother never smoked. My aunt did, but not all the time, and never in the house. She made the sound again, and I could hear the crackle in the center of it. The baby continued to cry. "Anyway, you need things, and it seems silly to buy things when we have things—for you—right here in the basement, and I need the room. So I'll just plan on seeing you this afternoon."

"Wait!" My mind raced. I thought about how long it would take to walk across town in the snow. And trudge back. I calculated a schedule and shook my head. How could I make any of this work? "But," I said. "How can I get everything back over here? Do you have a car?"

Another long hissing sound. "No," she said with a dull laugh. "Your father doesn't let me drive. It's unladylike, apparently. But your old sleds are in the basement as well. And we have rope. You're a smart girl. Mechanically inclined, I hear. Your teachers call all the time and tell me about it, so I'm sure you can figure out something."

I gasped. *"They do?"*

And she hung up.

I stood next to the phone for a long time, the hairs on the back of my neck standing up in alarm. My stepmother has been having conversations with my teachers. *What did she even say to them?*

⁓

Beatrice and I arrived a little after one. I had hoped my father would have returned by then. I'm not sure why. Maybe a part of me hoped that he would be a voice of reason, but why would I think such a thing? My father was not a reasonable man. We knocked on the door. Beatrice bounced on her toes.

"I remember this house!" she said.

"Do you?" I said absently. When I was a little girl and my mother disappeared, my aunt and my father simply didn't mention it. They hoped I would forget. And I didn't, obviously I didn't . . . but, to be truthful, sometimes I *did*. I went entire days without thinking about my mother. It's a fact that seems astonishing to me now—the older I get, the more I realize that I can't get through an hour without thinking of her at least once.

The door opened and my stepmother stood in the entryway. I expected her to be dressed impeccably, the way my mother always was. But no. Even though it was the afternoon, she was still in her robe—it was made of a shiny fabric with embroidered flowers and tied tightly around her middle. Seeing her standing up for the first time, I could see that she was tall—even taller than Auntie Marla was—and far more voluptuous. Her hair—a chemical blond—was pinned in rollers and fastened with a sheer scarf. She crossed her arms over her ample chest and stared down at Beatrice and me the way an ancient god would peer down from her mountaintop at misbehaving acolytes. She was pretty, too, despite the look of contempt pressed into her face.

Beatrice, despite her earlier enthusiasm, was suddenly shy. She slipped behind me and hung on to my coat.

"Is my father in?" I asked. It suddenly didn't feel safe for

Beatrice and me to walk into the house with this hostile woman all by ourselves. I hesitated.

"No," she said, turning her back to me and walking through the entryway. "Business trip."

"And the children? Our . . ." I didn't know what to call them. My brothers? My half brothers? I wasn't sure.

She didn't even glance back. "I took them to my mother's," she said. "I have no intention of you meeting them." I held on to Beatrice's hand.

The living room looked nothing like it did before. My mother's crocheted window sashes and table runners were gone, as were the pictures on the wall of the four of us pretending that we were a happy family. Gone, too, was the photograph of my mother's parents standing in front of their old farmhouse in their Sunday best. The furniture was different, and the walls had been covered in a patterned paper that I did not care for.

"Well," my stepmother said. "Let's have you get your things. I haven't got all day."

I told Beatrice to sit on the couch with the comic books she had brought with her, and made my way to the basement. It was mustier than I remembered. It looked as though no one had swept or aired it out in a long time. The boxes were heavy, but not overly large or awkward. Five in all. Each had my mother's name on them in my father's handwriting, each partially obscured by another marking pen's scribbles over it.

"This everything?" I asked.

"Yep," she said, not meeting my eye. "I hope you're not expecting me to help. My back can't take it."

"I wasn't," I said as kindly as I could. "I'm small like my mom, but I'm strong like her too."

"I'm not sure you should be angling to be like your mother," my stepmother snapped, and went back up the stairs, leaving me to haul boxes on my own. I saw our old sleds, each made of wood slats over metal runners. If I gave Beatrice the lighter one, we could make it home okay. I found a bottle of mineral oil and a rag and greased the metal to help it slide over the snow more easily. In my head, I made a quick plan for how the boxes would stack, and which knots I would use, and then got to work. I hauled the sleds outside, and then, one by one, brought box after box upstairs and lashed them onto the sleds.

I returned to the living room, my coat already on, my bag slung across my shoulders. Beatrice was absorbed in her comics. My stepmother sat across from her, reading a magazine. If Beatrice and I had not been sent away, if we had been allowed to be a family, maybe this is what it would have looked like. Both my stepmother and Beatrice turned the page in synchrony; they both tilted their heads to the left. I wondered if it could have worked. Perhaps Beatrice's cheerfulness would have eased my stepmother's anger. Perhaps a house full of children would have softened my father. Perhaps . . . but then my stepmother looked up, caught my eye, and the sharpness returned.

Perhaps not, I decided.

I realized with a sudden and inexplicable ache that this might be my last time in the house. My breath shook for a moment, and I did my best to calm it. I found myself, all of a sudden, crowded with memories. My mother in her coveralls. My mother in her embroidered dress. My mother playing cards with my aunt at the table, both tipping their heads back and laughing. My mother in the nude on the bed, my aunt rubbing oil into her wounds (two bite marks where her breasts had been; the shiny red remains of targeted burns; I know, obviously, that it wasn't a monster that gave her those wounds, but oh! Memory is a funny thing). My mother tottering inside, returning from the hospital. My mother unconscious and bleeding on the floor. This house was filled with my mother. And also—

I gasped.

My aunt.

The last time I saw her.

"Um," I began. "Is it okay if I go see my old room?"

She asked me to take her secret treasures. She asked me if I had a hiding spot.

My stepmother frowned. "Whatever for?"

My mother never knew.

I slid my hands into my pockets to keep myself from fidgeting. "Just to see it," I said. I tried to keep my face neutral. Blank. Just like my mother. I rocked back on my heels in what I hoped was a nonchalant sort of way.

My stepmother tucked her magazine under one arm. "Suit yourself," she said, walking out of the living room and toward the stairs. She kept talking without turning around. "Don't expect me to see you out. I'm going to take a bath. Saturdays are supposed to be for me, you know." As though all of this had been my idea. As though I was trading on her goodwill. She turned at the top of the stairs and closed the bathroom door behind her. I waited until I heard the taps turn on. I hurried upstairs. Beatrice didn't follow. I don't think she looked up from her comic book even once.

It didn't look anything like it used to, my room. The clouds my mother had painted were gone, as was the old advertisement poster declaring JOIN THE WAVES that my aunt had given me. Also gone was the soft lavender paint on the walls. Instead, the walls were white, nicked and smudged by the rough play of rambunctious boys, and toys were everywhere.

I opened the closet and knelt on the floor.

The loose panel was still loose. I reached in and pulled the contents out—several notebooks, a series of drawings, a hand-bound book of paintings that Sonja had given me long ago, and the dragonish booklet and bundle of letters that my aunt had given me. I didn't look at any of it. I didn't linger. I just stuffed the lot of it into my bag, replaced the panel, and hurried out.

My stepmother had already retreated into the bathroom, with the thundering taps. Beatrice looked up from her comic book.

"Does our room look the same?" she asked.

"No," I said.

She pinched her lips together. "Then I don't want to see it."

"You don't have to, Bea."

Beatrice looked around. Everything was dingier than it was before. And uglier. I never realized how much care my mother had put into the house, how much of *herself* was in every bit of it, but the loss of her in this space was palpable.

Beatrice and I walked home in the snow, pulling the weight of my mother's memories behind us.

[From The Daily Cardinal, November 19, 1963]

UNIVERSITY CLINIC RAIDED
BY FEDERAL AUTHORITIES

Administration officials at the University of Wisconsin, Madison, campus remained tight-lipped on Monday regarding the weekend raid of the Student Health Center. Witnesses report seeing several vans arrive on the street, as dozens of federal officers and a handful of state law enforcement agents entered the building early Saturday morning.

The clinic had been under fire of late for distributing information to students that was outside the purview of the clinic's mission statement, and had been cited by the state in recent years for various charges of indecency, vulgarity, unlicensed medical practice, and libel. The clinic fought each state action, and all have been either overturned by the courts or withdrawn. Saturday's action appears to be an escalation, as well as an apparent coordination of state and federal prosecutors.

Reporters requested comments from the representative of the governor's office, the state health department, the Dane County Sheriff's Department, and the regional offices of the FBI and the U.S. Marshals, and none have responded as of press time. The spokesman for the chief of the Madison Police Department, however, did issue the following statement: "Let this be a message to anyone else who wants to set up a temporary, illegal medical unit, these so-called 'clinics for the curious.' Stop what you're doing. We're onto you. And we're willing to prosecute every last one of you before you corrupt another unsuspecting young person."

28.

It took a long time, but slowly, I made my way through my mother's things. I ironed each dress, reshaped each hat, set the stockings outside. I soaked the gloves and hand washed each scarf. I spent hours each night examining my mother's knot-work, the mathematics of each twist and whorl, the logic under-pinning the progression of those concentric loops. The knotwork showed up in her hand-tied laces, in the complicated interwoven eyelet patterns that she had stitched in a decorative spray on the side of her skirts, or the devilishly intricate braiding that she did on her waistbands and belts. There was a meaning, I was sure, to my mother's obsession with knots, a sincere belief at the core of it. But for the life of me I couldn't figure out what it was.

I found her notebook with her diagrams and equations, and her stack of books with her scrawled annotations. Even then, my mother seemed to be gathering evidence to support a hypothesis that she never wrote down. I did not know her rationale. I did not know her point of view. My mother was as sphinxlike as ever. All I knew was that it was beautiful. All of it was so, so beauti-ful. Her loss was a chasm in my life, a hole in the universe where my mother should be.

Slowly, I either wrapped each piece in tissue paper and hung it at the back of the closet, or I set it out to be eventually sold. I found nearly enough winter gear in the boxes marked "Alex-andra," and what we still needed, I was able to buy from the proceeds of selling some of my mother's more elegant dresses at the local consignment shop.

We were fine for now. I couldn't think about how we would

manage in the future, which remained impossible to imagine or plan for. All we could do was leap.

My father's phone calls had all but ceased, and I didn't hear from him until late December. The only thing he gave us was our monthly allowance and silence. I was glad at first, but after a while, it just felt strange. I hadn't expected to miss him. I called my father's house more than a few times, but no one ever answered.

He called four days before Christmas. He could barely say hello, he was coughing so hard.

"Dad?" I said to the explosive hacking on the other end. "Is that you?"

"Of course it is," my father barked. "Who else do you have calling you on this phone that I pay for?" He coughed again. "Actually, that's not a bad question. Who *do* you have calling? I don't want you taking advantage of this situation to make terrible choices and humiliate your family."

"It's nice to hear from you too," I said drily. "Every time I call the house, no one answers. Is everything okay?" I tried to keep any hint of petulance out of my voice. I tried to hide the yawning need inside me, so enormous it threatened to swallow the whole earth. He'd told me I wouldn't be alone. He lied.

"What kind of question is that? Of *course* everything is okay. Why the hell wouldn't it be?" He made several loud swallowing sounds. I hoped it was water for his cough, but I knew it likely was not.

Beatrice played outside, building forts in the snow with the neighborhood children. She had homework to do and her grades were slipping, but I didn't have the heart to call her back in.

Finally I couldn't stand it anymore. "Do you have any plans for Christmas, Dad? Will we be seeing you?" I don't know why I even asked. We never saw him.

He ignored this question. "I ran into your math teacher at the club," he said, and I knew he meant "bar."

"Did you, now?" I said, my voice neutral. "Did he tell you I shouldn't even be in that class, and I'm just being used as free labor? Honestly, they should give me a salary."

"It's crass for young ladies to discuss money," my father said. "Your mother should have taught you that." He gave a humorless laugh that sounded more like a snort. "You've always been too sharp for your own good. Even when you were little. Your teacher informed me that he wrote you a recommendation to attend the university. Under duress, I'm assuming. You know how I feel about your continued education. Waste of time. Waste of resources. You're ready to be a productive citizen right now, do your part in this great American economy. Also, this is how girls land good husbands, and isn't that what you want? It's foolish to wait too long, and miss your chance. I don't know why you turn up your nose at that. Why you insist on getting above yourself. I told your mother not to fill your head with ridiculous notions, but she didn't like to listen either."

I bit my lower lip to keep myself from speaking. I took a long, slow breath through my nose. "Well, what a nice chat this has been. Anything else, Dad? Or maybe I should call you Mr. Green."

"*Cheeky,*" my father said, his voice drowned by another wave of coughing. I waited a long time for it to pass. Finally, "I can't make you change your mind, I'm assuming."

"About school, Dad? No." I had already submitted my applications. I had already applied for scholarships. All I could do now was wait. "Turns out, I love mathematics more than marriage." *Just like Mom,* I wanted to add. But I didn't.

My dad coughed again. "That librarian stopped by. At my *office* and everything. I never did like her."

"Mrs. Gyzinska?"

"I suppose that's her name. She has a tendency to stick her nose where it isn't wanted. She always has. The first time your mother got sick, that insufferable woman showed up at the hospital and henpecked and harangued the nurses until they let her sit in the room every day, where she filled your poor mother's head with nonsense. After a while, the nurses called me to complain that your mother wouldn't stop reciting poetry, all thanks to that damn librarian. I had to call the administrator and he put a stop to it."

"Poetry?" I asked. The room swam. I leaned against the wall. *"The woods decay,"* I recited. *"The woods decay and fall."*

"She's gotten to you too, I see."

I could see my mother's face in my mind's eye, morphing from phase to phase. My mother before her illness, all rosy cheeks and smiles. My mother when she came home *wrong*. My mother sunburned and strong in the garden. My mother with her face twisted with anger, and that hard, sharp slap. My mother with grey clouds in her eyes and caves in her cheeks. My mother shrinking, hollowing out. The husk of a cricket, blowing away.

I recited:

Coldly thy rosy shadows bathe me, cold
Are all thy lights, and cold my wrinkled feet,
Upon thy glimmering thresholds, when the steam
Floats up from those dim fields about the homes
Of happy men that have the power to die,
And grassy barrows of the happier dead.
Release me, and restore me to the ground.

"I hate that poem," my father said.

"Mom loved it," I said. I closed my eyes. "She asked me to recite it too. In the hospital, before she died. Every day, over and over and over again."

I would never have admitted this to him—not at the time, and not ever—but I agreed with my father. I hated that poem too.

My dad was quiet for a long time. "Well, that was her all over." Another swallow. Then another. "I'm calling because, contrary to what you likely believe, Alexandra, I do care about you.

The whole country is starting to lose its mind. Protests at lunch counters and schools and chaos at the capitol and union goons mucking up profitable businesses and riots at those bars for . . . you know . . . *those* fellows, and nice young girls getting it in their heads to start doing whatever the hell they want without a thought to their families or their futures. And other things. Worse things. Things I can't even talk about, and you shouldn't either. Our country is in danger of losing its head. The crazies are here now, in this town, *our town,* with their flyers and their underground meetings and secret societies. And then marches, and riots, and total chaos. It's happening now. And you need to protect yourself."

"Dad, are you hearing yourself? This is insanity. This hasn't been a single march anywhere near here. Not one. I would have seen it. Or riots. Whoever is telling you these things has no idea—"

"Look," he said. His voice became sharp and desperate. "Some ideas are dangerous, okay? And some notions upend people's lives. Families get ruined. We tried to keep it all away from you, your mother and I. We agreed that innocence is safer. I wish you had found yourself a nice man and were engaged already. It would be a huge relief, frankly, if I knew you were well in hand. I told your mother she should be molding you more appropriately for matrimony, but she never listened to me. I thought running a household would be good for you. Keep your eyes on the ground and give you some practice for a good, solid future. But no, you had that librarian filling your head with mathematics and college and other horseshit. And now here we are."

I felt dizzy. I sank onto my heels and the phone cord pulled tight. "I'm not sure what you expect me to do."

He sighed. "Don't go out after dark," he said. "And stay away from that library lady. She has a history that you can't even fathom. I hear even J. Edgar Hoover is scared of her."

"No one is afraid of little old ladies, Dad. Don't be absurd."

"You're so naïve. Listen to your father. Listen to your teachers. Don't talk to strangers. I won't always be here to protect you, you know."

I bit my lip. He wasn't protecting us. Did he know he was lying, or did he think I wouldn't notice? I wasn't sure it mattered either way. Still, he was paying for our apartment until August, and the groceries still came every Saturday and I had my allowance arriving like clockwork at the bank, and I wasn't about to gamble with that money. "Okay, Dad," I said.

"I'm glad we had this talk, Alexandra."

"It's Alex," I said. And I hung up.

Could they come back? From a scientific perspective, the answer is obvious. It is not unusual for an organism to return to the ground of its making, as is the case for the northwestern salmon, or to the place of its transformation, as is the case for the horned toad. Why should it not be so with dragons? That we have not seen a mass return of the mass dragoned gives us no indication as to whether we will. Indeed, it is from folklore, and its oblique—and often fearful—relitigating of the stories of its dragoned daughters from long ago, that we can glean that sometimes they certainly did return. Were the battling dragons in the deep reaches of Uther's castle merely a misinterpretation of a couple of bickering aunts? I tend to think that perhaps they were. Was the dragon Vishap, living for decades on the top of Mount Ararat with her brood of children (both dragon and human), merely a kindly mother and foster mother, making a home for her heart's beloveds? It is difficult to say. But as I conclude this paper, I must offer a note of caution to my colleagues, to my superiors, to the United States Congress, and to my country: It serves no one to close our eyes and stop our thinking. There is so much that we do not yet understand, and there is a great deal of work to do. When faced with the collective trauma and grief and fear that gripped this nation as we watched thousands of women step out of their very skins and transform into creatures of tooth and claw, of heat and violence, there was an inexorable pressure to simply look away and refuse to speak of what happened and forget. Forgetting was frankly easier. But without questions, there can be no knowledge. What does the river do when the salmon returns? Does it dam itself up and bar any entrance? What does the tree do when the butterfly returns to the leaf where it once was egg, once was larva, once was chrysalis? Does it quake in fear, or does it welcome its wanderer with open arms? So what should a town do when the mother who once escaped into the sky, in a scream of rage and fire, decides to return? What should this nation do if they all come home?

—"A Brief History of Dragons" by Professor H. N. Gantz, MD, PhD

29.

The morning of March 23, 1964, began like any other day: with Beatrice pouncing on my bed wrestling me awake until we both fell on the floor.

"You're late! You're late! You're late!" she sang. Loudly. I held my finger up to my lips to remind her that we needed to keep it down. It was only five in the morning, and the walls of our apartment were thin.

"Late for what?" I yawned.

"The day!" Beatrice crowed. "You're late for the day!" She spun about the room.

I rubbed my face. Five was as good a time to start as any. I wasn't done with two of my problem sets, and I needed to mail them in by Friday.

"Fine," I said. "Put your uniform on and wash your face. I'll make breakfast."

After eggs and toast and instant coffee for me, I slipped an art smock over her school uniform and set her to work at her art table while I completed my physics homework.

Outside, a siren sounded. I made myself a third cup of coffee and finished my work and affixed stamps to the envelope and readied myself for school.

Beatrice pressed her face against the window. The sky was red and gold. "Today's the day!" she called to the world. "Today's the day!"

"What are you even talking about," I said absently as I hunted for a clean pair of socks. Beatrice wouldn't say.

Outside, the claws of winter were only just starting to recede. Snow piles, once looming along each sidewalk like trembling mountain passes on the brink of avalanche, were now collapsing into great dark puddles that pooled on every street. We all wore heavy galoshes to and from school, slipping into flats as soon as we arrived. I walked my bicycle as Beatrice skipped to school. "Today's the day! Today's the day!" she sang at the top of her lungs.

I was starting to get annoyed. We arrived at her school. I crouched down to rebuckle her boots and resnap the barrettes securing her hair above each temple. This was a futile gesture. She would be a rat's nest by noon.

"I'm so happy." She hugged me tight. "I love you so much, Alex. What a good day it is!" She lifted her face to the sky, then skipped up the stairs and went into the building without looking back.

"Weirdo," I said, smiling in spite of myself and feeling my breath suddenly catch. I loved her *so much*. And every once in a while, the immediacy of that love would catch me off guard and knock me flat. Whatever happened when I graduated, I told myself, it was me and Beatrice. Me and Beatrice against the world.

I swung my leg over my bike and kicked it forward, skimming across the wide, dark puddles, leaving long, smooth tidal waves in my wake.

⁂

Once at school, we all found our way to our classrooms, and the PA system made the same announcement that it had made every single day for the last month. *"Any . . . erm . . . unusual sightings or rumors need to be reported to the authorities immediately."* None of us took it seriously. It was, to us, like the grim warnings about possible Russian spies or the advertisements for prefabricated fallout shelters or the occasional air raid drill. We were old enough to know that the posters warning of reefer madness were fully bogus and that there were plenty of girls who went parking with boys in cars and still maintained their grade-point averages and their status in school. There were a lot of falsehoods in this world, and it seemed a large percentage of them were posted in hallways and announced on the school's PA system. I tuned them out.

Sister Leonie, my French teacher, smacked her desk with a textbook, exhorting us in French to pay attention.

"*Oui, ma soeur,*" we said meekly.

There was another announcement in the middle of third period. I didn't listen to it. My bra itched and my back hurt. I wasn't sure why.

The bell rang and I went to calculus. Mr. Reynolds grimaced when I walked through the door. "You're late!" he said. But I wasn't. That's just how he greeted me most days. What he meant to say was "I needed your assistance at some point earlier, and you failed to materialize."

I was about to respond, but the bell started to ring and did not stop. Air raid drill. Mr. Reynolds nearly jumped, his expression transforming quickly from alarm to exasperation. "Well for crying out—" He threw a notebook onto his desk with frustration. "We just had one of those." He glared at me, as though it was somehow my fault. "These boys need to get ready for their state exam. My reputation's on the line."

What reputation? I thought waspishly. I opened the door and saw students filing into the hall.

"You know what to do," the teachers called out, as everyone sat on the floor with the wall at their backs and a book clutched above their heads. Mr. Reynolds directed the boys in my class to do the same. I didn't sit down. There was something about this drill that didn't seem right. Suddenly, I became acutely aware of the distance between Beatrice and me. I tried to ignore the twist of anxiety in my gut.

"Well?" Mr. Reynolds said, motioning to the floor.

"I'm sorry, sir. This will only take a minute," I said. I showed him my empty hands. "Forgot my book." I dashed back into the classroom and looked out the window.

There weren't any fire trucks parked in front, but I could hear the sirens coming from far away. Which was odd. Usually it was the firefighters who would arrive early and set the alarm in the first place, and then pace the hallways, giving kids tips on the best ways to use a biology textbook to protect a human skull from nuclear annihilation. They mostly were able to do this with a straight face. In any case, it was a planned event. This didn't look planned. If the firefighters weren't administering the air raid protocol, who was? Was this an actual air raid? I certainly hadn't heard any planes.

The fire truck finally arrived, followed by a second, and they screeched to a halt. The firemen poured out, but they didn't come inside. Instead they crowded on the sidewalk, shoulder to burly shoulder, and looked up at the top of the building. One man pointed. Their mouths were open.

"Alexandra!" my teacher shouted.

"In a minute!" I called back, but I didn't move. The firefighters fixed their gaze a couple stories above the window where I peered out. And then their faces tilted in unison up and up and up, and then began to trace a slow arc over their heads. It took a moment for whatever they were looking at to reach the angle of my vision, and even then I couldn't really see it clearly. Something large. And flying. Whatever it was, its surface reflected the sunlight so brightly that I had to squint and I couldn't watch it head-on, I could only catch its shape through the corner of my eye. It flew too low for a plane. And anyway, it had been on the top of the school. Hadn't it?

The firefighters gave the all-clear and the bell rang and everyone stood and filed back into the classrooms. I didn't move from the window.

"Alexandra?" my teacher said.

I watched as the firefighters climbed back into their truck.

"Alexandra, I think you were about to hand back the tests?"

More sirens sounded. The truck tore off toward the west. Two police cars squealed around the corner and followed it, their lights flashing.

"Alexandra, are you listening to me? These students have questions about their tests."

They told us to be good children. I had always been a good child. I always did as I was told. But now . . . I turned and faced the classroom. The boys in my class all stared at me, a look of bewilderment on their dull faces. My teacher held the instructor's manual as though it was a life preserver. He gestured to the stack of exams on the desk.

"Well?" he said.

Once, when I was very small, my mom taught me how to set my face. How to erase the mad or the sad or the disappointed. "Not too eager, not too happy, not too anything. Just pleasant. And unflappable. You can get a world of work done with a pleasant face. Nobody interrupts and nobody gets offended. Like this, darling." And she showed me.

I set my face. "Of course, Mr. Reynolds," I said smoothly, even though I wanted to light him on fire. "Don't worry about a thing." And I passed out the tests. The boys who liked their scores tried to smile at me. The boys whose scores were embarrassing tried to assuage themselves by embarrassing me with more side comments and crass remarks. Didn't matter. Didn't work. My face was set. After the last test landed on the last desk, I walked to the board and wrote out the three problems that literally every boy in class got wrong. They weren't particularly hard. Just tricky. I knew Mr. Reynolds couldn't do them without consulting the manual.

"Mr. Reynolds," I said sweetly, "I'll leave you to it, if you don't mind, and I'd appreciate it if you would write me a hall pass. I believe I need to go to the nurse's office."

I didn't, actually. I was perfectly fine. But his combined discomfort was worth the lie. He opened his mouth without speaking, and then closed it again, clearing his throat. He tried again.

"Are you sure?" he said.

"Quite sure," I said. I lowered my voice. "Lady reasons," I said. The color drained from his face. He looked as though he was about to pass out. My face remained stubbornly neutral, as though it was carved from the side of a mountain. Was I the immovable object, or was I the unstoppable force? Perhaps I was both. Perhaps this is what we learn from our mothers.

"Just one moment," Mr. Reynolds said.

It didn't take much to convince the nurse I was sick and had to go home. I didn't even have to finish my sentence.

"Oh, of course you're sick! Just look at you! So pale! So wan!" the nurse wailed. "And the dark circles under your eyes. You poor sweet thing!" I must admit this stung a bit. Still, I hadn't gotten a decent night's sleep in months. I nodded weakly, and pretended to call my dad on the phone, and told her I'd wait outside for him to pick me up. "A touch of sun on my complexion . . ." I began. That's all I had to say. She shooed me out and told me that a bit of foundation and rouge would work wonders and that I didn't have to worry about getting in trouble because it would be our little secret. I thanked her and hurried outside, where I grabbed my bike and started down the road, in the same direction that—

Well, I wasn't entirely sure. But I knew that *something* had been on the roof and *something* had launched itself into the air and arced across the sky and *something* had those firefighters scratching their heads. I wasn't going to think *dragon*. I wasn't going to think anything. I was already thinking of myself as a scientist. There can be no assumptions in science: only questions, data, and more questions. I would have an open mind and an unbiased demeanor and would simply record observations and remain obedient to the facts. I pedaled my bike as fast as I could go, following the data.

30.

I caught sight of the object on Sycamore Street and followed it across the park and down Seventh Avenue until it landed first on the roof of a house, and then settling in the front yard. A house on Chestnut. My old street.

My old house. I had planned to never go back.

And yet, there I was.

And yet, there she was.

A dragon.

She sat in the front yard on her bottom, her tail curled around her body like a scarf, as she rummaged through her purse.

I slid off my bike and let it drop on the ground.

She, the dragon, well. She was . . . *enormous.* But the word *enormous* doesn't even come close to clarifying the *experience* of being near that dragon, or the *feeling* of her enormity. She bent the air around her. The ground beneath my feet seemed to wobble. Waves of heat poured off her skin, making what was left of the snow piles dissolve into the waterlogged grass. She had sat on one of the Adirondack chairs, though it couldn't sustain her weight. Shards of blue painted wood scattered under her wide rump and winding tail. Her scales were black and green and shot through with silver. It was not so much that she shone, but rather, that she seemed to own the light, allowing it to shimmer and vibrate on the scintillating scales skimming her bulk as she saw fit.

She lowered her head. Cocked her chin slightly to the left. Held my gaze.

And she was my aunt. I knew it before she even opened her mouth. I knew it even as I heard the air raid drill at school and the ridiculous announcement on the PA system. I knew it even as I saw her massive shadow streaking away as she soared unseen overhead. I knew that she was the one who haunted Beatrice's dreams. Of course it was my aunt.

I cleared my throat. The dragon nodded. She let her purse fall to the ground. She pressed her forepaws to her heart.

"Alex," my aunt began. Her voice caught. Her large eyes became bright with tears.

I didn't know dragons could talk. I didn't know they remembered who they were. I didn't know they carried purses and recognized family members or could cry. I clenched my teeth, feeling my cheeks get hot. If all that was true, *where the hell had she been all this time?*

"Alex," Auntie Marla said, wiping her cheeks. An attempt at a sharp-toothed smile. "Honey, it's me."

My head swam. "You're too late," I said, and gasped. I had not anticipated those words, nor was I even aware of myself thinking or feeling such a thing. I felt myself start to shake, and felt the pricking sensation of unshed tears of grief and loss and frustration erupting in my eyes. My vision blurred. My anger heated me down to my bones.

"Your mother?" she faltered. Her large, dragony eyes partially closed. She interlaced her talons together as though in prayer.

"Dead," I said through my teeth.

The dragon sank her face into her paws, her talons pressing against her skull. She began to sob. Her tears exploded in puffs of steam the moment they hit the ground. Her body shook, and the ground vibrated through my feet. "When?" she asked without looking up.

"Long time." I almost spat it. "It'll be three years in June."

"I should have known," the dragon whimpered. "I should have felt it."

"I agree," I said, my voice all barbs and venom.

If that dragon was hoping for sympathy, she was crying in

front of the wrong teenager. I reached down into the gravel border along the sidewalk and grabbed a good-sized rock. I chucked it at the dragon's belly. It bounced off. She didn't seem to notice.

"You left us!" I shouted at her. "You left my mother alone. You left all of us alone. You abandoned us, and for what?" My voice cracked, and I'm sure the neighbors could hear, but I decided not to care.

"She should have come with us." My aunt's dragon tears continued to stream, great boiling buckets from her elongated eyes that splattered on the walkway. Steam clouded the yard, massing into a thick, white cloud, offering us a modicum of privacy. "Maybe she would have lived. When I saw it was just you and Beatrice in that little apartment, I hoped . . . *well*. I hoped that she had followed us later."

"She *never* would have left Beatrice and me alone. *Never*. Not in a thousand lifetimes. She loved us and cared for both of us. She hung on to every single day. My mother was more mother to my sister than you ever were. She was the only mother Beatrice ever knew."

My aunt shifted her body, resting on her back haunches and uncurling her spine toward the sky. The undersides of her wings were red. Her needle-sharp teeth shone like gold. "That isn't true," she said. Her long eyes looked at me closely. I felt as though they could see all the way inside. "You've been her mother as well. I can smell her all over you. You have held her and fed her and loved her. Taught her right from wrong. Washed her hands and read her stories. Haven't you? She's yours, and you are hers."

"Beatrice is my sister," I said automatically.

"Poppycock," my aunt said. "You may not be her mother. But you're her *mother*. That's just the fact."

Sirens approached. They were getting closer. I looked behind me and saw a pair of eyes peeking around the edge of the curtain in one of the neighbors' houses, squinting through the low cloud. Mrs. Knightly, if I remembered right. I never did like her.

"I must fly," my aunt said. "I'll be back. Tell Beatrice I'm coming." She brought a taloned paw to a treacherous mouth and blew me a kiss. And then she launched into the sky, causing such a quake in the sidewalk I nearly lost my balance.

"DON'T BOTHER," I yelled. "WE DON'T NEED YOU. WE DON'T WANT TO SEE YOUR FACE. WE ARE FINE ON OUR OWN."

"WE'LL SEE," my aunt yelled back as she skimmed over the tops of the trees. Her scales glinted and shimmered and shone. And then she was gone.

I sat on my father's front steps for a long time. I knocked on the door and rang the bell. No one answered. The curtains were drawn. And the house seemed—sterile, somehow. Or not sterile, exactly—but in stasis. The house didn't seem to breathe. No toys in the yard. No pictures taped in the windows. Nothing to indicate that children lived there.

I didn't particularly want to talk to my stepmother. But I did find myself wanting to talk to *someone.*

Across the street, Mrs. Knightly continued to peek around the edge of her curtains. She was the lady who tattled on me if my knee socks were down and tattled on me if she saw me wipe my nose with the back of my hand and tattled on me when she saw me push a neighbor boy down after he made fun of Beatrice. I wasn't sure of her opinion on dragons, but I certainly knew her opinion of me. It wouldn't take long for her to phone my father at work. It wouldn't take long for him to arrive.

Ten minutes, as it turned out.

He stopped on the walkway and dropped his briefcase on the ground.

I hadn't seen him since that day we moved into the apartment. He seemed . . . it was hard to say. He was like a drawing that was partially erased. The lines of his body were smudged and faded. His hair was almost gone—had he been balding before? I couldn't remember. His face was grey.

"Alexandra," he said. His voice was fading too.

"It's Alex," I said. "Did you know—"

"When did you realize it was her?"

"Just now. She was sitting right there." I pointed to the broken chair. "I saw something flying over the houses and I followed it here."

He frowned. "You must not have seen the paper. There was a photograph. Of Marla. A week ago. They published a retraction and an apology the next day. Called it a hoax, which of course was nonsense. I knew her instantly. I don't know how. It was blurry and distant, but there she was." His gaze slid over to the broken remains of the chair and the spongy grass in a crater of melting snow. "So she came here, did she?" I nodded. He nodded back. "Makes sense. She liked it better here than her own sad house."

We didn't say anything for a long minute. His chin sagged into his neck. His lips were dry. I remembered him looking much bigger than this. Did he shrink? Even his shoulders could barely maintain the weight of his wrinkled shirt. He cleared his throat.

"Would you like to come in?"

I didn't answer, but rose to my feet. He unlocked the door and let me inside.

It was a mess. Much worse than when I was there in October. Dust clung to every surface, and grime insinuated itself into the cracks. The air was stale, and musty, and the trash needed to be taken out. Much of the furniture was gone, too. The walls were almost entirely bare, with only bare nails and dusty rectangles to show where framed pictures had been.

"Your new wife?" I said.

"Gone," he said. "And the kids. They live at her mother's. It's for the best."

"I see," I said. I didn't ask how long ago. He could have told us to move back home, but he didn't. Instead he was paying for his house and an extra apartment and probably his wife's upkeep as well. I tried not to let it hurt me. I took a deep breath and set my face. He wouldn't see me upset.

"Beer?" my father asked, as though I were a man.

I blanched. "I don't drink, Dad," I said.

"Good," he said. "I'll have something stronger." He waved for me to sit down at the table—it was sticky and covered with bits of paper—and he came back with a tall glass of scotch and nothing for me. There were cobwebs in the corners. The windows were thick with grime. Some husbands were devoured on the day of the Mass Dragoning. Others, like my father, simply languished. I slid my eyes toward the door.

"Have you given any more thought about that job I mentioned?" he said, reaching into his pocket and finding his pack of cigarettes.

"I told you, Dad. I'm going to college."

His laugh sounded like the bray of a donkey. "With what money?" he said, his first puff leaking out of his mouth.

"I'll figure it out." I crossed my arms across my chest and pressed my back into the chair. "Anyway, that's not why we're talking. My aunt is back. And she's a dragon."

"*Alexandra!*" My father held up his hands, and he cast his gaze aside, suddenly too embarrassed to look me in the eye. "That's none of my business." He flushed scarlet.

"Yes it is," I insisted. "Whether you like it or not, you're Beatrice's legal father. And mine too, obviously. And that dragon is hanging around. And says she'll be back. Doesn't that bother you? What if we got hurt? Or worse?"

I didn't say out loud what I meant by *worse*. I thought about Beatrice's drawings. The dragons everywhere. My father would say nothing if Beatrice . . . *changed*. If she took to the sky and never came back. *But my world would end.* I closed my eyes for a moment, doing everything in my power to keep from crying.

"Well. I'd be sad, obviously." He took another sip of scotch.

"You are, you know. Important." Another sip. "You may not believe me, but I do care about you, Alexandra. And your little, um, Beatrice." He set down his glass. He didn't look at me.

We sat for a long moment, saying nothing.

I rolled my eyes. "Well, Dad. This was fun. Maybe we should see each other again in a few years." I stood. He put his hand on my hand. He turned his body away and rested his forehead on his other palm, cupping his face. It took me a while to realize he was crying.

"The wrong sister left," he said, finally, wiping his eyes. "It should have been your mother. I told her that myself. That very day. She knew it was coming, and told me so. She could feel it. We both knew it was only a matter of time before her cancer came back, and maybe it wouldn't have, if she let herself change. I told her to tell Marla to do the right thing—that she should be the one to be the grown-up, and resist the childish urge to run away. Or fly away, rather. She should have stayed. Marla could have raised both of you and my Bertha—" His breath caught. "She could have—" He shook his head. "Well, she probably would have kicked me out eventually, but I would have known that she *lived*. Even if they both had . . . well *you know* . . . and left, it would have been preferable. I could have made arrangements for you and Beatrice when you were still little enough to be raised properly in a new family. Instead, we spent those years waiting for the cancer to come back. Watching her die by inches. She knew I would be bad at this. She knew I wouldn't be able to bear it. This is all her fault." He drained his glass.

I turned away and looked at the wreck of the house. The shine was gone. Back when I was a kid, every surface glowed. Now it was all dust.

"I have to go, Dad."

"Wait." He stood, drained his glass, and stumbled toward the basement. He returned with a wooden box, about the size of a loaf of bread. It had vines and flowers carved into the edges. He shoved it into my hands. He couldn't even look at me. "It belonged to your mother. I didn't keep it with the rest of her things because . . . well, my wife, you see, has sticky fingers. You'll notice your mother's jewelry is gone. And this, well, it's special. Handmade. Your mother told me specifically that she wanted you to have it when you were old enough. I figure now is as good a time as any."

"What's in it?"

"No idea. Couldn't bear to open it. We weren't . . . close by the time she died. Not by a long shot. Didn't feel right to look inside. She said it's for you. So it's for you." He shoved the box into my hands and then turned on his heels and went to his room. He took the bottle with him.

This was the last time I saw my father. Later that week, while he was at work, my father had a heart attack and collapsed at his desk. He didn't make it to the hospital. Two days later, in the middle of the night, his house caught on fire while the rest of the neighborhood slept. Lit cigarette from a passing vagrant, the paper said. "Let that be a lesson to us all on the dangers of smoking," the editorial said. But that didn't explain the fact that his bedroom window, along with its surrounding wall, had been somehow wrenched free and torn off the house. It was found the next morning resting against the large oak tree by the alley.

~ ༄ ~

I didn't open the box, either. I also couldn't bear to look inside. Maybe my dad and I weren't so different after all. I sat with it on my lap for a long time, my fingers lingering at the latch. Finally, I gave up and put it in the back of the closet.

31.

That night, at dinner, Beatrice nearly dragoned. Right in front of me. Her eyes grew large, then wide, then gold. She blinked once, and then blinked again with a nictitating inner eyelid, a pale blue membrane languidly sliding across the circumference of the eye. One talon curled from her index finger. She watched it grow with fascination, then, in a state of wonder, lifted her face to the sky as she slowly brought her hand to her sternum.

I dropped the pan holding our dinner onto the floor.

"Beatrice," I gasped.

"Today's the day," she whispered. Gold face. Her tongue glittered.

I leaped over the table and grabbed her in my arms. She was so hot she blistered my skin. I didn't care. I hung on for dear life. My hands burned. My arms burned. My neck. My cheek. And oh, my heart. Everything burned.

"*Stop!*" I pleaded. "Oh, Beatrice, please stop." I held her tight, wrapping my arms around her body so far that they wrapped around myself as well. "Mama was all alone and oh, god, please don't leave me alone. You're a girl, you're a little girl, you're my little girl. Don't go." My voice caught. I began to sob. I held her so tight she gasped. "Please don't, Beatrice. I can't bear it." My tears fell on her neck and quickly turned to steam.

Beatrice shuddered in my arms and sighed. And then, quite quickly, she cooled. Her whole body went limp. Her head rested heavily in the crook of my elbow, like she was a baby. She blinked. Blinked again. Then looked at me with her little-girl eyes—not gold anymore, but big and brown. And bloodshot now—from transformation or from crying, I couldn't tell. I didn't let go.

She frowned. "But." Beatrice stopped, slightly disoriented. She licked her lips. She looked at the ceiling. Her thoughts, I could see, moved slowly, as though she was wading through deep, deep water. Tears began to trickle down her temples and pooled in her ears. She took in a breath, staccatoed by sadness as the realization of what just happened at last began to settle. "But why?" she said at last.

I sank to the floor, pulling Beatrice onto my lap. I stroked her hair. I kissed her cheeks. They were still hot, but not injuriously so. The food cooled on the floor. Somewhere, in another apartment, a radio droned and droned. I held Beatrice close, my body rocking back and forth.

"Do you want me to tell you a story?" I asked. She didn't respond, but that didn't matter. I closed my eyes, too much of a coward to hold her gaze. Did I know to feel shame yet? I think deep down, I probably did. "Once upon a time," I said, "there were two sisters. Both good. Both bad. Equal parts of each. They took care of one another, and worked hard, and both tried their best, and mostly it was good enough. They loved each other so, so much. One day, they heard the dragons' call. 'Come with us,' the dragons said. 'Come play with us. Be one with us.' The dragons called and called and they would not shut up. One sister answered the call. She took off her skin. She stepped out of her life. She became a dragon. The other sister didn't. She had work to do and people to care for and things to learn. She loved the world and everything in it and didn't want to leave her life behind. She stayed as she was, but she missed her sister, more and more each day, a great yawning sadness, until she couldn't bear it anymore. Her heart broke in half and she died of sorrow. The end."

Beatrice's eyes scanned the room, finally settling on my face. They narrowed skeptically.

"Is that a real story?" she asked.

"Of course it's a real story," I said. "I told it to you, didn't I?"

"Are you telling it right?" she asked.

I started to get annoyed. "Of course I'm telling it right. It's my story. This is the only way to tell it. That's how stories work."

Beatrice looked up, met my eye, held my gaze for a good long time. She wiped her nose with the back of her hand. "Did Mama tell you that story?" her breath catching slightly.

"No," I said. "I had to figure it out for myself. It took me a long time to understand." I looked at her. I took her hands in mine, kissing her knuckles. "But I understand it now. I understand what Mama lost. I understand what she did for her family. No more dragoning. *Please.* Beatrice, if you dragon, there is no more *us.* If you dragon, then you'll fly away, and maybe you'll forget me, and I'll be all alone. I don't know how to be alone. Don't leave me, Beatrice, promise me you won't."

"But what if—"

"Promise me you won't." I was emphatic.

She looked at me. The corners of her mouth quivered downward even as she struggled to stay neutral. "But," she paused. Her lips shook. She put her hand on my cheek. "What if you told the story wrong? What if it was *staying a girl* that made that sister die of sorrow? Maybe if the dragoned sister stayed, then she would have died too. Maybe they would both die of sorrow."

What would have happened if my mother had dragoned? What would have happened if she followed her sister into the sky? Would she have died? I forced that thought away. It did me no good to think it. I gave Beatrice a hard look. I stood and lifted Beatrice onto my hip even though she was way too big. I brought her to the kitchen sink to wash her hands and face. "I think you weren't paying attention to the story."

"Maybe *you* weren't," Beatrice said.

"Time for bed," I announced.

It wasn't, actually. It wasn't even six o'clock yet. The sky was light. Kids were playing outside. Beatrice went to the bathroom to brush her teeth. She was asleep inside of twenty minutes. It appeared that dragoning was tiring. Or almost dragoning. Or dragoning-undragoning. It was hard to tell. I sat down next to her and laid my hand on her forehead. She slept deeply, her breathing slow and easy, but she was hot to the touch. A fever? Post-almost-dragoning sickness? What even happened to a person when they nearly dragoned and then didn't? I didn't know. I went to the only source of dragoning information I had. I climbed up on the kitchen counter and reached into the space between the cabinet and the ceiling, and pulled down the sack where I had hidden my aunt Marla's bundle of treasures.

I set the letters and pictures aside and pulled out the booklet, *Some Basic Facts About Dragons: A Physician's Explanation.* It had been so long since I last looked at it. But now I stared. Under "Researched and Written by a Medical Doctor Who Wishes to Remain Anonymous" was my aunt's handwriting: "Also known as Dr. Henry Gantz. You can't fool me, old man."

I put it down, cradling my head in my hands.

The old man by the river. I thought he had been observing a cow. Why on earth would anyone take extensive notes on a cow stuck in a cranberry bog? And then I thought he was simply bird-watching. *My god,* I thought. *I've been so stupid.*

If I had Mrs. Gyzinska's phone number, I would have called her right away. But I didn't. One thing was clear, though: I needed to get to the library as soon as possible.

~

Later that evening, just after sundown, when the sky was still washed over with purple and gold and bursts of rosy light, my aunt showed up outside my apartment building. She waited on the sidewalk using a large concrete planter as a stool. I stared at her from my window, but she did not look up. Instead, she pulled out her knitting from her purse and began working on what looked like a sweater, her needles dancing swiftly in her talons.

I went outside. Everyone else on my block headed in the opposite direction—running from their cars into doorways. Everyone else hurried away. Likely calling the police. There was a dragon about, after all. Marla didn't seem to care. I looked down the street and gasped. Another dragon lingered under a leafless maple tree, gazing wistfully into an upper-floor apartment window, her neck unfurled in a graceful sway, her head bobbing up and down. Her paws were pressed against her heart.

How many were there, anyway?

Aunt Marla didn't look up. Her eyes focused on her knitting. I cleared my throat. She still didn't look up.

"What did you do?" My voice rasped terribly. I tried to set my face. It didn't work nearly as well as before.

Marla continued to knit. "I can hardly tell what you mean," she said mildly. The sweater was beautiful. The sky was beautiful. My aunt was so beautiful I thought I'd die of it. It was cold out, but I didn't need a coat. The heat pouring off my aunt was all the warmth I needed.

I closed my eyes and took a long breath through my nose. I wanted to throw something at her, but I didn't think it would do any good. I almost lost my sister, and there was only one person to blame. If I could be Saint George with his steed and spear, I would pierce my aunt through the middle without thinking twice. "Beatrice is the only family I have and I love her more than you could possibly know. She nearly . . . *changed* today. She nearly turned into one of you. I'll ask it again. *What did you do?"*

She looked up. Held my gaze. And smiled a dragonish smile, all gold and glitter.

"That's not how this works, my love. Whatever happened to Beatrice originated with *her.* I had nothing to do with it."

"I don't believe you." I wanted to kick something.

My aunt tilted her head. Her eyes flashed. "I already told you. Long ago when you were little. It's just magic. All of us got some. It calls to us—all the time really, but sometimes louder than others. And some of us are better than others at tuning it out. Years ago, it called quite loudly—an insistent wail, sounding through the whole country. It was louder than it ever had been before and no one really knows why. A lot of us answered, for reasons that should be fairly obvious. Thousands and thousands of us made the leap. All at once. It called and I answered and I didn't look back. Your mother could have—it called to her too. Maybe she nearly did. It's impossible for me to say. What I do know is that your mother *should* have answered it. But she didn't. And now here we are. If Beatrice nearly changed today, it means she is simply answering the call that's been speaking to her since she was born. Even when she was a baby I could see it on her face. That girl's been part dragon since the moment she kicked in the womb. You really want to stand in the way of nature?" she snorted. "Good luck."

"This is ridiculous," I said.

The dragon down the street began to sing. A lullaby from the sound of it. A window opened and a man shoved his head out. "Get out of here! I already told you! You left and we don't need you! Go away or I'll call the cops!" The window slammed so hard the glass shattered. The dragon seemed to deflate. Her head fell heavily into her paws and she began shaking with sobs.

I glared at my aunt. I crossed my arms across my chest. "Listen. This is *my* family and *my* rules and *my* life. Beatrice is my sister and we only have each other. I'm going to college next year somehow, and Beatrice is going with me and *that is the end of it.* You can go back to . . . well, wherever you were. We will be *fine* on our own. We've always been *fine* on our own." Even as I said these words, I knew they weren't true. We had been fine on our own for all of two and a half years, but only when someone else was paying for it. And the truth of it was we weren't really all that fine.

There was no good answer, but I certainly wasn't going to voice my doubts to a goddamned dragon. I turned on my heel and stomped back to the building door. It wasn't until I opened it that I realized my aunt was laughing at me. I turned at her and glared.

"Oh, honey. You are so like your mother. Big plans but no thought to the details."

My face grew hot. *How dare she?*

"Did you ever wonder how your mother paid for her education? Or rather, *who* paid for her education?" The dragon began winding the unknit yarn back into its neat ball and zipped her needles and sweater back into her voluminous purse.

I started to say something, but nothing came out. Obviously I knew. *But that wasn't the point.* I was practically grown, or felt grown, but the longer I stayed near my aunt, the more childlike I felt. And the more I felt it, the more angry it made me, and the more childish I became.

Marla tilted her head and pressed her hands to her heart. "She was my little sister, after all." Her eyes shone. "There was nothing I wouldn't do for her, nothing I wouldn't sacrifice. I gave up the work I loved, the life I loved, and I did it happily." She shook her head and sighed. She opened her purse and hunted around until she found a handkerchief (really, it was a scarf that had been folded to look like a handkerchief) and began to dab at her eyes. Then she extracted a lipstick and a mirror from her purse's outside pocket and began to reapply. She gave me a hard look. "I've been gone too long. I've neglected my duties. I realize that now." She stopped, held my gaze for a long time. "I know it's hard for you to accept, Alex, but we are family, and you need me. You've *been* needing me. And now I'm here."

Ridiculous, I thought. *No thank you.* What kind of help could a dragon give me? Light my future on fire? Fly Beatrice to school and back? For all I knew, her only intention was to abandon me yet again. My life had no room for dragons in it.

"I don't want—"

I was about to tell her I didn't want a single thing from her, but several police cars and fire trucks came tearing around the corner and raced toward us. My aunt looked up and called to the other dragon.

"Clara, honey," she said. "This isn't a time to linger. Either he'll come 'round or he won't, but you can't force it either way."

She turned to me, sliding her arm into her purse's hook and securing it in the hinge of her elbow. "We'll be back tomorrow."

"Don't bother," I said. But my voice was lost in the great *whoosh* of wings and heat and wind. Despite their tremendous bulk, they launched skyward with astonishing speed, shaking the earth and cracking the sidewalk as they kicked off. In the air, my aunt flew close to the other dragon. Their necks stretched forward and their heads tilted toward each other, resting gently jowl to jowl. Their taloned claws curled round each other with a tenderness that I would not have thought possible.

The fire trucks and police cars screeched to a halt and the officers came out. The dragons flew swiftly over the low-slung buildings and empty trees, sliding into the clouds, bright with the lurid colors of sunset. They were—oh, god—*so beautiful*. I shivered in spite of myself. And then, in the space between a breath in and a breath out, they vanished. Obscured by clouds, maybe. Or some sort of magic. It was hard to tell with dragons. I'm sure I must have made a sound—a small gasp or a wounded sigh—because one of the officers turned to me. His eyes were red and his cheeks were wet, but his face had hardened.

"Nothing to see here," he said.

"What?" I said.

"Move along." His voice was cold, and rigid.

I went inside.

The next day, I swiped Mr. Watt's newspaper and read it in the girls' bathroom at school. There was no mention of the dragons. There was a report of several police units being called to investigate a "suspicious disturbance." But that was all. I guess I wasn't surprised. It wasn't polite to speak of such things, after all.

Dear colleagues,

I would first like to thank our beloved librarian for delivering this message to you. It has been some time since my unceremonious removal from the National Institutes of Health, and my fall from grace thanks to the actions of the House Un-American Activities Committee. I lost my title and my license and my lab, but I retained my soul, ethics, and backbone, and I protected the names and work of my colleagues and friends in the collective. It will remain, above all else, my most important achievement.

Inside this package is the totality of my research, conducted during my, shall we say, extended sabbatical. I have become more unorthodox in my research methods, and have been more courageous and receptive in my quest to gather data. I have, in my travels, been invited on several occasions to meet with and examine members of several different dragon communes, where I was permitted to conduct extensive interviews (yes, contrary to our earlier hypotheses, speech and cognition and memory are fully intact), full medical examinations (including bloodwork, skin samples, basal temperature—we are going to need better thermometers—a full mapping of dentition, basic neurological testing, as well as a thorough analysis of cardiac and pulmonary functioning), not to mention notes on the social and emotional structures of dragon subculture. I had the great fortune to bear witness now to sixteen different dragonings, five of which were planned in advance by someone who could feel the change coming and permitted me to gather extensive data. (Photographs are included; films are available in the vault at the library. You know which one.)

All told, I have now interviewed over a thousand dragons, all around the world, and I can tell you that a good number of our early hypotheses are in error. This, of course, is exciting news.

There is no greater moment for a scientist than to be proved wrong or to be alive at a time when settled science is turned on its head. It is then that the researcher realizes that the world is so much more interesting than it was even a day before. I can tell you with certainty, for example, that dragoning has nothing to do with motherhood—less than half of the dragons I interviewed were mothers. It has nothing to do with menstruation—232 of the dragons I interviewed were postmenopausal, and 109 had already undergone radical hysterectomies, and an astonishing 74 were women by choice, and by the great yearnings of their hearts, and were not labeled as such at birth, and yet are women all the same. They dragoned too, just as their sisters did. "There are more things in Heaven and Earth, Horatio, than are dreamt of in your philosophy," Shakespeare tells us, and I am here to tell you that this is true. My friends, I have borne witness to things most wondrous strange, and I attest that still more wondrous things are on their way.

We are on the cusp, I believe, of another large-scale trans-formation. I can't tell you when. But it is my belief it is coming. I have been working with dragon communities and impressing on them the damage that was done—to their homes, to their families, even to the soul of our nation—not by the shock of their transformation, but the shock of their leaving. The damage of the lies the nation told itself in their absence. I contend that it was not the loss that hurt the culture, but the pressure to ignore that loss. The pressure to forget. But what, I wonder, would happen if people weren't allowed to forget? What would happen if the reality of their dragoned relatives became impossible to ignore?

Please, my friends, read my research. Analyze my findings. Criticize as you see fit. Tell me where I've failed. But do take it seriously. And get ready. Your patients will need you. So, too, will your communities, your country, and indeed the whole world. It is about to change.

Thank you for your work,
Henry Gantz

32

After that, the number of dragons showing up in my town increased. Almost every day, *someone* knew *someone* who saw *something*. People whispered and muttered. Rumors started to flow.

An emerald-green dragon with long, pink eyelashes and a razor-barbed tail started appearing every Tuesday at two o'clock in the yard next to an old folks' home. Sometimes she craned her neck to look into one particular room, but mostly, she simply sat quietly and waited. No one knew for what.

A ruby dragon started sitting outside the window of a History of the Novel course taught at the local community college. The professor tried shooing her away, but when that was unsuccessful, he handed her a stack of books and told her when the next paper was due and informed her that he didn't allow goof-offs in his classroom. The dragon immediately got to work.

Another dragon, whose scales were the exact color and scent of a perfectly ripe peach, took it upon herself to find a comfortable place to sit right outside the window of the nursery where the local hospital housed its newborns. She didn't even look in the window. She just sat, leaned her cheek against the building, and began to sing. There likely would have been an attempt to scare her away, but her song was so soothing to the newborns that the nurses insisted she not be moved. The babies who listened to the dragon's lullaby gained weight faster, took a nipple more vigorously, and were generally more placid and content, making for an excellent work environment. That . . . *thing*, the nurses insisted (they wouldn't say "dragon"), was going to stay. And that was that.

None of these incidents made the local paper. No television

or radio stations attempted to cover it. Giant creatures descended on a small town in Wisconsin, and no one considered it news. It was dragons, after all. People got red in the face just thinking about it.

It wasn't just my town, either. This was happening across the entire country. Due to news blackouts on the subject (not enforced by any agency or rule, but ardently adhered to by the journalists themselves—or their editors or outlet owners), no formal paper trail about what was later referred to as the Great Return exists, aside from a few local government inquiries and one congressional inquest, all heavily redacted still. However, since then, academics and researchers have been steadily collecting contemporaneous diary entries and letters, homemade films and snapshots, and thousands of hours of recorded interviews, and have carefully created a list of corroborated, verified incidents, with widespread agreement as to their veracity. In the first week alone of the Great Return, a total of 77,256 dragons either visited or fully returned to their former homes.

For example:

In East Los Angeles, a young woman celebrating her *quinceañera* in the backyard of her aunt and uncle's house was just about to cut the cake when a dragon the color of seafoam landed lightly on the roof of the carport. The music stopped. The girl dropped her plate on the ground. Several elderly women shouted at the dragon, in both English and Spanish, ordering her to leave the premises at once. The dragon didn't move. She kept her eyes on the girl. The girl stepped forward. Her uncle told her to go inside. The girl did not. She couldn't look away from the dragon. There was frosting on her left hand. She smeared it lazily across her filmy skirt. The dragon drifted to the ground. She stood perfectly still, her lovely neck outstretched, her paws pressed against her heart. The assembled family and friends gave her a wide berth. The girl began to cry. Several witnesses agree that her eye makeup smeared and her nose ran. The dragon said nothing. Instead she bowed to the girl and set a pair of very pretty high-heeled shoes at her feet. The dragon kissed the girl's hands, lingering for a moment. And launched without a word.

In southeastern Montana, two smallish dragons arrived at a midsized sheep ranch and immediately made themselves useful. They tuned the trucks and rotated the tires and put a new roof on a grain shed. They dug up a new plot for the summer's vegetable garden and dredged the pond. The rancher, an elderly widower who wasn't known in town for his conversational skills, quietly built a pole barn behind his house where the dragons took up residence. As it turned out, the dragons were excellent with sheep.

During services at the Good Shepherd Missionary Baptist Church in Cullman, Alabama, two little girls in their Sunday best, with multicolored ribbons tied in their hair, peered out the east side window and gasped. They were, of course, immediately shushed, and services continued for another two and a half hours. The girls knew better than to speak up—everyone would see it soon enough. It was customary at Good Shepherd to follow services with a meal, which was to be followed by a Bible study and hymn sing. This was normally organized by the women in the congregation, who had already anticipated a fine midday and planned to serve the food out of doors. But when they exited the church side door, they found the meal already set up and ready to be heaped onto plates. A dragon stood next to the long table, three aprons tied together and looped around her wide middle. She clasped her taloned hands together. "Good day to you, sisters," the dragon said tentatively. "It's nice to see you again." They hesitated, but only for a moment. There was a meal to be served, after all.

In Kansas, a group of three dragons got wind of an older farm couple who had suffered a stroke (the husband) and a broken leg (the wife), and so the dragons worked ceaselessly (it appeared that they do not sleep) to finish the harvesting of the winter wheat. The wife, with her leg in a cast, sat on the front porch and watched. Her skin had a permanent sunburn and her mouth had a permanent scowl. She did not speak to the dragons. When they finished, one approached the old farmhouse. It was an onyx dragon, with emerald eyes. She stood by the porch, her posture excellent, her fingers interlaced as though praying as she had been taught, and her breath in her throat. The wife stared at the dragon for a long time. She said nothing. She grabbed her crutches and hobbled inside. The dragon left in tears.

On the North Carolina Outer Banks, an early-season hurricane laid waste to a sleepy fishing town on the water. Four dragons arrived with tools and lumber (no one knew where they got them) and quickly built a shelter. Five more scoured on and under the waves and retrieved thirty-two lost fishing boats, rigging and all. No one spoke to the dragons except one elderly gentleman, who hobbled close to a bright yellow dragon with quills all up and down her back. The dragon held very still as the man approached. The man had dark skin and white stubble and eyes that could take in the whole ocean at a glance, and often did. He stood in front of the dragon for a long, long time. He brought his hands to her face. She closed her eyes. He laid his cheek to her cheek. "Welcome home, child," he said.

In Chicago, a group of dragons arrived in the nick of time at an orphanage that had gone up in flames after a kitchen fire had gotten out of control. It was an ancient, flimsy building with terrible wiring, and the one exit had been blocked by burning debris. The dragons went in like a conquering brigade, saving every child before the first fire truck arrived. Two children, both girls, and three young nuns dragoned that very afternoon, in the back garden of the church next door, just as neighbors arrived with food and blankets and plans for caring for the displaced. It happened in a flash, the dragoning—a shock of heat and mass and light and energy. And then, as one, the dragons flew away.

Around the country, dragons could be seen along roadsides, in abandoned lots, or simply strolling in the parks. They were alone, those dragons. Or in pairs. Or in small groups. In all my research, I never encountered a group of more than five, despite some of the wilder rumors at the time of entire towns being suddenly overwhelmed by an invading dragon population. There were dragons who took it upon themselves to assist migrant populations living hand to mouth in tin shacks in the fruit fields of California and dragons who forced their way into sweatshops in Queens, threatening to burn them down during the night if working conditions didn't improve immediately, and dragons who walked alongside marchers in Nashville and Atlanta and Birmingham, simply using their quiet presence as a dare to anyone who might wish to make trouble.

There were dragons who showed up in ladies' sewing circles.

And dragons who attended labor meetings.

And dragons who marched with farmworkers.

And dragons who joined anti-war committees.

No one knew what to do with them at first. Newspapers didn't report it. The evening news remained silent. People averted their eyes and changed the subject. Cheeks flushed; voices faltered. Most people simply assumed that if they just ignored the dragons they would go away.

The dragons did not go away.

33

I was still rattled the day after Marla's unplanned visit, so I did something I had never done before in my entire life: I cut class. After dropping Beatrice off at the front steps of Saint Agnes (*No dragoning at school,* I told her. *I mean it*), I went home and called the main office, fraying my voice and adding in a few fake coughs just to complete the picture. "Touch of the flu," I told the woman who was volunteering that day. "Something going around." I could hear Mr. Alphonse shouting in the background and the poor woman sounded like she was going to cry. Silently, I resolved to never work in a high school.

I grabbed Dr. Gantz's book and shoved it into my book bag and I walked over to the library. Mr. Burrows sat at the front desk. He was reading through a large binder, shaking his head as he turned the page. He looked up at me, smiled, and said, "Miss Green!" but then he frowned. "Shouldn't you be in school?"

I had spoken to Mr. Burrows a thousand times, but I realized with a start that I had never really *seen* him. He was just another adult. But today, as I approached his station at the circulation desk, I actually *looked.* He nibbled on the edge of his pencil as he curled over a book that he kept on his lap, mostly hidden from view. I watched him as he shook his head and wrote something on the page. He was a small man. Nervous and kind. He was the only man I had ever seen who kept a basket of yarn and crochet hooks at his desk. He did experiments making hyperbolic planes and Möbius loops and topographical conundrums and something called a snark and various three-dimensional approximations of four-dimensional objects. He had explained all of them to me before, but I had never actually listened. I was too busy with the weight of my life to pay attention to anything else.

I startled him when I said hello, but he recovered quickly enough.

"Mr. Burrows," I said. I paused a moment as he twirled his nibbled pencil in his hand. "What's your job?"

He blanched. "I'm sorry? I don't know what you mean. I'm a librarian." He made a weak gesture toward the stacks as though this was all the explanation he needed.

I reached into my bag and set Dr. Gantz's book on the desk. He stared at the book. He stared at me. I watched his Adam's apple go up and down. I rested my elbows on the desk and leaned my chin on my fists.

"I guess I'm just curious." I blinked slowly and watched his face become pale. "What was your *other* job?"

He stood. His hands shook slightly. "You know, Mrs. Gyzinska has returned from her travels. She's downstairs. Let's go visit her, shall we?"

Mrs. Gyzinska already had our coffees poured—cream for him and black for me—and waiting for us when we arrived. How she knew I was coming remains a mystery to me to this day.

"Sit," she said, sipping her coffee. "You have questions, I gather."

"I'm guessing he's not a librarian, right?" I said, pointing to Mr. Burrows with my thumb. He blushed. "Not really, I mean."

"No," she said, an indulgent look on her face. "At least not by training, though I would like to point out that he has excellent instincts. Mr. Burrows is a planetary physicist, and an excellent one—beautiful, elegant science, an intellect of pure creativity and insight." His blush deepened but Mrs. Gyzinska didn't relent. "I helped fund his research during his post-doc at Princeton, and it was money well spent. He's an expert on the Jovian moons, and had a little side project tracking the movement of dragons on and around said moons, and was blacklisted as a result. And then, unfortunately, he got on the bad side of a few overly keen congressmen, and is now a bit on the lam, poor thing. It happens. His new name fits him, I think. Michael, dear, you don't actually have to be here for this. Thanks for bringing her down."

Mr. Burrows scurried out of the room. I picked up my coffee and swallowed it in several gulps. I handed her the book. She smiled and gave the cover a loving pat.

"You should definitely keep this. They're quite rare. Chock-full of absolutely incorrect information too, as it turns out. Henry will be the first one to say so. The beautiful thing about science is that we do not know what we cannot know and we will not know until we know. It requires an incredible amount of humility to be willing to be wrong nearly all the time. But we have to be willing to be wrong, and proven wrong, in order to increase knowledge overall. It is a thankless, and essential, job. Thank goodness." She sipped her coffee, gazing fondly at Dr. Gantz's book.

Well. That was frustrating. What I needed was information, and what I had was garbage. I glared at the book, as though it had been incorrect on purpose, and wanted to give Dr. Gantz a piece of my mind. "Is he here?"

She frowned. "Unfortunately, someone spotted him about a month ago, recognized him, and called the police. Thankfully I had gotten wind of it, and packed him off to an instructor I know at the medical school in Madison. He's happy as a clam, actually. He even has access to a lab—a real lab! And he's assisting at a, um, rather unconventional clinic. I think they've appreciated having his help—he's been at this for longer than most. Things are starting to get . . . *interesting* over there."

This was too much. I rested my forehead on the table and covered my head with my arms. "Mrs. Gyzinska," I sighed. "I just don't know what is going to happen next. I don't know what I'm supposed to *do*."

"Oh, piffle," she said with a wave of her hand. "What kind of talk is that? You're going to do exactly what you've been doing. You're going to take care of that girl of yours, and throw yourself into your work, and excel in every way that you choose to excel, and you will simply live your life. You'll elevate mathematics to an art form and conduct science like a symphony, and I honestly expect nothing less of you. Other people will come and go as they please, and live the lives they choose and I'm not sure why it would affect you one bit. You're upset because your aunt has returned, yes?" She drained the last of her coffee.

I sat up and stared at her. "How did you," I managed. I had no words after that. I shouldn't have been so surprised. After all, they put my aunt's picture in the paper.

"You've figured out her connection to our Dr. Gantz, of course. You always were one to figure things out. He owes her an apology, I'm afraid, but you know how men are. Children, essentially. Listen, I've known Marla since she was a teenager. She's always been bigger on the inside than she is on the outside. Her life has never entirely fit her. Even now. Even as a dragon. That's the thing about dragoning—it doesn't solve everything. The body changes, but the self is still the self, with all its original problems and consternations—and yet, still with its capacity to learn. We're never stuck in one spot. We're always *changing.*"

My head swam. "I'm stuck," I said. "I feel *so stuck.*" *Weights on my ankles,* I thought. *And weights on my wrists.* I felt as though I was nailed in place.

"You're not," Mrs. Gyzinska said kindly. "Everyone feels that way from time to time, but I assure you, you're not. You're just not looking at the whole picture."

"I can't lose Beatrice." I was in tears now.

Mrs. Gyzinska rapped on the table with her knuckles, her expression inscrutable. "Then don't," she said, as though it was that simple. "Honestly, it's not that hard. There's very little we can control in this life. All we can do is accept whatever comes, learn what we can, and hang on to what we love. And that's it. In the end, the only thing you can hope to control is *yourself.* In this moment. Which is both a relief and a huge responsibility, both at the same time." She opened her desk calendar.

"Which reminds me, you have two exams coming up this week. Since you've decided to play hooky, perhaps you should take this opportunity to study. I informed your professor at the beginning of the semester that I expected you to be his top student, and I do hate being wrong. Let's hop to it, shall we?" She stood. "I have business to attend to in the office. Your materials are in your cubby." She turned, opened a locked cabinet, and pulled out a large white binder with no markings on it—just like the one that Mr. Burrows was reading earlier. "You can page through this, too, if you can stand it. It is a collection of Dr. Gantz's more current research on the topic of dragoning. But I'll warn you. I have nothing but respect for Henry, and I've been his supporter for nearly forty years. But that man is *wordy*." She rolled her eyes.

She patted me on the back as she passed, and closed the door behind her.

I didn't study. I spent the entire day reading Dr. Gantz's research.

Mrs. Gyzinska wasn't wrong. *So wordy.*

34

On the first of April, I learned I had been accepted into the University of Wisconsin as an honors student. I spoke to the director of Student Life on the phone to discuss my housing options, given my family situation. He informed me that I couldn't live with Beatrice in the dormitories because children were not allowed, and I also couldn't live in married housing, as I was not married.

"Well," I said. "That leaves me in a bit of a pickle. I'm curious. What do other students do who find themselves in a situation of unmarried motherhood, but who wish to pursue their educations, unhindered? Is there any plan for them?"

The director exhaled. I couldn't see him through the phone, of course, but he sounded like he rolled his eyes. "Well," he said. "I'm sure I don't know. I expect they drop out." I could tell he had nothing more to say to me. I thanked him and told him I'd find another way.

Fortunately, a few days later I learned I had secured a partial scholarship. Not enough to cover everything, unfortunately, so I was still contacting potential apartments, part-time employers, and babysitters. Mrs. Gyzinska made phone calls on my behalf as well.

"Don't say yes to anything yet," she advised me. "Every institution has its hidden wellsprings of money, and I am determined to find at least one more spout to flow in your direction. Leave me to it."

I did. I didn't have the energy to do anything beyond what was directly in front of me, and even then I could hardly focus.

My aunt came by most days, just to say hello, and look at Beatrice through the window as she slept. I wasn't ready to let them meet yet. Beatrice, of course, had no memory of Marla. She wasn't even a year old when . . . *well.* When everything changed. Her only mother was our mother. And yet. The memory of Marla holding Beatrice in those moments before she transformed, of Marla kissing each finger and marveling at her plump cheeks and sleeping mouth and damp curls, rattled in my mind and disrupted my thinking. That memory wasn't mine, of course, but I carried it anyway. Did Marla's heart break when she laid a sleeping Beatrice back in her bed? Did she press her hand to her mouth as she hurried out of the baby's room to stop herself from sobbing? Yes. Probably. I felt my own heart break every time I thought of it.

Still, I wasn't ready to forgive her. I wasn't ready to welcome her into our life. I know I was being cruel. But I was a teenager: cruelty was the only leverage I had.

Despite my keeping her at arm's length, even then I knew that having a dragon hanging around the place had its advantages. There were no longer men whistling at me as I mounted my bike. They tipped their hats now, if they looked at me at all. Also, our landlord became much more amenable, and was suddenly quick to open a drain or fix a leak. I was certain my aunt was responsible. I never said thank you. I couldn't give her that. I was distracted, anxious, and ruder than normal. I trudged through school in a blurry haze.

The death of my father weighed strangely on me. How does a person mourn a man she barely knows? I inherited nothing, outside of the money that he had already transferred into my account and the rent he had already paid. Nothing went to Beatrice, either. No surprise. My stepmother didn't invite us to the funeral. For all I know, she didn't even hold one. She simply sent me the envelopes filled with my monthly cash allowances—marked April, May, June, July, August—tucked together in a file folder, with a note on top that said, "Your father had these laid out for you on his desk. Don't expect anything else." She didn't sign it.

All I had from my father was that small wooden box. Weeks went by, but I hadn't been able to bring myself to open it. It remained where I had first stashed it—at the back of the closet, under a carefully arranged pile of junk. I couldn't bring myself to even look at it.

That same week in April, dragons began showing up at the high school. Every day. There were only a couple at first. Then they came by the dozen. Dragons milled around the schoolyard and sunned themselves on the roof. They bummed cigarettes off kids who looked like they might have an extra, and smoked by the back doors. The garbage trucks refused to come after a while—because how, really, could they work under these conditions—but it ended up not being a problem. The dragons put themselves in charge of sanitation, carrying the dumpsters to the municipal landfill twice a week. They picked up litter and kept the grass cut and weeded the gardens. They even brought buckets and rags and washed all the windows. Over the course of the month, the school began to gleam. Crocuses peeked up along the walkways. A newly turned garden patch for vegetables appeared next to the football field. No one mentioned the savings to the school because it wasn't polite to discuss dragons.

It was school policy at the time—communicated in vague terms in hastily produced pamphlets handed out in homeroom as well as periodically announced over the PA system—that we were to pointedly ignore the current dragon infestation. Under no circumstances were we allowed to strike up a conversation with or even acknowledge that the dragon was there. If a dragon was in your way, you simply *went around.* You didn't mention it. The dragons never behaved threateningly so there was never a need to close school. They didn't interrupt classes. They were simply *there.* The nuns told us that nothing good could come from stopping to chat. They were dangerous women, after all, who had succumbed to dangerous things.

But, as April pushed toward May, I started to notice that there were girls who didn't simply go around when a dragon was in their way. There were girls who paused for conversation. Who sought out the dragons. The dragons took notice and started bringing blankets and picnic baskets. They organized kaffee-klatsches and discussion groups with girls and dragons behind the gymnasium and in the parking lot. They passed around cigarettes and snacks, and sometimes shared books. I have no idea what they talked about. I was not interested. They called to me, they invited me over, but I pretended not to hear. Anyway, my days were numbered at that school. I was bound, I felt, for bigger things. A whole universe of science to discover with infinite questions to ask. I was hungry for knowledge and I didn't think I would ever be full. There was nothing of interest left for me in that building.

Which is why I was so shocked when, five days before the prom, Randall Hague cornered me on our way out of calculus class and asked if I would be his prom date. His voice was halting and stilted, his syntax strangely formal. He kept his hands in front of his chest as though he was holding a hat. And even more shocking: I was so flustered that I inexplicably said yes.

It wasn't that I disliked Randall. I just had no opinion of him whatsoever, despite having known him since kindergarten. I wasn't even sure if I'd be able to pick him out of a lineup. He was one of those boys who simply faded into the background. But then, there he was with his stuttery "I'd be honored," and there I was with a short "Yeah, sure, why not." And that was that. He shook my hand gravely, as though we had just conducted a business transaction, and then we both went to third period. I had never gone to a school dance before. But, apparently, I was going to prom. I wasn't sure how I felt about it.

Beatrice, on the other hand, was beside herself with enthusiasm. She jumped on the bed and turned two cartwheels across the apartment, knocking over a lamp. The old man in the unit below us bashed on his ceiling with a broom.

"Wait," she said, suddenly pausing her exuberance. "What's prom?"

"It's a dance," I said. "And a party. People dress up."

"You should dress up as a dragon!" Beatrice crowed.

"No dragons," I said absently. It was a pat response at this point. Like a reminder to look both ways before she crossed the street. "Besides, it's not that kind of a party."

"What kind of party is it?" she asked.

"A fancy-dress party," I told her.

"So dress fancily," she said very patiently, as though I was too slow to understand the obvious. "As a fancy dragon." I glared at her and she crumpled, just a bit, which made me feel bad, so I sat down next to her on the bed and held her hands.

I explained how prom worked. How girls wore long gloves and high-heeled shoes and dresses that rustled when you walked and boys wore something called a tuxedo, which no one really understood. She was disappointed. Beatrice loved anything involving a costume.

"And besides," I said, "I wouldn't dress up as a dragon even if it was. They're just—" I stopped myself in time. I nearly said "vermin," but that was unkind. Nothing good could be gained from insults. I pressed my lips together. "The dragons are a distraction. Anyway, it doesn't matter. What I need is a pretty dress."

Fortunately, I had some. One by one, I pulled out my mother's dresses, which I had wrapped in tissue paper stuffed with sachets, and laid them on the bed. I removed her hats and shoes from their protective sacks and arranged them into ensembles. Beatrice clasped her hands and gasped reverently. The apartment was suddenly filled with the smell of rosemary. The dresses were old-fashioned, but they were lovely all the same.

I tried each one on—along with matching purses, shoes, and gloves—while Beatrice commented on their various qualities and defects. She asked me to walk across the room, turn, sashay, and say something interesting.

"I want you to look fancy," she said. "But I also want you

to look like you. Put on that one and then say something about math. You look most like you when you talk about math."

The dresses fit—my body was exactly the same as my mother's had been, a fact that astonished me. We were cut into the same shape. Or we were, until her body was reduced to kindling and ash and wind. *(The woods decay, the woods decay and fall.)* I shivered. Would my body betray me the way hers did? Would I leave behind the ones I loved the most?

"I'm wearing the pink one," I told Beatrice. It was pink silk with a tulle slip and a lace overlay on the skirt—hand knotted in a complex pattern that looked almost like constellations. I tried it on and twirled for Beatrice, who twirled right along with me.

"Pink is always the very best one," she said with authority. "That's just science." And she went immediately to her art table to draw a picture of me in a pink dress, riding a dragon. It was the first dragon picture she had drawn in a month. It bothered me, but I decided not to argue, and I did hang it up on the refrigerator when she was done, if only to humor her into going to bed on time. Later, I took it down and was about to throw the picture into the trash.

I paused.

The dragon was black and green. Little hints of silver grey shot through the dragon's body. It looked just like Marla. How much did she understand? I took the picture and put it under my bed, next to my mother's carved box.

⁓

It was the night of prom, and Randall Hague, per our arrangement, approached the front door of my apartment building, driving his father's car. He wore a dark suit, the kind you wear to a job interview, or a funeral. I barely recognized him, which wasn't unusual. I met him outside because I didn't want him seeing what our apartment looked like. It wasn't that I was ashamed of it, I just never had invited anyone in other than the occasional babysitter. And also Mrs. Gyzinska, but she wasn't exactly invited. Sometimes, a person just gets used to keeping the world at bay.

The dress was made of taffeta and chiffon and tulle and it whispered when I moved. A lace shawl made from silk threads, hand knotted by my mother, was draped around my shoulders— it was the color of the sky. I wore my hair in pin curls like my aunt, and I wore red lipstick like my aunt. I didn't intend to look like her, but maybe I did in a way. Unconsciously, I found myself taking a wide stance. I found myself wishing I wore army-issued boots.

Beatrice, I knew, was watching me through the window, along with Mrs. Darga, the widow who lived in the brick building next to ours. I liked her, and so did Beatrice. She often babysat. Both her son and her daughter died during the war. Her daughter was a nurse and her son was an airman, and both were shot by enemy soldiers, in different countries. Despite that sadness, Mrs. Darga was an unflappably cheerful woman. She was about the size and texture of a tree stump, with a large bun growing out the back of her head like a burl. She often arrived with trays of pierogies and golabki and bowls of cabbage soup, and told us emphatically that if we didn't eat everything immediately we would surely starve and die on the spot.

Through the window, I heard Mrs. Darga say, "*Córuchna,* that may be your new papa," to which Beatrice responded with uproarious laughter and a loud, "DON'T BE RIDICULOUS." I reddened, hoping Randall Hague didn't hear.

He parked the car, came round to the passenger door, and was about to open it without a word, when he thought better of it, turned on his heel, and faced me. It wasn't that he was an ugly boy. Just . . . utterly forgettable. He offered his hand, and once again I shook it. His expression was grave and serious.

He reached his hand toward my dress, and then thought

better of it, and shoved it in his pocket instead. "Your dress is very beautiful," he said, a flush rising in his cheeks.

"Thanks," I said. "It was my mother's."

His expression changed to panic. "Oh!" he said. "Mothers!" He smacked his forehead. "I almost forgot." He returned to the car door, yanked it open, leaned inside, and rummaged around for a bit. He reemerged with a small box. He shoved it into my hands. It was a corsage of pink carnations with a ribbon to hold it to my wrist.

"Thank you," I said.

"My mother said I had to give you one," he said. "She picked it out." He motioned to me to put out my hand so he could secure the ribbon.

"Oh," I said. "Well, thanks to your mother."

"I helped," said Randall Hague, his flush deepening. He opened the door and ushered me into the car, and we sat in silence as he inched down the street, his face tense as he eyed any and all possible mishaps that might assault his father's car, slowly making our way toward the school.

There were dragons lining the roof of the building when we arrived. More than I had ever seen at once. I didn't see my aunt, but that didn't mean she wasn't there. I peered upward, trying to differentiate their faces in the slanting light and deepening shadows, but it was difficult to see. The dragons didn't say anything. They didn't move. They just pressed their hands to their hearts. They had good posture and kept their feet sensibly apart with a slight bend to the knee, and their chins tilted upward. They held purses and craft bags and document caddies and what appeared to be sack lunches. One held an old-fashioned suitcase. Their eyes were clear and wide and *searching*.

I shivered. I waited for Randall to come around to the other side of the car to let me out. It never made any sense to me why this was considered good manners. No one came to open his door, after all. It wasn't like it was hard, opening doors. Still, I waited, with my ankles crossed and my gloved hands folded on a frothy pink skirt that wasn't even mine. Or at least it wasn't mine originally. I guess it was mine now. I was literally standing in my mother's shoes. I wasn't sure how I felt about that. I readjusted the shawl over my shoulders.

Randall opened the door and offered me his hand. I took it and stood. His hand felt cold, even through my gloves. And impossibly damp. I gave him a squeeze to show that was quite enough, thanks, and clasped my hands in front of me instead, like I was praying. I don't know why, but I looked up, and realized that one of the dragons was watching me with interest. She gave me a curt nod before returning her gaze to the sky.

I didn't know what that was supposed to mean.

Randall noticed me noticing, and wrinkled his nose in disgust. "Ugh," he said. "It's bad enough that they make a nuisance of themselves during school. But did they have to come to *the prom?*" There was a distinct whine that I decided not to notice. My mother, long ago, said there was nothing worse than whiny men. She couldn't have been talking about my father—he rarely spoke. I think she was just speaking in generalities. I wished I had paid closer attention.

"I rather like it," I said. He looked at me in confusion. "It's like an honor guard, you know? Look how stately they are. And dignified." I found myself suddenly thinking about Mrs. Gyzinska.

"Honor guards are *men*," he said scathingly. "And anyway there's nothing dignified about a . . ." His voice trailed off and he cleared his throat. He couldn't even bring himself to say it.

"A dragon?" I prompted. It seemed impossible, but his flush actually deepened. "I don't know why people get so squirrelly about that word," I said. "It's like how they make the boys take a separate health class so they don't have to hear about menstru—"

"Ah!" He slapped his hands to his ears and looked like he was about to faint. "Please let's change the subject!"

"Fine. In we go," I said, walking forward while keeping my hands to myself. He offered me his arm, but I just gave a vague smile and did not take it, quickening my step instead. I paused and glanced up at the sky. One by one, a few planets and the brightest stars began to assert themselves. My back hurt. Above the building a larger flock of dragons circled overhead, swooping and swirling across the darkening blue. It wasn't quite evening yet. But night was coming.

35

The prom committee chose a "Romance on the High Seas" theme that year, primarily because it allowed them to reuse the decorations from the school production of *The Pirates of Penzance*. Blue cellophane covered the light bulbs and blue streamers suggested frothy waves on either side of the gym. Four girls from my literature class had turned a French flag, a Union Jack, an American flag, and a Jolly Roger into capes tied across their shoulders with ribbon, and each held a pirate hat in their hands—not to be worn, of course, as it might interrupt the lines of their coiffures.

Everyone was so *happy*. Or at least the girls were. They moved through the crowd like birds, all color and flutter and flounce. Their hips swayed with each step, causing their skirts to ripple and flow about their legs, as their smart heels clicked daintily across the floor. They linked arms with their friends, resting their pretty heads on shapely shoulders. They waved at one another, and waved at *me,* a fact I found astonishing. In fact, they lit up when they saw me, each lipsticked mouth spreading into a wide smile. No one had ever smiled at me like that in all my years at school. Granted, I had never smiled that way either. The girls in the flag capes bowed and curtsied at one another. They broke into pairs and slid their arms around one another's waists and grabbed one hand and stepped out an abbreviated waltz. I gasped. I had to look away. They were too beautiful to bear.

I smoothed the bodice of my dress with my hands and let my fingers skim the pink chiffon. My mother's dress. It fit me perfectly. My body became what her body once was. Before the first cancer. Or the second. Before the cancer ate it. Before it became ash and air. Before it blew away.

There were no dragons in the gym. Or anywhere inside the school. Still, we all knew they were on the roof. Standing guard. We all knew they swooped and swirled through the skies overhead. Every once in a while, one would appear at one of the windows—a bright flash of color, of tooth and scale and muscle and eye—and vanish just as quickly.

"You need punch," Randall said suddenly. "My mother said I'm supposed to bring you punch."

I wasn't thirsty, but Randall was already marching away. *Such a strange boy,* I found myself thinking, wondering why I had ever said yes to the whole business. By the time Randall made it to the refreshments table—manned by Mr. Reynolds and two science teachers—he blended in so well with the other boys, all getting punch for their dates, that I couldn't have picked him out if I tried. I turned my attention to the dancers.

Sister Leonie and two other nuns prowled the dance floor, inserting a measuring stick between the couples, making sure the dances remained chaste.

"Leave room for the Lord," Sister Leonie said, in both English and French, just to show she really meant it.

Randall returned with two glasses of punch, spilling a little bit on his shoe. I sipped it gingerly.

Girls began to clump together in greater numbers, leaving their dates alone on the sides of the dance floor, holding coats or wraps or purses and not entirely knowing what to do with them. The boys shifted their weight from one foot to the other, some heading to the chairs along the back wall to sit. The girl clumps drifted toward me, each one a riot of ruby reds and emerald greens and dark golds—the girls were all glitter and color and light. They flashed their teeth. They batted their eyes. They danced in groups of three, then seven, then thirteen, a tangle of arms and skirts and loosening hair. The bangles on their wrists glinted. The rhinestones around their necks winked prettily against their shining skin. The boys slumped on the sidelines and held their hands at their eyebrows, shading their gaze from the glare. One by one, the boys began to scowl. I wasn't sure why. *Just look at them,* I wanted to explain. *If you could choose to surround yourself with that much beauty, wouldn't you do so in a heartbeat?* I had never thought about it before. *Yes,* I thought. *I know I would.* I pressed my hand to my heart. My skin was hot. My whole body pulsed.

The band consisted of the art teacher and the art teacher's brother and three guys on horns who graduated the year before and an older lady who played the drums. They were not very good. They had their eyes on the growing clumps of girls. They missed notes and dropped beats and sometimes forgot the words. No one seemed to notice.

"I love your dress, Alexandra," one girl called out to me as she waltzed in the arms of her friend. It looked so much more fun than dancing with someone like Randall—the swish of skirts and the click of heels. I took a sharp inhale and brought my hand to my cheek.

"Thanks!" I called back. "My friends call me Alex," I added, which wasn't exactly true—I didn't have any friends—but oh! I wished it was true. I had never felt lonely at school before. But now . . .

One girl smiled at me—like a sudden burst of light. I thought my knees might give way. "Alex is a beautiful name," she said, blowing me a kiss. I wish I knew her name. I wish I remembered. I fingered the knots on the lace my mother had made, feeling tied to the ground, and tied to this life, in a way I had never noticed before.

"Your shoes are perfect," a girl from another clump enthused.

"Your hair is so pretty with that rose clip!" An entire girl clump began twisting their own locks mindlessly, like small children.

"I'm so glad you came!" Another clump, from across the room. More girls left their dates. They moved together, inexorably bound, like the amassing of innumerable particles in the formation of a star. What makes such things happen? Safety in numbers, maybe. Or maybe this is how small things become something impossibly large. Or maybe they just all preferred the company of girls. And really. Why wouldn't they?

The air shifted, slightly. I felt it in my hair first—a dry, sharp sensation, like static electricity. I was afraid to touch anything in case I might experience a shock.

The clumps drifted in, and complimented me and everyone else, and drifted away. They swirled, split apart, and pulled back together—a dance of attraction, accretion, ignition, and acceleration. The girls sashayed with their arms wound together, with their cheeks resting against one another, with their hair winding into complex love knots. They were beautiful, and dizzying. I was not part of it, of that sense of intimacy and closeness, of any of it. I never had been. My mother didn't have friends, either. She had her sister, and no one else. I had my sister, and no one else. I had no idea how to even do it. I was always the girl who stood apart. A lone star in a sea of galaxies. I was always happy to be the girl who stood apart. Or, I had been. Now I wasn't so sure.

A dragon paused at one of the west windows. Leaf green. Eyes as red as apples. She winked. Randall noticed me looking. He furrowed his brow and his mouth became grim. "They *better not* ruin prom," he grumbled. "It's our big night. It wouldn't be fair."

I looked at him. "How would they *ruin* prom?" I asked. "They're just dragons."

He choked. Reddened again. But he steeled himself and decided to muscle through. "You know. By being . . . those things." He drained his glass. "And all their related nonsense. In public, and everything. Where anyone can see. It shouldn't be allowed. My father said they wouldn't have let any of this stand during the war."

I laughed out loud. "What are you talking about? Of course they would have," I said. "They wouldn't have had any choice."

Randall reddened, and not from embarrassment this time. He did not like it when I laughed at him, that much was obvious. He hardened his mouth. "Well, you know. There's, well, rules during a war. And honor. And, you know. Armies that follow orders. With guns." He glared at the window.

"Randall Hague, that is the most foolish thing I've ever heard." I didn't know why he was making me so mad. But something about the way he was talking to me made rage grow in my chest, hot and bright and enormous. I thought I would never be able to contain it. "Bullets don't have any effect on dragons. It's not a matter of letting anything stand. It's a matter of accepting that the world isn't the same as you thought it was before. We thought there weren't any dragons. And then there were. We thought the dragons were gone. And now here they are. Any choice we think we have in the matter is an illusion."

Randall glared at me. "That's a very un-American sentiment."

I snorted. "Oh, really." I handed him my glass and folded my arms across my chest. I tried to set my face, but I believe my expression was harder and sharper than I intended. Randall blanched and backed up slightly. "Explain how." I held up one finger before he could start. "But please use a clear thesis and logical arguments backed up by examples. I am very much looking forward to hearing your conclusions, and I'm sure you will appreciate my unvarnished feedback in response." He flinched. It occurred to me briefly that this may be the reason why I didn't have very many friends. I decided not to care.

"Uh . . ." Randall said.

"No need to rush." I looked at my watch. "I'll wait."

I didn't have to. Another group of ribbons and skirts and pretty arms swirled by and grabbed me by the shoulders. "Ladies only!" they crowed. "The boys can watch and learn." And I was pulled into the tangle of arms and skirts and stockinged legs, absorbed by the gravity of girls.

Dragons settled at each window looking into the gymnasium. They pressed their paws against the glass. No one seemed to notice this. I couldn't look away. The girls were too busy dancing, utterly taken in the moment. The boys were too busy scowling, utterly enraged by the moment. I was both present and separate, both observing and observed, both here and everywhere, both now and then. A dichotomy, and a paradox. I was in all moments, all at once. The music played and played, looped in and around itself, pulling in tight. The girls twisted and shimmied, then wound their way from one end of the dance floor to the other, threaded together through the touch of their hands. Two boys fought near the refreshments table, one boy bloodying the other's nose, only to be knocked straight into the bowl of punch and then crashing into a sticky puddle on the floor. No one else looked up at the dragons. I couldn't stop looking at the dragons. I thought of that day in the hospital, when my mother died, and how I wanted my aunt to come crashing through the window to save us—an explosion of rage and grief and vengeance. An explosion of hope and care and connection. All at the same time. She didn't come then, and the dragons stayed in their places. Again, I found myself in all moments at once, past and present and worrying future, the threads of time and space looping through my experience, intersecting with one another, forming a knot at the center of myself, where each touched each—each place, each moment, each heartbeat, each discrete unit of time, each twist in the thread of my life. The music pulsed. Two hands took my hands and twirled me around, setting the world spinning. When my mother died, she was only a husk of what she used to be—paper and dust and air. *(The woods decay, the woods decay and fall.)* Another girl looped her arm around my waist, and I felt the heat of her hip pressing against my hip, and the earth shifted under my feet, making me dizzy. I saw a dragon when I was four years old and on that day I learned to be silent; I was given no context, no frame of reference, no way in which to understand my experience, and the adults in my life hoped I would forget, and by doing so, nearly forced me to forget. A girl ran her gloved hand along my sweaty collarbone and down my arm. I shivered. My aunt nearly destroyed her house and flew away from her life and my cousin became my sister, and an entire section of my family was erased forever. Or so I thought. A girl pressed the backs of her fingers on my cheek, and gazed at my face. I felt the skin on my neck begin to flush. There were galaxies in her eyes. There were dragons who explored the cosmos, and dragons who explored the sea, and dragons who settled deep in the jungle—they left and they did not look back. We thought they weren't coming back. *They weren't supposed to come back.* And yet. Here they were. The music enlarged itself. I could feel it in my bones. The dancers swirled. They were entrancing, these girls. And entranced. They moved like a single organism—or, rather, they moved with a single collective mind. A hive of girls. A swarm of women. A murmuration of dancers. They threw their heads back in ecstatic joy. Pleasure radiated from their bodies in waves—pleasure at the simple fact of being *this very person,* at *this very moment,* living *this very life.* Cheeks flushed. Lips reddened. Fingers lingered on fingers and hips curved against one another through the frothy rustle of skirts.

I was part of them. But I was separate, too. I was aware of myself being separate. It *hurt.* But it was *interesting,* too. The memory of that moment is tangled with all my other memories—my own Gordian knot. The flush of those cheeks and the plump of those lips intersect with my mother's last rattling breath, my father slumped by the bottle, the look on Sonja's face when she was taken away, the shuddering sobs of Beatrice in my arms, they all are stuck and unstuck in time, experienced all at once. I reached. I wept. I longed. I grasped. I spun away.

In the windows the dragons sighed. And how could they not? They were beautiful, these girls. They were so, so beautiful. And maybe so was I. I lifted my arms and began to twirl. It felt so good, just for a second, to let go. Completely.

The guitar player stopped playing. So did the drummer. The horns hadn't noticed. They pushed doggedly on.

"Stop it this instant!" Sister Leonie gasped.

"Girls," Mr. Reynolds called. "Stop dancing."

They didn't.

I looked closer. I began to observe the way a scientist observes: dispassionately, and set apart. Even with only partial music, the girls' dancing increased in fervor and intensity. I stood still. I watched. And then I understood. Their mouths glittered. *(I touched my mouth. It didn't change.)* Their eyes widened. *(I touched my eyes. They were as they always were.)* They lifted their faces to the sky. There was a smell of cinnamon and clove and phosphorus. Hot smells. Maeve O'Hara's fingernails lengthened and curled prettily into points. Loretta Nowak's smile turned gold. I suddenly found myself wishing I had a notebook to write it all down. Record the observations. Follow the data. I looked at the windows. The dragons had begun to tap the glass.

"Oh dear," I said.

Marlys Larsen found Betty Shea's pretty mouth and kissed it hard. The nuns were transfixed. No one, save the dancers, moved. Alice Cummings stared in wonder at the talons growing out of her open-toed shoes. She ran her thumb down the front of her prom dress and sighed as it fell away. She stepped forward. Bare feet. Bare legs. Slightly lopsided breasts, but lovely all the same. A delicate curl at her pubis—even the trickle of blood making its way down the curve of her thigh was beautiful. I nearly choked. She was *so beautiful.*

Randall Hague, with his two glasses of punch in his hands, found his voice. "HEY NOW," he shouted.

"Shut up, Randall," I said. I pressed my hands to my heart. There was so much beauty. My knees started to wobble.

I noticed with a start that the music had stopped. I didn't know when. Time didn't mean much anymore. The girls may have been dancing to silence. Or they may have been dancing to music they made themselves. Was it true that my mother could have dragoned? I thought about the nuns at school and Mrs. Gyzinska and my stepmother and the widow lady minding Beatrice at this very moment. Did everyone hear the call? Would I? Would I go if I did? Could it be that some people heard it but didn't understand it? Could it be that some women weren't called? I ran my hands along my mother's lace, each knot like a promise. I imagined her fingers tying each one. A knot connects two disparate things into one immutable whole. Was I my mother? Was my mother me? Was she here with me, her fingers on the knots that my fingers now held? I didn't know. I was dizzy. There was so much beauty everywhere.

Eunice Peters suddenly had teeth made of diamonds. She didn't seem to notice. One of the nuns began turning green. No one noticed that either. In that tangle of cries and motion, of heat and change, of transformation and velocity, I stood, rooted to the ground, perfectly still. A fixed point in an otherwise chaotic universe. The dragons held vigil. The moment swirled around me. *They would all change,* I understood, deep in my bones. *And I would not.* I didn't know why. But I knew it was true.

Alice slid her thumb between her breasts, and my heart broke. I looked away. I couldn't bear to see them go.

The room grew hot. Faces flushed and skin slicked. A dragon blinked on the dance floor. Alice wasn't Alice anymore. Or no. She was more than Alice. She was Alice unbound. She was Alice compounded by Alice. She was infinite degrees of Alice. She opened her brand-new wings. She let out a scream of joy. It shattered the windows.

Glass shards, hard and bright as memories, rained suddenly down. They spangled and glittered on the ground.

The dragons flew in.

New dragons flew up.

Dresses littered the floor. Undragoned girls danced in the nude. Girls with dragon eyes and dragon mouths. Spikes erupted from vertebrae. Tender skin grew bright scales. Talons curled from painted toes.

I stepped away. The boys couldn't move. My hands were my hands and my mouth remained my mouth and I wasn't dragoning at all. My hands were on my mother's knots. I couldn't let her go. I walked backward, one slow step at a time. Maeve dragoned. Eunice dragoned. Marlys and Loretta and Emeline and Betty and six nuns all dragoned. I stepped right into a large black and green dragon. It was my aunt.

"Marla," I whispered. Beatrice hung around her neck. Little-girl arms. Little-girl legs. Dragon eyes. A dragon mouth. My head swam.

"No, Beatrice!" I shouted. "Absolutely not!"

Don't leave me when I can't follow, my heart sobbed. *Don't leave me alone. Please.*

The brick wall groaned. Two boys screamed. The back side of the gym collapsed.

My aunt gave me her paw. "This place is going to get dangerous in a minute. Let's go." I climbed onto her neck, holding Beatrice in the circle of my arms, and my aunt leaped into the night.

36.

There was no graduation that year. Really, they shouldn't have given us our diplomas at all since we simply missed the entire last month of school. Almost a third of my graduating class disappeared. I should put that word in quotation marks. "Disappeared." That was the official line. But they didn't disappear. We knew exactly what happened to those girls. And for the most part, we knew exactly where each of them went.

And it wasn't just my school. Girls across the country, once again en masse, dragoned that May. They called it the "Little Wyrming," but only when reporters were trying to be cute. Girls as young as ten and as old as nineteen dragoned that day.

The scale of the transformations was not even close to the numbers of the Mass Dragoning of 1955. Nationwide, well under thirty thousand girls stepped out of their skins and set their teeth against the sky. Many regions had no dragonings to speak of. Instead there were concentrated pockets scattered at random across the country. Another difference: while some girls opened their wings and struck out, like their dragon mothers and aunts before them, to seek their fortunes in the oceans or the mountains or the jungles or the sky, many, many of them stayed where they were.

The girls whose families kicked them out (alas, this was common) created communes in the parks, or they took up residence in abandoned factories or barns. Most of the dragoned girls attempted to continue with their educations, and went to school as normal the following Monday, forcing their overly large bodies into the narrow gates of schoolyards, only to be stopped by police, or newly formed anti-dragon brigades, or in some cases the National Guard. School principals and head teachers did not take kindly to potentially unruly students with the ability to breathe fire. The thinking went that the risk of insubordination with dragoned students was incalculable. How on earth could they be educated when they couldn't be subdued? principals wondered. At first, most schools took a hard line. Letters to the editor in newspapers across the nation were exclusively dragon-related for months. Tearful groups of concerned mothers of the non-dragoned went on television and demanded that their daughters be safe from any dragon influences at school. They asked for America to please *think* of the *children*.

HUMANS ONLY signs read.

Librarians, on the other hand, were far more sympathetic. And flexible. And very soon, small learning communities, geared toward the specific educational needs for recently dragoned young women, began to form in libraries around the country.

My town was one of the communities with a heavy transformation burden. The morning after prom, dragons were everywhere. In the parks. Loitering on bus benches. Sunning themselves down by the river. Or taking long strolls along country roads, before remembering suddenly that they knew how to fly. Little old ladies shooed dragons away from their rose bushes and their fruiting trees. Old men insisted that they stay off the lawn. Police officers told people to move along. But no one in an official capacity made any sort of plan as to what to *do* with the new dragons—most of whom were still minors. There was no consistent policy. The president of the United States, while giving an address talking about "new challenges" in vague terms, refused to even say the word *dragon*. But by the way he stammered, everyone could tell he was thinking it. The nation, once again, decided to carry on as though everything was normal.

Nothing was normal.

Older dragons—from the Mass Dragoning and other spontaneous transformations along the way—continued returning in larger numbers to their home grounds. Not all of them. But in significant numbers over time. Here and there. The dragons would simply *arrive.* There was no announcement of their arrival, and no pattern either, and yet, Mrs. Gyzinska always seemed to know when a new batch was about to show up. She had a large covered picnic area installed next to the library, and hired two former social workers (both transformed) to coordinate support and services to returning dragons. She also applied for (and received) several large grants from different foundations, which funded the creation of communal living spaces for dragons in several decommissioned factories around the Midwest. The dragons seemed to appreciate this. They weren't there to make trouble. They stayed in the communal spaces for a little while, but then they simply *got to work.* Some went to family farms and helped with the planting. Others took it upon themselves to volunteer with food distribution in poor communities. Others could be found mucking along riverways, pulling out the discarded remains of industrial refuse and coaxing back the green.

"Well, I for one am not surprised," Mrs. Gyzinska told me when she stopped by the apartment to give me my graduation present—or more of an end-of-school present. "We can't solve our problems unless we all work together. *All* of us. And heavens. Do we ever have problems."

Dragon crews showed up to repair the gym. They fixed the cars that had been overturned accidentally on prom night. They formed sewing circles in the park and donated sweaters and baby clothes and blankets to the local charity center.

"Ignore them," city officials said, without saying *who* exactly people were supposed to ignore. As though by ignoring them, eventually the dragons would go away.

They didn't go away.

Gentlemen, I am as surprised as you are to find myself called back in front of this committee, though I suspect for different reasons. I know that this is a difficult time for many of you—change is hard, after all. It is painful to let go of the things we once thought were true. We have reached, I believe, the mystic's Cloud of Unknowing. Or Kierkegaard's saltus fidei. His leap of faith.

As a scientist, it is a strange thing for me to stand in front of you and declare that science has no answer. But really, science rarely gives us answers. Rather, science gives us the means by which we may ask more questions: it provides context, connection, and background. It compounds our curiosities. We may stick a pin through the thorax of a butterfly in order to stop its wings and allow us to examine it closely, but by doing so, we will never observe those very wings pressing against the skin of the air and fluttering away. We will never know which direction that butterfly might choose to go, or what it would seek to do next. Science can only teach us so much.

You brought me here because some of you have daughters who dragoned. One of you has a recently dragoned son. Three of you have dragoned sisters. Dragoned neighbors. Dragoned colleagues. A dragoned wife. I know it is a lot to take in. I know that there are some of you who cling to the belief that dragoning is not only a cataclysmic tragedy, but that it is surely biologic in nature, and therefore must have a biologic antidote.

I am here to relieve you of that notion.

I am here to ask you to accept that which you cannot change.

I am here to point you to the fact that once upon a time, humanity worshipped the Divine Feminine, and that in that time all of humanity was in the thrall of her power and strength, both procreative and destructive, both fecund and barren, both joy and terror, all at once. If there is one thing I have learned in my years of research, it is that the answer is never just one thing. The particle is the wave, is the particle, is the wave. In the end, the entire universe is the marriage of opposites.

You have brought me here, gentlemen, in hopes of conquest—in an attempt to rein in this feminine largeness, to shrink it down and force it to acquiesce to your paternal control, to allow our culture to forget that any of this dragon business ever happened. This, my friends, is an impossibility. While it is true that there is a freedom in forgetting—and this country has made great use of that freedom—there is a tremendous power in remembrance. Indeed, it is memory that teaches us, and reminds us, again and again, who we truly are and who we have always been. The dragons are here to stay. Let us remember everything that brought us to this moment. Let us remember all those we have lost. Let us remember our loved ones as they were so that we may accept them as they are, just as we accept our country—changed, flawed, and growing—as it now is. Just as we must accept the world.

Personally, I think it's rather marvelous.

—From the opening statement given by Dr. H. N. Gantz (former chief of Internal Medicine at Johns Hopkins University Hospital, and erstwhile research fellow at the National Institutes of Health, the Army Medical Corps, and the National Science Administration) to the House Committee on Un-American Activities, March 12, 1967

37

The first semester of my freshman year at the University of Wisconsin was already well underway when my diploma finally arrived in the mail. It took the post office a very long time to locate my new address, and I suppose I shouldn't blame them. My new home was not . . . a typical sort of residence. Mail service was spotty.

The envelope was crushed and rumpled and the diploma itself looked as though someone had spilled coffee on it, but still, there it was. My name written in scripty letters. Highest honors. Despite the loss of my mother. Despite my father's abandonment and abdication. Despite raising an irascible little girl all alone. Despite the deep wound of grief. Despite everything.

I would have called my father to let him know, but of course my father was gone. So I called Mrs. Gyzinska instead.

"I wondered when I'd hear your voice," Mrs. Gyzinska said. And then, "Have you stopped in on Dr. Gantz, like I asked? I spoke to him last month, and he was asking about you, again."

I hadn't. I just didn't have time. I had thought I would hit the ground running when I arrived at the university, and that every secret of the universe would simply fall into my lap, and that I could catch new scientific discoveries as easily as a child catches fireflies in a jar, and would untie mathematical knots with a single tug. As it turns out, college is a lot of work. Dr. Gantz operated in an out-of-the-way laboratory in the medical school. He wasn't on the directory, but Mrs. Gyzinska had given me the number for his basement office. I just hadn't had time to call yet.

"I'm still just trying to keep my head above water," I said.

"No matter," Mrs. Gyzinska said, and I could easily picture

her waving my discomfort away. "See that you do so, though. Eventually. You'll be glad you did."

She waited for me to speak. I swallowed. I just didn't know what to say. It felt strange, suddenly, to say *why* I had called or *what* I needed from her—was I looking for approval? for validation?—and I found myself experiencing a wave of deep embarrassment, and then annoyance for feeling embarrassed.

Mrs. Gyzinska noticed my pause. She cleared her throat decisively and continued. "I've been meaning to get in touch anyway, but several"—she paused, and I could hear her knuckles rapping the wood of her desk—"several *interesting* projects have been occupying my time." I knew she meant her efforts with the new dragons. While there were a handful of schools that defied the state order banning dragons from attending primary or secondary institutions, I was fairly certain that my old school was not among them. Of course Mrs. Gyzinska would move heaven and earth to accommodate any dragon patrons. She was not one to suffer any impediments to a person's education. Especially a girl person's education. Or, in this case, a dragon person.

I found out later that she commissioned the construction of a prefabricated airplane hangar in the empty lot next to the library, for the dragons who hadn't been welcomed back by their families and didn't have anywhere to go, and then installed elephant doors at the western entrance so they could come and go freely. She converted the auditorium into a classroom of sorts. She put up a sign by the front door that said THIS LIBRARY IS FOR EVERYONE, and dared the anti-dragon campaigners to tell her otherwise (and god help them if they did). She was known to clock the occasional protester on the library steps with a swift swing of her very heavy purse. That's the thing about Mrs. Gyzinska: she could sneak up on a person.

I told her about Beatrice and her new school. I told her that it was already November and she hadn't gotten into trouble even once—a personal record. I told her about the books that Beatrice had been reading lately, and that she had been learning to paint and to build complex metal sculptures that turned in the wind, and was recently dabbling in fired ceramics. I didn't mention how she had access to things like metal forges or high-temperature kilns or how on earth such things were safe for a child of her age. But Mrs. Gyzinska didn't ask about any of that.

"Well," she said. "Beatrice is the sort of little girl who will always have an outsized presence in the world. I, myself, have always expected tremendous things from her. And how is . . ." She paused for a long time. "How is the *rest* of your household, my dear? Your . . . larger members."

Goddamned librarians, I thought. *How on earth can she have known?*

I shouldn't have been surprised. Of course she knew. She was Mrs. Gyzinska, after all. I sighed.

"Fine," I said. "They're all . . . I mean. We're still getting used to one another. They are extremely helpful, actually. But it has been an adjustment." I grimaced slightly. "Or, I mean to say that it's been an adjustment *for me,* mostly. Beatrice, of course, is thrilled. But for me . . . after everything that's happened. It's still a lot for me to take in." Was I too ambivalent? Did I sound too uncomfortable? Biased, even? Probably. These still weren't easy things to talk about. I took a slow breath. "It's strange. After I was so desperate for so long raising Beatrice on my own with no help, now that I have help—and honestly I have *so much* help. I have help coming out of my ears, and, well, sometimes flying overhead . . . And I know they mean well, *I do.* It's just sometimes *too much help* can feel"—I searched for the word—"irksome." I was being mean. I knew I was. And ungrateful. I was suddenly horrified that Mrs. Gyzinska might judge me for it. "That's the wrong word. It's just *a lot.* Does that make sense?"

Instead, she chuckled, low and gravelly, followed by a series of dry coughs.

"Indeed," she said. Again she coughed, hard, covering the

receiver with her hand to block out its severity, but I heard it all the same. My father coughed in the exact same way. "Sorry about that. It's cold season. Not like a little cold could stop me."

She could not have known—and neither could I—that a little cold *would* actually stop her, a little over a year after that conversation. What would start as a cold would become pneumonia, which would end her life on Christmas Day, 1965. The memory of what was to come and the memory of what was actually said that day are now, for me, inextricably linked. A memory inside a memory. The sharp and the soft coexisting in the same small space. Now, where I am, in *this* moment, I can't think about that conversation without wanting to cry.

I told her about the diploma—graduated with highest honors.

"Yes, I know," she said, coughing again. "I wish your mother could have seen it. I know she and I had our differences in the end. But I cared about her deeply. I know what your education meant to her, and what she was willing to do to ensure that it could persist. She would have been very proud of you, Alex. On some plane of existence, I feel confident that she is, even now."

All of a sudden, I couldn't look at the diploma. I missed my mother so much, I could barely trust myself to speak. I held my breath to stop myself from collapsing.

"Mrs. Gyzinska," I managed. "I just. I mean. Thank you. For all of it."

She coughed again. "Well. What I did was nothing and remains nothing. The only thing that matters is what happens next. And I suspect it will be fairly interesting. Don't you?"

We exchanged a few small pleasantries—what I was studying, which professors were terrible, and some books she had read recently. And then we said goodbye. We exchanged letters after that, but this was the last time I ever spoke to her.

I went to the roof of my building where we had set up a little open-air living room, with an old, elements-resistant rug. Several ratty chairs and a couple very sturdy benches surrounded a large brick fire pit. I gathered sticks from the kindling bin and newspaper from the paper bin and assembled it into a workable shape and lit it. I had a good blaze fairly quickly. I stared at the diploma for a long time, thinking about my mother, her body reduced to paper and husk and wind. And my father, disappeared into work, then disappeared into a bottle, and then into nothing. I thought about our house, so meticulously maintained by my mother, now disappeared in a bright moment of heat and smoke and flame.

"Here you go, Mom," I said. I pressed the diploma to my heart and then put it in the fire pit and watched it burn. *"Here at the quiet limit of the world,"* I recited, *"A white-hair'd shadow roaming like a dream / The ever-silent spaces of the East / Far-folded mists, and gleaming halls of morn."*

My mother's love of the Tithonus poem confounded me while she was alive, and it confounded me when she was gone, and it continues to confound me after all these years. It never stopped me from reciting it and holding it close. The words that she whispered became the words that I whispered. I wore them uncomfortably, like a dress that fits in theory but still feels off. Does memory decay? Does it shrivel and dry up and collapse? Is it a cricket in the pocket of the goddess, alive only through the force of misplaced love? If I held on to my mother's memory, did that mean that she was still with me? Did it see what I saw, or feel what I felt? I was a motherless girl, but my mother was with me *all the time.* It still wasn't enough. I closed my eyes and smelled the smoke and listened to the paper burn. I watched it in my mind's eye, trying to find my mother's eye as I did so. I hoped she saw it. I hoped she saw *me.* I hoped my mother became larger than herself in death. Larger than a dragon. Larger than everything.

38.

I was not, by any means, a typical student at the university. First, I lived a fair distance from any student housing, on a block of old factory buildings and warehouses. We were the only residents. Second, I had a ten-year-old to raise. One whose gaze was set firmly on the sky and who daily demanded to be allowed to dragon.

"Not yet," I said every day. "Please, not yet." Though my emotional reaction to the notion was becoming—and I noticed it at the time—less fraught. It felt like more of a delay to the inevitable. Moreover, the distinction of corporeal form began to feel more and more arbitrary to me. Perhaps this is a function of college life: we inexorably shed ourselves of our closely held preconceived notions. Or, perhaps more likely, Beatrice was simply wearing me down. Each day I saw the look on her face as she watched a local pod of dragons make their daily flight over our heads as I walked her to school, a look of pain, and hope and longing. None of the elementary schools in the area allowed dragoned students to attend, which provided me my original excuse to delay any major transformations—her access to education was a bottom line for me, and must be protected at all costs. But how long would that be the case? There were dragons attending universities, after all. And dragons attending church. And dragons meeting friends in the park. And dragons demonstrating at the Capitol. Every day between our home and school, Beatrice saw dragons assisting tree-trimming crews or beautifying the side streets or working alongside the sanitation department.

Dragons, it seemed, were everywhere.

Not to mention the dragons who lived in our home.

⟡

Back in May, before I arrived at school, on that terrible and wonderful prom night, with flocks of newly dragoned girls tossing their dresses on the ground and joyfully taking to the sky, my aunt Marla whisked me out of the collapsing gym to safety. We landed on the sidewalk in front of my building, breathing hard. Beatrice had undone her partial dragoning, and the process exhausted her so that she sat down on the stoop and instantly went to sleep. My aunt looked at me, her eyes suddenly wild. She had just remembered something.

"Your father didn't find out, did he?" my aunt asked urgently. The night air was choked with sirens. Dragons circled the sky. A car sped down the street and squealed out a U-turn at the sight of Marla on the sidewalk. "About the accounts?"

"What accounts?" I asked.

She pressed her paws to her mouth. "What of hers do you still have? Show me everything," she said.

Marla explained that she had insisted my mother open an account in her own name before she got married, in my name when I was a baby, and then another one when Beatrice was a baby. All three were in a bank in Madison, out of reach from my father.

"We started it with what our parents had left for us—their savings, the dregs of their farm after the bank had its share, a measly life insurance policy—and then we both contributed, every month. Your mother had to hide it from your dad, but it wasn't all that hard since he never paid any mind to the household accounts because he was, and I mean this very sincerely, a sexist, useless oaf. The money I kicked in, though, was nothing compared to what your mother *did* with it. I told you, remember? I told you she was a sorceress with numbers, and I wasn't kidding. She made it grow just by looking at it." Marla's eyes brightened with tears. "We never touched a dime. She said we could use them at the right moment. I believe that moment is right now. Show me what you have."

I went in and Marla stood outside and stretched her long neck up so that her head rested in the window. Beatrice was delighted. She could barely keep her eyes open, but still she was delighted. A dragon. A *real* dragon. Right here in our apartment. Well, just her head, but *still*. What a wonderful day.

(*What do we call her?* Beatrice asked before she fell asleep again.

She's my aunt, I told her. *Mother didn't like mentioning it. It was too sad when she left.* I wasn't ready to tell Beatrice the whole story. I didn't know when I'd be ready.)

After spending too many minutes rummaging through the haphazard folders that my father had dropped off over the years— bank crates containing birth certificates and baptismal records and the like—it finally occurred to me to open mother's carved box. The one my father had handed to me back in March, still hidden under my bed. My hands shook as I held it on my lap. Marla's eyes grew wide.

"Oh," she said, her voice barely more than a whisper. "I made that for her. A lifetime ago."

I undid the latch and opened it, awash all at once with the scent of rosemary, marigold, and thyme. I closed my eyes for a moment and took it in. The box appeared to be simply a place for mementos and keepsakes—old photographs, a hymnal, several rings, a bone carving of a startled-looking fish, a necklace with a seal pendant, tiny dolls made entirely of knots, and an ancient slide rule. I noticed the false bottom right away. I lifted it out, along with the first contents, and found two manila envelopes underneath, both of which contained the relevant information on the accounts, along with the name, address, and phone number of the nice man who managed them both.

The next day, my aunt insisted that she fly me to Madison first thing, despite my protestations. (*No one will give us a passing glance,* she insisted. *Not with this many dragons crowding up the sky.* She was incorrect. Everywhere we went, people stopped and stared. One old lady took our picture. A man threw rocks, though he could not hit us.) Marla waited with Beatrice outside as I went in to meet with the banker. He was about the age of my father, with delicate, tapered fingers and a rather dusty wool suit. He had been my mother's friend at school, and the moment he saw me, he clutched his heart for a moment.

"Surely you must be told all the time that you're the exact image of her," he said breathlessly. I merely smiled. Actually, no one had ever told me that. He showed me the files and explained that he was simply following my mother's precise algorithmic instructions, which accounted for the fund's success. "She was a marvel, your mom. An absolute marvel," he said with wonder. Included in the portfolio was a share in a small farm that produced a tiny profit every year, because my mother insisted that money should be tied to the land, and a building in an industrial area that was both out of the way and also not too far from campus. And was between tenants, the manager said apologetically.

I still hadn't found an apartment. Mrs. Gyzinska's search for untapped funds had been fruitless thus far. I looked at the map. The building was a short bike ride to campus.

"Great," I said. "Let's keep it that way for now."

And I moved in.

With my sister.

And four dragons—Marla, Clara, Jeanne, and Edith.

Clara the singer. Jeanne the construction specialist. Edith the caretaker. Marla, who made sure that everything worked. Their presence was my aunt's idea—or should I say, her demand.

"You're going to need some help," she said in a matter-of-fact sort of way that I found instantly annoying. "And we're here. Alex, I spent far too many years not intervening when I should, and not speaking out when I must. But I'm your aunt.

And I'm . . ." She couldn't bring herself to say *Beatrice's mother,* but the words still hung there—still unacknowledged, and still true. She closed her eyes for a moment before recovering. She crouched down and held my gaze. "And I'm *here now,*" she said. "And I insist."

The dragons were large, obviously. And loud. Big opinions, big voices, a massive presence. Beatrice took to all of them right away, gawping at her reflection in their shiny scales or climbing up their backs and hanging on to their long, lovely necks. She sat on their laps and told them stories and was delighted to have someone new to talk to. I, on the other hand, was accustomed to the controlled, hidden world that I lived in with my sister. That I maintained and managed all by myself. It was me and Beatrice, rulers of our own little universe. And then, quite suddenly, I had to *share.*

It took me a long time to make peace with it.

When we first moved in, we knocked out several extraneous walls and ceilings to allow greater freedom of movement for the larger residents. The dragons had decided to learn the art of brickmaking, harvesting the clay from southwestern Wisconsin (the colors are prettiest there) and using their own resources to fire the kilns. They then used the bricks to build a large oven and subsequently took up the practice of breadmaking. They became quite good, selling their wares to high-end restaurants and cafés and at their little stand at the farmers' market. People in Madison, as a general rule, tended to be far less leery of doing business with dragons than folks back home. It's a university town, after all, which leads to a certain level of open-mindedness. There was even a sort of Madisonian who went out of their way to buy bread specifically from the dragon bakers and then would speak loudly of how *proud* they were to be doing business with *dragons* and wasn't it *just terrible* that *some people* couldn't see past their own *prejudice?* My aunt loved this sort of shopper, as they could always be relied upon to buy something extra. And also, they left tips.

"Income is income," Marla liked to say. "No matter how insufferable the source."

It was her hope that their efforts would generate enough business to keep us financially afloat once my mother's money ran out—we had enough to fund the rest of my education, and save for Beatrice's education, and to cover the living expenses of two girls and four dragons for a while. But eventually we would need a different source.

I was grateful, frankly, for my father's ambivalence toward my mother and his laziness when it came to the duties of being a father. If he had known about my mother's accounts, he would have liquidated them for sure—and swallowed every drop. I was also grateful that my aunt was there to explain what all of it meant. When I turned eighteen right after prom, I became my own custodian. I inherited all that my mother left me, but I also inherited my own life. It was a strange feeling. I also became Beatrice's guardian, in point of law in addition to point of fact. It shouldn't have made a difference, but it absolutely *did*.

The dragons, it turned out, were simply part of the package.

And they were handy. They put in plumbing and fixed the electricity and even put in an automatic dishwasher, which felt like a modern miracle. They found cast-off furniture and flew it over, decorated tastefully, and built tables and comfortable chairs and tall bookshelves. Marla built a clothes washer and several woodstoves, which kept the individual rooms warm in the winter. They set up tools and a workbench in one area of the building, and planted a vegetable garden outside in the yard. They set up bedrooms for Beatrice and me that were separate for privacy, but with adjoining doors to allow for closeness. They built me a study with a telescope and a chalkboard for working through big problems, and built a climbing gym for Beatrice. They even built a greenhouse on the roof, with a large lounging patio next to it, lined with potted fruit trees and berry bushes and a climbing grape vine along the back wall.

I wasn't entirely comfortable, but even I had to admit that we definitely could have done worse.

⁓

The morning after my conversation with Mrs. Gyzinska, I grabbed my school bag from one of the sturdy pegs next to what used to be the delivery entrance.

"Are you off to class, Alex dear?" my aunt called from the other side of the building.

I sighed and pressed my forehead to the bricks. *Be kind*, I reminded myself firmly. *Be kind, be kind, be kind.* Everything Marla did seemed to annoy me. She was just always *there*. And she *cared so much*, it made it hard to breathe. Plus, she was just so *dragony*. My circumstances had not allowed me to be a regular teenager, but now, from time to time, all my years of deferred teenage petulance seemed to well up inside me, unbidden, so I did my best to pull myself together to keep from saying something I might regret.

I shouldered my bag, the strap crossing my body, the weight of my studies resting on my hip. I didn't really feel like having a conversation. I appreciated the fact that I had four enormous babysitters to fuss over Beatrice and cook her dinners and braid her hair and help her with her homework and make sure she brushed her teeth, yet I was still . . . icy with my aunt.

She was the one who left, after all. Left Beatrice in her crib. Left her sister. Left me. *For years.* And, as yet, she hadn't apologized.

And, as yet, I hadn't entirely forgiven her.

"Alex?" My aunt's large head peered into the hallway. I jumped. "Did you hear me?"

"What? No, I didn't. Sorry. I must be deep in my head. Homework, and you know. And . . . math stuff." That wasn't true. I still don't know why I felt like I needed to lie, but I lied all the time. Force of habit, perhaps. My aunt's eyes narrowed.

One of the side effects of having been married to a drunk was that not much got past her. She said nothing, clearly deciding to let the matter slide. "I'll be home late," I said, giving her half a smile. I pushed the heavy door open with my boot. "Please don't let Beatrice dragon while I'm gone."

Lately, Beatrice had learned how to partially dragon and return to her little-girlness at will. It always happened in bits and pieces—glittering fangs erupting out of her mouth, or golden scales shimmering up and down her arms. Once she developed talons in the middle of practicing the recorder in music class. It was difficult keeping that child in shoes, what with the occasional talon bursting through at the toes. Sometimes, she made her eyes dragon, just to freak out the boys at school. And she got good at it too. Her dragon aunties, as she called them, were mystified by this—none of them had known it was possible. And whether this was a function of the plasticity of childhood—and by definition, temporary—or if it was something specific to Beatrice, was a mystery. There was scant research on the subject, and it was simply impossible to get good information. I knew this would change eventually—it had to—but it didn't change the fact that we were largely flying blind in regard to the long-term effects on Beatrice's health and well-being. Maybe she would be able to continue to dragon and undragon as often as she liked. Maybe she would get unintentionally trapped in a form she did not wish. Maybe there would be consequences. There just was no way of knowing.

I worried about it.

My dragon housemates worried too. We wanted Beatrice to have a regular childhood—well, as regular as it could be while living in an old warehouse full of fearsome guardians.

My aunt cleared her throat. "Just so you know, there will be some ladies—"

"Dragons, you mean," I said, more scathingly than I meant.

My aunt gave me as mild a smile as is possible for a dragon. "Yes, of course. Dragons. Visiting. Later tonight, after Beatrice goes to bed. Anyway, they were friends of mine, once upon a time. They haven't been back since 1955. Interplanetary exploration. One put herself right in the eye of Jupiter's storm. Just amazing. I thought you might have questions, given your interests. If you wanted to stop by and meet them—"

"We'll see. I'm signed up for the observatory tonight. Lots to do. Don't know how long it will take. Got to go."

And I walked out the door without looking back. I was being unfair. I knew I was being unfair. And unkind. My aunt wanted us to be a family. But Beatrice was my family. How much family did one person need, anyway?

The third-floor window wrenched open and Beatrice's face peeked out.

"Bye, Alex!" she called, waving madly.

"Young lady," I heard Edith admonishing her from inside. She often got saddled with Beatrice duty. "You are already *thirty minutes late for school.* Get your shoes on this instant!"

"But I'm hours and hours early if school was in Hawaii, Auntie Edith," Beatrice cackled. "Let's fly to Hawaii!"

Beatrice referred to all four of our dragon housemates as "the aunties" inside of a day of our moving in together. Even Marla was Auntie Marla to her. As the months went by, I continued to notice the way that Marla lingered while brushing Beatrice's hair, or the way she pressed her paws to her heart at the sound of Beatrice's voice.

I had to tell her. But I wasn't ready.

"Be smart at school, Alex!" Beatrice waved with a grin. She shut the window. I knew for a fact that she had no intention of finding her shoes. Beatrice preferred to be on her own time. I sighed. If it weren't for the dragons, it would be me wrestling with Beatrice. Demanding rule-following. Demanding submission. It was a relief, frankly, to leave that behind.

I tried to feel grateful for the dragons.

It was a one-mile walk from my building to my first class. Sometimes I biked and sometimes I took the city bus. But when

I had time, I preferred to walk. It was November, but still oddly warm. The trees were bare, and the brown turf was brightened with frost, but the sky was a brilliant blue and the sun shone warm and clear. I closed my eyes for a moment and lifted my face, drinking in the heat and light.

Without meaning to, I thought about the dragoning girls. I thought about their dresses on the floor, their discarded skins lightly tumbling away like cicada husks. I did not hear the call that day, at prom, when many of my classmates did. I did not transform when they transformed. My body was still my body. I was still *me*. And yet. My back ached and my fingertips ached. All the time. My bones creaked like cranked-down springs. My back was my back, but sometimes I felt phantom wings. My hands were my hands, but sometimes I felt phantom talons. And phantom fangs. And inside my belly, a fire burned. I couldn't explain it. I had no way of getting good information. I had no way of knowing what was happening to me—or if anything was happening at all. Maybe my aunt was wrong. Maybe some women are *not* magic. Maybe all my symptoms were psychosomatic. The brain is powerful, after all.

It didn't matter. I didn't want to dragon anyway. I liked my body the way it was.

I mean. I was pretty sure.

39

On my way to school, I saw Sonja.

I didn't believe it was her.

I had imagined her so many times ever since that afternoon when my father hauled her away, I had begun to question whether she had ever been real in the first place. I would see her out of the corner of my eye on the stairs, or in the locker room, or at the drinking fountain. Several times, I thought I saw her at the library, or on the street, or driving a car. Each time, at my second look, I would realize it was just another blond girl, or a brunette, or a girl of a different race entirely. Once I thought a middle-aged woman with children was Sonja. And another time it was a man in a suit. And another, an elderly nun. Each time I would shake my head or give my hand a little slap. *Pull yourself together,* I told myself sternly.

I stopped on State Street to grab something to eat—my aunt had been right, of course, and I realized I was hungry the moment I left the house. State Street was overrun with people again, and it was difficult to maneuver through the crowds and barricades. Another protest. Two of them, actually. On one side of State Street were the anti-dragon protesters (THE WISCONSIN IDEA NEVER INCLUDED MONSTERS! read one sign. DRAGONS ARE DUMB read another), and on the other side were the dragons and the dragon supporters. (MY BODY, MY CHOICE declared the sign held by one dragon. OUR LIVES ARE BIGGER THAN YOU THINK read another. REAL MEN LOVE DRAGONS insisted the sign held by a scruffy-looking ponytailed man gazing hopefully at a nearby dragon.) I stopped for a few minutes to say hello to friends who were handing out flyers and demonstrating in favor of dragon acceptance—a boy from my astronomy class, and two girls who were in my mathematics seminar, and a dragon named Milly from my physics study group.

After a few minutes, the boy—Arne was his name—peered over my shoulder and squinted into the crowd. Then his face lit up.

"Oh, hey!" he called out, waving madly and beckoning someone over. "Guys," he said to us, "come meet my cousin."

My mouth was full of cheese sandwich when I turned, and gasped. The din of the crowd—with its chants and music and blasting horns and beating drums and shouting—fully ceased, and was replaced by a high, thin ringing in my ears. A young woman approached. She was smiling at Arne. She hadn't recognized me yet. Her hazel eyes were stark against her pale skin, and her white-blond hair had been tied into a braid that hung down her back. It was . . . *oh god.* Her face. *Sonja's face.* The whole world stopped. *Sonja's face.* My cheeks got hot. *Sonja's face.* I couldn't breathe. *Sonja's face.* My vision wobbled, and the street, the people, the signs, the buildings, and the wide, wide sky all at once, began to swim. I tried to speak, but nothing came out.

"Oh, my god," Arne said. "Alex, are you choking?"

After a few swats on my back from my friends, and then being fully turned upside down and shaken by Milly the dragon, the chunk of sandwich lodged in my esophagus popped violently forth. I dropped to my knees and heaved a few times. I wiped my face on my jacket and stood. *Sonja's face.* I became suddenly aware of myself in ways that I hadn't been for a long time. My hair, much longer than I preferred, curled below my shoulders and was covered mostly by my hat. (I had never once in my entire life thought about my hat, nor had I ever bothered to wonder if I happened to look dumb in that hat, but in that moment, my only thought was *Oh good lord, do I look dumb in this hat?* over and over again, like an infinite loop.) There was cheese sandwich stuck in my teeth, and I was fairly certain I hadn't washed my corduroys in well over a week. Possibly a month. I was wearing a sweater that Clara had knitted, which frankly wasn't one of her primary skills, so while it was certainly warm, it was also lumpy and misshapen and a terrible shade of rust. I became uncomfortably aware of my hands, and suddenly realized that I had no idea where I should put them, and I noticed that I was likely standing weirdly, but I suddenly couldn't remember how people organize their bodies in order to stand like regular people. *Sonja's face, Sonja's face.* How could everyone hang around acting normal when Sonja was—

"Alex?" Sonja said. Her spangle freckles had darkened since I saw them last, and stood out on her skin like jewels. Her cheeks and lips had brightened in the bite of the November wind. She was wearing a fringed jacket and boots that had been hand-painted with flowers and mountains and trolls, and a University of Wisconsin T-shirt. *For crying out loud,* I thought. *We go to the same school. She's been here the whole time.* Sonja blinked. She was crying. "It's you! Alex, I can hardly believe it."

"Sonja," I managed, but I didn't have to say anything more, because she had thankfully thrown her arms around me and pulled me into a hug. She smelled of cinnamon and clove, and a dark, metallic smell that I would later identify as her paints from her art studio. Even in that moment, I noticed the colors embedded in the cuticles around her nails.

"Aren't the rest of us going to be introduced?" Milly complained. Arne apologized and gave everyone's names, and suddenly I remembered to look at my watch.

"*Shit,*" I said. "I'm late." I didn't want to leave. I hesitated, hugged Sonja once more, and then I hugged her yet again, and it felt as though the world ceased its spinning for a moment and everything stopped—the wind, the shouts of the crowd, the peppered questions from my friends, all of it gone. What was time, anyway? The only thing that could possibly exist was *now.* There was only *this very second.* Everyone around us shivered and stamped their feet in the cold, but all I could feel was the warmth of her body in my arms, the heat of her cheek against my skin. It hurt to step away. I pointed at Arne. "He can give you my number," I said to her, my voice harsh and desperate. "I wrote you so many letters, and—" I clenched my teeth and stopped. I didn't trust my voice. Sonja took my hand. And my other hand.

"I did too," she said, shaking her head. "My grandmother didn't let me send them. She said it would get you in trouble. I wrote to Beatrice too. Alex, I kept them all. Every single letter. I have a whole box. I was so scared you would forget me." She hugged me again. "I can't believe it's you."

The crowds surged around us. Young men threw rocks and fights broke out between the opposing sides. I found out later that there were several arrests that day. A small fire burned at the center of the street. People swore and jeered at one another. I didn't notice any of it. I held Sonja's hands in mine. I couldn't bear to let go.

"Call me as soon as you can," I said. "I have to go, but I need to see you. As soon as possible. I have so much to say."

I turned on my heel and headed to class at a run. I paused, briefly, to look back, and saw that someone had given her a sign that said WE ARE ALL PRECIOUS with the silhouetted figures of people and dragons holding hands. She held it aloft, like a flag.

I don't think my feet touched the ground for the rest of the morning.

Over the next month, I saw her every single day, many times a day. We had no classes in common—she was an art student, with a minor in literature, and her classes were all in an entirely different section of campus—but we had breaks around the same time and could meet in the library, or in a nearby diner, or in one of the lounges. We walked along the lake and sat for hours on a bench, watching the snow blow across the thin sheets of newly formed ice. She came to my house and met my family. It was the first time I ever called them my family. Marla tried to play it off, but I could see her turn away and wipe her face with the tip of her tail and then hunt through her purse for a handkerchief.

And it wasn't just when Sonja was around. I became more present with everyone. I stopped and had conversations with Jeanne. I helped Edith with the bread. I asked Marla about engines. I didn't roll my eyes when the four of them lounged together with their limbs entwined, reading literature out loud—Dickinson or Shelley or Proust.

My aunt, obviously, was thrilled with this development and made sure to compliment Sonja and invite her to dinner whenever possible. Beatrice insisted that Sonja sit next to her at the table and occasionally showed off her partial dragoning—but only occasionally since it exhausted her so, and because the other dragons objected so vociferously. Beatrice then insisted on organizing drawing workshops with Sonja, or playing board games on weekends, or inviting Sonja to sit out on the roof with our dragon aunties and roast marshmallows. Sonja and I sat for hours up there, feeding the fire and watching the stars, or the snow, the weight of her body leaning against mine and my cheek resting on her shoulder, talking about the world and everything in it until the deepest part of the night.

We spent every minute together we could. There weren't enough minutes in the day. In a lifetime.

Her grandfather had died two years earlier, but her grandmother lived and painted nearby in a small apartment in Madison not too far from campus. Sonja went to see her every Sunday. Mrs. Blomgren didn't want to see me, though—my father was the one who evicted them, after all, and some hurts are difficult to let go. I tried not to take it personally. Sonja never mentioned her mother, and I still hadn't asked. She regarded my dragon family shyly at first, and then with a growing curiosity, and then closeness. She helped with the breadmaking and learned about their brickwork. She even took up glassmaking.

"She fits right in, don't you think?" Marla said one evening while we were finishing the dishes. Sonja and Beatrice were on their bellies on the floor, drawing pictures of castles. Sonja rested her cheek on her fist and glanced over at me. She smiled. I blushed. Marla flared her nostrils and suppressed a grin of her own. "As I said," she muttered.

Did my grades suffer? Maybe a little.

Maybe it was worth it.

40.

Finals came, and went, and I pulled enough all-nighters to get my name at the top of the list when my professors posted the scores. My sour-faced recitation instructor offered me a lab assistant job. "It's the sort of thing that a student who is likely pursuing a doctorate might be interested in. I assume that means you." Even when he was complimenting me, it sounded like vinegar in his mouth. I said yes before he finished his sentence. I started volunteering a few nights a week at the astronomy lab. Mrs. Gyzinska, somehow, knew all of this, and sent me an old copy of *Ideas and Opinions* by Albert Einstein (it had been inscribed to her on its publication day with a personal note from the man himself—was there anyone that librarian didn't know?) as well as a small potted plant. She enclosed a note that said, "This seemed appropriate," and nothing else. Meanwhile, Sonja's grandmother had forgiven me enough to knit me a scarf, and stitched a little felted troll at the end.

All in all, it was a successful conclusion to my first semester at the university.

I hadn't forgotten my promise to Mrs. Gyzinska to pay a visit to Dr. Gantz. All semester long, I put it on my calendar and cleared some time. And each time, I found myself hesitating, and avoidant. I needed to see him, I knew, and not because of my promise. I had *questions,* many of which kept me up at night. But I wasn't sure if I wanted to know the answers.

The day before Christmas break, I found the dumpy little building on the corner of the medical school complex and made my way down several flights of stairs to Dr. Gantz's office.

I hadn't called and hadn't told him I was coming. It didn't matter.

"Ah! A visitor!" he exclaimed. "Please come in!"

I'm not sure if it was the fact that I had previously met him in the dark, but he looked much older than I remembered. Shockingly old. His head was mushroom shaped and nearly entirely bald, with age spots scattered across his scalp. He had brown eyes that were likely warm once, but were now blurred nearly blue by the cloud of glaucoma. His tissue-paper skin folded over itself and his knotty fingers crawled across a stack of paper covered with tightly packed numbers and diagrams.

"Do you remember me?" I asked.

"How could I forget? You thought that dragons were cows." I blushed, but he didn't notice. "Or maybe it was birds. Honestly, I was a wee bit concerned that maybe our Helen was incorrect in her assessment of your potential."

I shoved my hands in my pockets and deeply wished I hadn't come. "I've often thought the same thing, to be fair," I admitted.

A smile cracked across his round face, like a jack-o'-lantern. "I've been hoping to see you, actually. I do wish you hadn't waited so long—I'm not getting any younger, you know. Men my age drop dead without a moment's notice. Mrs. Gyzinska, thankfully, has kept me informed of your academic successes this semester." *Of course she did,* I thought in amazement. "Congratulations." He raised his teacup toward me as a salute. "You're well on your way."

He motioned for me to sit and immediately began busying himself with the electric kettle, calling out to the secretary to bring a small bottle of milk and two mugs.

"No, really," I protested. "It's not necessary. I don't want to be any trouble." (I had a question, deep in the center of myself, that wriggled and itched. But I wasn't ready to ask it. Not yet.)

"Nonsense, nonsense," he said. "Make yourself at home. I get so few students stopping in. We might as well make it an occasion." He called for the secretary again. Hearing nothing, he shuffled off to find a teapot. And tea. And apparently a bottle of milk. I sat in the office chair and waited.

The walls were a riot of artwork and esoteric charts and old documents and framed photographs. A few old maps. Printed broadsides. There wasn't a square inch that wasn't occupied. Odd contraptions and instruments littered the shelves, along with heaps of assorted fossils and bowls of shining scales. An open wooden box sat on the floor, filled with what looked like massive teeth. There were sculptures and stained glass and whirligigs. Nothing looked like it belonged in a scientist's office. There were several medieval engravings depicting dragons attacking villages or sitting serenely on mountaintops or guarding the mouths of caves. He had about a dozen photographs of ancient carvings and pictographs, as well as another photo of a tapestry that appeared to show both male and female dancers in mid-transformation. He had three separate pieces showing the anatomy of dragons: one modern, one from the Enlightenment, and one taken from an Egyptian papyrus. He had one blurry photograph of a woman halfway through her dragoning. Her hands were clouds. Her dress hung in strips. There was a look of fierce joy on her face.

The kettle sang and the professor trundled in and began to busy himself with the making of tea.

"As I said, I've been waiting for you to come by," he said. "But more so, I've been hoping that you might do me the honor of extending an invitation to *your* home. I know that sounds bold. But I've been in this business a long time, and I have some . . . *questions* for you. Or rather, some points of curiosity, regarding the structure and organization of your household." He stirred the boiling water into the leaves and covered the whole thing in a cozy. He set a timer. He noticed me staring. "Tea requires precision, you see, when made properly. I'm a scientist, after all. And details matter." He winked.

I folded my hands across my stomach and pressed. The smell

in the office—Lysol and dust and underground mustiness—was making me nauseated. Or maybe it was nerves. "How much did she tell you?" I didn't have to say who *she* was.

He sat at his desk and steepled his fingers, resting his chin on his fingertips. He grinned. "Oh. Heavens. Everything. About *you,* certainly. Probably more than you know yourself. That's Helen all over."

"I read your pamphlet," I said. "*A Physician's Explanation of Dragoning.* I had a question and—"

"I hope you instantly forgot everything you read. Even a year after I wrote it, I realized that a good percentage was wrong. Now I feel that most of it is."

I nodded. "Clearly." I tapped my chin a few times with my fingertips—a nervous gesture I had developed that Marla insisted would give me pimples if I wasn't careful. "My aunt gave it to me a long time ago. When I was a little girl."

"Yes, your aunt," he smiled. "Marla. She was part of the group I studied. It's amazing how science can work sometimes—a pebble can give us insight into the nature of the mountain. Or a single, whizzing particle can intimate larger truths about the stars. I was fond of Marla. And her . . . special friend. I was there on that terrible day when her heart broke forever."

"Well," I said, frowning. "Not forever, exactly. Edith lives with us now."

His eyes twinkled. He pulled out a steno pad and wrote something down. "Now that, young lady, I did *not* know." He paused and clapped his hands. "I know something that Helen Gyzinska does not. This *never happens.* How marvelous!" He bounced in his chair a few times and added another sentence. "I wonder how they found one another in the end."

"No idea," I said. "I never asked." I shifted uncomfortably.

He resumed writing in his steno pad. "Are they still in love?" the doctor asked, his voice light and neutral. He didn't look up.

The question startled me. *In love?* I had never asked that either. They were simply adults who had somehow come into my sphere and invaded my life and were helpful in their way. I hadn't once considered their internal lives or motivations or feelings. All four dragons slept together in a heap, cuddled in a nest that they built in the corner. Tails curled around middles and arms and legs entwined. I never asked them to name this, and they didn't do so for me. They just worked together and cared for one another and admired one another's skills and service and humor. They just held one another close. They sweetly bid goodnight and kissed one another in the morning. And they were all good mothers to Beatrice.

In love. I turned the concept around in my head, trying to get a sense of its size and shape and mass.

"Yes," I said, understanding for the first time. It felt like a burst of light in my head. "Very much so. All four of them are very much in love, I believe." I pressed my hands to my cheeks. I hadn't hugged Marla since she returned, but I felt an ache to do so now. I thought about Sonja. If those dragons were in love, then *what was I?* I spent every day with Sonja. I spent every minute I could. We clung to each other. Still. There was a bit of a fog when it came to putting a name on what it was that I felt, what it was that we were to each other. I suddenly had a profound need to know, but I did my best to put that thought aside and save it for later. I was talking about my aunties. I looked at the doctor in the eye. "It's incredibly nice, actually."

"Well, of course it is," he said, writing something down. "That's love for you. It's why we're all here, after all. And why we hang on."

I was quiet for what felt like a long time. *It's time to tell him why I've come,* I told myself. I held on to the arms of my chair the way a castaway clings to a lifeboat, like the world around me was wind and wave and the ocean's abyss.

The timer rang and the good doctor made us tea. "I'm assuming you take milk. I simply assume that everything is better with milk, but then I am from Wisconsin, after all."

He handed me a mug. The tea was nearly white, and the separated cream floated on top in a thick pool.

I grimaced. "Doctor Gantz," I said, "there's something I need to know. My father, before he died, told me that my mother should have dragoned. He thought that maybe the cancer wouldn't have taken her if she had, and then maybe she wouldn't have died." My voice shook.

The doctor sipped his tea. He thought a moment before he spoke. "I've heard that hypothesis," he said, finally. "I don't think there's any evidence for it either way."

"So he's wrong?" I said. My throat felt constricted as though wounded, as though I had swallowed a fish hook. I did my best to remain impassive. I don't know how successful I was.

Dr. Gantz set his cup on his desk. "No, I'm not saying your father is wrong, I'm just saying that we can't know if he's right. Our knowledge is so limited. Look, there are those who insist that the ability to dragon is sex-specific, and moreover that its expression is subject to the will of the individual—in other words, it's bad women making bad choices. That's a misreading of the data in order to support a foregone conclusion and a limited point of view. Fortunately, we have enough evidence to reject the first notion out of hand—sex-dominant, sure, but the human-dragon organism is far more complex than we previously thought. I do subscribe somewhat, and with reservation, to the theory of *choice,* however, though with the caveat that some individuals find the need to dragon so powerful that it becomes an inexorable force. They couldn't stop it if they tried." He shrugged. "It's multifaceted, this condition." He sipped his tea again. "As for your mother. One could certainly argue that perhaps the cancer itself prevented her changing. But I'm not sure I believe that. One could similarly argue that the change itself would have interrupted the progression of her cancer because of the reorganization of tissues and cells. Perhaps that could be true if she was actively sick, but her cancer was in remission in 1955. Dragons have died of all sorts of things—pneumonia, heart attacks, organ failure, and, yes, cancer. Just because they live longer than us, and have profound differences in their anatomy, respiration, metabolism, and other systems, it doesn't mean they can't also get sick and die someday. Your mother died of cancer. What form she was in at the time is irrelevant, but that doesn't make her loss any less painful. Does that help?"

This bothered me deeply for reasons I couldn't quite name at first. I sat up in my chair, my body tilted forward. Was I being aggressive? Maybe. "My mother's body," I said carefully, *"wasn't irrelevant."* My cheeks felt hot.

"Of course not. I didn't mean to suggest so." He sipped his tea again, closing his eyes and collecting his thoughts. He seemed unbothered by my sudden anger. Maybe he was used to being the target of people's rage. "One could argue that perhaps she never felt the urge to transform in the way other people did. But that, too, I find doubtful. More likely, she did feel the urge to change, and powerfully so, and yet chose to stay anyway—she chose that very body, that very life, despite its limitations and despite the fact that it would be cut short far too soon. Even imperfect things can be precious, after all. The choice *itself* is precious. The smallness and the largeness of an individual life does not change the fundamental honor and value of every mani-festation of our personhood. I think it does no good to wonder if your mother chose rightly or wrongly. There's no such thing, you see? The only thing that is relevant is the fact that she *was*. She *lived*. She raised you and Beatrice as best she could and as long as she could and loved you every second. And her life mattered."

I still had more questions, but I wasn't sure I had the strength to ask them. Maybe it's true that the cancer would have gotten her in the end either way. Or maybe she was afraid of what a life unbound might be. Or maybe she didn't trust my father to raise me on his own. Or, simply, my mother loved me *that much*. Was it fear or love that made her stay? There was no way of knowing.

The only thing that was certain was that I missed my mother. I felt a surge of grief hit me like a wave.

I looked at the clock. "I'm due in the lab in a bit, so I have to go fairly quickly. I'll talk to my aunt Marla and we'll see when you can come by for a visit. I'm sure Mrs. Gyzinska told you about my sister."

He lit up. "Yes! A most interesting case. I have yet to come across a similar situation, either in the current literature or in any of the historical documents. Truly an extraordinary child. Has she ever *fully* transformed and then returned?"

"Not fully. Usually she only changes in bits and pieces. If she has ever fully changed, I have not seen it. We usually tell her to return to her little-girl self. Just in case."

The doctor wrote something down. "And why is that, do you think?" he said.

No one had ever asked me that before. I opened my mouth, but nothing came out. I thought about my mother's rules. Her silences. The sudden anger. The slap. She told me I would understand someday. But I didn't. Instead, that slap came out of *me* in oblique and unexpected ways. In my explosion of anger at Mrs. Gyzinska that day in the library. At Beatrice when I saw her notebook full of dragons. It came out in my terror of being alone. My mother's fear became my fear, whether I wanted it or not. The realization of this made me gasp.

"I can't lose my sister," I said, as large tears pooled and slid down my cheeks. I was astonished. I hadn't meant to cry.

"What on earth makes you think you'll lose your sister?" He shook his head in a state of bafflement and wrote something down. *"A lifetime of research and still no one understands the basics,"* he muttered under his breath. He scribbled something else on a separate scrap of paper and regarded me through a narrowed eye.

"Beatrice and I only have each other," I murmured, which didn't answer his question. The words were automatic, and for the first time, I realized how hollow they sounded. I had been saying these words for so long that I had never considered how quickly a comforting truism can become a limitation—or a trap.

The doctor leaned forward. "Well, first, it's clear that this belief is no longer true. There are others in your life—indeed, you live in an entire household of others, all of whom would gladly risk everything to protect and care for both you and Beatrice. The two of you are part of something larger than yourselves. How marvelous! Would that all of us were so fortunate. While it is perfectly understandable that you once worried that your sister's dragoning would precipitate her removal from your life, I think recent events should have disabused you of that notion. At this very moment, human and dragon families—both blended by birth and created by circumstance and shared bonds—are caring for one another and sitting down at dinner and making plans and occasionally squabbling and carrying on with their lives, just as they always have. You are holding on to a fear that is no longer relevant to the current reality. Leave it behind!" He drained his teacup and sat in silence for a long moment. I looked at my hands. "Essentially, you have a choice: you can force your sister to remain in the form you know, or you can accept her as she wishes to be. But ask yourself, is it really so terrible to have another dragon in the house? Will you not simply fight just as hard on her behalf, and protect her interests, and hold her in love and care, just as you always have?"

"But school . . ." I began lamely.

He tossed that idea away with his hand. "Small-minded bureaucrats!" he snorted. "Don't even get me started on that ilk! I've been battling similar buffoons my entire career."

I didn't know what to say. I looked at the clock. I was definitely going to be late. But I wasn't quite prepared to leave. I gulped the last of my tea, which for some reason made Dr. Gantz suddenly look unreasonably happy.

"More tea?" he said.

"No thank you. I have to go." I pulled my bag onto my shoulder. Dr. Gantz put his hand on my arm.

"My advice? Let her dragon. Maybe she'll stay that way. Maybe she won't. But there's no point in preventing a chrysalis from opening if it's ready. Indeed, doing so could kill the creature inside. I would prefer a world with Beatrice in it, regardless of her form," Dr. Gantz said. He steepled his fingers and pressed them to his chin. "And, if you don't mind, I would love to be permitted to come and observe her transformation. For science. It could be she is not as unique as she appears, but the research right now is scant. The only way we challenge poor thinking and bad ideas is through the careful examination of the facts and the publication of data. I have always believed this." He interlaced his fingers as though in prayer. "Please," he said.

I will admit it now: I took a dim view of Dr. Gantz's request. "I'll think about it," I said. My voice was flat. At the time, what I meant was *no*. It was one thing for me to throw caution aside and allow my greatest fear to happen to the person I loved the most, regardless of the consequences, and without knowing what the emotional, biologic, or situational fallout might be (and yes, I was beginning to understand, with greater clarity, that my fear was likely unfounded), but to agree to have a man we barely knew sit and watch? For something this . . . *private*? And take notes? And maybe try to get it peer reviewed and published? Well. *We'll see.* Science was all fine and good, but scientists also need to know when to notice that enough is enough. I didn't want my sister to be anyone's lab rat, no matter how well intentioned.

I didn't say any of this to the doctor.

"Thanks, Dr. Gantz," I said. "I'm so glad we had a chance to meet."

And I left.

41

I didn't tell Marla and the aunties about Dr. Gantz's advice right away. I could barely put it into words inside my own thinking. The very notion of not being able to braid Beatrice's hair, or hold her on my lap, or hang on to her hand as we walked, felt like a needle in my heart. And while I hadn't told anyone about the nature of my questions with Dr. Gantz, I did, unfortunately, tell Aunt Marla about his desire to come by the house and meet the family. I thought she would reject it out of hand. Instead, she and Edith were inexplicably thrilled by the prospect of seeing him again and catching up on old times, and called him immediately to invite him to Christmas dinner. We were already hosting Sonja and her grandmother—and who knows how many extra dragons, as well as some of the other vendors from the farmers' market—and really, what was one more? I was miffed, I must say, about the prospect of having too many people around the table on Christmas. It had always been Beatrice and me, just the two of us. And now we were *many*. And it took some getting used to.

Beatrice remained in school for another week after my term ended, as her break didn't start until the day before Christmas Eve, a fact that struck her as deeply unfair. I had carefully arranged my schedule first semester with an open space around three-thirty so I could continue picking Beatrice up from school every single day and walking her home. Just like old times. Before moving. Before the dragons living in our house. I wanted Beatrice to know that at least some things would never change.

Except one change—now Sonja came with me.

Snow drifted slowly from the late-afternoon sky as we waited outside the school. We sat at the edge of the playground, in view of the front door, sitting side by side on one of the benches. The bell hadn't rung yet, but the sun still hung low over the trees, and we knew it would be dark soon. Several mothers milled about in front of the school, checking their watches, stomping their boots on the ground to warm up their toes. They ignored us. Neither of us was a mother as far as they could tell, which made us deeply uninteresting. Which was fine. I only wanted to talk to Sonja anyway.

Though it turned out I didn't have very much to say.

"You're quiet," she said. There was no petulance in her sentence, no note of disappointment. She was simply stating the fact. She reached her arm across my back and held me close for a moment.

"I know," I said. Dr. Gantz's advice had settled in the center of my guts like a heavy stone. I carried that weight for days. I barely ate. I hadn't slept. I had taken to tiptoeing into Beatrice's room at night and lying on the floor next to her bed, just as my mother had done, my face turned toward the window, my eyes full of stars. "Too much on my mind, I guess."

I turned to Sonja. Thick snowflakes clung to her hair and eyelashes. They gleamed in the slanting light. She was so pretty I could hardly breathe. I took her mittened hand in mine. And then, I leaned in close and kissed her. Her cheek. Then her forehead. Then her mouth. Did anyone notice? Did anyone see? I didn't know, and I didn't care. What else could I do, in the face of that much beauty? The smell of clove and paint. The smell of cinnamon and something else—something dark and slightly acrid, like smoke. Her chapped lip, her cool cheek, her pale hair clinging damply to my skin. There was no one else in the universe. We were a universe of two.

I could be this happy all the time, I thought first.

But what about Beatrice? I thought next. *Doesn't Beatrice deserve to be happy?*

The stone in my abdomen grew even heavier.

The bell rang and the children streamed out—running to their buses or their bikes or heading home in little packs. Sonja and I stood and separated (though even in the space between us, a thread pulled). I watched Beatrice emerge from the front door. She held her hand over her eyebrows like a visor, looking out. Her shoulders deflated as she spotted us. She carried her knapsack like it weighed a thousand pounds, her footsteps trudging through the snow.

I did this, I thought. *I am doing this.* I tried to keep my thoughts on the present. But it was difficult.

"Hi, Beatrice, honey," Sonja said.

"Nice to see you too," I said. Beatrice walked right past us. No hug. No thousand stories. No impromptu songs. She didn't leap onto rocks or pirouette on park benches. Her dragon aunties had combed out her curls and wound them into two tight buns on the sides of her head, like a Valkyrie, into which Beatrice had stuck four pencils, two crayons, six markers, and a compass. I was surprised her toothbrush wasn't in there. Beatrice scowled and kept walking home without a word. Her eyes got dragony with emotion, but returned to normal before I said anything.

How many times had I begged her to refrain from dragoning at school? And for what? Was it worth it? Beatrice sniffed and rubbed her eyes. Golden scales appeared briefly along the back of her neck and vanished.

I had three dragons in my physics class and another four in my Western civ recitation. There were dragon student workers in the library and several in the nuclear engineering lab and at least two professors who had dragoned in the middle of their lectures at some point in the semester and had simply returned to their notes and proceeded as normal. How many times had I wanted to tell Beatrice all of this? Nearly every day. But I didn't want to confuse her, so I kept this information to myself, which made her feel more alone.

"Would you like to stick around for a little while?" I asked. "It looks like some of your friends are playing in the playground."

I wasn't actually sure if those were her friends. I realized with a start that she hadn't been playing with other children lately. "Sonja and I could play too."

"No, thanks," Beatrice said. Her normally active face was leaden and slack.

"Oh. Okay," I said, trying as hard as I could not to sound hurt, but clearly failing. "I'm sorry you had a hard day."

Beatrice glared again. Dragon eyes. Dragon mouth. They went back to normal. "I *didn't*. It's just . . ." She looked at the ground. "The other kids in my class don't have their big sisters walking them home. Like babies."

Sonja squeezed my hand and let go. She put her arm around Beatrice for a moment. "You know, Beatrice, I was planning on walking home with you, but I completely forgot that I have to help my grandmother move something very heavy." She caught my eye and raised one eyebrow. Sonja was always a particularly perceptive person. Far more so than I ever was.

She leaned over and kissed my cheek. "You two have a lot to talk about," she whispered, her lips brushing my ear. My skin buzzed, heating me through. And she walked away in the snow, her touch lingering on my body, like a ghost.

Beatrice gave Sonja a brief wave, and then stumbled forward under the weight of her backpack. I leaned over and hoisted it off her shoulders and carried it instead. "I'm sorry, Bea," I said. "I keep doing everything wrong."

"It's fine. Just forget about it. I want to walk by myself." She quickened her pace to walk ahead of me. I didn't try to match it. I just let her walk on, observing the upward thrust of her step, the slight arch to her back. As though she was waiting for the moment that her wings would simply erupt. Waiting for that moment to fly away, unhooked from the limitations of gravity, her silhouette etched against the sky. I knew what it was like to be left behind—when my aunt dragoned, when my mother died, when my father shunted us into that apartment and didn't look back. Each left a gap, a lack, a hole in the universe where love should be. What would it be like for me if Beatrice left? I imagined myself standing on the ground, watching for her—craning neck, shaded eyes, a squint creased permanently into the face. Was that what my life would be?

When we arrived home, Beatrice wrenched the heavy steel door open with surprising strength and ran toward the stairs, pausing briefly to look back at me, point, and say, "Don't follow me," and after a pause she added, "please," and then sprinted away. I could only watch her go.

Dragons were protesting all over the country. So too were the families of dragons. And the supporters of dragons. And what was I doing? I went into the great room and found everyone hard at work, baking bread and shaping cookies and marinating the meat. They sang carols and encouraged one another.

I listened as Beatrice stomped up the rickety stairs and slammed her bedroom door behind her. I leaned against the brick wall and slid my bottom down to the floor. I rested my chin on my knees and did my best not to cry.

My aunt looked up and noticed my face.

"Alex," she said. "Alex, honey. What's wrong?" The other dragons stopped what they were doing. They wiped their paws on towels and surrounded me, their faces flooded with care and concern. *My family.* Of course I couldn't do this alone. Of course I needed to discuss it with them. I sighed, and I reached out and put my hand on Marla's paw. She squeezed my fingers.

I rested my chin on my knees and pulled my ankles close to my body. "Ladies," I said. I stopped and shook my head. "I mean, my darling aunties. If you could have stopped yourself from dragoning—you know, like a switch—would you have done it?"

Marla made a sound as though she was kicked in the stomach. She crossed her forelimbs and turned away from me.

"What about you, Jeanne? If some doctor showed up and said, 'Here's some medicine to make you un-dragon!' Would you take it?"

"Hell, no," Jeanne said. "I know where you're going with this, but I really think our situation is—"

I didn't let her finish. "How about you, Clara?" Clara looked up at the ceiling, avoiding my eyes. "Did you ever try just . . . *not being a dragon?*"

Clara shook her head. "Of course not," she whispered, pursing her lips. "Don't be silly."

"Edith," I said. "You found Marla in the unlikeliest place, and she was the love of your life. You had a plan to make a go of it after your time in the service. It would have worked too. But even then, it was too much to hang on. Your dragonness welling up inside you, wasn't it? A deep and unstoppable—"

"Joy," Edith gasped, finishing for me. She nodded, blinking rapidly, as though keeping her tears away. "It was a profound joy." She sighed, looked at Marla, and took her hand. "I thought Marla would follow me. That day, ideally. Like sunshine following the rain. And it would be joy forever."

Marla pressed her paws to her face. Her breath stuttered and her body began to shake. I pressed on. "You didn't though, Marla. You felt it then, the call to dragoning, a great and inexorable need, and you said no to it. For a while anyway."

My aunt sighed deeply. "My parents died. And I had a sister still in high school. And she needed me. I couldn't leave this life. I couldn't say yes yet."

"And I couldn't say no," Edith said. "I shouldn't have *had* to. It was too *wonderful.*"

I considered this. "What did it cost you, Marla?" My aunt pressed her forehead to the ground. She shuddered. "It cost me terrible," she said. "I had my sister. I had you. I had Beatrice. And that was wonderful. But it still cost me terrible." Edith and Jeanne knelt on either side, curling their arms around her.

"I understand," I said. I pressed the heels of my hands against my cheekbones and covered my eyes. I couldn't look at them. "I understand it all now. Ladies, we have a problem. Beatrice is miserable. We all know it. It's getting harder and harder for her to keep from dragoning. Everything in her is just crying out for it. All day at school. All day at home. *All the time.* She can't go on like this. It's hurting her."

I stood up and shoved my hands into my pockets, my ribs shaking a bit. Edith reached over and laid her paw on my foot. She looked at me steadily, her eyes damp with love and concern. Clara draped her tail on my shoulder. Jeanne extended her neck and pressed her forehead to mine. Reassuring me that she was there. Even when my mother was alive and the four of us lived together, I never had family like this. I wasn't alone. I would never be alone. I stepped close to Marla and knelt down in front of her. Finally, she met my gaze.

"She's in her room, and frankly I think it's good to give her a little privacy. Ladies, it's time. I've been resisting it, but I've been wrong. We have all been wrong. Beatrice needs this. She needs the freedom to own herself. She may dragon and she may not, but that needs to be her choice. There can be no more rules. No more limitations. She can partially dragon, or fully dragon, or go back and forth forever, or get stuck any which way. It's not up to us. It's up to Beatrice. If the school doesn't like it, then tough." I suddenly felt so exhausted, I thought my bones would turn into mush.

"But Alex," my aunt said.

"What about her education?" Edith gasped.

"Then we teach her at home," I said. "Eventually the schools will let her come back. I'd rather she learn at the library than spend one more day this unhappy. She doesn't have to dragon today, but she needs to know that she *can.*"

"It's just," Jeanne said. She paused and pulled out an embroidered handkerchief. "It's just, we love her so much. We were adults when we changed. We knew what we were getting into. What if she changes her mind and can't return?" She blew her nose in a tremendous roar.

I shrugged. "If there is one thing that Beatrice knows, it's her own mind. Always has. And if she gets stuck, that's her nature asserting itself. If she can go back and forth, well maybe some children can go back and forth. Hell, maybe some women can. No one knows anything because no one is willing to talk about anything, and so no one bothers to ask these questions, much less answer them. Myself included. That's stupid. I live in a household of dragons. My hesitation makes *no sense*. If any child should be comfortable dragoning if she damn well feels like it, it's Beatrice."

My aunt held my gaze for a long time. "If she dragons and can't re-girl, you're saying you don't mind that I'll manage her schooling?"

I felt something shift deep inside me. I leaned close to my aunt and threw my arms around her. She turned her head, keeping the boiling drops away from my non-dragoned skin. "I love you so much," I said. "Of course I don't mind. She's your daughter, Marla. It's time she knows that. It's time she understands what you suffered, and what you gave up, and how much you loved her. She's your *daughter*, Marla. And so am I. You're just as much a mother to me as my own mother was. I wish I could have understood this earlier."

I found myself scooped up by my dragon aunties. My shoes dangled about three inches off the floor. Their bodies were smooth and quite warm. It felt nice, actually, being held up by people who loved me. I couldn't remember the last time this was true.

⁂

It didn't happen right away. We all moved through the rest of the day in a state of alert, waiting for the change. Instead, Beatrice, suddenly relaxed, helped with the decorations and putting icing on the cookies. She cleaned her dishes and helped with the sweeping and brushed her teeth without prompting and went to bed without a fuss. The next night was Christmas Eve, and we attended a special Midnight Mass in the snow outside the cathedral with other mixed-state families. Both Beatrice and I rested in the arms of one of the dragon aunties, the furnace in their bellies keeping us warm. I half expected her to dragon then, right there in front of all those people. But she didn't. Beatrice was asleep before the second reading.

The next morning, Beatrice was up like a shot and raced to open her presents under the tree. Our building was thick with the smells of cinnamon and cloves, of apples and roast turkey, of sugar and chocolate and cream. Sonja and her grandmother and Dr. Gantz all arrived for our Christmas Day celebration at two in the afternoon. Immediately it was clear that Dr. Gantz was rather taken with Mrs. Blomgren—he became oddly flustered and stumbled on his words, his cheeks flushing each time she spoke. We had invited Mrs. Gyzinska as well, but she informed us that she had caught a cold and couldn't come. (She didn't tell us that she was in the hospital. I had to find out later.) We sang and read stories and Beatrice played a song on her flute and Sonja sang Norwegian folk songs as her long fingers plucked chords and harmonies on her grandfather's old mandolin. The dragons were tender with one another, and Sonja and I sat with our arms around each other on one section of the couch. No one told us we couldn't.

The dragoning began after the dinner and songs, but before Edith presented her beautifully crafted Yule log, with layers of chocolate cake and ganache and thick cream, along with spun sugar made to look like holly leaves.

"Is anyone ready for something sweet?" Edith asked everyone. She swayed a bit from wine and laughing.

Beatrice stood. "Yes, but." And then she stopped. She pressed her hands to her heart. My eyes went wide. I reached over and grabbed Sonja's hand.

"Oh," Beatrice said, her eyes growing gold. *"Oh."*

"Beatrice?" I asked.

Jeanne, thinking fast, began to move the furniture out of the way. Clara ran and filled a bucket of water, just in case. Dr. Gantz took out his steno pad. He reached over and pulled a camera out of his bag and handed it to Sonja. "Please take as many as you can. Do try to keep the camera steady. This is for science, after all." I don't know how he knew to give this job to her. Perhaps it was her unflappable demeanor and her clearly solid hand. In any case, I still have the photographs, all these years later. They remain remarkable.

Dr. Gantz asked question after question, and wrote things down whether he got an answer or not.

Beatrice said nothing. I watched her tilt her face upward, her rib cage heave in and out. Her mouth was open, as though her soul was escaping in sighs. She had a look of unabashed joy on her face. I crept closer, kneeling to the ground. I put my hand on her hand—it was so hot it hurt, but I held on anyway, lacing my fingers with hers. I kissed her cheek. My lips blistered just a bit.

"It's okay, Bea," I said. "It's okay. It's you and me, together. Nothing ever changes that. You are you, and I am me, and we are us, and that is pretty great." She turned, opened her eyes. They were wide, and large, and gold. They glittered so brightly, I squinted.

"Alex," Beatrice gasped. Her skin stretched. Her tongue shone. I still have scars on my hands from when I grabbed both her hands in mine and held on tight. I didn't let go for anything. Light poured from Beatrice's skin. "Did you know, Alex? Did you know how big the world can be? Did you?"

Oh, Beatrice. Yes. I finally did. And I still do.

Her skin fell away like petals. She let out a roar that rattled the bricks, sent books off the shelves, and vibrated in my bones.

As expected, Beatrice was expelled from school. Marla, Edith, Jeanne, Clara, and I all marched into the principal's office, with Beatrice reluctantly in tow, and demanded that she be allowed to remain in class. When the principal refused, we demanded that he put his refusal in writing. Journalists and photographers from the university newspaper (all friends of Sonja's) waited in the hallway. They lobbed questions and took photographs and splashed the whole story on the front page the following morning. By the next week, the Milwaukee paper had picked it up, then Chicago, and by the end of the month, similar stories had been reported across the country. It seemed that we were not the only ones willing to make a fuss about maintaining educational access for a recently dragoned child.

Still, Marla and the other aunties enjoyed homeschooling and shared the duties equally, and Beatrice took to the concept with unexpected enthusiasm. Jeanne built a learning nook in the corner with a dragon-sized desk and several bookshelves and even a makeshift lab for science class. Clara taught home economics and history, while Edith was in charge of literature and rhetoric, and Marla handled math and car repair. Jeanne was in charge of both science and gym class, and don't even ask me what the latter entailed. Something that Beatrice referred to as "fire dancing" and honestly the thought terrified me, so I just changed the subject. It turns out my mother was partially right—sometimes it really is best not to ask questions.

Through their contacts at the farmers' market, they found other families with dragoned children, which meant that Beatrice had both peers and compatriots—and later, study groups.

She organized games and schemes similar to the ones she spear-
headed in our old neighborhood, but now her playmates could
fly. And breathe fire. I gritted my teeth and hoped for the best.
Beatrice, now unburdened and unfettered, became infinitely
easier to live with. She continued to transition between her girl
and dragon forms, though the process was sometimes arduous
and left her exhausted for the better part of a day. She generally
preferred being a dragon and girled only occasionally. She said
she sometimes enjoyed the sensation of being *small*. I understood
this. I was also *small*. And I did enjoy it. Beatrice laughed easily
and helped often and filled every space she occupied with light.
Her mind was an endless river of ideas and concerns and questions and *plans*. She wanted to understand the whole world. This
isn't to say things were perfect. But they were *good*. All of us
would say so.

For me, this signaled a profound shift in how I understood
my life. I wasn't in charge of Beatrice anymore. Marla and the
aunties were. Not only that, I wasn't alone in managing my own
life. Marla and the others helped me manage my finances, and
they made sure I got enough sleep, and insisted that I eat balanced meals and take my vitamins. They fussed when my cheeks
got sallow or when I developed a cough. They entertained my
friends and they pretended not to notice when Sonja slept over.
They advised but didn't pry; they listened but didn't judge;
they cared but didn't coddle. They asked for my input when it
came to Beatrice's interests or behavior or learning. Because we
shared these responsibilities, it meant that I, for the first time,
could simply be a student—fully engaged in the life of the mind
and the practice of inquiry, without the burden of worry. Marla,
once again, became the pillar that held up my life. A future
opened in front of me, full of possibilities, all made possible by
their support.

Gratitude is a funny thing. It feels so similar to joy.

I met with professors to discuss the possibility of graduate school. I wrote to Mrs. Gyzinska to get her advice on the

subject (she had several thoughts) and I even wrote to Mr. Burrows—though he wrote back using his real name from his new laboratory at the University of New Mexico. I began to make plans for what my future might be—what once felt like a mad dash to the end of a cliff now felt like an interesting path in a beautiful wood that may or may not lead to the top of a mountain. And yes, the chances of my arrival at that destination were uncertain, but *oh!* What a mountain! And oh! What a view! And what a pleasure it was to keep moving forward.

The new semester began, and I threw myself into my studies and inquiry. I worked at the lab and joined research teams and even secured funding for projects of my own. I volunteered at the observatory every Tuesday and Friday night until past two in the morning. Sonja came with me on Fridays—she'd study, or make art, or just lounge or nap on the couch deep in the night until my shift was over. From time to time, I took a break just to touch her face, or her hair, or drape my arm across her back. I didn't hide the fact that we were together. If anyone had a problem, no one said. Sometimes, letting it be known that you live in a household full of dragons has certain benefits.

Often, after my shift ended, Sonja and I stayed out the rest of the night. We were restless, and *awake,* walking along the paths by the lake until the sky turned red and dawn came. I wanted to spend every moment with her. I wanted each moment we had to bend and loop with every other possible moment.

An infinite tangle of time.

A quantum love knot.

The thing about a first love is that it so rarely lasts, but it always feels as though it *must.* I hung on to every second I had with Sonja. Each one felt precious to me. Each one felt like a treasure that could be easily lost.

When did I notice that Sonja had begun exclusively drawing dragons, painting dragons, etching dragons onto the faces of small pieces of tumbled glass, carrying them in her pockets like touchstones? When did I notice her gaze wandering past where

I stood, and tilting upward to the sky? I didn't want to think about it. I didn't ask about it. I tried to tell myself that it wasn't happening.

One Friday at the beginning of February, Sonja arrived late. Her cheeks were flushed and her eyes were bright. But it was February, after all, and that night it was a shattering cold. There were four other students present, all boys, and all of whom took turns to explain the equipment to me (despite the fact that I had trained each of them) or to explain the theory to me (I had seen their notes, and no thanks) and to offer to check my mathematics (I politely declined). At one point, when one boy tried to explain to me how lenses worked, I said, "Thanks, friend, but your explanations are as useful to me as gum in my hair. Why don't you do the group a favor and *zip it.*"

"Geez, Alex," he breathed. "Don't bite my head off." All four of the boys made a hasty exit shortly after. The graduate student managing that night—a tall young man from North Dakota—had, once again, fallen asleep at his desk. This wasn't unusual for graduate students. On their best days they were both gaunt and sleep-deprived, powered solely on coffee. I didn't have the heart to wake him, so I buttoned up the observatory for him instead, replacing equipment and shutting down machines and checking the inventories. It was good to have something to do. Sonja stayed put in her corner, bent over her notebook, a look of wild joy on her face. I couldn't see what she was drawing. Every once in a while she looked up and caught my eye and smiled. Every time, she took my breath away.

We woke the grad student, who looked around the room in utter panic until I explained that I had done all his tasks for him and he could just lock up and go to bed. Sonja and I grabbed our bags and left him to it.

Once we got into the hall, Sonja took my hand. "I'm not ready for the evening to be over, are you?" I turned and faced her. I took her other hand. I stepped closer.

"No," I said, my voice more breath than anything else.

"Let's go to the roof," Sonja whispered. "I want to show you something."

It didn't occur to me that it was, at that moment, below zero, and that it would be icy and dangerous up there. I just nodded, my heart in my throat. Sonja started walking backward, pulling me along with her hands.

I didn't know what she wanted to show me. I did know that I wasn't ready to go home.

I shivered as we stepped outside. The black sky overhead glittered with stars, each one crisp and clear and cold. It was one of those rare nights where the dropping temperature squeezed out every droplet of excess moisture that might fog the air and muddle the seeing, and the wind had decided to make itself perfectly still. My breath clouded and my eyelashes froze. It didn't matter. My belly was hot and my bones were hot and my skin seemed to radiate. Sonja Blomgren reached over and placed her hands on my cheeks. Her fingers were cold but her palms were hot. I didn't want to go inside. Her cheeks were flushed with anticipation. (*For what?* I didn't ask. *Oh god, why didn't I ask?*)

"The sky is perfect," I said. "Would you like to stargaze with me?"

The best way to stargaze is to lie flat on your back and look directly up, so that the center of your vision is on the darkest part of the sky. Some years back, some astronomy students outfitted a trunk on the roof for stargazing, stocked with boiled-wool blankets to protect our bodies from the cold roof and the cold wind, and a few old pillows for comfort. We lay down, cuddled in as best we could, and looked up. Sonja held my hand. Her eyes were filled with stars. Lake Mendota was still fully frozen, and even from way up here, we could hear the tympanic bows and deep cracking of the ice—a cold, lonely sound. We could also hear the music from several dorm parties and the sound of young men running outside, playing testosterone-fueled games in the dark.

After a bit, Sonja Blomgren rolled toward me, resting her cheekbone on her knuckles.

"My father had this mad idea," Sonja said, her eyes still pointed upward toward the sky and not looking at me. She ran her fingertips along my cheek absently, as though her skin was memorizing my skin. "After my mother dragoned. He brought me to my grandparents' house on the south shore of Lake Superior and told me that he wasn't going to say goodbye because he would be back, and he would bring my mother with him, and then all of us would live together. Maybe on an island in the lake. My grandparents gave him their blessing to go find their daughter, but they thought he was nuts. And he was. He thought we could maybe live on one of the lighthouse islands or just in a cabin with the big lake on one side and thick woods on the other. And Mom could just be a dragon and do her dragony things, and I could just be a little girl with both of her parents who both loved her, and he would fish or hunt or grow our food and we would all be happy. It was ridiculous. First off, he couldn't fish. He was too impatient and far too squeamish. He had never hunted in his life. Same problem. And the only garden we ever had was just a square of dirt and weeds. He couldn't even grow asparagus, which is the easiest thing in the world. My dad was a carpenter, not a pioneer. Second off, my mom left for a reason. She didn't say goodbye to me and she didn't say goodbye to her parents and she certainly didn't say goodbye to my father. It's hard for me to accept that, but I know it's true. And, what's more, she hasn't come back for a reason."

She sat up. She kept her gaze on the sky. There was a slick of tears curving along her bottom lids. Her eyelashes had tiny ice crystals adhered to each strand, flashing in the low light. My cheeks were hot. My lips were hot. I couldn't move and I couldn't say anything. I knew I *should* say something. But my mouth was full of ashes.

Sonja bit her lower lip. "That day when all the girls changed? I was at a slumber party. Me and five other girls. My friend's parents were at a wedding and we had the house to ourselves, so obviously we all helped ourselves to the liquor cabinet. We went outside in our skivvies and lay out on the lawn chairs and looked at the sky. My head was muddled. I kissed my friend Joanne, like a real kiss, and she lay next to me on the lawn chair, her skin pressed against my skin, her hand in my hand, and it was the best feeling in the whole world. We watched the sky for over an hour. And then, very suddenly, she told me she was sorry. She stood." Sonja's voice trembled. She took in a quick breath, as though stifling a sob. "And then *she changed*. Everyone *changed*. I watched them fly away, one after another, and I stood in the backyard alone. It was one of the loneliest days of my life. My friends all changed. All of them. They left me behind."

Above our heads, the stars glinted and burned. I reached my arm under Sonja's back and held her close.

I found my voice. "A long time ago, before she dragoned, my aunt told me all women are magic. She told me that we all hear the call and that some people answer and some don't. But I don't know. I was *there* that night at prom. I watched how happy they were. And those girls *changed*. We were all dancing together and it felt *so good* to be dancing all together, and then their eyes changed and their mouths changed and they stepped out of their skin and they went away. And left me behind. I didn't hear *anything*. Nothing called me."

I didn't say what I was thinking. *Am I not enough? Was I not good enough?* But even in that moment, I knew these were the wrong questions. Instead, I knew I needed to ask, *What life will I choose? What life do I want?* In my heart, I already knew the answer.

Sonja held my hands in her hands. She brought her mouth to my cheek and rested her lips there. I felt her breath. I felt her kiss. Our mouths were open and our arms wound together, like a knot. Her lips were warm. Then hot. Her skin was hot. My lips burned and my bones burned and my heart burned and burned and burned.

Oh, no, I thought. *Oh, Sonja.* I wrapped my arms around her and held on tight. *Don't go where I can't follow.*

After the kiss, we lingered close for a long moment. Our flushed cheeks touching. Our hands resting gloved palm to gloved palm. Sonja pulled away. She looked at me for a long time, her grey eyes glittering. "Sometimes, I think about my mother. How many drawings do I have of her face? How many paintings and sculptures? I can't keep track of them, honestly. But it helps me to make sure I remember her face, and my father's face. It comforts me to remember the vast amount of love they had for one another. Even though their love wasn't enough. Because sometimes love isn't enough." She slid her hand under my hat and wound her fingers in my hair. I buried my face between her scarf and her long neck. "I didn't hear the call that night with my friends. But I *wanted* to. And I *kept* wanting to. So when I got to college, I went out of my way to make friends with dragons. I thought that might trigger something. Nothing happened. Not for a long time."

"Well, then," I said. I didn't let go. "Maybe that's your answer."

She dropped her arms, stepped back, and regarded my face. She shook her head. "Oh, Alex. Don't you see? I *do* feel something. Now. It started the day I found you again. I felt something inside. Like my life was more than itself. That I was more than myself. Maybe that's a different sort of call." She took another step back. Her eyes were now gold, and shining. There were rubies in her mouth.

"Oh, Sonja," I breathed. *"Are you sure?"*

"My father died looking for my mother, but my mother *wasn't even here.* I think—actually I *know*—that she launched to explore the stars. I think she's still there. Deep in space." Her neck elongated. Talons pierced her boots. She was so beautiful I thought I'd die. She kissed me once more, on the mouth. Her coat began to smoke and singe. My lips burned. She pulled her clothes apart with a slight tug and held a talon on the skin between her breasts. I looked away. The night was cold. The stars were bright. Dragons skimmed the windswept lake and the air was full of the calls of men. Beatrice was home. Beatrice needed me. *This* me. Unless she didn't. Maybe she wouldn't need me forever. Maybe asking what Beatrice needed was the wrong question. What did *I* need? What did *I* want? What did *I* want my life to be? The ground moved under my feet in waves. *Sonja Blomgren creates earthquakes,* I thought, and it never felt more true. Sonja pressed her talon into her skin and began to draw it down.

"I want to be bigger than myself," she said, closing her eyes. "I'd like to find my mother. I'd like to explore the stars. And beyond the stars. I want to swallow the universe with my eyes. Come with me, Alex. I can't stay here a moment longer. I can't stay in this body a moment longer. This is not the life I choose. I choose something *else.* I love you so much, Alex. Won't you come with me?"

How do I pin this memory down? How do I wind each detail, each strand, each filament together? I remember the squeak of my shoes against the impossible cold of the compressed snow and ice. I remember the ache in my heart and the heat in my body. My back hurt. My skin felt tight. My vision swam—with tears? Or something else? I remember the smell of Sonja as she had now become, no more rosemary, but ash and caramel and smoke. I remember the sheen of her scales, the glow of her eyes, the glint of each tooth, each edge, each claw. A drunk young man on the ground catcalled and hooted. A car's horn blasted and another car peeled away. Sonja hovered in front of me, a riot of light and beauty, a crack in the universe. It was all I could do to keep standing.

She reached outward, her scales shimmering in the low light. What could I do? I took her paw between my palms. I stroked each scale with my thumb. I bowed my head as though in prayer.

"Well?" Sonja said.

43

By the spring of 1965, a year after the Little Wyrming, a majority of the girls who dragoned that day were living, once again, with families. For the most part, this was due to a change of heart in the families of origin, who sorrowfully sought their homeless and abandoned daughters and begged forgiveness. Once these reconciliations became public, and once the images of happy, reunited families became part of the public consciousness, the sense of urgency regarding the well-being and moral development of dragoned girls living on their own began to increase. Social service agencies dedicated to finding flexible foster families who were ready to take on the physical, spiritual, and moral needs of a transformed girl popped up around the country, seemingly overnight.

Once the families were reunited or built anew, parents started advocating for their daughters. And they weren't prepared to take no for an answer.

By 1966, high school principals began defying their district decrees and welcoming the dragoned girls back to school (either moving classes out of doors, or holding special classes in the auditoriums or commons or gyms, or in the case of some schools, fitting each window with outdoor perches to allow outsized students to participate in class but also have freedom of movement). The first dragon-friendly primary school announced itself in 1967. And in 1969, a group of eight thousand souls—both human and dragon—situated themselves in front of the White House, demanding equal education for their dragon daughters.

The optics were terrible. No politician ever wants to appear to be anti-education. President Nixon, new to the job, was not a tremendous fan of dragons generally, but even he knew a losing argument when he saw one. He and the First Lady invited a well-heeled family (long-standing Republican donors) and their Radcliffe-educated dragon daughter to the White House lawn for a well-publicized luncheon. The weather was fine, the chat genial, and promises were made. From Nixon's point of view, the promises were empty, obviously, and meant to placate worried parents and provide himself with political cover over making any real change. He had no idea what was coming next.

The citizenship question, along with the schooling question, were both answered unanimously and heralded as the law of the land by the Supreme Court in 1971. Bogus death certificates were vacated, social security numbers were reissued, and dragons became full persons under the law. They applied for library cards, driver's licenses, and bank accounts and registered to vote. They took full advantage of both the rights and sacred duties of full citizens. They created spaces for themselves in the highest institutions of learning, graduating summa cum laude from famous universities, and then putting those degrees to work. Dragons later litigated cases in front of state and district courts, arguing on behalf of others who, like them, were once denied a voice. They took jobs as social workers, park rangers, scientists, engineers, philosophers, farmers, and schoolteachers. They were impressively adept as builders, and were in high demand as their strength, dexterity, flight, problem solving, and ability to breathe fire made them veritable Janes-of-all-trades. Not only were they helpful and hardworking and highly skilled, but they also kept costs down.

Even as anti-dragon sentiment persisted, and still persists even today, the effect the dragons had on both local and national commerce cannot be understated. No matter what a person's point of view, it's hard to begrudge a booming economy.

Beatrice only had to learn at home for just under two years, until her school relented and allowed the return of dragoned children. For her, it didn't last. Once she learned what it was to learn on her own, it was difficult—and nearing impossible—for her to remain in school for too long. The yoke of sameness felt like a heavy prison indeed, and the boredom of remaining chained to a desk all day was more than she could bear. Even after the schools opened up to accommodate students like her, she remained unwilling to attend them.

"Why would I waste my day learning what *they* want me to learn, when I can just go to the library and learn *everything?*" I didn't have a good answer to that. As time went on, Beatrice was still able to move back and forth—fully dragon and fully girl—with some ease, though the transitions exhausted her more and more as she aged. Still, her fluidity persisted through her adolescent years and into adulthood. Dr. Gantz published six papers on the subject. There were others he found who were similarly situated, but they were few and far between. Beatrice was, is, and ever shall be, exquisitely special.

By 1980, there were four dragon members of Congress, eighteen dragon CEOs of major corporations, and 422 cities, towns, or incorporated municipalities had at least one elected dragon member to their governing bodies. Dragon-centered nongovernmental agencies began doing work all over the world, in advocacy, peacemaking, animal welfare, environmental protection, and the rebuilding of infrastructure in countries injured by armed conflict. In the autumn of 1985, the Norwegian Nobel Committee shocked the world by awarding the Nobel Peace Prize to the dragon founder of one such NGO. The organization in question—Guardian Dragons—had been established ten years earlier by a young dragon from Wisconsin, who made it her mission to broker peace and safety in those delicate regions in the world where the machines of war came perilously close to civilian life. She kept her name a secret, opting to publicly use the moniker the Loving Leviathan as a way of protecting her family back home. The work of peacemaking, unfortunately, is not without enemies. Originally, the mission of these dragon workers was to position themselves near imperiled villages and spirit children out of harm's way. Eventually, though, the dragons learned that by increasing their speed, they could intercept bullets and bombs, rendering both harmless. They became skilled defusers, and lightning-fast fliers, sending any bullet ricocheting back. Because of their excellent sense of smell, and their ability to hover over the ground, they also helped rid entire regions of the scourge of land mines. Guardian Dragons became, around the world, symbols of powerful nonviolence, as their techniques of passive protection forced seething warlords, self-aggrandizing dictators, and sociopathic CEOs back to the negotiating table, their efforts to rule by force, fear, and coercion thwarted—perhaps forever.

Newspapers around the world either hailed the choice as obvious and overdue, or they condemned it as dragonish bullying, and splashed breathless headlines, decrying the so-called Ascendency of Serpents and the Diminishment of Man and other histrionics. Commentators on news programs debated it endlessly. But it's hard to argue against the possibility that war, as we have known it, was finally coming to an end. Congress put forward a resolution honoring both the Guardian Dragons and its anonymous founder, only to receive the first veto of the Reagan administration, for fear of offending the president's favorite dictators and war profiteers. (The veto was overridden. Unanimously.) Radio reporters ruminated on whether the Loving Leviathan would give a speech at all, since doing so anonymously was against the rules. Refusing to do so would mean refusing the prize, and therefore the substantial award check—and like any nonprofit, the Guardian Dragons was perennially strapped for cash. She would be foolish to turn her back on the money.

On December 10, 1985, dignitaries from around the world, both human and dragon, began to arrive in Norway. Security concerns at the University of Oslo, and around the Domus Media, where the ceremony was held, not only put law enforcement and the Norwegian military on high alert but placed the entire nation on edge. It was unheard of, of course, for there to be violence at the Peace Prize ceremony. But given the vitriol and gnashing of teeth among the practitioners of war and the dealers of bloodshed, no one could really say for sure how this particular ceremony would end. Many attendees wore bulletproof vests under their gowns and jackets. Just in case.

Dinner was served. The laureate's table, as is traditional, occupied the middle of the room, with the prime minister, the Nobel Committee, and various other government and cultural officials all carefully eating their beautifully presented food. But no dragon. Was she coming? People in the banquet hall began to whisper.

The committee chairman, as is traditional, called the ceremony to order and gave his yearly speech, with its attempts at humor. The guests indulged him with wan smiles. A film showed dramatic moments from the Guardian Dragons' heroic efforts, plus interviews from rescued families, protected villages, and the negotiators of progressive new peace deals, hailed around the world for their innovations in protecting human rights and human dignity as well as establishing new protocols to empower the citizens of the region. When power belongs, not to the violent, and not to the wealthy and well-connected, but to the people, a different sort of future begins to present itself. A lasting, global peace seemed not only possible, but probable.

The crowd was moved. Several dragons wept. The committee chairman called for the laureate, who entered from a side door. She was a beautiful dragon. Though surprisingly small. All potential energy and compact heat. She seemed to vibrate with excitement. She was accompanied by a slight woman with very short hair, lightly shot with grey. They embraced tenderly, the woman resting her hand on the dragon's face and giving her a kiss on the cheek. They were standing very close to the microphone. The banquet attendees heard the woman say, "You are my favorite sister, honey. I'm so proud of you." They heard the dragon reply, "Last I checked, I'm your only sister. But thank you."

The crowd leaped to their feet, applauding until their hands were raw and red. Makeup smeared. Men with hardened faces wept. The dragon cleared her throat, and the attendees took their seats once again.

"Thank you so much for being here," the dragon said. "Thank you for sharing in our collective commitment to peace. I want to talk to you about the work we are doing, and the people that we all can help save. But first, I should probably introduce myself. Officially. In public. For the first time. My name is Beatrice. Beatrice Green. And I'm so happy to meet you."

44.

As I write these words, my head swims a bit, but I attribute much of that to the indignities of old age. My joints creak, my back is bowed, my hair has paled, wisped, and fallen away. Every day, I am lighter, weaker, more fragile, my skin like rice paper crinkled over a skeleton made of grass. So it goes. I was an astrophysicist once, and perhaps I still am. I built mathematical models to better understand the composition of stars, using that foundation to predict larger and larger structures, moving toward a unified understanding of the movement of the universe. Every day, there were galaxies in my eyes. I claimed a life that was bigger than I was, a presence in the world that was larger than the one I was told that I could have. I held the threads of the universe in my mind and attempted to pull them together. I could have dragoned with my first, precious love. But I didn't. I chose *this* work, *this* path, *this* life. This precious life. Would that I could have chosen both.

My path sent me to universities all around the country and the world, giving lectures, presenting papers, probing the universe, and coaxing her to reveal her absolute truths, until, at last, I chaired the Department of Physics back where I started, at the University of Wisconsin, and where I remained until my retirement. My lovely wife, Camilla—a loudmouthed and often profane ceramic artist from Rome—complained bitterly about the weather and complained passionately about the food, but loved living near my dragon aunties, who still occupied the same building and still made their living baking bread. Camilla tenderly cared for each of my aunties in their old age, minding the house and tending the garden and managing the kitchen and cooking massive vats of food (all her grandmother's recipes), and making sure everyone—from the aunties to their nurses to the various neighbors and even the mailman—was fed. Her sculptor's hands were gentle and kind. She caressed their faces and adjusted their beds, and held their hands as they slipped away. They loved her as if she was their own daughter. This shouldn't have surprised me, but it did. Sometimes, the expansive nature of family takes my breath away.

Camilla—*oh, heavens.* It pains me now to write her name. The wound is too fresh. What can I say, other than that our life was beautiful. That she was beautiful. Her work was beautiful. She made the world more of itself and tied me to it—tied my mind to my body, tied my heart to hers. An unbreakable knot. Sometimes, I feel that we are all tricked by love, and its rigid requirement of pain. We find the love of our lives and cleave to our beloved when we are still quite young and do not yet understand that we must, by our nature, die someday. In any successful marriage, one partner must face the reality of being very old, and very alone. What is grief, but love that's lost its object?

If I had known how this story would end, would I have done anything differently? Would I still have loved her, body and soul? In my mind's eye, I can see Camilla asking me that very question.

Oh, my darling, I feel my heart answer. *I wouldn't change a single thing.*

She passed away only a month after my retirement, just as we planned to set off around the world. I still see her face glittering in the stars from time to time. Which is why I've taken to sleeping in the hammock at night. Beatrice remains out of her mind with worry. She fusses over me endlessly. Sometimes she flutters down and carries me indoors, cradling me in her arms as I did for her, as my mother did for both of us, once upon a time. Once again, the past and the present wind together: they loop, they twist, they pull in tight. Tension and response, filament and friction and time. A knot. There was so much that my mother understood, even as she got so much so very wrong.

I built a house on the lot where I first saw a dragon. The original house was long gone. So was the chicken coop. Beatrice accused me of being morbid, living so close to where our parents lived miserably together—even though that house, too, is long gone. I told her that my choice has unity, though I didn't explain why. I never told her about the old lady's transformation—about the scream and the scrabble and the thud. I never told her about that quiet, awestruck *Oh!* Is it strange that I never did? Perhaps it is. Even now, with context and understanding, that memory remains a hard, bright, dangerous thing. Broken glass in the shelves of my mind. Still, that memory is mine. And I cherish it, regardless.

Now *I* am the old lady with the chickens and the garden. The one who gives out snacks or chats or a beautiful basket of eggs to any wandering child who stops over for a bit of company. Perhaps this is my destiny—to be the one sensible thing in an often senseless world.

My house now is filled with pieces of my life. Every room contains elements of my mother's knotwork—from the curtains to the table runners—each modeled after her notes and diagrams. I even managed to find a copy of her senior thesis, housed in the archives of the Department of Mathematics, a treatise on the topic of topography, which is now displayed on my dining room table. When my stepmother passed, I inherited a box of my father's old hats, which now occupy a shelf along the crown molding, each quiet and empty and somehow diminished. Every corner of my house has Camilla's artwork—her sculpted platters and her undulating vases and her lovingly hand-built nudes. Each piece is imprinted by the touch of her hands, the closest thing I have to the memory of her body. I have painted the walls of my study with images of Norwegian mountains and flowers and trolls, in memory of the youth I shared with Sonja. I have built gazebos and high roosts for Beatrice and any other dragon who wishes to stop by or just rest their wings for a while. Every day I work in the garden. I hand out books to furious girls in memory of Mrs. Gyzinska, and write their recommendations when they apply for college. And I have learned to fix engines as a tribute to my aunt. Retirement is wonderful, after all. And filled with diverse occupations. I highly recommend it.

I woke this morning in the hammock, which meant that Beatrice had not been by. She was out changing the world again. Speaking. Organizing. Intimidating politicians or world leaders or clergy members to change their minds and make the planet a better place. Beatrice my cousin. Beatrice my sister. Beatrice my child. And now, perhaps, Beatrice my mother, caring for me as my body fails. I feed the chickens and water the beans. I pick a bowl of ground-cherries and hunt for eggs. And then I rest on the lounge chair in the garden and look at the sky.

Birds circle overhead. Dragons, too. Beautiful things. There is so much beauty.

Nearby, a dog barks.

Nearby, an engine hums.

I close my eyes and listen to the drone of cicadas, calling to one another from tree to tree to tree. Memory is a strange thing. It reorganizes and connects. It provides context and clarity; it reveals patterns and divergences. It finds the holes in the universe and stitches them closed, tying the threads together in a tight, unbreakable knot.

I learned this from my mother.

And now I will teach it to you.

ACKNOWLEDGMENTS

An acknowledgments page is, by its nature, incomplete. There are a thousand people that likely should be thanked for their assistance and kindness and care in the creation of any book, and a thousand times a thousand more that we have likely forgotten. I will say that I would not have been able to push forward if it weren't for the encouragement of one writing group—Martha Brockenbrough, Olugbemisola Rhuday-Perkovich, Laurel Snyder, Laura Ruby, Tracey Baptiste, Anne Ursu, Kate Messner, and Linda Urban—or the kind and incisive critiques of another—Lyda Moorehouse, Naomi Kritzer, Theo Lorenz, Adam Stemple, and Eleanor Arnason, also known as the Wyrdsmiths.

I need to thank Steven Malk, my fearless agent, who wholeheartedly encouraged me in the writing of this frankly bonkers book, despite the fact that it was a stark deviation from my other work and well outside my comfort zone. "Have fun with this," he told me after I showed him some early pages showing the enthusiastic devouring of a hapless husband. "Make some trouble." So I did. And I'd also like to thank my lovely editor, Lee Boudreaux, who believed in this story from the word *go*, and whose boundless enthusiasm gave me the courage to shape it into what it became.

I'd like to thank the kind librarians at the Central Library in Minneapolis, as well as the shockingly thorough library at the Minnesota Historical Society. I'd like to thank the Freedom of Information Act, which allows anyone, even dirtbag authors like me, to read through the transcripts depicting the real-time horrors of the House Un-American Activities Committee during McCarthy's heyday, so that we might never repeat that shameful history.

And thank you to my wonderful family—my husband, my kids, my siblings, my parents, my cousins, and my found family of neighbors and friends—who have to live with a person often hijacked by her own imagination, and wounded by the world. The work of storytelling requires a person to remain in a state of brutal vulnerability and punishing empathy. We feel *everything*. It tears us apart. We could not do this work without people in our lives to love us unceasingly, and to put us back together. I feel so lucky to be surrounded by boundless love. I owe the universe a great debt to be held in such care.

I often say that I write my books by accident, and I almost always mean it. This book is no different. This book would not exist if it weren't for a marvelous editor and anthologist named Jonathan Strahan, who kindly asked me to write him a short story about dragons for a new book. I had convinced myself that my writing days were behind me but said yes because Mr. Strahan is just so darn *nice,* and what kind of trouble could I get myself into, really, with just one more story? And then I, along with the rest of America, listened with horror and incandescent fury to the brave, stalwart testimony of Christine Blasey Ford, as she begged the Senate to reconsider their Supreme Court Justice nominee and make a different choice, and I decided to write a story about rage. And dragons. But mostly about rage.

Stories are funny things, though. We think we know what they will be when we begin, but they have minds of their own. They are so like our children in this way. I thought I was writing a short story. I wasn't. This story very quickly informed me that it wanted to be a novel. Who was I to argue? I thought I was writing a story about rage. I wasn't. There is certainly rage in this novel, but it is about more than that. In its heart, this is a story about memory, and trauma. It's about the damage we do to ourselves and our community when we refuse to talk about the past. It's about the memories that we don't understand, and can't put into context, until we learn more about the world. And I thought I was writing about a bunch of fire-breathing, powerful women. And while those women certainly are in this book, it isn't about them. It's about a world upended by trauma and shamed into silence. And that silence grows, and becomes toxic, and infects every aspect of life. Perhaps this sounds familiar to you now—times being what they are.

This book is not based on Christine Blasey Ford or her testimony, but it would not have existed without that woman's bravery, her calm adherence to the facts, and her willingness to relive one of the worst moments of her life to help America save itself from itself. Her actions didn't work, but they still mattered. And maybe that's enough, in our fervent hope that the next generation gets it right.